THE RESCUED MATE

SHIFTERS OF THE THREE RIVERS 4

KIRA NIGHTINGALE

ÉDITIONS SPOTTISWOODE

Book Cover by 100 Covers

Edited by Brigitte Billings

Published by Éditions Spottiswoode

First edition 2024

ISBN (ebook): 978-1-998510-00-9

ISBN (paperback): 978-1-7382838-9-7

DEDICATION AND TRIGGER WARNINGS

Dedication

Most of this book was written in Scotland during a visit there in summer 2024. I love Scotland. I was born and brought up there, and there is something about the land that calls to me. I hope to some day write a series set there. But not today. This book, book 4 in the Shifters of the Three Rivers series, was the first time I wrote different main characters. I wasn't sure I could love anyone as much as I do about Mai and Ryan, but Shya and Mason proved me wrong. This book is for new characters, new adventures, and Scotland – you inspired me, as you always do.

Trigger Warnings

This book contains some adult themes and lots of spice. There are characters dealing with grief in this story as well as domestic violence, arranged marriage, and attempted suicide.

CONTENTS

Chapter One

SHYA

 days ago

The Louis Vuitton heels were calling to me. They were perfection. A blossom slingback pump with a three-inch heel. Slim, pretty, powerful; they were everything I needed for my meeting with Ellen tomorrow. As nominated leader of the humans on the town council, I had to work closely with her, but she was possibly the most annoying human I had ever met. Every little detail had to be discussed, every angle considered.

I was more of a just-get-it-done kind of girl. And tomorrow, my parents had asked me to push through the new rules for our security protocols. My parents wanted the rules updated to reflect the heightened risk of attack from outsiders these days. Ellen was not keen because she thought it sent the wrong message to the humans and tourists in town. She had a point. Bridgetown worked because it was marketed as a haven for humans and Shifters to live together. Tourists came here to drink with Shifters, go rafting with Shifters, get served their meals by Shifters ... and we put on a friendly face for all the paying humans who then went home and told their friends that the news reports were wrong, and Shifters were just people who grew fur and claws every now and again.

The Wolf Council supported our mission here. There had been too many voices in the human government recently demanding that Shifters be put in cages, to be tamed and controlled. The more tourists we made happy here and in the conclave cities down South, the more human allies we had who realized those voices were talking bullshit when they said we were a species that could not live safely side by side with humans. What we did here was important for all Shifters.

But recent events meant we needed to update our security. Tristan, our old Beta, thought Shifters were infinitely superior to humans and had had enough of bowing down to the pets, as he saw them. He'd plotted to kill my parents and take control of the Pack, and when that failed, he escaped with a lot of our people. He was still out there, still hated humans, and still wanted my parents dead. This meant I needed to get Ellen on board and put these new measures in place. The last thing we needed was an attack where a human was killed. It would scare the tourists off and would be used by those in government who wanted to enforce segregation between the species.

So, I needed to have my armor on. Just like Clark Kent's glasses, my shoes were my disguise. Not many people realize this, but shoes have a superpower. Slip on my favorite rainbow sneakers and I can run for miles. My sky-blue sneakers can kick Martin, my trainer, in the head, and he's six foot five. Given I'm five foot three, that's some feat. And my green satin Manolo Blahnik's turn me into a powerful Pack princess who can take on the world. Shoes are my armor, my shield against other people realizing I'm not up to the job. I step into the right pair, and I become exactly who I need to be for that day.

"I see you've found them."

I turned to see Marnie smiling at me. "They arrived yesterday. I made sure to order your size."

I grinned back at Marnie. She always seemed to know exactly what I needed, sometimes even before I did. That's what made her such an incredible friend as well as a successful businesswoman.

Marnie had opened Marnie & Summer's Shoe Emporium shortly after moving to Bridgetown, turning her passion for footwear into a thriving business. She was a human in a predominantly Shifter town, and she'd quickly become a beloved figure in the community. Her warm personality and killer instinct for fashion had won over even the most skeptical werewolves.

"Marnie, you're a lifesaver," I said, admiring the shoes once more. "These are precisely what I need for tomorrow's meeting."

She leaned against the counter, her hazel eyes twinkling. "Ah, another showdown with Ellen?"

I groaned. "Is it that obvious?"

"Only to someone who knows you as well as I do," she laughed, her chestnut hair catching the light as she shook her head. "So, what's on the agenda this time?"

I slipped off my everyday flats and tried on the Louis Vuitton heels. "The new security rules."

Marnie nodded understandingly. "Ah yes, I heard her talking about those in Josie's cafe this morning. Those are definitely the shoes for you, then. Go on, have a look."

Marnie had had her own run-ins with Ellen when Marnie and

Summer first arrived here. Ellen had wanted to buy these premises for her own yarn shop but with another yarn shop already in Bridgetown, the town council had liked Marnie's proposal for a shoe shop better. Ellen had not been happy and had let everyone know about the new single mom in town who stole her shop.

I walked over to the full-length mirror just as the bell above the door chimed. Summer walked in, her school backpack slung over one shoulder.

"Hey, Mom! Hi, Shya!" she called out, her gray eyes lighting up.

"Hey, sweetie," Marnie replied. "How was school?"

Summer dropped her bag behind the counter, but before she could answer, she caught sight of my new shoes. Her eyes widened. "Shya! You look amazing in those!"

As Summer moved closer, I caught a whiff of her scent. Today, it was distinctly human, but there had been times over the last five years when I'd sworn I'd detected a hint of Shifter. Marnie refused to talk about Summer's dad and would just say that it was best for all of them that he was gone (though she'd never elaborate if "gone" meant living somewhere else or dead). I wondered if he'd been a Shifter, though, despite it being extremely rare for Shifters and humans to be able to have children together. I pushed the thought aside for now, focusing instead on the excited pre-teen in front of me.

I looked at the shoes in the mirror and did a twirl. "You think?"

"Absolutely! You'll win Ellen over in no time in those!"

I glanced over at Marnie. "Does everyone know about the meeting?"

Summer nodded seriously. "Oh, yes, Ellen's telling everyone how she's going to shoot down the 'ridiculous new proposals that have no place in our community.'" Summer did an almost perfect job at imitating Ellen's nasal voice.

"Wonderful," I deadpanned. "I definitely need these shoes, then."

Marnie laughed. "I'll get the box for you."

I turned back to Summer. "You got any exciting plans for the weekend?"

Summer's cheeks flushed slightly, and she glanced quickly at her mother before answering. "Um, not really. Just helping out here in the shop and maybe doing some studying."

I raised an eyebrow, sensing there was more to the story. "Studying, huh? Any particular subject?"

Her blush deepened. "Just ... you know, general stuff. I picked up a few new books from the library."

Marnie chuckled softly. "These are books numbers twelve and thirteen this month."

I had a feeling she knew exactly what—or who—was behind Summer's sudden interest in reading. I made a mental note to ask Henry if he had any plans this weekend.

My phone buzzed in my pocket. It was a message from the boy himself.

You better get back here. Visitors just arrived.

Visitors? Odd. Henry normally warned me about exactly who was at the house.

"Everything okay?" Marnie asked.

"Yeah, I might need to run, though. Can you keep the shoes for me?" I didn't want to run with the box. I shuddered to think of what would happen if I dropped it.

"Don't worry. I'll add them to your account and get Summer to bring them up to the house for you."

"You're the best, Marnie."

"And me!" Summer said, "I'm the one being volunteered to bring you the shoes."

Given it would give her the opportunity to see Henry and talk about her latest books, I suspected she was secretly pleased with the idea, but I kissed her on both cheeks, European style, making her giggle, and said, "You're the bestest, Summer," making her giggle even more.

I waved goodbye at them and the gorgeous shoes that would soon be mine and jogged out the door.

Chapter Two

SHYA

The scent wafted down the driveway. I inhaled deeply, noting the intoxicating aroma, a tantalizing blend of cedarwood and musk that could only belong to one person: Mason.

Damn it!

The last thing I needed right now was to see Mason Shaw, hear Mason Shaw, or smell Mason fucking Shaw. He had the ability to send my brain into a Mason fog. I couldn't think properly when he was around.

As his scent wove its insidious threads around me, as it always did, I felt my body respond instinctively. My heart beat faster, and an annoyingly pleasing warmth spread through my core. I hated that he had this effect on me. And it was getting worse. I was seeing Mason in my dreams now. Like, every fucking night. Each dream was more vivid and explicit than the last, as if my subconscious was determined to torment me with what I couldn't have. The way he would touch me, the way he made me feel; it was addictive. All I could think about was his chiseled jaw grazing my neck as he whispered exactly how he was going to fuck me. And he used those words, too. No romantic sweet nothings, no promises of unending passion. No, in my dreams, Mason told me exactly, in explicit detail, what he was going to do to me. And instead of being appalled at his language, I woke up each night horny as hell.

Maybe if I got a new vibrator, thoughts of Mason would disappear? I'd been using the same one for years now. Ever since my parents made it abundantly clear that having sex before my mating ceremony was a hard—no pun intended—no. I'd been sat down when I was fifteen and told that no matter how appealing someone might be or how much I wanted to, I could not risk the future of this Pack by sleeping with whoever I wanted. If the mate bond sealed, that person would be the future Alpha of this Pack, whether they wanted it or not. I had to trust my parents to help me choose the best person for the Pack, and as had happened for my parents, hope that the fated mate bond sealed during the official mating ceremony. If not, well, not everyone found their fated mate, and at least my parents will have chosen someone suitable to be my partner to help me rule this Pack. But I couldn't help but wonder what was under Mason's pants, what that bulge in the front would look like. What it would feel like.

I had to stop doing this. I couldn't get caught up in my Mason fog anymore. I was the daughter of the Pack Alphas, and I had work to do. I sped up. I would just have to find out what he wanted and send him on his way. I didn't have time to daydream about his hands roaming my body, his lips kissing lower and lower until—No! No more daydreaming!

This morning, I had a meeting scheduled with Edmond, the werewolf my parents had chosen as my future mate. I had to focus on that. Both my parents thought he was the perfect match for me.

I wasn't so sure, but Edmond certainly possessed qualities that made him an ideal partner and co-leader of the Pack. He was, first and foremost, loyal to Bridgetown. We'd had our share of traitors recently; first Tristan, then Elise, who'd tried to kill Ryan and Mai while they were hiding out here. The new werewolves my dad and Tristan had brought in to help us when we thought there might be a war with the Three Rivers Pack had all left with Tristan. Now, everyone was on edge, wondering who might be next.

Edmond, though, came from a Bridgetown family that was as old as mine. He was raised like me, taught to always put the Pack first. He understood the importance of unity and would do anything to protect our people. He had a sharp analytical mind, which allowed him to assess situations quickly and make well-informed decisions, and it helped that he was always cool under pressure, a trait that was invaluable in our world.

I wasn't attracted to him, although he was definitely handsome in an accountant-who-secretly-works-out kind of way. This was what had convinced me I was doing the right thing. I didn't want to fall in love. Didn't want someone to have that power over me. Not after what had happened with Tristan.

Memories of my past with Tristan flooded my mind, transporting me back to when I was an 18-year-old, sheltered within the Pack and surrounded by my parents' enforcers. I remembered the thrill when I realized that Tristan had noticed me, that he was paying special attention to me. Me!

It started with small gestures, like bringing me my coffee in the morning, just the way I liked it, or leaving a single flower on my desk. He would always find a reason to be near me, offering to help with my training or volunteering to accompany me on errands. Tristan made me feel special, like I was the only person in the world who mattered to him. At eighteen, it had been intoxicating.

One day, he surprised me with a picnic in the woods, just the two of us. He had prepared my favorite foods, including caprese sandwiches and strawberries, brought a blanket for us to sit on, and wine to drink. As we ate and talked, Tristan told me that we were fated mates, destined to be together forever. He said he could feel the bond between us, and that it was only a matter of time before I felt it, too.

I had been so naive, so excited by the idea of being Tristan's fated mate. The idea of having someone who loved me so completely, who wanted to share their life with me, was everything I had ever wanted. I believed every word he said, and I couldn't wait for the day when I would feel the bond, too.

It really had been that easy for him. I fell for the fantasy, the attention. For the gorgeous older Beta who wanted me to be his mate. It took me at least another six months before the doubts started to creep in.

My parents had been delighted that Tristan and I were involved. They adored him. But I started to see how he acted around them was different to how he acted with other members of the Pack. With my parents, he fully supported their vision of Bridgetown as a tourist spot for humans to come and learn and interact with Shifters. With others, with me, though, the way he spoke about humans and the future of our Pack made me uneasy.

I remember the first time I really noticed it. We were walking through town one evening, and a group of human tourists passed by, excitedly taking pictures.

Tristan's lip curled in disgust. "Look at them," he muttered, his voice low enough that only I could hear. "Gawking at us like we're some kind of circus attraction. They have no idea of the power we possess."

I felt chilled by his words. "But isn't that the point?" I asked hesitantly. "To show them we're not a threat?"

He scoffed. "But we are a threat! We should be ruling them, not pandering to them."

Then, after a Pack meeting about increasing human-werewolf integration in town, I heard him talking to some of his friends. "They're leading us down a path of weakness. We're diluting our true nature. Werewolves are apex predators, not tourist attractions or pet dogs for humans to coo over."

I tried to argue, to defend my parents' vision, but Tristan always had a way of making his words sound so reasonable, so right. "Use your brain, Shya. How long before humans decide they want to control us? Study us? We need to show them our strength before it's too late." He'd looked around at his friends, at the others nearby listening in. "When I'm Alpha," he said, his voice low and intense, "things will be different. We'll reclaim our rightful place. Humans will learn to fear us again, as they should. And you'll be by my side, Shya. My mate, my queen."

The possessiveness in his voice, the way he spoke about humans as if they were inferior beings, it all started to make me deeply uncomfortable. But every time I tried to talk to him about it, Tristan would brush me aside, telling me I just needed time to understand, that once our mate bond fully formed, I'd see things his way.

Gradually, I began to see how Tristan manipulated others in the

Pack. He'd whisper doubts about my parents' leadership, plant seeds of discontent about our relationship with humans. To the younger wolves, he'd talk about the 'glory days' when werewolves didn't hide their nature, when they were truly free.

"Imagine not having to pretend to be weaker than you are. That's the future I see for us."

As I watched him work his charm on others, saw how easily they fell under his spell, just as I had, the unease in my gut grew. I began to realize that the Tristan I thought I knew, the one who brought me coffee and left flowers on my desk, was just a mask. Behind it lurked someone far more dangerous, someone whose vision for our future filled me with dread.

When I went to my parents, they thought I was just getting cold feet. They couldn't believe their beloved Tristan, who was so charming and supportive, would turn on them. So, I'd done the only thing I could do. I'd sneaked out of Pack territory and gotten really drunk at a human bar where no one would recognize me.

Fortunately, it turned out that Derek Shaw, head of intelligence for the neighboring Three Rivers Pack, was there. He'd asked if I was okay, gave me his card. I hadn't thought much of it at the time, but I'd gone home determined to find some proof about Tristan to show my parents. That's when I found he'd been in touch with someone in Three Rivers, and they were plotting to take over both Packs. I'd remembered Derek's card and called him. After that, I'd worked as an agent for Derek, passing him information when I could. We'd eventually worked out that Brock Madden in their Pack was conspiring with Tristan, and we'd stopped their plot, but Tristan escaped and took a lot of our Pack with him, ones who bought into his vision of the future.

I'd been burned pretty badly by the whole thing. Tristan had taught me how easy it was to manipulate feelings. He taught me not to trust myself or what I felt. I had been convinced that he was my fated mate, but I'd been wrong. Now, I couldn't help but question every emotion, every attraction I felt. I didn't want to make the same mistake again, didn't want to give my heart to someone who might betray me and the Pack again.

That's why I had to push my feelings for Mason aside. I couldn't risk getting caught up in another whirlwind romance, no matter how much my body and heart wanted him. My wolf thought I was a being an idiot. For her, it was straightforward. I wanted Mason. I should have Mason. But I had to focus on my duty to the Pack, on my arranged marriage to Edmond. It was the right choice, the logical choice.

I was walking up the steps to the front door when I heard raised voices coming from the study. I crept closer to the door.

"You have got to be fucking shitting me!" Mason's voice was full of disbelief and anger.

Damn it!

I was guessing Mom and Dad had just told him about my upcoming mating ceremony to Edmond.

Well, he had to find out sooner or later. Though I had been hoping it would be after the event. Mom and Dad would give him some time to cool down and then send him on his way.

Me? I was going to take the coward's way out and hide in my room until he'd gone.

CHAPTER THREE

SHYA

I closed my door as quietly as I could and leaned against it. Phew! Crisis averted. My nose wrinkled. Mason's scent was getting stronger, radiating his feelings loud and clear through the house. Where was he goi—? Wait, he couldn't be coming here, could he?

I scrambled away from the door, my heart pounding in my chest. The idea of Mason coming to my bedroom was both thrilling and terrifying.

I listened, the sound of footsteps growing closer. What the hell was I going to say to him? I just wouldn't open the door when he knocked; that was it. I'd pretend I wasn't here. Not exactly a great look for the future Alpha of the Pack, but I didn't care. There was no way I could see Mason right now.

The door burst open, and there he was.

Okay, so Mason Shaw is not a knocking-on-doors kind of guy. Good to know.

All the breath left my body as I stared at him. He stood in the doorway, his imposing figure filling the space, his anger filling the whole room. He was in the prime of his life, his body honed by years of training and Shifter genetics. Power coiled within him, ready to pounce at a moment's notice.

His pale blue eyes stood out against his dark hair and blazed with a deep, almost electric sheen. Those eyes, usually so warm and inviting, were now filled with a fury that sent shivers through me. His jaw was clenched tight, the muscles in his face taut with tension. His full lips, which I had so often admired, were now pressed into a thin line, emphasizing the sharp angles of his chiseled features. His hands, strong and capable, which were usually holding something—a pen, a knife, a tennis ball, anything to keep his fingers busy while he thought—were balled into fists at his sides as if he were barely restraining himself.

My gaze traveled down his body, noticing a set of intricate tattoos on his left arm. I'd never seen them before. Mason had always worn long sleeves. Now, his white shirt was rolled up, and the dark ink stood out against his tanned skin, winding patterns that immediately drew my eye.

The air between us seemed to crackle with tension. I couldn't tear my eyes away from him, couldn't breathe, couldn't think. All I could do was stand there, transfixed by the raw power and emotion emanating from him.

"There you are." He stalked toward me, his movements fluid and purposeful, like a predator closing in on its prey. I instinctively backed away, my heart beating rapidly now as I tried to keep a bit of distance between us. I moved backward, never taking my eyes off him until I felt the wall pressing against my back.

He kept coming at me, though, stopping mere inches from me, his body so close that I could feel the heat radiating off him.

Mason leaned in, his face hovering just above mine. His eyes roamed over my features, studying every detail as if he were committing them to memory. I couldn't look away, couldn't escape the intensity of his gaze.

Then he raised his arms and placed his hands on the wall. One next to my head and the other by my hip. He'd caged me in without actually touching me. The gesture was both thrilling and unnerving. If I tried to escape, I'd have to touch him to do it. And I wanted to. I so wanted to close the distance between us and feel his skin on mine.

I had to break this spell.

"You're in my bedroom."

Way to state the obvious, Shya.

Mason didn't respond. He just continued to stare at me, his eyes boring into mine. I could feel my knees going weak.

I tried again. "*Why* are you in my bedroom?"

He didn't answer right away, but his eyes darkened. "You seem to be under the impression that you're going to mate with someone else."

I blinked, surprise and confusion washing over me at his statement. "I'm not under the impression. I *am* going to mate with someone else. With ..." My mind went blank for a moment, and for the life of me, I couldn't remember his name. "Edmond! Yes, Edmond!"

Mason's lips curved into a smirk, a hint of amusement dancing in his eyes. "No. You're my mate. You know it. I know it. There is no Edmond in this relationship."

I shook my head, trying to clear the fog that always seemed to settle over my thoughts when he was near. "Edmond is a logical match. He is exactly what this Pack needs," I argued.

It was hard to focus on my responsibilities, on the duty that had been drilled into me since birth, when Mason was so close. His presence was overwhelming, consuming every part of me until all I could think about was him.

"Is he?" Mason challenged. "What about you, Shya? What do you need?" His voice was so silky smooth, it sent a thrill straight to my core. I opened my mouth to respond, but no words came out. What did I need? In that moment, with Mason's body so close to mine, I couldn't think of anything beyond the desire that coursed through my veins. And I knew he could smell it, the bastard, from the smug expression on his face.

Mason leaned in even closer, his breath ghosting over my lips. "What is it that *you* need?" he asked again, his voice whisper soft. "Whatever it is, I can give it to you. You need me to lick your pussy until you come all over my face? You need me to fuck you from behind, my cock plunging into you again and again until you're screaming my name? Tell me, princess, what it is that you need."

I couldn't think clearly, could barely breathe. I had never, ever had anyone talk to me that way before. It was crass and shocking and explicit, and all I could focus on was the way his lips moved as he spoke, the way they seemed to beckon me closer. I wanted exactly what he had said, wanted it so badly I thought I would faint with pleasure if he actually did it.

My eyes dropped to his mouth, and I felt my own lips part slightly in anticipation. I wanted to close the distance between us, to give in to the longing that had been building inside me for so long.

In that moment, something within me snapped. The rational part of my mind, the part that had been telling me to resist, the one whose job it was to protect my heart, went silent. All that remained was the overwhelming need that consumed me, the desire that had been building since the moment he'd stepped into my room.

I surged forward, closing the distance between us as my lips crashed against his. Mason's arms wrapped around me, pulling me impossibly closer, as if he wanted to meld our bodies into one. I moaned against his lips. Every nerve ending in my body felt alive, electrified by his touch. Mason's hands roamed over my body, tracing the curves and lines of my form as if he were committing them to memory.

I trembled, and a low growl rumbled from his throat. His hands drifted lower, squeezing my hips as he pulled me closer. I could feel a fire starting to burn low in my belly, and I was already wet with anticipation. Mason's hand continued its descent, slipping beneath my jeans and into my panties. I gasped against his lips as his fingers grazed my clit, sending shockwaves of pleasure coursing through my body.

"Fucking hell, the princess is so fucking wet already."

I clutched at Mason's shoulders for support. His thumb gently flicked my clit, and I gasped into his mouth.

"Yes, my princess likes it." He smirked as he slid a finger inside of me, and I honestly thought my whole body was going to explode. The sensation was unlike anything I had ever experienced. He pumped his finger in and out, his thumb still slowly stroking my clit, and I could feel a building heat within me. Then he added another finger, and I knew I was going to explode. The sensation was so intense, his fingers filling me so completely as he stretched them apart as he slid them out before thrusting them back inside of me.

It was as if Mason had unlocked some primal, untamed part of me that I never knew existed. My fingers dug into his muscles, his skin warm and firm beneath my touch. I wanted more; I wanted him, all of him. I could feel the orgasm building, the heat and intensity growing. I couldn't hold myself up any longer, my legs weak, and I clutched at him for support.

"Mason," I gasped.

He grinned as his other hand stroked my hair, his touch gentle yet possessive.

"That's it. Come for me, princess."

I could feel his dominance, the way he took control of me without even trying. And I loved every second of it. My hips rolled, wanting more, needing more. He slid another finger inside of me, stretching me further. I cried out into his mouth, my body arching toward him in pure, unadulterated need. Mason's eyes never left mine as the most amazing orgasm I'd ever had exploded within me. His thrusting fingers matched the rhythm of my whimpering cries. The pleasure built up and crashed over me, over and over again, sending waves of ecstasy coursing through my veins. My body writhed and bucked against his hand, every nerve ending exploding with exquisite pain and sweet release.

I was dizzy with pleasure and need, my body trembling from the intensity of my climax. But I wanted more. I wanted all of him. I wanted that connection that could only be achieved through mating. Mason's eyes locked onto mine, his face a mix of hunger and dominance.

"You want me," he smirked, his voice full of cocky confidence.

I did. I really did. I opened my mouth to agree when a voice from the doorway snapped me out of my Mason fog.

"Shya Little!"

My eyes widened in panic. My mom, like my actual mom, was behind Mason at the entrance to my room.

Oh, the ever-loving Goddess! This couldn't be happening. I was going to die of embarrassment.

Mason's gaze never left mine as he gently slid his hand out of my jeans, and then the arrogant bastard winked at me as he sucked the fingers that had been inside of me.

Holy fuck!

I tried to push Mason away, but he didn't move.

Fine. I ducked around the side of him and walked to the middle of the room, trying to put as much distance between him and me as possible.

What the hell had I just done? What had I been thinking?

I hadn't been thinking, that was the problem. Mason and his fucking brain fog had struck again.

I couldn't allow this to happen again.

Mom's face was shocked as she watched us both; she knew exactly what had happened here. My whole body was burning. I couldn't believe my mom had just caught me with Mason's hand down my panties and a blissed-out post-orgasm look on my face. Could this get any worse?

"I think it is time you left, Mason Shaw," Mom said coldly.

Mason didn't move. Most people moved when Mom gave them an order.

"I'm not done talking to Shya."

Mom looked furious. "I tell you to leave, you leave."

Okay, so yes, it could indeed get worse. My mom and Mason were going to start a war between our two Packs, right here in my bedroom.

"I ..." Oh Goddess, how the hell did I tell him to get lost after what he'd just done to me?

I pulled on my years of training to be an Alpha, straightened my spine, and made my face go blank.

"Mason, I might have feelings for you, but it doesn't change anything. I will be mated to Edmond. It is what is best for this Pack, what is best for me."

Mason crossed his arms. "Bullshit."

I blinked. No one in this Pack ever talked to me like that, and definitely not in front of my mom.

"Excuse me?"

"I called bullshit. Mating with Edmond is not what's best for this Pack, and it certainly as fuck isn't what's best for you."

I drew myself up and met his eyes. "You are entitled to your opinion, of course. But I am going through with this, and I think it would be good if you left now."

"I bet you do." He stalked toward me, and I only just stopped myself from stepping back. "I'm betting things become much clearer when I'm around. You know exactly what you want and what you need, and for some reason, that confuses you." He leaned down toward me, his face right in front of mine. "You can't deny what's between us forever, princess. This isn't over. This is just the start."

With that, he turned and stalked out of my room.

CHAPTER FOUR

MASON

I strode out of Shya's room, my jaw clenched, and my hands balled into fists at my sides. The taste of her still lingering on my lips did nothing to calm my anger. Nor did the memory of how her green eyes clouded with desire or how her curly auburn hair had been a wild halo around her face as she came all over my fingers. She wanted me as much as I wanted her; I was sure of it. But fucking politics and family duty were stopping her from admitting it. I could still feel the phantom touch of her body against mine, the way she'd been so fucking responsive to my touch. Shya might be fighting our connection, denying what was meant to be, but now I had a taste of her, I wouldn't give up. I couldn't. She was mine, and sooner or later, she'd have to accept that fact.

My wolf snarled in frustration, urging me to go back.

Ours. Mate.

I ignored him when I saw Michael waiting at the front door. As the other Alpha of the Bridgetown Pack, he had a reputation for being fiercely protective of his people and his family. His expression was a clear indication that he had something to say.

Fucking great.

"Mason." His chin jerked in my direction.

I didn't have time for this, had no desire to be lectured by Michael, but we had come here asking for his help in tracking down information on ripple, the drug that was wreaking havoc across all Shifter communities. We needed their help.

"Michael."

"I understand, I really do. I know you have feelings for Shya, but I need to ask you to respect her decision. She will be Alpha here someday and is doing what she was born to do: putting the Pack first."

I met Michael's stare, my own eyes hard. Couldn't they see the damage they would do to her if they forced her into a marriage with someone who wasn't her fated mate? How could they do that to their own daughter? I resisted the urge to argue, to tell him that Shya's happiness should come first, knowing it would be pointless right now. Michael's belief in his family's duty was unshakable, and any attempt to convince him otherwise would only strain the tenuous relationship between our Packs just when we needed them. I'd come back in a few days. Sit down with Michael and Camille and make them see sense.

I held his gaze a moment longer, knowing I was pushing the boundaries. He was an Alpha, and I should have lowered my eyes the second his met mine, but I was done respecting these traditions. Not if it meant Shya was going to end up in someone else's bed.

Without a word, I turned and walked out the door. Derek was waiting by his SUV, his arms crossed and his face blank. I knew he'd heard everything, but he didn't ask questions, thank fuck, just opened the driver's side door and slid behind the wheel.

I stared out the window as we pulled away from Bridgetown, my mind racing. My wolf was still restless, pacing in the back of my mind, but I pushed him down, focusing on the anger that simmered just beneath the surface. I had to get it under control.

I pulled out one of the tennis balls that were stashed in all of my brothers' cars. They knew me too well. I thought best when I had something to do with my hands. The familiar texture of the fuzzy yellow surface grounded me as I began to squeeze it rhythmically.

I hated feeling out of control. Anger was a dangerous emotion for a werewolf, especially one as strong as me. It was like a wildfire, threatening to consume everything in its path if left unchecked. I'd seen what unchecked rage could do, both to the wolf and to those around them. I'd vowed long ago never to let myself get to that point.

The ball compressed and expanded in my grip as I focused on my breathing. In, out. Squeeze, release. Each repetition helped to calm the storm brewing inside me. I could feel my muscles relaxing incrementally.

The anger wasn't gone, just contained. It was a constant battle, one I'd been fighting for years. Part of me wanted to let the rage flow freely, but the rest of me knew better. Control was everything. Without it, I was just another monster.

Derek glanced over at me, his brow lined with worry. "Want to talk about it?"

"No," I replied, my tone curt and dismissive. I appreciated my brother's concern, but talking about Shya and the clusterfuck that was our relationship was the last thing I wanted to do.

Derek nodded, his eyes returning to the road. But after a few moments of silence, he spoke again.

"I know you don't want to hear this, but maybe Michael has a point. Shya has a responsibility to her Pack, and you can't expect her to just abandon that for you."

I clenched my jaw, my fingers tightening around the tennis ball.

"She's my mate. I won't let anyone else have her. Not even you."

Derek frowned at me but kept his voice calm. "Yes, I worked with Shya. Yes, I ran her as an agent, but if you really think I have any feelings for her besides seeing her as a kid sister to look out for, then I'll pull this car over, and we can have at it."

I sighed. Derek had a point. I knew his fated mate was Sofia. Hell, everyone knew it, well, apart from maybe Sofia. But my possessive instincts for Shya were on full steam right now. She was going to be mated to someone else, for holy fucking sake.

I grunted. And that was as much as an apology as he was going to get.

"You think I don't understand? I understand perfectly, Mason. But you need to think about this. You can't just storm in and take her away from her Pack. That will start a war."

I didn't reply, hoping he'd get the message that I didn't want to talk about this.

"So, what's your plan here, Mason? You've got two options, as far as I can see."

I glanced over at him, raising an eyebrow in question. Derek could be fucking annoying with his calm precision all the time. He never seemed to have issues keeping his anger under control, not since he served in the army. It was a skill they had instilled in him and one he excelled at. I wasn't too proud to admit I envied his talent and found it unbelievably irritating at times, but it meant he was good at looking

25

at things logically. At seeing things others didn't.

"Option one," Derek said, holding up a finger, "Shya gives up her position in Bridgetown as Pack princess and comes to live with you, a lowly PI, in Three Rivers. She becomes your mate and leaves her Pack behind. She has trained to be an Alpha her whole life, so maybe she'll be happy doing what? Being your secretary? Or maybe one day she wakes up and realizes she could be running the Pack a whole lot better than Ryan and Mai and decides to make that happen."

"And option two?" I asked, already knowing the answer.

"You give up everything," Derek said, his voice serious. "You leave Three Rivers, leave our Pack, and move to Bridgetown. That means that, in time, you'll become the Alpha of the Bridgetown Pack and take your place beside Shya."

I barked out a laugh, the sound harsh and bitter. Me? Running a Pack? The last thing I wanted was that sort of responsibility.

"Of course," Derek continued, "I'm sure that'll go down well with the Bridgetown Pack. An outsider, a rival, coming in and taking over as their Alpha. I'm sure they'd welcome you with open arms."

"Your sarcasm's on fire today."

Derek dipped his head. "Thank you. Seriously, though, it would be a fucking nightmare. You'd face challenges, have to deal with a lot of resistance. You'd be isolated, constantly fighting off schemes to remove you from power."

I sighed, rubbing a hand over my face. Derek was right. Neither option was viable, not really. Shya and I were caught between two worlds, two Packs, and there seemed to be no way to bridge the gap.

"You need to ask yourself if she's worth it."

My wolf snarled at the suggestion. Of course she was fucking worth it. I'd do anything for our mate. But now that I was calmer, I knew Derek was just looking out for me, like always.

"I won't lose her, Derek. But I don't know how to make this work."

Derek nodded. "Well, you've got time to work it out. The mating ceremony isn't for another couple of weeks."

He was right. I had to focus on the task at hand. We had come to Bridgetown for a reason, and I needed to put my personal feelings aside and concentrate on finding the information we needed to take down Brock.

I slipped the tennis ball into my pocket and straightened in my seat. Shya and I would find our way to each other, I was going to make sure of that, but first, I had a job to do.

CHAPTER FIVE

SHYA

T^{oday}

I walked down the hallway toward the dining room, my footsteps muffled by the plush carpet beneath my feet. I hadn't been able to concentrate since Mason left four days ago. I thought the Mason fog only worked when he was nearby, but after the mind-blowing orgasm he'd given me, he was all I could think about. It was the first time anyone had touched me like that; hell, the first time anyone, apart from me, had touched me there. It had been eye-opening. Was it always like that? Would I feel that way every time Mason touched me? How the hell did anyone get any work done when they knew someone could make them feel that way? That was just his fingers; what would it feel like to have *him* inside of me?

These thoughts kept going round and round in my head and it was throwing off my game; I was starting to get seriously annoyed about it. It didn't help that reports had been coming in of a battle brewing between the Three Rivers Pack and Brock's forces.

I paused outside the dining room door, taking a deep breath and composing myself. I couldn't let my family see the turmoil that Mason had caused. They needed me to be strong, to be the leader they raised me to be. I had on my Shya-kicks-butt white Dior slingback pumps today for precisely this reason, and I needed their superpowers to start working. With a final shake of my head, I pushed open the door and stepped inside.

"Shya!" Tucker's excited voice rang out, and before I could react, my little brother barreled into me, wrapping his arms around my waist in a tight hug. I stumbled back a step, a surprised laugh escaping my lips.

"Hey there, Tuck," I said, ruffling his hair affectionately. "What's got you so excited this morning?"

Tucker grinned up at me, his eyes sparkling with mischief. "You'll never guess what happened this morning! I was out in the backyard just after dawn, and I found this really cool bug. It was huge, like the size of my hand! And it had these crazy colors, like rainbow wings! And Dede said she could catch it, but I knew she wouldn't be fast enough. She's only six!"

I listened as Tucker chattered on, his enthusiasm and innocence a welcome relief from thoughts of Mason fucking Shaw, and especially me fucking Mason Shaw. I felt the tension in my shoulders ease, and a genuine smile spread across my face. No matter how troubled the world seemed at times, Tucker's presence always brought a ray of sunshine into my life.

"So, then," Tucker said, bouncing on the balls of his feet, "I tried to catch it, but it was too fast even for me. I chased it all around the yard, and I almost had it, but then I tripped over a rock and fell into a

29

muddy puddle, and Dede laughed so hard she wet her pants!"

My eyes widened. "Oh dear!"

"Nah, even that didn't stop her laughing! Not even when Henry came and dunked us both in the bath!"

"Well, it sounds like you had quite the adventure," I said, tapping Tucker's nose playfully. "I hope you didn't track mud all over the clean floors, or Mom'll have both our hides!"

Tucker giggled, hugging me tighter. "I didn't. I promise. Henry carried me on his shoulders!"

As if on cue, Henry walked into the dining room, his nose buried in a book. At seventeen, he had grown into a lanky young man, his frame not yet filled out but hinting at the strength he would one day possess. His watchful brown eyes, so like our mother's, flickered toward Tucker every few seconds, a silent check to ensure his little brother was safe and sound.

"Hello, Shya. Tuck." He nodded to each of us before sitting down at the table.

Henry had always been the quieter one, his thoughtful and soft-spoken nature so different from Tucker's exuberance and the rebellious streak I'd had when I was a teenager.

Despite his shyness around strangers, Henry possessed a fierce protectiveness when it came to our family, especially Tucker. The incident with Tristan last month had only intensified it, and I knew that Henry would go to any lengths to keep his little brother safe from harm.

I caught a glimpse of the book's title as Henry lowered it to his lap: *The Art of War* by Sun Tzu. Hmmm. Another effect of Tristan taking Tucker—Henry had given up his previous favorite fantasy books, and now all he read was about war strategy. I needed to spend more time with him, help him feel safe again, and go back to just being a teenager and not a general-in-training.

I shooed Tucker to his chair just as our parents came in. Mom and Dad had been mated for over two decades, but the love and affection between them were as strong as ever. They moved in perfect sync, Dad's hand resting gently on the small of Mom's back as he guided her to a seat at the head of the table.

As Dad pulled out Mom's chair, she smiled up at him, her eyes shining with adoration, and I felt a pang of regret. Would I ever have that with Edmond? My parents were fated mates and were the epitome of what an Alpha couple should be—strong, united, and deeply in love. I knew they hoped that Mason was wrong, that as soon as I mated with Edmond, our mate bond would reveal itself, and Mason would be a distant memory. It was how it happened for them. They were betrothed by their families, but it wasn't until they went through the mating ceremony that their fated mate bond came to life.

"Good morning, everyone," Dad said as he passed a dish to Mom. The Pack's cook had outdone himself this morning, with platters of crispy bacon, fluffy scrambled eggs, and golden pancakes drizzled with maple syrup already on the table. Despite the mouth-watering spread before us, no one touched their food until Mom and Dad had filled their plates and taken their first bites.

"So, what's on everyone's agenda today?" Dad asked, his tone light and casual.

Tucker, his mouth full of pancake, mumbled something unintelligible before swallowing and grinning. "I'm gonna catch that bug today! And then I'm gonna show it to Dede!"

31

"Just be careful out there, Tuck. I don't fancy giving you and Dede another bath!"

"It was a minor miscalculation! My reflexes are awesome; I'll soar over the rock next time like a flying wolf ninja!"

I couldn't help but smile as an image of Tucker's wolf dressed in black clothes, with a black headband tied round his head, doing ninja rolls around the backyard popped into my head.

Henry cleared his throat, setting down his fork. "I've been thinking about the Pack's training regimen," he said, his voice steady, but I could detect a hint of nervousness in my brother. "I'd like to propose some changes, maybe implement some new techniques I've been researching."

Dad raised an eyebrow, intrigued. "Oh? What kind of changes did you have in mind?"

Henry straightened in his chair. "Well, I've been reading about how some Packs in the conclave cities integrate more diverse fighting styles into their training. Incorporating elements from human martial arts, maybe even some parkour for agility. I think it could give us an edge."

Dad nodded slowly, a small smile forming on his lips. "That's an interesting idea, Henry." He paused, his eyes studying Henry for a moment. "It is not the way we have done it, but a great leader carves their own path. I don't see any problem with trying it out for a while. Why don't you put together a detailed proposal, and we can discuss it later?"

Henry's face lit up, though he tried hard to remain stoic. "Thanks, Dad. I'll start working on it right away."

I pushed my plate away. "Are there any updates from Ryan and Mai about the situation with Brock's Pack?" I asked.

There. That was calm, no mention of Mason at all. They didn't need to know about the knot in my stomach at the thought of what he was facing in Three Rivers.

Dad's expression grew somber. "Last I heard, they were preparing for a battle. They're going head-to-head with Brock's army today."

My stomach dropped, and I had to hold my wolf tight inside. Mason was out there, fighting alongside his Pack, and the thought of him in danger made my heart clench with fear. He could die today, and I was here sipping coffee. She was trying to get me to run out of here to be at his side, but I knew my parents would never allow it.

Mom's brow furrowed as she looked at me. "If the worst should happen, we've agreed to take in any survivors from the Three Rivers Pack. They're our allies, and we can't leave them to fend for themselves. Preparations are being made to accommodate them all."

I would have to approach this carefully. I needed to pretend that it was no big deal. If they knew I planned to sneak out of here as soon as breakfast was over and join the Three Rivers Pack for this fight, they'd lock me in the cage room until it was all over.

"Have we heard anything about the expected size of Brock's forces?" I said, keeping my voice even.

Dad shook his head. "The reports have been inconsistent, but it seems like Brock has managed to gather a significant number of followers. Ryan and Mai are facing a formidable challenge."

"Father—"

"No, Shya. Your Mom and I agreed. This is an internal Three Rivers issue. We won't put our people on the line for this, and Ryan and Mai have not asked."

I nodded, my heart racing despite my outward calm.

Mom reached across the table, placing her hand over mine. "I know you're worried, Shya. It's natural to be concerned for our *allies*, especially given the gravity of the situation."

Allies, huh? She was being careful not to mention Mason, too.

"You have nothing to worry about, Shya," Tucker piped up. "Ryan and Mai will kick Brock's butt!"

I forced myself to smile, even though my thoughts were whirling. I had to go and help them, but I'd have to be careful, bide my time, and wait for the right opportunity to slip away unnoticed.

Chapter Six

SHYA

There was a sharp knock at the door, and Danni, our Pack Beta, walked in. She was good at her job, well liked in the Pack, but whenever I saw her, I had this urge to take her out and get her drunk. She was so uptight all the time. I knew she felt she had a lot to live up to, that she had a lot of trust to rebuild after Tristan, the previous Beta, betrayed us all, but she really needed to loosen up.

"Good morning, everyone. Michael, Camille, I have the briefing notes ready for you both to go over. Shya, Summer is here with a package for you. Do you want me to send her in?"

My shoes! I'd forgotten all about them. Fucking Mason fog.

Dad arched an eyebrow at me. "Not more shoes?"

He didn't see the point of having so many pairs of shoes. He had his smart shoes, his comfy shoes, and his sneakers; anything else was being opulent.

I took a different view. I'd been working since I was twelve. My parents wanted me to learn what everyone did in a Pack, so I would spend six-month stints with different people, doing entry-level tasks, from running errands and inputting data for the enforcers to being a kitchen helper, cutting up food and washing dishes in the Alpha House and some of the restaurants in town to being an admin assistant to our Pack lawyers and accountants. I had done everything and worked my butt off doing it before and after school and around my Alpha training. None of them paid much, but they paid.

When I turned eighteen, my parents had created a position for me here, a sort of Alpha-in-training post where I shadowed them and gradually took on more and more responsibilities, like the town council meeting this evening. Even though we owned the Alpha House, my parents insisted I pay for rent and food so that I would always be able to appreciate what other members of our Pack faced financially. I didn't take holidays and had no one to spend the money on. I rarely ate out, and, apart from Marnie and I having a girls' night every fortnight, I didn't go out, so most of what was left sat in my bank account or got spent on shoes. I didn't just want the shoes. I needed the shoes. They were my armor, my superpower; they helped me be the best version of myself.

"Yes, more shoes, Dad. I work hard for my money, and I get to spend it how I want."

"And the girl wants shoes," Tucker sang.

"The girl always wants shoes," Mom replied as she winked at me.

Damn straight, the girl always wanted shoes.

"Send her in, please," I told Danni.

A moment later, Summer walked in, carrying a sleek shoebox. Her ash-blonde hair was braided neatly, and her eyes darted around the room, landing briefly on Henry before quickly looking away. A faint blush crept up her cheeks.

"Hi, Shya," Summer said, her voice slightly breathless. "I've got your shoes."

"Summer," I replied, taking the box from her. "You're a lifesaver!"

"Hiya, Summer," Tucker said, faking casualness. He was up to something. "I saw you in the library yesterday. You seemed pretty cozy with Jake Anderson."

The room fell silent, with all of us adults trying to subtly listen in while pretending to be engrossed in our food. Jake Anderson was Ellen's son and was notorious for having bullied Henry in middle school. Jake was human and had tried to push all of Henry's buttons, trying to get him to "go wolf," as he called it, and snap. As the Pack Alpha's son, Henry was expected to remain calm and in control at all times. He could not be seen to be fighting anyone. It would have been devastating for our reputation and the tourist trade here to have the Alpha's son attack a human. Mom and Dad had refused to get involved, saying it was important that we all learned how to handle difficult situations. It took two years before Henry was confident enough to shut Jake down, and Henry—and, by extension, Tucker—both hated him.

Two pink dots appeared high on Summer's cheekbones, and she quickly glanced at Henry before looking away.

"Oh, really?" Summer replied, her voice level despite the color in her cheeks. "And what exactly did you see, Tucker?"

Tucker lifted his chin. "You two were sitting really close, whispering over some books. Looked pretty intense. You do know he's a total douchebag, right?"

"Language, Tucker," Mom murmured.

Summer, however, didn't miss a beat. She turned to face Tucker fully. "Well, Tucker, since you're keeping such close tabs on my study habits, I'll fill you in. I'm tutoring Jake in Chemistry. Principal Walters asked me to help him improve his grades so he can stay on the soccer team." Summer continued, her voice light but with a hint of challenge, "If you're so curious, maybe you'd like to join us next time? I could always use someone to fetch snacks and sharpen pencils. I'm sure I wouldn't mind having an assistant."

Tucker crossed his arms, glaring at Summer. "He's still a total douchebag."

Summer winked at him. "Maybe. But he's a douchebag who pays me to tutor him. I don't mind taking his money if it means I can go to the movies once a month."

And there it was again, a quick flick of her eyes over to Henry and then away again. Boy, she had it bad.

There was another knock at the door, and Danni popped her head in. She mouthed one word at me, "Edmond," then disappeared again.

Chapter Seven

SHYA

I really needed to take the girl out for drinks; maybe she could come the next time Marnie and I hit the town. Danni had been giving me a heads-up for the last couple of weeks whenever my fiancé was about to arrive, and I was eternally grateful to her. She somehow knew that I needed a moment to compose myself before I saw him.

I took a deep breath and turned as I heard footsteps approach. As always, Edmond looked impeccable in his tailored charcoal suit, not a hair out of place. His 6'2" frame carried an air of authority, shoulders broad and posture perfect. His dark hair was neatly combed, accentuating his strong jawline and high cheekbones, but his steel-blue eyes, usually so controlled, held a touch of tension today.

Behind him stood his brother, Garrett, a study in contrasts. Where Edmond was polished, Garrett was raw energy. He was slightly taller than Edmond, maybe 6'3", with a muscular build that spoke of hours in the gym rather than board rooms. His dark blonde hair was artfully tousled, giving him a roguish appearance that was amplified by the perpetual hint of a smirk on his lips. Garrett's eyes, a shade lighter than Edmond's, held a mischievous glint that always made me slightly wary.

"Shya," Edmond said. "I hope I'm not interrupting."

"Not at all," I replied, forcing a smile of my own. "We were just chatting."

Garrett leaned against the doorframe, a cocky grin on his face. "Hey there, Shya-girl. Looking good, as always."

"Garrett, I didn't expect to see you here."

Edmond cleared his throat, shooting a pointed look at his brother before turning back to me. "I was hoping we could discuss the arrangements for next week's Pack BBQ."

Of course. Always business with Edmond. I suppressed a sigh. "Sure, let's step outside."

I nodded to my parents before leading the way into the hallway, trying to get us far enough away that everyone wouldn't be eavesdropping. With Garrett trailing behind me and Edmond, I waited for a spark of something, anything, to hit me. Something to hint at a possible fated mate bond between me and Edmond. I knew my parents were convinced it would happen as soon as we were mated, and Edmond was a good choice for me. Calm, considerate, cool under pressure. He held the respect of members of our Pack, both human and Shifters. He would be accepted and looked up to as my partner Alpha. But there was nothing. Not even a twinge in my core.

Edmond cleared his throat again, pulling me from my thoughts. "Thank you for seeing me, Shya. I know how busy you are, but there are some logistics we need to work out."

I raised an eyebrow. "Logistics? It's a BBQ, Edmond. We've done this before."

"Yes, but this year, there will be more humans than ever before," he explained, his face a mask of calm efficiency. "There are tourists coming here especially for the BBQ. We have been marketing it for months in the conclave and human cities. So, we really need to ensure everything goes smoothly."

I couldn't help but sigh. "What did you have in mind?"

"Well, for starters, we need to consider dietary restrictions," Edmond began, ticking off points on his fingers. "Not everyone can handle rare meat like we can. Then there's the issue of activities. We need to make sure they're inclusive for both Shifters and humans."

I felt a flare of frustration. We'd been holding this annual BBQ for the last ten years. He had been to all of them. He had never seen humans getting food poisoning or werewolves hunting or scrapping in the middle of the town park. But now he was the presumed future Alpha, he was so concerned with every little detail, even when my parents and I had worked it all out years ago.

"It'll be fine, Edmond. We have everything in place."

Edmond's lips tightened slightly. "Shya, this event is crucial for Pack relations. We can't afford any misunderstandings or accidents."

"Accidents?"

Was he serious?

"What are you worried about? That some of us will suddenly Shift and start chasing the humans around?"

"Of course not," Edmond replied, his voice still infuriatingly calm. "But we need to be prepared for any scenario. It's what good leaders do."

"And if nothing else, Edmond is a good leader," Garrett said, glancing back down the hallway. I couldn't tell if Garrett was being sincere or if there was a hint of bitterness to his words.

Either way, Garrett was right; Edmond was a good leader. I tried seeing it from his perspective. I'd been training to be an Alpha since birth. My parents had only arranged our mating in the last couple of weeks. Edmond was learning on the go and wanted to do the best he could do. He had always been meticulous and well-prepared. This was the first Pack event after he had been announced as my fiancé. I bet it was giving him hemorrhoids just thinking about all the things that might go wrong and look bad on him.

"Look," I said, lowering my voice and putting my hand on his arm. "It'll all be okay. We've got this; we've done it plenty of times before, but I'll talk to Mom. Maybe me and you can have a meeting with her this week and go over every last detail."

I would hate every second of it, but if it gave Edmond peace of mind, and meant he lightened up a bit, it would be worth it.

Edmond nodded, a small smile playing on his lips. "That would be helpful. Thank you, Shya."

Garrett grinned at me. "I can't think of anything worse than a logistical meeting about a fucking BBQ. You guys live real exciting lives, you know that, right?"

A look of exasperation crossed Edmond's face, a crack in his normal calm, controlled exterior. "Someone has to do it, Garrett. We can't all spend our time partying with our friends."

"Yeah, but your life would be hella more fun if you did, bro. Tell him he needs to loosen up, Shya, otherwise your sex life is going to be the most excruciatingly boring experience you've ever had. Have you even heard of reverse cowgirl, bro? Trust me, all the ladies love it, and you don't have to do any of the work. Isn't that right, Shya-girl?"

But of course, all women were exactly alike. Have breasts? Then you must enjoy exactly the same things. Of course, being a virgin, I had no idea if I loved it or not, but I was pretty sure Garrett had just ruined reverse cowgirl for me forever.

I narrowed my eyes at him as Edmond turned to his brother. "Garrett, Shya is your future Alpha. You talk to her like that again, and I'll cut off your allowance."

Garrett got an allowance? Interesting. Tucker got an allowance, but he was seven, and he had to do chores for it. Henry, like me, had been working since he was twelve.

Garrett held up his hands. "Man, I was joking! This is precisely what I mean; you and Shya need to both loosen up. Learn to take a joke, bro."

I wanted to shut Garrett down, but I was surprised to find that I was intrigued to see how far Garrett could push Edmond. Was there life under his robotic exterior? What would it take for him to lose his cool and explode? I was tempted to let this go on, but Edmond and I hadn't really talked since the announcement.

"Garrett, give me and your brother a moment, would you?"

A look of irritation flashed in his eyes before Garrett plastered a smile on his face. "Sure thing, Shya-girl. I'll be in the car."

I waited until Garrett was out of earshot before smiling softly at Edmond. "Brothers can test your patience, can't they?"

"Indeed. I apologize for his behavior. Garrett can be ... challenging at times."

"It's okay," I said, searching for something to say. "So, um ... how have you been since the announcement?"

Edmond straightened his already immaculate tie. "I've been well, thank you. Busy with preparations."

An uncomfortable silence fell between us, and Edmond seemed to find the wall behind me fascinating.

"And ... how do you feel about it all?" I ventured, hoping to break through his professional facade.

He blinked, as if surprised by the question. "It's a great honor, of course. I'm committed to fulfilling my role to this Pack to the best of my abilities."

I wasn't sure whether to laugh or feel completely dismayed. He sounded like he was giving a press conference. He wanted to mate with me to the best of his abilities? Could he be any less romantic?

I nodded, trying not to let my disappointment show. "Right, of course. But I meant ... personally. Are you ... happy about it?"

Edmond's eyes met mine for a brief moment before darting away. "I believe it's a wise decision for the Pack. We'll make a strong team, Shya, of that I have no doubt."

Which only made me question what he did have doubts about.

"And you?" he asked, his voice carefully neutral. "Are you ... satisfied with the arrangement?"

I forced a smile. "Like you said, it's for the good of the Pack."

Edmond nodded, looking relieved. "Excellent. I'm glad we're on the same page."

Another awkward silence descended. I found myself wishing for Garrett's inappropriate comments—at least they'd felt real.

"Well," Edmond said, checking his watch, "I should be going. Garrett's waiting, and I have a meeting in an hour."

"Of course," I replied, stepping back. "I'll be in touch about the meeting for the BBQ."

"Thank you. I'll have my assistant send over some available times." He hesitated for a moment, then awkwardly reached out and patted my shoulder. "Take care, Shya."

As I watched him walk away, with his straight back and measured steps, I couldn't help but wonder if this was what the rest of my life would look like—polite conversations, careful touches, and a partner who treated our relationship like a business merger.

No, I had to trust my parents knew better than me about this. I'd once picked Tristan, after all. After the ceremony, once the fated mate bond was in place, I was sure it would all be different.

I closed my eyes for a moment as the memory of Mason's warm lips on mine, his fingers pumping inside of me, flashed unbidden in my mind.

No! I quickly pushed it away. I couldn't afford to think about Mason, about what could have been. I had a duty to fulfill, a Pack to protect. And if that meant marrying Edmond and living a life of careful control, then so be it.

I snapped upright when Danni charged round the corner, her face flushed and her eyes wide with alarm.

"Tristan's here! He and his men are attacking the town!"

I heard Dad's chair fall onto the floor from the dining room.

"Where?" he asked, striding into the hallway.

"They're spread out across the west end of town," Danni replied. "Ivan and some enforcers are holding them off, but they're outnumbered."

Dad nodded. "Danni, gather the rest of the enforcers and have them meet me at the west end."

Danni turned and sprinted away as Summer came running toward me, followed by Mom, Henry, and Tucker.

"My mom! She's in town, opening the shop!"

Mom whirled to the children. "Henry, Tucker, I need you both to Shift, then take Summer and hide in the forest. Stay together and stay hidden until one of us comes for you."

Henry nodded, his face pale but determined. He grabbed Tucker's hand, pulling him toward the door. "Come on, Tuck. Summer! Let's go."

"I can't! I have to go and get Mom!"

"We'll make sure she's safe, Summer," I told her. "Go with Henry!"

Dad turned to face Mom and me. "Shya—"

"I'm ready."

He studied my face for a moment, indecision in his eyes. Then he jerked his chin. "Let's go."

Chapter Eight

SHYA

As we burst out of the Alpha House, the gravity of the situation hit me like a physical blow to the chest. Our Pack was under attack, and every second counted. The bell in town was toiling, and my phone was vibrating, our warning system kicking in. It would tell humans and Shifters alike to take cover.

Dad's face was grim as he turned to Mom. "I'm—"

"Go!" she interrupted. "I'll be right behind you."

Dad took off, sprinting toward the sound of fighting, his powerful strides eating up the ground.

Mom turned to me. "Shya, I need you to make sure the humans in town are safe. If any of Tristan's men get past us, they'll head there. You'll be our last line of defense."

Tristan hated humans with a passion; he wouldn't hesitate to slaughter every last one of them if given the chance.

I nodded. "I won't let you down."

She gripped my arm, her fingers digging into my skin. "If they break through our lines, you get the humans out of there. Do whatever it takes to keep them alive."

Mom pressed a quick kiss to my forehead before racing after Dad.

I didn't have time to watch her go. Marnie would be in her shop. I kicked off my Dior pumps—I wouldn't be able to run fast enough in them—turned, and sprinted toward the east side of town, a cold knot of fear twisting in my stomach.

Adrenaline raced, and I could feel it sharpening my senses. In the distance, the sounds of battle drifted over the town. I wanted to turn around and fight with my parents, but Marnie and the rest of the humans needed me, and I wasn't going to let them down.

As I neared the center of town, the familiar sights of the local bakery and the old-fashioned barbershop with its red and white spinning sign blurred past me. The usually bustling streets were empty, the shops closed up tight in the face of the impending danger. Good. Everyone was inside.

I was passing the hardware store when movement caught my eye. Two men I didn't recognize stepped out from the alley beside the building, their eyes fixed on me.

I slowed my pace and caught sight of three more emerging from behind the parked cars that lined the street.

Shit! They were boxing me in, cutting off escape routes. I came to a stop in the town square, next to the old stone fountain of a wolf and human sharing food at its center.

That's when I saw Cliff. He'd been one of Tristan's most loyal followers, and I'd never liked him, even when I was dating Tristan. He'd always been too sycophantic, too eager to please Tristan by any means necessary. Cliff, with his bulky frame and close-cropped blond hair that made him look more like a military grunt than a werewolf, stepped out from behind the fountain, dragging Marnie by her hair.

My heart clenched at the sight of my friend. Marnie's usually neat chestnut hair was tangled and matted with dirt and blood. Her face was a canvas of bruises, her left eye swollen nearly shut, and a nasty cut marred her cheekbone. Her clothes were torn and disheveled, as if she'd put up a fight. A trickle of blood ran from the corner of her mouth, staining her lips crimson.

I felt a surge of anger. Marnie was tough, but she was still human. She couldn't heal like we could. The fact that they'd hurt her so badly, knowing this, made my blood boil.

Marnie's eyes met mine, and I saw a flicker of fear in them.

Cliff's gaze never left mine. "Well, well, well. If it isn't the princess herself."

"Cliff. And here I was enjoying my day."

"Run, Shya! It's a trap! Forget me; go now!" Marnie yelled.

Cliff yanked Marnie's hair, eliciting a pained gasp from her. "Shut up, bitch!" He said it so casually, like it was something he said every day. "Look who we found. Your little human friend here thought she could say no when we told her to come out and play."

"Let her go, Cliff," I said, keeping my tone bored and uninterested. "This is between us. Marnie has nothing to do with it."

Cliff's smirk widened. "Oh, but she does. I'm here to prove a point, you see. To drive home the fact that you will always be weak, will always be defeated because you think of humans as more than just pets. Your attachment to them will be your downfall."

To the left and right, four more men dropped down from the tall oak trees that surrounded the square, completing the circle that now trapped me. I recognized some of them—werewolves who had once been a part of our Pack before they'd followed Tristan in his rebellion.

If I could distract them, could Marnie make a run for it?

I looked straight at her. "You know what I do in my rainbow sneakers?"

She tensed slightly, then gave an almost imperceptible nod.

"Fucking focus, Shya!" Cliff growled. "You're surrounded. There is no escape. You're too predictable, you know that? Rushing to protect your precious humans."

I circled around him, drawing attention to myself. "At least I'm playing for the right side. What's your excuse? Boredom? Or are you compensating for a tiny dick?"

His eyes flared with anger, and I knew I had him.

"You're fighting a losing battle," he taunted, stepping toward me and loosening his grip on Marnie. "Humans are fragile, expendable. Why waste your strength on them?"

"Because they matter," I replied. "Now!" I shouted at Marnie, then lunged at two werewolves to the right. I threw a punch into the first one's jaw and used the momentum to follow through with a roundhouse kick to the second one's head.

Marnie didn't hesitate. She threw a punch to Cliff's groin, and when he shied away, she yanked out of his grasp and bolted. She came straight at me, jumping over the first werewolf as he hit the ground, and darted away.

Cliff swore. "For fuck's sake! You guys are fucking pathetic!"

"You want us to go after her?" one of the werewolves to the left asked.

"No," replied Cliff. "Let the stupid bitch go. We have what we came for."

I had a horrid feeling he meant me. I tried not to show the panic that was weaving its way through me. There was no easy escape for me; I was going to have to fight my way out. I swept my eyes over the men, assessing them. They were all big, heavily muscled, and battle-scarred. None of these guys wanted to be brought down by a female, and definitely not one as pampered as they all thought I was. Maybe I could goad Cliff into fighting me by himself. One-on-one, I could kick his ass. He'd always been too quick to get angry in a fight. It made him sloppy.

"I'm flattered, Cliff. All this for little ol' me? What? You didn't think you were tough enough to take down the Pack princess alone?"

Cliff's lip curled in a sneer. "You think you're tough? Think you can take me?"

I forced a laugh. "Fuck, yeah! I'm not the one who had to bring nine of his buddies to take on one little girl."

One of the other werewolves growled, stepping forward menacingly. "Shut her mouth, Cliff! The bitch talks too much."

Cliff held up a hand, stopping the man in his tracks. "Easy, Des. All in good time."

He turned back to me, his eyes glinting. "You want a chance at this?"

I rolled my shoulders, warming up. "You talk too much, Cliff. You always did. We doing this or not?"

Cliff narrowed his eyes, but he smiled. "I'm going to enjoy watching you beg for mercy."

I shifted my stance, preparing for the fight of my life. I might win against Cliff, but the others weren't just going to walk away. I was outnumbered and outmatched, but I refused to show them my fear.

"Bring it on," I growled, my eyes flashing with challenge. "I'll show you what an Alpha's daughter can do."

And with that, he attacked.

I met Cliff head-on, my fist slamming into his jaw. He staggered back, but I didn't have time to savor the small victory.

Cliff yelled, "Fuck it. Get the bitch!"

And then they all came at me from all sides, a whirlwind of fists and feet.

I let my instincts take over, my body moving on pure muscle memory. Mom and Dad had trained me for this since the time I could walk. They knew that being an Alpha's daughter, I'd have to fight for my life, and they made sure they prepared me for it.

I ducked and weaved, landing blows where I could and dodging those I couldn't. A fierce joy surged through me as I felt my fist connect with flesh and bone, as I heard the grunts of pain from my opponents.

But for every hit I landed, I took two more. They were relentless, a tide of fury and aggression that threatened to sweep me away. I could feel my strength starting to wane, my breathing coming in ragged gasps.

Cliff and his men pressed their advantage, sensing my growing fatigue. They came at me harder, faster, their blows raining down like sledgehammers. I felt my ribs crack under the onslaught, felt the blood trickling down my face from a gash above my eye.

Still, I wasn't going to yield. I was an Alpha's daughter, and I would not go down easily.

My vision was starting to blur, my limbs growing heavy and unresponsive.

I saw Cliff's blow coming and knew I would be too slow to dodge it. His massive fist caught me square in the temple, and the world exploded into stars.

I felt myself falling, my body crumpling to the ground like a puppet with its strings cut. The last thing I saw before the darkness claimed me was Cliff's sneering face, his eyes alight with glee.

Then, there was nothing but the void, a yawning abyss that swallowed me whole. As I spiraled down into unconsciousness, a single thought echoed through my fading mind.

I had failed. The humans were defenseless now, at the mercy of Tristan and his thugs.

And it was all my fault.

The darkness took me then, and I knew no more.

CHAPTER NINE

SHYA

I clawed my way back to consciousness, my head pounding and my thoughts scattered. I blinked open my eyes, trying to focus through the haze of pain that enveloped me. A wave of scents hit me, so strong that it nearly made me gag. Every smell seemed to be amplified, and the most overwhelming of all was the stench of blood.

It was everywhere, the coppery tang of it filling my nostrils and coating the back of my throat. Some of it was fresh, still warm and pulsing with life. But there were older scents, too, blood that had dried and crusted over hours ago.

Other scents mingled with the blood—sweat, fear, anger. It was a nauseating cocktail, and it took every ounce of my self-control not to retch.

I couldn't make sense of where I was. The world seemed to be moving, shifting and swaying in a way that made my stomach churn even more. I tried to sit up, but my body wouldn't cooperate. I blinked, realizing my hands and feet were bound, the rough fibers of rope digging into my skin.

Panic shot through me, hot and sharp. I struggled against my restraints, my breath coming in short, desperate gasps. Where the fuck was I? What had happened?

Memories came back to me in fragmented pieces, like shards of a broken mirror. The town square. Cliff and his men. The fight.

I remembered the blows raining down on me, the sickening crunch of bone, and the coppery taste of blood in my mouth. I remembered the moment when I knew I was beaten, when the darkness had rushed up to claim me.

So how had I ended up here, trussed up like an animal?

I forced myself to take a deep breath, to try to calm the racing of my heart.

Remember your training. I could hear Dad's voice in my head.

Right. I needed to think, to assess my situation, and find a way out.

I looked around, my eyes slowly adjusting to the dim light. I was in the back of a van, the metal walls shuddering with each bump and turn in the road. The engine roared, and I could hear voices murmuring nearby, though I couldn't make out the words.

I tested my bonds again, hoping to find some give in the ropes. But they held fast, biting into my wrists and ankles with every movement and tying me to the side of the van with a bolted-on clip. Whoever had tied me up knew what they were doing.

Frustration and fear warred within me, but I pushed them down. I needed to stay calm and wait for an opportunity.

It was another five minutes before I felt a presence looming over me. I looked up and recoiled. Tristan was crouched beside me, smiling.

I went for him, my hands reaching to rip the smile off his face. The bolt clanged but held fast, my hands inches away from Tristan. He hadn't moved; just kept smiling as he watched me try to get to him.

"Look who's finally awake." His hand brushed a strand of hair from my face. I knocked it aside. "Hush now, you're finally where you belong."

His words sent a chill through me.

The scent of blood was strong on Tristan—blood and sweat, old adrenaline, and spikes of fear. Then, I caught a scent that was achingly familiar, even through the chaos. It was my father's scent, as recognizable to me as my own heartbeat.

For a moment, hope surged through me. If my father was here, maybe there was a chance. Maybe we could fight our way out of this together.

But as quickly as the hope had come, it faded. It wasn't my father's scent; it was the smell of his blood.

Ice-cold fear gripped my heart. Was he hurt? Dying? The thought was too awful to think about. The world was starting to spin again, the edges of my vision blurring and darkening. I tried to hold on, to ask Tristan about my dad. Tristan was saying something, his lips moving, but I couldn't hear him over the roaring in my ears. I caught one last glimpse of his face before the darkness claimed me once more.

Cold had seeped into my bones, making my muscles shiver and ache. I blinked open my eyes, wincing at the dull throb of pain in my temples.

I was lying on something hard and cold, the surface sucking all my heat away. For a moment, my vision swam before it righted itself.

Slowly, painfully, I pushed myself up to a sitting position. Everything was sore. Ribs, legs, head. Nothing had escaped the fists and feet of Cliff's men. When I got out of here, I was going to hunt them down and make sure I paid every one of them back.

I squinted, trying to work out where I was. Thick metal bars surrounded me on all sides. So, a cage then. How original of Tristan. The floor was a sheet of metal, cold and unyielding. The space inside the cage was barely big enough for me to stretch out. The cage had been placed in a tent, a large one, by the looks of it, though it was empty of everything except my cage and a chair and table set to one side of the closed door-flap.

Outside, I could hear the sounds of the forest—the rustling of leaves in the wind, the chirping of birds, the scurrying of small creatures in the underbrush. No voices, though.

Fear clawed at my throat, and I forced myself to take a deep breath. I rattled the cage door, then felt along all the bars. The gaps between them were too narrow for me to squeeze through. The floor had been welded onto the bars, and the roof of the cage was, like the floor, a solid piece of metal.

Shit. I was well and truly trapped.

The flap of the tent swished open, and Tristan stepped inside. He looked me up and down, assessing.

"You're awake," he said, his tone smug and self-satisfied. "Good. I was starting to worry Cliff might have hit you a little too hard back there."

I glared at him through the bars of the cage, my hands clenching into fists at my sides. "What the fuck, Tristan? Where am I? Where's my family?"

He waved a dismissive hand as if my questions were nothing more than pesky flies to be swatted away. "Your family's not important right now. What matters is that we got what we came for. You."

He stepped closer to the cage, his eyes glinting with a fierce kind of pride. "The attack was a success, Shya. We took Bridgetown by surprise, and we got you out. That's all that matters."

I felt a rush of anger rise up inside me, hot and potent. "All that matters? What about Bridgetown? My family, my Pack?"

"Like I said, not important. The only question now is just how much of a fight will you put up before you acknowledge I'm your mate?"

I laughed, a sharp, bitter sound. "You can't honestly believe I'm going to fall for that again. You tried once; it didn't work, Tristan. Not then, not now."

I thought he might be angry, but Tristan seemed unfazed, his posture relaxed and confident. "Once you've accepted me, we'll go back to Bridgetown and make things right."

I narrowed my eyes. "Make things right? You mean with the humans?"

"You treat humans as our equals. And we werewolves tie ourselves in knots, trying to make them feel safe. We have become so much less than what we really are. And why? Why do we pander to them? We've been brainwashed, Shya. We've been told that the peace with the humans is the only thing that matters. That if they saw us for real, they'd only see monsters. They'd rise up, try to kill us all. So, we have to make ourselves less so that they can pretend to be more.

"Werewolves have become so afraid of them that we've been neutered, reduced to pale imitations of what we should be. But what if it wasn't that way? What if we let ourselves be our true selves? The blood that runs through our veins is blood to be honored, not hidden away. I say we take back control. We live how we are supposed to live and fuck the humans. They want to rise up against us? Let them. We'll show them what it means to be truly scared. We'll finally show the humans what we really are. Bridgetown should no longer be a Disney fucking tourist town but a proper Shifter town. For real werewolves."

I stared at him. "You've gone mad! Bridgetown is a symbol of peace between humans and werewolves."

He scoffed. "Yes, that is precisely why we have to hit there first. You have to ask yourself, Shya, what's so bad about war? I have no doubt who will end up on top. It's time that the humans bow down to Shifters. That's how it's supposed to be."

I shook my head, my hands gripping the bars of the cage until my knuckles turned white. "I'll never agree with any of this."

Tristan stepped closer. "You won't just agree, Shya. You're going to believe, truly believe."

There was something in his eyes, a resolve and certainty that shook me to my core. He had no doubts that he could make me fall in line, that he could twist my mind to match his own warped vision.

Without another word, he turned and left, the tent flap fluttering closed behind him. I sank back down to the floor of the cage, my heart pounding and my thoughts racing.

Tristan was insane, that much was clear. But what scared me was the absolute conviction in his voice when he spoke of his plans. He truly believed that he could bring about this new world order with Shifters ruling over humans.

And he expected me to be by his side when he did it.

Chapter Ten

MASON

M y wolf was going fucking crazy, desperate to find any trace of Shya. His need to protect her, to ensure her safety, was a pulsing, living thing, threatening to overwhelm me. I could feel his panic rising with every passing second, and it took all my concentration to keep him in check as we pulled up to the Bridgetown Alpha House. Losing control would not help find Shya.

The scene before us as Derek and I got out of the car was one of chaos and confusion. People stumbled about, their faces etched with a mix of shock, pain, and disbelief. Some were visibly injured, nursing wounds, and leaning on each other for support.

I turned to Derek. "Let's start at the medical wing. If anyone knows what happened, it'll be Camille, and that's where she'll be."

We made our way through the throng of people, following the scent of blood that grew stronger with every step.

As we entered the medical wing, the atmosphere shifted from chaos to something far more somber. The fluorescent lights cast a cold, clinical glow over everything, and the air was thick with grief. There were dead here, the dead and their families.

Two enforcers I didn't recognize stood guard outside a room. I headed toward them just as Ivan popped his head out of the door. He saw Derek and me, nodded to the guards, and then disappeared inside again.

Right.

I followed, Derek behind me.

The room was small, just a single bed next to a window. Camille, Henry, and Tucker were gathered around the bed. Camille's eyes were red-rimmed and haunted, but her back was straight as she looked down at the bed. Henry and Tucker stood on either side of her; Henry looked to be in shock, his face pale and stricken. Tucker had obviously been crying recently, but I recognized the rage flowing through him now. I could see it in every strained muscle of his small body. He would need watching. Ivan, stoic as always, stood guard by the door, his face grim.

There was one more person in the room. Michael lay on the bed, his body still and lifeless, a black sheet covering him from the waist down.

Fuck!

I'd hoped it hadn't been true. That there had been some mistake. But there was no mistaking his body, fragile and broken, his chest unmoving and his eyes closed forever.

Camille finally looked up. "Mason," she said, her voice dull and lifeless. "Derek."

When she didn't say anymore, I stepped closer to the bed, my eyes taking in the gruesome wounds that marred Michael's body. His throat had been torn out, the flesh ragged and bloody. Deep gashes ran along his arms and torso.

"What happened?" Derek asked, directing his question to Ivan.

"Tristan and his men, about forty of them, attacked the west end of town. They killed the sentries posted on our border, so we had little warning. They came out of nowhere and caught us off guard. I was there with several enforcers, trying to hold them back, but we were losing ground."

He paused, his eyes shifting to Michael's lifeless form. "That's when Michael arrived. He tore through the attackers like they were nothing. For a moment, it seemed like we might push them back.

"But while Michael was focused on the main group, Tristan came up from behind. He was in his wolf form. He was fast, too fast. He ..." Ivan's words faltered, his eyes closing briefly.

"Tristan severed Michael's hamstrings," Camille said, her voice hoarse with grief.

It was a coward's move. Sneaking up behind and cutting the hamstrings meant Michael would have been on the ground. A bad position to be in when faced with a wolf.

"I arrived just as Michael fell, unable to stand. I tried to reach him. I tried, but ... Tristan ... I watched him tear out Michael's throat. I was too late. There was nothing I could do."

I think I was the only one who noticed Tucker's eyes flash green, his wolf coming to the fore.

"I'm going to kill Tristan," Henry stated, his fists clenched at his sides. He looked like he'd just woken up from a nightmare to find he hadn't been dreaming, which was probably exactly how he felt.

I understood their need for revenge, but the last thing we needed was Shya's brothers going after Tristan right now.

"Your family needs you right now," I replied, staring hard at Tucker and hoping he'd get the message, too. "You need to step up and look after them first."

Henry glared at me, and for a moment, I thought he was going to hit me. Then the fire died down, and he nodded once. "Pack always comes first."

Good. There might be some advantages to that mantra being drilled into this family after all.

Tucker averted his eyes, and I had no clue what he was thinking. I turned to Camille, keeping my voice gentle. "Michael was a great leader and an even better father and mate. His loss is a tremendous blow."

She nodded. "He died as he lived; protecting our Pack, protecting our people."

"Tell me about Shya."

Camille's eyes filled with fresh tears, and she seemed to crumple for a moment; it was all too much for her to handle. "They took her. Tristan's men ... they grabbed her off the main street during the attack."

My heart stalled, a cold fear gripping my chest. "How?"

Camille shook her head, her voice breaking. "When the attack started, I sent her to town to protect the humans. We have fifty tourists in town this week, plus the humans of Bridgetown. They are innocent in all this. Reports say she was surrounded by ten of Tristan's men. They were waiting for her. They took her."

My wolf threw himself against my insides, a growing sense of urgency and desperation taking hold. He wanted out.

Calm. We need more information.

Hunt. Hunt now.

63

Soon. We'll hunt soon.

Derek suddenly spoke up. "Tristan's men. They were waiting for her?"

Camille nodded. "It seems that way."

He turned to me. "They knew she would be sent into town. The goal was Shya. The rest was a diversion."

Ivan nodded grimly. "I believe your appraisal is correct. As soon as they had her, a message went around, and Tristan's forces scattered."

Tristan had orchestrated this attack with a singular purpose—to take Shya. I was going to rip him limb from limb. No one touched my mate.

I don't know what Derek saw in my face, but he jerked his chin at Henry and Tucker.

Right. Rage was not a good look in front of them right now.

Derek passed me a tennis ball from his pocket. I took a deep breath and took it. This whole thing was such a fucking mess. This family needed to concentrate on the things they could do, and that started with making sure this Pack was defended.

"Camille, I know how much you're hurting right now, but your Pack needs you. They need their remaining Alpha to guide them through this crisis."

Camille's eyes flashed with pain, her gaze snapping back to Michael's body. I could see the internal struggle playing out across her face, her grief and need to be beside Michael warring with the responsibility she now had as the sole Alpha.

"I can't leave him," she whispered, her voice cracking. "Not like this."

I placed a hand on her shoulder. "Michael would want you to be strong for the Pack. For your children. They need you now more than ever."

Camille closed her eyes, taking a deep, shuddering breath. When she opened them again, there was a flicker of resolve in their depths, a glimmer of the fierce Alpha I knew her to be.

"You're right." She nodded, her voice steadier now. She turned to Ivan, her demeanor shifting, a quiet authority settling over her. "Ivan, gather the enforcers. We need to secure the borders and make sure all of Tristan's Pack is gone. Ask Danni to oversee it. After that, coordinate with the medical staff. Make sure everyone who is injured is taken care of. Tell the humans nothing. The less they know of this, the better. And send word round that all Pack werewolves are to meet here in two hours. We'll need to tell everyone what happened."

Ivan nodded, his posture straightening as he recognized the command in Camille's tone. "Yes, Alpha."

I was proud of her. She wasn't falling apart.

Camille's attention then turned to, her eyes narrowing slightly. "Mason, I appreciate you coming here, but we are officially in mourning now. We are locking our territory down. It is a private affair. Bridgetown Pack only."

And she went too far.

"You have got to be kidding me. I'm here for Shya. We need to pool our resources and find her."

Camille shook her head. "The Bridgetown Pack will handle the search for Shya. She is our responsibility."

My wolf snarled within me, and I had difficulty pushing him down. "Shya is my mate, Camille. I won't sit by and do nothing while she's in danger."

Camille's eyes flared. "You're not part of this Pack, Mason. I can't tolerate outsiders right now. Not after this. We will protect what is ours, and Shya is ours. *We* will find her."

I stepped forward, my frustration mounting. How could she be so blind? How could she turn away help to find her daughter?

Derek placed a hand on my arm, his voice low. "You won't change her mind. Not at the moment. They're circling the wagons. They need to feel safe, secure, in control. You push too far on this now and there won't be any coming back from it."

I paused, Derek's words piercing through the haze of my own anger. I looked at Camille, really looked at her, and saw the devastation etched into every line of her face. She had lost her mate, the father of her children, and now she was being forced to put aside her own mourning to lead her Pack. She needed to feel her family was back in control of this. Derek was right; if I pushed this right now, I'd lose any hope of getting their cooperation in the future.

Derek squeezed my arm. "Let it go for now, Mason. We'll find another way."

I nodded reluctantly, accepting that I wouldn't find the support I needed here. The Bridgetown Pack was closing ranks, and I would have to search for Shya on my own.

CHAPTER ELEVEN

MASON

As we left the medical wing, I wanted to ram my fist into the walls. Camille was being short-sighted. She needed all the help she could get. Instead, her instincts had gone the other way. Closing ranks, shutting down all outsiders. Part of me understood it. They'd just had their whole world ripped away. Michael dead, Shya taken. Outsiders had done that, and they needed to protect what was left right now before they faced the world again. But that didn't help my mate. She was out there, in Tristan's hands, and the best chance of getting her back was if we worked together.

A figure was waiting for us by the door, and for a moment, I flashed back to Michael standing there, waiting to tell me to leave Shya alone.

This person was no Michael, though. While they shared a similar tall and lean build, this man possessed none of the distinct presence that set Michael apart. His dark blond hair was meticulously styled, not a single strand out of place, and his blue eyes held a calculating intensity that seemed to evaluate everything they fell upon. He stood with an air of unwavering authority, his posture rigid and controlled, as if he had been trained to maintain a perfect stance at all times. I had a feeling that this could only be Edmond D'Estry, Shya's fiancé.

His smile, though perfectly practiced, didn't reach his eyes when he said, "Mason Shaw, I presume. I'm Edmond D'Estry, Shya's intended mate."

"I know who you are," I growled.

Edmond's expression hardened. "Yes, I imagine you do. I'm here to let you know that the Bridgetown Pack appreciates your concern for our Alpha family, but we do not require further assistance. This is a matter for our Pack to handle internally."

I stepped forward, my anger rising. Had he been listening to my conversation with Camille, or had he come to that conclusion himself? Either way, I didn't have time for his diplomatic double-speak. I valued straight-talkers in my business and my life.

"What you're trying to say, Edmond, if you stop pussyfooting around, is that you want me to back off. You intend to find Shya yourself."

There was that smile again, polite and perfect, even when his eyes remained hard. "I can see why Shya likes you. You must seem like a shiny new toy to her, rough around the edges, telling it like it is. It's different from what she's used to. Unfortunately, some of us have to live in this world, have to understand the nuances of politics and diplomacy, and apply them to complex situations such as this one. I'm sure she has enjoyed your company while it lasted, but Shya is our Alpha-in-waiting and as such, once she is found by us, she will need to elevate her mind once again."

"And now you're calling me stupid, and I'm guessing you're hoping that I'm too dumb to realize it."

His smile widened, like I was a puppy who'd just learned a new trick. "No, I was very much hoping you'd realize it. It's more satisfying that way. I just want to be very clear. Shya is a member of the Bridgetown Pack, and as such, her safety and well-being are my top priority. I will personally lead the hunt for her and bring my future mate home."

"Shya is not your mate," I growled. "She belongs to me."

Edmond's eyes flashed, a hint of possessiveness in his gaze. "Shya and I are promised to each other, Mason. Our union is what's best for the Pack, and I will not let anyone, least of all a coarse, boorish outsider, interfere with that."

I'd had enough. First Camille, now this fucker. All their posturing was pointless. Finding Shya was the only thing any of them should be working on.

I moved, slamming Edmond against the wall, my forearm crushing his windpipe. "Shya is out there, in the hands of that fucker, Tristan. That's all that matters. You're wasting time with your fucking games."

He pushed against me. I didn't budge.

Derek placed a hand on my shoulder, his grip firm and grounding. "Mason, don't do something you'll regret."

I kept my focus solely on Edmond. "Understand the nuance in this: I'm going to get my mate and kill Tristan. Try to stop me, and I'll kill you, too."

Edmond's eyes narrowed as he choked out, "Leave, Mason. The Bridgetown Pack … will handle this. Your presence … here … is no longer welcome."

I released Edmond, letting him crumple to the ground. I turned to Derek, my anger so close to the surface now. "We're wasting time here."

Derek nodded, and we headed for the SUV.

"Can you believe that guy?" I fumed. "And that's who Michael and Camille want her to mate with!"

Derek's face was grim. "They just lost their Alpha, and they're trying to protect what's left of their Pack."

I scoffed, my frustration mounting with each step. "By shutting out people who can help them find Shya? It's bullshit, Derek, and you know it."

"I know," Derek replied, his voice calm and measured. "So, how do you want to play this? You want to march back in there and start a war? I'll be right behind you, Mase, if that's what you want to do."

I shook my head, my mind racing with thoughts of Shya and the danger she was in. "I don't care about their politics or their power plays. All I care about is finding Shya and bringing her home."

"Then let's find her."

And just like that, my anger, so big and wild up to now, focused down to a laser point. I had a mission. I had a target. It was time to go hunting.

As we approached the car, I heard footsteps behind us. I turned to see Henry and Tucker striding toward us.

"Mason, wait!" Henry called out as I slowed. "I wanted to say sorry about my mom. She's just ... she's not thinking straight."

I sighed and put a hand on his shoulder. He didn't need to hear my thoughts about his mom right now. "She's going through a lot."

"I know, but we need help. We should be reaching out to our allies, not sending them away. That's why my parents cultivated relationships with other Packs. So that they'd be there in times of need."

"Grief affects people in different ways, Henry," Derek said. "She'll come around. She just needs some time."

Tucker shook his head, his little face scrunched up in anger. "We don't have time! I'm gonna find the asshole myself. He has to pay for hurting our family."

I looked at Tucker, really looked at him. He was like a tiny missile ready to go off. Someone had come into his territory, attacked his family, murdered his dad, and taken his sister. His wolf would be demanding retribution. He was a born Alpha, and if I didn't try to shut this down now, Shya's brother was likely to get himself killed.

I had to take him seriously and not sugar-coat it. "Tucker, you need to stay here and keep your mom safe. Your Pack has been hit hard. It won't just be Tristan who is circling now. You'll have threats inside and outside the Pack to deal with. Any enemies you have be wondering if you are down and out, and they're going to test to see how weak you are. You're going to be needed here to show everyone that the Alpha family is not prey, that you're still strong, still capable. Let me find Tristan and make him pay for what he's done. I'll bring Shya home."

Tucker's eyes flashed with a fierce determination as he took in what I was saying. Then he lifted his chin. "You'd better find her. I know where you live, and I've been saving up all my spitballs!"

I didn't smile even though I wanted to. Instead, I nodded solemnly. "I swear to you both, I will find Shya or die trying."

Tucker kept his eyes on mine for a long moment before saying, "Okay. Go find my sister."

I jerked my chin at Henry, then Derek and I got in the car.

We didn't get very far. As Derek pulled out of the Alpha House driveway and started down the road, a small figure darted in front of us, arms outstretched. Derek slammed on the brakes, the tires screeching against the asphalt.

It was a girl, probably no more than twelve years old. She wore a faded blue denim jacket over a bright yellow T-shirt with a cartoon sunflower on the front. A small, colorful bracelet adorned her left wrist, its beads catching the light as she moved. She stood defiantly in the middle of the road, her long brown hair whipping around her face in the evening breeze.

"What the hell?" Derek muttered, but I was already getting out of the car.

"You're Mason Shaw," she announced, her voice clear and unwavering, before I could say anything.

"That's right. Do I know you?"

She smelled human, but I didn't recognize her. The girl shook her head, her eyes never leaving mine. "No, but I know you. You're going to find Shya."

I raised an eyebrow. "And how do you know that?"

"Because you think you're her mate, and that's what proper mates are supposed to do," she said firmly. "So, if you were thinking of not finding her, I'm telling you, no, ordering you, to go find her."

This was sounding eerily familiar. I narrowed my eyes at her. "Are you friends with Tucker?"

She narrowed her eyes right back at me. "Who I'm friends with is no concern of yours. You need to focus on finding Shya."

I blinked. Seriously, who the hell was this girl? Did everyone in Bridgetown have supersonic hearing?

Her expression softened for a moment. "Please. Shya is ... she's important. To me. To my mom. To all of us. You're the best chance we have to bring her back."

"She's important to me, too. I promise you, I'm going to do everything in my power to bring Shya home."

She nodded, seemingly satisfied with my response. "Alright then. But I'm warning you, if you don't, you'll have me to answer to. And I can make a hell of a lot more spitballs than Tucker."

I inhaled. She definitely smelled human but if she was, there was no way she could have heard my conversation with Tucker. Which opened up a whole load of questions that I didn't have time for right now. "I'll bear that in mind."

I got back into the car, my resolve stronger than ever. Derek gave me a questioning look.

"Looks like we've got another set of marching orders," I said, my voice filled with grim determination. "Let's go find my girl."

Chapter Twelve

MASON

The tension in the room was high as Derek and I sat across from Sam, Ryan, Mai, and Waylen in my office at Shaw Investigations. Derek sat with his arms crossed, his gray eyes scanning the room. Sam, his twin, leaned back in his chair, his shoulder-length brown hair falling over his brown eyes, so different from Derek's disciplined appearance.

Mai sat next to her mate, looking grim. She was friends with Shya and knew what it meant that Tristan had taken her. Ryan had his arm draped protectively over the back of Mai's chair. Waylen fidgeted restlessly in his seat, ignoring Derek's scowls. Derek liked calm. Waylen was anything but calm; most days, he was more like an excited puppy.

My usually tidy space was now cluttered with maps, notes, and empty coffee cups. We'd been here for hours, going over everything we knew about Tristan. I would stop at nothing to find Shya, but right now, we had fairy fuck all.

Ryan and Mai had turned up two hours ago to help, but even they were just as frustrated as I was.

Ryan leaned forward. "There's nothing here. Tristan's covered his tracks too well."

"Er, hell no!" Waylen frowned, adjusting his glasses. "No one defeats Waylen the Wizard! Especially not an ass-eating dickhead like Tristan."

Mai raised her eyebrows at Waylen, a small smile playing on her lips. "An ass-eating dickhead?"

He waved her comment away. "I'm searching for him; that means I get to call him what the hell I want."

Mai raised her hands in surrender, her dark hair falling over her shoulders. "Sure thing, Waylen."

My fist clenched on the armrest of my chair. "We're running out of time. Who knows what that fucker is doing to her."

Sam shifted in his seat. "We'll find her, Mase. We won't stop until we do."

I looked at him for a moment. "We? You forgetting something?"

He tilted his head, his brown hair falling into his eyes. "We won't stop until we're dead?"

"As much as I appreciate the sentiment, you're leaving for the Wolf Council today."

This year, it had been the Three Rivers' turn to nominate someone for the Wolf Council, the body that oversaw and enforced our laws, maintaining the peace between werewolves and with the humans. Mai had told them Sam would be representing our Pack, and he was supposed to meet Talia Johnson in eight hours.

"Fuck the Council! I'm here until we bring Shya back."

Ryan glanced at Mai, then over to Sam, his blue eyes serious. "While I agree that the Council can go fuck themselves, we can't afford to piss them off right now. You don't show, and we'll have half the Council and their enforcers on our doorstep tomorrow morning."

"Ryan's right," I said, though the words tasted bitter on my tongue. Having Sam by my side would have been a comfort, but I knew we had to play this smart. "We need you on the inside, figuring out who the mole who was working with Brock is. They might have information on Tristan."

Brock and Tristan had been plotting together for months, and now that Brock was dead, it was possible the mole was still in contact with Tristan.

Sam locked eyes with me. "I don't like it," he said, "but I get it. I'll start digging around at the Council, see what I can find."

Ryan lifted his chin in approval. "Good. We'll work on it this end."

I turned to Ryan and Mai, my eyes serious. "I appreciate the help, I really do, but the Pack needs you both right now, more than ever."

Mai's brow furrowed. "This is our priority, Mason. Everything else can take a back seat right now."

Derek sighed, running a hand through his hair. "Mase is right. The attack on the Pack by Korrin and the battle with Brock have everyone on edge. They need to see their Alphas, to know that you're here for them, that you'll keep them safe."

Ryan's jaw tightened, his eyes flashing. "We can do both."

"It's not just about protection. It's about stability, about showing them that even in the face of this crisis, the Pack is strong, united. You can't go off hunting right now." Derek leaned back. "Besides, Mase has me. And with me by his side, who else does he need?"

Mai's eyes sparkled with amusement. "The Mason and Derek show, huh? Tristan won't know what hit him."

Derek grinned, his muscular frame relaxing slightly. "Damn right, he won't. We'll show him what happens when you go up against the Shaw brothers."

I turned to Waylen, who had been uncharacteristically quiet, his fingers flying over the keyboard of his laptop. "Waylen, tell me you've got an idea, something, anything, on how to find Tristan or where he might have taken Shya."

Waylen's shoulders slumped, his frustration evident as he looked up from the screen. "It's like that fuckhead vanished into thin air. But I've got some more trails to go down. No one beats me, Mason, no one. I'll get him."

I felt a wave of disappointment wash over me, but I refused to let it show. We had to keep pushing, keep searching. "Keep at it. Check everything, no matter how small."

Mai's eyes lit up with a sudden thought. "What about AJ? The bear Shifter working for Tristan?"

I frowned, trying to recall what we knew about AJ. "What about him?"

"AJ's not working for Tristan by choice. Tristan has his mate hidden away somewhere, using her as leverage to force AJ to do whatever Tristan tells him to do."

Derek raised his eyebrows. "So, if we can find AJ …"

"We might be able to get him to turn on Tristan, give us the information we need," I finished, a glimmer of hope sparking in my chest.

Mai nodded. "Exactly."

"It's worth a shot. If AJ can lead us to Tristan, it could be the break we need. And we've come up with fuck all else in the last few hours."

"You'll need to be careful, Mase," Ryan said. "AJ's not just any bear Shifter. He's cursed; his bear is insane. When he Shifts, he has no control. His bear just wants to destroy anything and everything in his way."

Mai nodded, her expression grim. "Ryan's right. Dealing with AJ is dangerous. You'll need to be cautious, find a way to get through to him without triggering his bear."

Waylen, who had been tapping away at his keyboard, suddenly sat up straight. "Guys, I might have something. I've been tracking bear sightings ever since Mai's last run-in with AJ—I wanted to make sure he wasn't heading here. There was a bear sighting in the forest near Ayer's Cliff just a few hours ago."

"Ayer's Cliff? It's not known for having a bear population."

"Precisely. A good place for a bear Shifter to hang out undisturbed. Plus, the bear matches the description that Mai gave me."

Derek caught my eye. "It's a start. We can head out there, see if we can pick up AJ's trail."

I nodded, already mentally preparing for the journey ahead. "Agreed. If we can find AJ, I'll get him to talk. I'll get him to lead us to Tristan." No matter what it took.

Chapter Thirteen

MASON

I pulled into the old forestry car park, gravel crunching beneath the tires as I brought the car to a stop. The car park was a relic of a bygone era, a place where loggers and rangers once gathered before venturing into the dense forest. Now, it served as the starting point for our hunt, a gateway to the wilderness where we hoped to find AJ and, ultimately, a path to Shya.

I scanned the treeline for any sign of movement. Nothing. The forest was still. Watchful. I was a werewolf, fully at home here, but my wolf form was the undisputed king of this domain, the apex predator that ruled supreme over all other creatures.

Without a word, Derek and I began to strip off our clothes, leaving them folded in the car. The cool air kissed my skin as I embraced the familiar sensation of the impending Shift. I could feel the power stirring within me, my wolf eager to be unleashed.

I breathed in and let him out. My muscles rippled and reformed, bones reshaping and fur sprouting from my skin. The pain of the Shift spiked quickly, replaced by the exhilaration of my wolf taking over.

I shook out my fur, relishing the strength and agility that came with my wolf form. My senses were heightened, the scents and sounds of the forest flooding my consciousness. But above all, my wolf's mind was consumed by a singular purpose: finding Shya.

Derek's wolf stretched beside me, his unusual silver fur catching the last rays of sunlight.

Without a thought, I turned and loped toward the forest. Derek fell into step beside me, our paws treading silently on the soft earth. Together, we melted into the shadows of the trees.

Six days later, and we still hadn't found AJ. We'd picked up his trail late that first day, a faint scent carried on the wind that set our senses on high alert, and we had been following it ever since. We'd been relentless, pursuing him deep into the heart of the wilderness, far from civilization. The terrain was unforgiving, with steep inclines, treacherous ravines, and dense underbrush that seemed to clasp at our fur with every step. The weather had not been kind to us, with cold rain and biting winds chilling us to the bone, even with our thick fur.

The pursuit had taken its toll on us, both physically and mentally. We had little rest, snatching only brief moments of sleep when we couldn't go on any longer. Hunger gnawed at our bellies, a constant reminder of the energy we were expending in our chase. When we could, we took advantage of any small prey that crossed our path. Rabbits and squirrels became our sustenance, their meat providing the fuel we needed to keep going.

As we pressed on, the forest seemed to close in around us, the trees becoming denser and the shadows deeper. The sun struggled to penetrate the thick canopy, casting an eerie twilight over the landscape. My wolf loved it. This was his domain, his kingdom. He ruled here and had no doubt that we would find AJ soon.

We had picked up on the faintest traces of his passage—a broken twig here, a disturbed patch of earth there. Now, his scent grew stronger with each passing hour, and we knew we had to be close to closing in.

It wasn't long before my wolf stopped, his hackles raised. Next to me, Derek let out a low growl. He was near. Then, up ahead, a massive form burst through the undergrowth. Bear. AJ was a terrifying sight, his eyes wild and filled with a madness that chilled me. His eyes swiveled in our direction and focused on Derek and me. I snarled in warning. The bear roared, a deafening sound that shook the earth beneath our paws.

He wanted to dance? We'd dance.

AJ charged toward us, his massive form a mountain of heavy muscle and unbridled rage. The ground trembled under his weight with each step, the air vibrating with the intensity of his fury.

Yeah, I wasn't going to stand there and be run over by the big guy.

With a powerful leap, my wolf launched himself forward, closing the distance between us and the charging bear in an instant. I swung left at the last moment as Derek swung right, jaws snapping shut on the bear's thick fur.

The bear let out a roar of pain and fury, swiping a massive paw at me. I dodged to the side, narrowly avoiding the blow, while Derek circled around to harry the bear from behind.

The forest erupted into a cacophony of snarls, roars, and the clash of claws and fangs. We danced around AJ, darting in and out, our razor-sharp claws seeking to inflict superficial damage while avoiding his massive paws and powerful jaws. Derek and I worked in coordination, our movements synchronized from years of growing up and fighting together. When one of us distracted AJ, the other would strike, leaving bleeding wounds on his thick hide.

Our strategy hinged on weakening AJ gradually, giving him numerous small cuts that would sap his strength over time. We knew we couldn't overpower him directly, but through precision and agility, we could wear him down. My claws found their mark again and again, leaving crimson streaks across AJ's fur. Derek followed suit, his silver form a blur of motion as he attacked relentlessly.

AJ roared in frustration, his massive form heaving with exertion as he tried to land a telling blow on either of us. But we were too quick, too coordinated in our movements.

Suddenly, AJ made a swift move, swiping his paw with unexpected speed. I felt a searing pain in my side as his claws raked across my flank, ripping through fur and flesh. I let out a sharp yelp of agony but didn't relent.

Derek lunged forward, sinking his teeth into AJ's hind leg. I seized the opportunity and darted in from the other side, my jaws closing around AJ's neck in a vice-like grip. The bear Shifter thrashed and roared, trying to shake us off, but we held fast.

Time seemed to blur, the world narrowing down to this moment, this fight for survival.

And then—a sudden stillness. The bear's struggles ceased, and we looked into each other's eyes for a moment. I didn't know if it was my imagination, but I could have sworn I saw something resembling remorse in his gaze before he went limp in my jaws.

Chapter Fourteen

Mason

I glanced around AJ's campsite. It was clear that he'd been living a solitary existence here for some time. A small, weathered tent was pitched nearby, its canvas faded and carefully patched in places. Beside it, a few supplies were neatly stacked, including a worn backpack, a coil of rope, and a small hatchet with a well-worn handle. A couple of water canteens hung from a nearby tree branch.

Near the fire, AJ's cooking setup was simple but efficient. A grill made from an old metal grate was balanced on a couple of rocks over the flames, the rabbits that Derek had caught sizzling as they cooked. A battered metal pot sat nearby, likely used for boiling water or making simple stews. A few tin plates and cups were on a flat rock, ready for use.

A low groan drew my attention to AJ. He was back in human form, having Shifted while he was unconscious.

"Wakey, wakey, sunshine." Derek grinned down at him, a mug of steaming coffee in his hands. "You've been out for six hours."

His eyes fluttered open, confusion and pain etched across his face. "Fuck!" he groaned.

Derek and I had had time to prepare for AJ to wake up. As soon as AJ morphed into his human form, we'd done the same. Then we'd followed his scent back to his campsite and set about utilizing all his supplies. Both Derek and I were dressed in clothes we'd found in the tent, and we'd eaten most of his cans of tinned food.

AJ blinked up at Derek. "Who the fuck are you?"

"We're the guys who beat your ass, AJ." Derek tilted his head to one side when AJ just frowned at him. "You don't remember the ass-kicking, huh?"

AJ winced as he tried to move. Bruises and cuts covered his skin, but they'd heal when he next Shifted.

"You're wearing my clothes." AJ sat up, his eyes darting around at the campsite. "And you ate all my fucking food!"

I shrugged. "We've been tracking you for six days. It made us peckish. Besides, we figured you'd rather wake up to this than two naked men standing over you."

AJ eyed us warily. "Just who the fuck are you?"

"Mason Shaw. This here's my brother, Derek."

"You're werewolves."

I nodded. "That we are. And you're AJ, the cursed bear Shifter who works for Tristan Munroe."

AJ's eyes narrowed at the mention of Tristan's name. "You've gone to a lot of trouble to find me. So, why don't you cut the bullshit and just tell me what you want?"

A straight talker. I was beginning to like AJ. "We need your help. Tristan has taken someone important to me, and we're going to get her back."

AJ stood up and started to pull on the set of clothes we'd left next to him. "Well, good luck to you both."

He was a mountain of a man, standing at an imposing 6'4" with muscles that bulged beneath his skin, hinting at the immense strength he possessed in both human and bear forms. His dark blond hair fell onto his face, and a rough, untrimmed beard covered his jaw.

But it was his eyes that truly captured my attention. They were a deep, rich brown, almost black, and they held such a haunted look. This was a man who carried a heavy burden day in, day out.

I exchanged a glance with Derek before responding. "We figured, seeing as you work for the guy, that you might have some idea where we could find him."

AJ scoffed, shaking his head. "Look, I'm sorry you've come all this way, but you've got the wrong guy. I'm not getting involved."

I stepped closer. "Listen, AJ, we know about your mate. We know Tristan's holding her captive to keep you in line."

"You don't know shit. If I make a move against Tristan, he'll kill her. I'm sorry for your friend, I really am, but I'm not risking my mate's life."

"And what kind of life is your mate living now?" I challenged. "Tristan will never let her go, AJ. This is your reality and hers until the day you die. You're condemning your mate to a life under his control."

AJ's jaw tightened, his eyes flashing with anger. "What fucking choice do I have? I can't fight him alone."

"You're not alone now," Derek interjected. "You've got us. Two wolves, ready to fight by your side."

I nodded, my voice firm as I added, "This is the best shot you'll ever get to save your mate, AJ. Work with us, help us take down Tristan, and you get your mate back. Or continue living this life, barely surviving out here in the forest, being Tristan's lapdog, while you leave your mate to rot in his cages."

AJ was silent for a long moment, his look distant as he considered our words. Finally, he let out a heavy sigh. "My bear ... I can't control him when I Shift. He's a liability."

"Then you fight in your human form," I said, my determination unwavering. "With two wolves by your side. We're stronger together, AJ. Tristan won't expect us to come at him like this."

AJ's eyes met mine, a flicker of hope in the haunted depths. "You really think we can take him down?"

"I think this is the best chance any of us will have."

AJ's eyes shifted between Derek and me as he considered our words. I could see the internal struggle playing out behind his eyes, the desperate desire to save his mate warring with the fear of what Tristan might do if he betrayed him.

"I don't know," AJ said, his voice strained. "Tristan's not a man to be trifled with. He's got resources, manpower. Even if we manage to get to my mate, he'll come after us with everything he's got."

"He won't come after you on account of him being dead. I have no intention of letting Tristan survive this."

AJ studied my face. "He has your mate, too."

I showed him my teeth. "And he'll die because he touched her. You in?"

AJ's eyes widened at my words. For a moment, he seemed to be weighing his options, the desire for revenge and the chance to save his mate battling with the fear of what Tristan might do. But as he stood there, I could see a change come over him, as if a massive weight had been lifted from his shoulders.

Slowly, AJ straightened up, his posture shifting. His broad shoulders squared, and he lifted his chin, a fierce light igniting in his eyes. For a brief instant, I caught a glimpse of the bloodthirsty bear within him, the raw fury that lurked just beneath the surface.

"I'm in," AJ said, his voice low and steady.

Thank fuck for that.

"You know where Tristan is?"

AJ shook his head. "No."

Disappointment crashed into me a second before AJ continued, "But I know someone who might."

CHAPTER FIFTEEN

SHYA

My wolf hated the cage and the metal bars even more than I did, and when I Shifted to try to keep warm, she threw herself against the bars again and again until I forced us to Shift back to stop her from seriously injuring us. Ten days in this fucking tent, no food, barely any water. Just enough to keep me alive, plus a bucket in the corner to pee in.

I could feel myself getting weaker. Almost hourly, my muscles cramped. My head constantly pounded. But what was worse was the utter loneliness. It ate at me, hollowed me out from the inside. Werewolves were pack animals for a reason. We needed the comfort, the sense of Pack, of belonging to something bigger than ourselves. Stuck here alone, no Pack, no family, not even a fucking blanket to cuddle, I could feel the despair creeping in. I tried to hold on to myself, to some kind of hope. But each day it got harder to remember who I was outside this cage, harder to believe I'd ever get out.

I couldn't stop thinking about my family. What happened to them after I was taken? Were they looking for me? Were they even alive? Was Dad? I hardly dared to think about the memory of his blood on

Tristan. Had I dreamed it, or was it real? I searched my Pack bonds, but there were no answers there. The bonds were there, intact, but it was like there was a blanket wrapped over them. I couldn't feel anything from them, and I had no idea what could cause the bonds to feel that way. Mom, Dad, Henry, and Tucker … I needed to know that they were okay, that they were safe, but Tristan just dismissed the question whenever I asked. The thought of never seeing them again made me want to howl.

I tried not to think about Mason, but my thoughts always ended up on him. He'd been so angry when he left. What if that was the last time I'd ever see him? I missed his touch, his scent, the way his lips felt against mine. Would he be looking for me? I had to get out of here, had to get back to them all.

The sound of the tent flap opening became so damned important. Tristan's visits, short as they were, were the only break in the endless nothing. Some part of me started looking forward to them, and I hated myself for it. I couldn't stand the way my heart jumped at the first sound of footsteps, the way I stared at the entrance, waiting. I was disgusted with myself for wanting anything from that dickhead. But I couldn't stop the desperate need for something, anything, to think about besides my own messed-up thoughts.

My ears picked up the sound of footsteps, and my eyes swirled to the tent flap as it opened and Tristan walked in. I felt a now-familiar sickening twist of excitement and revulsion. Then I saw what he had, and everything else disappeared. In his hands was a tray with a bowl of chicken soup and some bread. The smell hit me hard; I was sure I started drooling. It was simple food, something I would've picked at before, but now it looked like heaven. My body howled for it.

Tristan smiled at me. "Hello, Shya."

I ignored him, my eyes riveted on the food.

His smile got wider. "You've been so good these last few days, I thought I'd give you a treat."

He came up to the cage slowly, eyes on me. Carefully, he picked up the bowl and bread and passed them through the bars.

"Eat," he said, "but go slow. You don't want to puke." His voice was gentle, concerned. It made it worse. This fake kindness, this act of giving a shit, it was cruel in its own way.

The soup was lukewarm, but I didn't care. I tore into the bread, stuffing it into my mouth.

Tristan watched, a smug look on his face. "You see, Shya? That wasn't so hard, was it? You need me. I'm the one looking after you, keeping you alive."

I glared at him but didn't stop eating. I hated that he was right. Right now, he controlled everything. My food, my water, my fucking life. But I swore to myself this wouldn't last. I'd find a way out, a way to beat him. For now, though, I just had to survive.

I kept eating, trying to ignore Tristan's presence. But he just kept talking, his voice smooth as silk.

"I know there's something special between us. I feel it. In here," he said as he touched his heart. "A bond, a connection. The Goddess herself brought us together. I was meant to become an enforcer, to rise to the position of Beta, just so I could be close to you, Shya."

I wanted to laugh in his face. Bond? Connection? The only things between us were the bars of this cage and his fucked-up delusions. But I didn't say a word, just focused on the last spoonfuls of soup.

Tristan kept going. "I know you feel it too, Shya. The pull, the attraction. It's the Goddess's will, her divine plan for us."

Divine plan? Like hell it was. This was his twisted fantasy, nothing more. I had to stop myself from rolling my eyes.

Tristan wasn't put off by my lack of response. He had this calm sense of patience about him, this self-assurance that made my skin crawl.

"It's okay, Shya. I understand. This is all new, overwhelming. But you'll see, in time. We're meant to be together. Nothing can change that. Not now." His smile was serene, like he'd already won.

I couldn't deny that his certainty, his unwavering belief, it was getting to me. What did he know that I didn't? What if he was right? What if I couldn't fight this, couldn't escape him? I pushed the thought away. I couldn't let him get in my head. I had to stay strong, bide my time. Sooner or later, he'd slip up. And I'd be ready.

After I was sure there was no soup left, I took aim and threw the bowl at Tristan. He'd been expecting it. He snatched it out of the air effortlessly and smirked at me.

"You always were a firecracker, Shya. I'm going to enjoy teaching you the correct way to behave for your mate." Then he turned and left.

I slumped back against the bars, my momentary surge of defiance draining out of me. I was alone again, trapped in this fucking cage with nothing but my own thoughts for company. And they were getting darker by the minute.

What if Tristan was right? What if there was no escape from this? My Pack, my family, not even Mason fucking Shaw, had any idea of where I was. The hopelessness of my situation was suffocating, pressing down on me like a physical weight. Being cut off like this, it was like losing a part of myself. I could feel it, the emptiness, the aching loneliness. It was a physical pain, a hollowness in my chest that nothing could fill.

I tried to cling to my anger, my hatred for Tristan. It was the only thing keeping me going, the only thing stopping me from giving in to the despair that threatened to drown me. But even that was getting harder. With every passing hour, every moment spent in this cage, I could feel my resolve weakening.

I curled up on the cold, hard floor, wrapping my arms around myself. With a bit of food finally in my belly, I could feel exhaustion creeping up on me. I closed my eyes and let sleep take me.

It was another three days before Tristan came back, punishing me for throwing the bowl at him. By then, I didn't give a fuck who delivered water and food just as long as it came.

"Are we going to behave ourselves today, Shya?" He smiled at me.

"Fuck you," I whispered, my voice weak.

His smile got wider. "Yes, please, Tristan. Those are the words you need to use, Shya, if you want what I have."

I hungrily eyed the bottle of water, hot bread, and bowl of stew in his hands. The smell was driving me crazy. It twisted in the air, slipped inside my senses, and made my stomach ache with need. I tried to maintain some semblance of control, but my eyes kept darting between Tristan's face and the food in his hands.

"Come on, Shya," Tristan coaxed, his voice sickeningly sweet. "It's just three little words. Then you can eat and drink. Doesn't that sound nice?"

I gritted my teeth, hating him, hating myself more for how tempted I was. The hunger gnawed at me, threatening to overpower my resolve. But I couldn't give in. I couldn't let him win.

"I'd rather starve," I hissed through my parched lips, even as my body screamed at me to give in.

Tristan's smile never wavered. He crouched down, bringing the food tantalizingly close to the cage bars. "Are you sure about that? It smells delicious, doesn't it? All you have to do is show me the respect I deserve."

The aroma of the stew intensified, and I could feel what little saliva I had pooling in my mouth. My hands shook with the effort of not reaching out, of not begging like he wanted me to. I clenched my fists, nails digging into my palms, using the pain to anchor myself.

"Go to hell."

Tristan tutted and shook his head. "Oh, Shya. When will you learn? I'm trying to help you. To take care of you. Why do you insist on making this so difficult? Do you really think you are being strong by saying no? Who wins if you starve, Shya? Not you. Not me. You want to fight me? You want to escape? You start by getting out of the cage. Say the words, Shya. And you can eat. Get your strength back. So when an opportunity does present itself, you'll be in a state to take it. Doesn't that seem a better plan?"

I hated that he knew exactly the right buttons to push. He stood up slowly, taking the food with him. My eyes followed every movement, a whimper building in my throat that I barely managed to suppress.

"I'll come back later," he said, his tone maddeningly patient. "Give you some time to think. Maybe you'll be more reasonable then. I'll leave the stew here, though." He placed the bowl and the water bottle on the ground, just out of reach. "To help you while you think."

I did think, and I said, "Yes, please, Tristan," when he came back two days later and every time after that.

Chapter Sixteen

SHYA

Sleep was my only respite. Always, I would close my eyes and try to picture Mason's face, to remember his scent surrounding me, his touch when he stormed into my bedroom. I would hold on to that as I sank toward oblivion.

Tonight, though, there was no oblivion. Voices filtered in from outside the tent, weaving themselves into my dreams until I wasn't sure if they were real or not.

"This is dangerous." It was a voice I didn't recognize.

"I'm well aware of how dangerous it is. But it's not working. She is compliant, but only for food. I need her compliant in everything. I need her to see the real me. To love me, worship me." That one was definitely Tristan.

"Why do you want this so much? She's a female. You could have any female here. Click your fingers and they'll spread their legs for you. Why this one?"

"Because she was supposed to be mine! I worked on her for months. Months of my time to get her to see we were meant to be, and after all that, she still turned against me."

There was a slight pause, then the voice said, "Ah, so that's it. She said no. And you can't handle it."

"It's not like that! Yes, it will be sweet as fuck to see her on her knees begging for my cock, which she will, and I will enjoy the hell out of fucking that bitchy mouth of hers, but she's my ticket to the Bridgetown Pack. They'll accept me if she's hanging on every word I say. I'll be able to take it over and reshape it in less than a year. If I have to fight them every step of the fucking way, it will take at least three years before I can launch phase three."

"Three years is too long."

"You think I don't know that? That's why you have to do this. We have to speed this up."

Another long pause, then a sigh. "Alright. It will take time. This isn't an overnight fix."

"Just do it. I want her in my bed by the end of the month."

"You slipped the powder into her food?"

"I followed your instructions to the letter."

"Very well. You'll have your wish. By the end of the month, you'll be able to click your fingers, and this one will ask exactly how wide you want her to spread her legs."

I wanted to get up, to rip Tristan's fucking eyes out. What the hell was he planning? I would never spread my legs for him, would never be in his bed. I struggled to open my eyes, but sleep's arms had me caught tight and kept trying to drag me down.

Then the world around me shifted, the colors bleeding together, the edges blurring. I knew I was dreaming, and the bars of the cage fell away, the tent disappeared, and I was standing in a meadow. Next to me was a hooded figure. I assumed it was a he, given how tall he was, perhaps six feet, but I couldn't be sure as his face was obscured by a deep hood that cast shadows across his features. His cloak was simple, midnight black, and reached down past his ankles, but his hands emerged from the folds of the cloak as he gestured, showing a jagged scar that ran from his left wrist to the base of his thumb. It looked old, the tissue puckered and white against his tanned skin.

He started chanting in a language I couldn't understand. The words seemed to echo, to vibrate through my bones. It was eerie, unsettling. I wanted to run, to hide, but I couldn't move. I was stuck, frozen in place, and I could feel my heart rate spiking in panic. His voice as he chanted was deep and resonant, each syllable precise and measured, and I watched his breath misting in the air despite the warmth of the meadow. The mist seemed to take on a life of its own, coiling around us both like spectral tendrils. I shut my mouth with a click. There was no way I wanted to breathe that in.

Come.

My eyes swung to the left, and there, standing in the midst of this strange, hazy dreamscape, was a wolf. It was looking right at me, its eyes glowing an unearthly blue. I felt this pull, this connection. He was calling to me, and I knew as long as I kept my focus on him, I would be able to move.

Come.

Without thinking, I took a step toward him, then another. The chanting took on an urgent, angry tone, and the mist tried to pull me back, its tendrils grasping for me, but I shook them off; I kept my focus on the wolf and the wolf only. On my next step, the world around me seemed to warp and twist. The meadow evaporated like the steam from a river on a warm morning, and my foot hit sand. I blinked; I was in the middle of a desert. I took another step, and the desert disappeared, and I was in a city with skyscrapers towering above me. I took another step, and it changed again. Nothing made sense; nothing was real. Nothing except the wolf. He was my anchor, my guide, leading me deeper into my subconscious.

The wolf led me through this maze of dreams, the landscape shifting and changing with each step. Trees sprouted from the ground, only to melt into wisps of smoke moments later. The sky changed color from a deep, midnight blue to a fiery orange, then to a sickly green. But through it all, the wolf remained constant, a beacon of stability in this chaotic world.

Finally, after what felt like hours, we landed next to a river, its waters black and mirror-smooth. The wolf paused at the bank, then turned to look at me. His eyes seemed to pierce through me, to see into the depths of my soul.

"Who are you?" I whispered.

The wolf turned to look at the river.

"You want me to go in?"

He lay down, put his head on his paws, and sighed.

Okay, then.

I stepped into the river, expecting to feel the cold bite of the water. But instead, it was like stepping into a warm bath. I waded in, the water enveloping me, soothing away the aches and pains of my physical body. I felt weightless, free, all my troubles washed away by the gentle current.

And suddenly, Mason was there with me, standing in the middle of the river, the water swirling around his waist. Shirtless, his skin glowing with an inner light, the sight of him took my breath away.

"Shya," he said, his voice echoing through the dreamscape. "I'm here. I'll always be here."

He held out his hand, and without hesitation, I took it. His touch was electric, making me tremble. He pulled me close, wrapping his arms around me, and I melted into his embrace. It was like coming home, like finding a piece of myself that I hadn't even known was missing.

"I'm coming for you," he whispered into my hair. "No matter what it takes, no matter what I have to do, I will find you."

I clung to him, my face buried in his chest. I could hear his heartbeat, strong and steady. It was a promise, a vow. In that moment, I knew nothing would stop him. Not Tristan, not the cage, not even the vastness of the dream world.

He leaned down, his lips brushing against mine in a kiss that was both tender and fierce.

And as our lips met, the river itself seemed to come alive, pulsating with energy in time with our heartbeats, as if responding to the force of our connection. My hands slipped down his chest. He wasn't wearing pants, and my fingers traced the hard contours of his abdomen, their path mimicking the ebb and flow of the river around us. I trailed my hand lower and squeaked when I closed my fingers around his hard cock.

Fuck me, it was big!

I looked down; I just had to see it. It was the most beautiful cock I had ever seen, hard, smooth, glistening in the river water.

Eek! How was that supposed to fit inside me?

And then I didn't care. This was a dream, and if the meadow could evaporate, then this big, beautiful part of Mason would be able to fit anywhere I wanted it to. I grinned back up at Mason.

"Like what you see, princess?"

"Oh, yes!" I breathed.

A ripple of pleasure flickered across his face as I stroked him for the first time. He tilted his head back, lost in the sensation, and I took this as an invitation to explore further. I moved my hand up along the length of him, squeezed the top of his cock gently before slowly pumping my hand up and down, the water lapping against us.

Mason's eyes darkened, and his lips found mine in an urgent kiss, drowning out the rest of the world. His hand trailed down my side, causing goosebumps to rise on my skin despite the warmth of the water. His touch lingered at my hip, gently pressing as his fingers traced an intimate path across my body. With each touch, each caress, I craved him more.

"Shya," he gasped, his grip on my waist tightening. His eyes met mine, wide and yearning. I felt an answering urge inside me, a primal desire that was as much a part of me as the beating of my heart.

"Mason," I muttered, moving closer to him, feeling his heartbeat against mine. The river was no longer just water. It was our world, our haven away from everything else. Here, there was no danger, no cage, no Tristan, no starvation, or mind games. Here, it was just me and Mason.

With a swift motion, he lifted me up, our bodies aligning perfectly. My legs instinctively found their place around his waist, my body reacting to him on a level I barely understood. His dark hair was wet and slicked back from his forehead, and his eyes glowed with an intensity that made my heart skip a beat. He was focused on me, solely on me, like there was nothing else in this world, only me. He cupped my face with one hand. "Are you sure?"

Would I be doing this if it wasn't a dream? Would I want to lose my virginity in a river? I had no idea. But I had never been more sure of anything in my life than that here and now, I wanted this, needed this. I nodded.

His eyes never left mine as he gently lowered my body down onto him. I gasped at the sudden invasion. There was a sharp spike of pain, but even that felt amazing. I forced myself to relax against him. And then pleasure like I had never felt before pulsed through me. My vibrators did not do justice to what this felt like. Feeling Mason push himself inside of me, filling every inch of me, felt divine.

His muscles tensed beneath me, and a groan rumbled deep in his chest.

"Fucking hell, princess, you feel so tight wrapped round my cock; it's fucking delicious," he moaned, his hands gripping my hips, pulling me closer as he started to move. The rhythm was slow, deliberate, his cock coming out of me completely before he thrust back inside. I wrapped my arms around his neck, clinging to him as the pleasure built, each wave stronger than the last.

His grip on my hips tightened as he buried himself even deeper inside me. My eyes fluttered shut as I surrendered completely to the sensation. The world felt distant and unreal. But Mason was very real; the feel of him inside me, the slick heat of his skin against mine. I was utterly lost in him, consumed by the intimacy of what we were doing.

His teeth nipped my neck, and I sucked in a breath. The tiny jolts of pain only added to my pleasure, and I tilted my head to give him more access. Mason's movements grew more desperate, and I matched them with my own. The intensity was building, each stroke bringing me closer and closer to the edge.

"Mason," I gasped out his name.

He leaned in, capturing my lips with his once again. His kiss was demanding, filled with heat and passion that was nearly overwhelming. His tongue danced with mine, exploring, possessing, driving me further toward the edge. His hands moved along my body, tracing desire-ridden paths that seared into my skin. My breasts hardened beneath the strokes of his thumb and finger, twirling and rolling my nipple, sending bolts of electricity coursing through me.

He thrust into me harder and faster now. It was all I could do to keep up with him. But I needed it. I needed him. "More," I begged. "Faster, Mason."

His eyes glowed with a predatory sort of satisfaction, and he picked up the pace, driving into me with a fervor that felt incredible. I clung to him, my nails biting into the muscles of his back. He groaned in response, his fingers tightening on my hips as he drove into me with a renewed ferocity. He was everywhere—in my mind, under my skin, filling every inch of me.

Each stroke of his cock hit exactly where I needed it, the feeling so intense that I thought I was going to explode. Then my climax hit me like a freight train, and I cried out.

"Yes," he growled into my ear, his voice ragged with desire. "That's it, princess."

He buried himself inside me one last time before he, too, found release. His own cry mixed with mine as he shuddered against me, his cock throbbing as he ejaculated inside of me.

His breath ghosted down my neck in hot pants as he leaned down and whispered raggedly, "You're mine, Shya. Don't forget that!"

In that moment, the dream shifted again, the river fading away until it was just the two of us, locked in an embrace that felt more real than anything in the waking world.

"Don't leave me!" I felt a surge of panic. I wanted to stay here, with Mason, forever.

He cupped the back of my neck and bent his head down so he was looking directly into my eyes. "Stay alive, Shya. I'm coming for you." He started to fade as he repeated his words, "I'm coming for you."

"No!" I cried out, trying to grab hold of him. But it was too late. He was gone, and I was alone again. Despair hit me in a wave. The thought of waking up back in that cage, starving and alone, made me want to scream.

I couldn't do it. Couldn't face that hell again.

So I didn't. I dove deeper into my own head, letting the dream swallow me whole. I could feel the real world trying to drag me back, but I fought it. Buried myself so deep that it faded to a whisper.

The dream changed, colors and shapes blurring until there was nothing. Just empty space. Peaceful, in a weird way. No cage, no hunger, no being alone.

I let go. Let myself drift in that void. Thoughts, memories, all of it faded. No fear, no pain, just … nothing.

I let the emptiness take me.

Chapter Seventeen

SHYA

Time crawled in the cage. Hours bled into days, days into weeks. I had no idea how long I'd been there, how much time had passed. The world had shrunk to the cold metal bars and the stale air of the tent. After my dream of Mason, I'd made myself exercise at least twice a day. Push-ups, squats, lunges, dips, anything to keep my muscles working and loose, but as the days wore on, it became harder to do. Tristan was keeping me fed, but just the minimum to survive. I had been hoping to build up my strength, starting at a hundred reps and going up, but the calories Tristan gave me weren't enough to sustain that. I found myself going from one hundred to fifty to ten, and even that left me feeling weak and dizzy. Even my wolf had gone quiet. She had shut down, retreated so deep inside of me that I knew she was there, but that was all I could get from her.

Tristan's visits became the only thing breaking the monotony. I hated myself for it, but I couldn't deny that I looked forward to them. To the food he brought, the sound of another voice. It was fucked up; I knew this, I really did, but it was all I had.

I slept a lot. I don't know if it was the exhaustion or if Tristan was putting something in the food, but I suspected I was sleeping at least three or four times each day, and thinking it was a new day each time I woke up. It was a known torture tactic designed to make someone feel disoriented and soften them up for interrogation. I tried not to think about why Tristan was doing it to me.

The dreams of the witch came every time I slept now. Chanting in my head, drowning out everything else. It filled my skull, pushing out any other thoughts ... of Mason, of my family, of exercise, of getting out of here. I couldn't escape it, even in sleep.

Mason never returned, but the wolf had been there too, at first. He was my one glimmer of hope. But each night, the wolf became harder to find, and when I did find him, he had faded a little more. Last night, his howls were in the distance, and I couldn't find him at all.

I chased him through the dreamscape, calling out for him and for Mason. But my voice was lost in the chanting as it got louder and louder, and the wolf slipped further away. I woke up reaching for something that wasn't there. Like always these days, when I woke, I struggled to remember what Mason looked like, his face blurring when I thought of him. The same happened when I thought of my family. I remembered Mom's scent as she curled up with me in the night when I had a bad dream as a child. Dad's voice, so authoritative in front of the Pack but so gentle and loving when he talked to me, or Henry, or Tucker. My brothers, their squabbling and jokes, the way Tucker was so full of life and adventure, and Henry so determined to be serious and grown up. These things I remembered, but their faces? Were Henry's eyes blue or brown? Did Tucker have a freckle just below his left eye or not? Was Mom's hair long or short? I had to think really hard to bring up the details, and sometimes, I couldn't find them at all.

Tristan's small kindnesses took on new meaning now. The blankets, the bowls of stew and chili, the gentle words. In the void of the cage, they shone like beacons as his words wormed their way into my brain. With his talk of fate, of being meant for each other, I'd started to wonder if there could be some truth to what he said. Some part of me recoiled at the thought. But another part, small but growing, considered his words more thoughtfully. He was here, bringing me food, looking after me. And he was so sure that we were fated mates. Why would he be so convinced of it if it wasn't true? What if I'd been wrong this whole time? What if my fated mate was right in front of me, and all I needed to do was accept it, accept him? He had the power to make me happy. I looked forward to his visits, didn't I? Didn't that tell me that maybe a part of me recognized that I was supposed to be his?

I found myself clinging to the thought of Tristan. He was the only thing solid in a world turned to smoke and mirrors. The only one who seemed to care whether I lived or died.

I paced the small space, my bare feet hating the feel of the cool metal, trying to find some sense of connection, of grounding. My nose wrinkled at my own scent. Dirt, sweat, grime; it was all caked on me now.

But it was all so insubstantial, so fleeting. The only real thing was the gnawing hunger in my belly and the relentless chanting in my head. There was no escaping it now. Day and night, the chanting continued. I knew I was losing myself, piece by piece. Forgetting who I was, who I had been. But Tristan was my anchor, my one constant in this shifting, shadowy world.

The rustle of the tent flap jolted me from my thoughts. I looked up, heart leaping as Tristan ducked inside, a plate of food in his hands.

"Hungry?" he asked, a smile playing at the corners of his mouth.

I nodded eagerly, scrambling to my feet. The scent of the food hit me, making my mouth water and my stomach clench. But it was more than just hunger that drew me to him.

It was the promise of connection, of someone who saw me, who cared. In this lonely, twisted reality, that meant something.

He waited until I said the magic words, "Yes, please, Tristan." I couldn't remember why I had to say those words anymore, just that if I said them, he would feed me and call me a good girl. He smiled as he passed the plate through the bars, and I knew I'd pleased him. I grabbed the plate eagerly. The aroma of roasted chicken and spices filled my nostrils.

"I brought your favorite today," Tristan said. "Thought you might need a little pick-me-up."

I tore into the food, savoring the rich flavors on my tongue. For a moment, the world narrowed to the meal, to the simple pleasure of a full belly.

But as I licked the last morsels from my fingers, I realized Tristan was watching me intently. There was something in his gaze, a glimmer of excitement or anticipation.

"I've been thinking," Tristan said, settling cross-legged outside the cage. "About the future of our kind. What it could be if we seized our destiny."

I looked at the plate, wondering if he would be mad if I licked it, and tried to focus. "What do you mean?"

"Look at us, Shya. Scraping by on the fringes, hiding what we are.

While the humans destroy our lands, our way of life." His eyes flashed. "It doesn't have to be this way."

Something stirred in me at his words; some remembered feelings. "They have their uses, though. It's important to keep the peace between us."

Tristan leaned forward, his face intense. "But why is that peace so important? Why are we always the ones expected to compromise, to hide, to bend to their will?"

I shifted uncomfortably, the question catching me off guard. "Because ... because we all compromise, both them and us. We all do it so we can work together for the betterment of all. If we don't, there could be war. Chaos. People, both humans and werewolves, will get hurt, will die horribly. There are more of them than us. They could win, Tris."

Tristan shrugged. "People are already getting hurt. Our people. Forced into the shadows, denied our rightful place, not allowed to be who we really are." He paused, letting the words sink in. "Everyone is so scared of the peace breaking, but would it really be that bad if it did?"

I stared at him. The idea of open conflict between humans and werewolves was unthinkable. It went against everything I'd ever been taught.

But a small part of me wondered if he had a point. How much had we sacrificed, how much had we lost in the name of keeping the peace?

Tristan must have seen the doubt flicker in my eyes. He pressed on, his voice low and persuasive. "Think about it, Shya. A world where we don't have to hide, where we can be open about who we truly are. Where strength and power are something to be celebrated, not feared."

It was a seductive vision, one that tugged at something deep inside me. To be free. Truly free. What would that feel like?

I shook my head, trying to clear the conflicting thoughts. "I don't know, Tris. It's not that simple."

He smiled, but there was a hard edge to it. "Nothing worth fighting for ever is. But I believe in us, Shya. In our potential. We're going to do great things, you and me. We're going to take back our freedom. We're going to make the other Packs listen. Fuck, Shya, we'll destroy the Wolf Council if we have to and rebuild our world, so it works for us. I know we can do this. And I know, deep down, you do too."

"I don't—"

"Think about it, Shya. Think about how we live now. This fear of humans, this misplaced desire to keep the peace, it's stripped us of our pride, our purpose. Made us forget that we are the superior species."

Superior. That didn't sound right. We weren't superior to humans, just like they weren't superior to us. But Tristan had said it, and he always knew best, so it must be right.

"Imagine it," Tristan continued. "Werewolves united, no longer bowing to human laws and limits. Taking back our rightful place."

I could see it, the vision he painted. A world where we didn't have to hide, where we could run free under the moon, hunt as we were meant to. It called to something deep inside me.

"They've taken so much from us," I murmured. The jobs lost to humans, the dwindling forests, the young wolves driven to scavenging in alleys.

Tristan nodded. "And they'll keep taking unless we stop them. Unless we reclaim what's ours. This is our destiny, Shya. Yours and mine. To lead our people into a new era."

I wanted to believe him. Wanted it so badly. To have a purpose, a place where I truly belonged. Where being a werewolf was a source of pride.

Tristan understood. He saw me, saw the potential in our kind. Together, we could forge a new path.

"Sleep well, Shya. You're nearly there. You can nearly see the truth." And with that, he rose and left, leaving me alone with my whirling thoughts and the lingering scent of the meal.

I lay down on the blanket, my mind racing. Tristan's words had struck a chord, had awakened something in me that I didn't quite understand. My eyes felt heavy like they did after every meal these days, and as I drifted off to sleep, the chanting in my head seemed to take on a new rhythm, a new urgency. It was like a drumbeat, a call to action.

And despite my reservations, despite a part of me that was screaming at me, I found myself wanting to answer that call.

Chapter Eighteen

SHYA

Today, Tristan had promised a treat, a surprise, just for me. I couldn't imagine what it might be, but the anticipation had me on edge, my heart racing at the slightest sound. He'd come earlier this morning with a bucket of warm water, lemon soap, and a sponge. I'd waited patiently as he opened the cage and put them just inside the door, with a blanket and a clean yellow floral dress. After he left, I'd washed myself for the first time in weeks.

The warm water was a shock to my skin at first, a sensation almost forgotten. As I dipped the sponge into the bucket and began to scrub, the scent of lemon filled my nostrils. The suds slid over my skin, washing away layers of grime and sweat.

I blinked, marveling at the sight of my own skin, pale and clean, emerging from beneath the dirt. This simple act of washing felt luxurious, decadent even. I savored the feeling of the warm water cascading over my body, the soft caress of the sponge wiping away all that had happened.

I felt lighter, as if the physical act of cleaning had also purged some of the emotional weight I carried. The clean dress, a pretty, delicate thing, felt like a gift against my freshly washed skin.

For the first time in a long time, I felt like me again. Not just a caged animal, but a person. It was a small thing, this act of washing, but it meant the world to me. And Tristan had done this just for me.

I pulled the dress on over my head. It fit perfectly, but I didn't expect anything else; Tristan knew me so well. I ran my hands over the smooth fabric of the dress, enjoying the sensation. I wondered what he would think when he saw me. Would he be pleased? The thought sent a little thrill through me.

I sat down on my blanket, clean and refreshed, and waited patiently for Tristan to return. Whatever surprise he had in store, I was ready. Ready to be good, to be pleasing, to earn my place in his world.

The sound of footsteps outside the tent sent my heart racing once again. I sat up straighter. The tent flap opened, and Tristan ducked inside, carrying a small folding table and two chairs.

"Shya, don't you look beautiful. Like a proper Alpha's mate now."

He smiled at me, and I smiled shyly back at him, happy that he approved, as he set the table and chairs up in the center of the tent, then disappeared outside again.

He returned a moment later with two plates piled high with roasted meat, fresh bread, and ripe berries. It was more food than I'd seen in such a long time, and the aroma made my mouth water. Tristan placed the plates on the table, winked at me, then vanished once more.

When he came back, he held a bouquet of wildflowers in his hand. The sweet scent filled the small space. He laid them gently on the table, then turned to me with a smile.

"For you," he said. "You've been so good, Shya. You've earned yourself a treat today. Come, eat with me."

He unlocked the cage door and held out his hand to me. I took it and stepped out tentatively, my legs unsteady after so long just pacing within the confines of this space. The tent felt vast and overwhelming compared to my cage. I sank into one of the chairs, wondering at the simple comfort of sitting at a table.

Tristan took the seat across from me, the plates of food between us. He gestured for me to eat.

I reached for the food, my hands trembling slightly. It was a feast compared to my usual meals. I wanted to do this right, though. To show Tristan I could behave correctly at a table and make him proud of me. I delicately tore a piece of the bread, savoring the fresh, yeasty smell, then popped it into my mouth and chewed slowly.

As I ate, I couldn't help but steal glances at Tristan. He watched me, a smile playing on his lips. In that moment, everything felt perfect. The food, the flowers, Tristan being here with me.

I knew I would do anything to keep this feeling, to keep Tristan's approval. He was my everything now.

"I've been thinking," I said between mouthfuls, "about what you said. About werewolves and humans. About our future."

Tristan's smile widened. "And?"

I hesitated. "I have some questions. I'm not sure open war is the answer. The risk is so high that our kind will suffer huge losses. Maybe there's another way …"

"Another way?" Tristan scoffed. "Like what?"

"Well, I don't know yet. I was just wondering if there was something else we could do. Some way to change the dynamics between us and humans. A conference with the humans where we renegotiate the terms of the peace? Or a meeting with other Packs to discuss the best way forward? Maybe it will take more time, but this way, there'll be fewer deaths."

Tristan's eyes narrowed. He leaned back in his chair, his posture stiffening. "A conference? Negotiations?" His voice was cold, cutting. "You think they'll listen to us? That they'll treat us as equals? After all this time, bowing at their feet, giving in to their demands? No, we need a show of strength, Shya. That is the only thing they will understand. We need to make sure there is no doubt in their tiny little minds about who is the predator and who is the prey."

I flinched at his tone. "I didn't mean … I just thought …"

"You thought what? That you know better than me?" Tristan stood abruptly, his chair scraping against the ground. "I've been fighting for our kind for years. I've seen what the humans are capable of, what they've taken from us while you've sat in the Alpha House and been pampered. But please, enlighten me with *your* wisdom."

Tears stung my eyes. I could feel the situation slipping away from me, Tristan's anger a force beating against my mind in time with the chanting that was always there.

"I'm sorry. I didn't … I'm sorry." I bowed my head, my hair falling forward to hide my face.

Stupid, stupid. Why had I questioned him? Why had I ruined this perfect moment?

"I spoke out of turn," I whispered. "It won't happen again. I promise."

Tristan was silent for a long moment. I could hear his breathing, heavy and controlled. Then, slowly, he sat back down.

"Shya, look at me."

I raised my head hesitantly. Tristan's face had softened, but there was still a firmness in the way he looked at me.

"I know you meant well, but you must understand, I know this world better than you. The humans will never see us as equals. They fear us, hate us. They'll never willingly give us what is owed to us. We have to take it."

He reached across the table, taking my hand in his.

"I'm trying to build a better world for us. A world where we don't have to hide, where we can be proud of what we are. But to get there, we have to fight. We have to be strong."

I nodded, swallowing back my tears. "I understand. I'm sorry for doubting you."

Tristan squeezed my hand before releasing it. "I forgive you. Just remember, I know what's best for us. For all of us."

Stay alive, Shya. I'm coming for you.

The words popped into my head, making me frown. The voice was so familiar. Who had said that?

Stay alive, Shya. I'm coming for you.

The words repeated, louder this time. Then the chanting in my head rose to a crescendo.

"Shya?" Tristan looked at me, concern on his face.

I shook my head, clearing my thoughts. "I trust you, Tris. Completely."

And I did. He was my guide, my leader. If he said we had to fight, then that was what we would do.

I would follow him anywhere, do anything he asked. Because he was my going to be my mate.

And his word was law. His expectations were my laws. His desires, my north star.

Without him, I was lost. With him, I was found.

CHAPTER NINETEEN

SHYA

Tristan studied my face and must have liked what he saw. He stood, holding out his hand. "Come. It's time you saw the camp."

My heart raced with excitement as I took his hand and stepped out of the tent. The world outside was so bright, expansive, so huge after my confinement. I blinked, trying to take it all in as my eyes adjusted to the light. The sun beat down on my skin, its rays warm despite it being late fall. I tilted my face upwards, savoring the sensation, and took a deep breath, filling my lungs with the forest air. It was invigorating. I felt alive, my body thrumming with energy.

I looked around and saw the outside of the tent for the first time. It had been pitched in a small clearing, a pocket of open space amidst the dense forest. The ground was covered in a thick layer of fallen leaves and twigs, the earthy scent of the forest floor rising up from underneath them. Pine trees towered overhead, their canopy filtering the sunlight into dappled patterns on the ground.

At the edge of the clearing, a narrow trail snaked into the trees, disappearing into the shadows of the forest. It was a well-trodden path, the ground packed down by the passage of many feet using it over time. The trail seemed to beckon me, promising a journey into my future with Tristan.

Tristan tugged on my hand, pulling me toward the trail. "Come on. The camp is this way."

I followed him, my feet sinking into the soft earth of the trail, and my energy soon dissipated. We walked for what felt like an eternity but must have been only ten minutes or so. Yet my legs ached from disuse, and my breathing got heavier and heavier. I briefly wondered why I'd stopped exercising, but that thought flittered away as quickly as it came. The ground was uneven, rocks and twigs digging into my soles. I stumbled more than once, Tristan's grip on my hand the only thing keeping me upright.

By the time the camp came into view, I was exhausted, my breath coming in short gasps. But the sight before me drove the fatigue from my mind.

The camp was a bustling hive of activity. Werewolves moved about, some in human form, others in their wolf skins. The air was filled with the sounds of growls, yips and laughter, and the scents—there were so many scents: sweat, smoke, roasting meat, the musky odor of different wolves.

Tents and makeshift shelters were scattered in an orderly pattern. In the center of it all was a large bonfire with people gathered around it.

I pressed closer to Tristan, my senses overwhelmed. It was so much to take in, so much noise and activity after the solitude of my confinement. Part of me wanted to run, to hide from this onslaught of stimulation.

"It's okay," Tristan whispered. "I know you'll do fine."

I took a deep breath, trying to steady myself. This was my world now. I had to make Tristan proud.

He led me forward, his hand firm on the small of my back.

As we approached the bonfire, my eyes widened in recognition. Among the unfamiliar faces, I spotted some I knew all too well. Members of my own Pack, people I had grown up with, trained with, people who left when Tristan did.

There was Kai, his dark hair pulled back into a messy bun, his eyes glinting with mischief as he caught sight of me. And Asha, her blonde hair braided down her back, her face split into a wide grin.

"Well, well, well," Kai drawled, sauntering over to us. "Look who finally decided to join the party."

"Shya!" Asha exclaimed, rushing forward to pull me into a hug. "I can't believe you're here! Tristan said you'd joined us; I'm so happy to see you!"

I returned the hug, my emotions a jumble of confusion, relief, and unease. Kai and Asha had been my friends in the Bridgetown Pack school. We'd grown apart after that, my parents training me for Alphahood and keeping a close eye on me while Kai and Asha had started jobs in town. But they were different now, their postures straighter, their eyes fiercer. They carried themselves with a new confidence, a sense of purpose that I didn't quite understand.

"Shya's one of us now," Tristan said, his voice carrying across the camp. "She's seen the truth of our cause, and she's ready to fight for it."

I shifted uncomfortably, Tristan's words sitting strangely in my gut.

"About time," Kai said, punching me lightly on the shoulder. "We always knew you were special, Shya. Destined for great things."

I smiled, Kai's words warming me from the inside out. Tristan had been telling me the same thing for weeks now, but hearing it from Kai, from someone who had known me before, made it feel more real.

"Tristan's been telling us all about you," Asha said, her eyes shining with admiration as she looked at Tristan. "About how you're going to help us change everything. With you on our side, the old guard will fall into place. We can get our Pack back and then show the humans who they've been messing with."

I glanced at Tristan. He believed in me, in my ability to make a difference. And if he believed it, then it must be true.

"Shya's a key part of our plan," Tristan said, his hand resting possessively on my shoulder. "With her by our side, we'll be unstoppable."

I nodded. Tristan's vision of the future, of a world where werewolves could live freely and openly, where humans knew their place and we ruled over them all, was a beautiful one. And I was so lucky that I was going to help make it a reality.

As Tristan led me further into the camp, introducing me to more of his followers, we approached a group of unfamiliar faces. A tall, muscular man with close-cropped blond hair stepped out of the group, his eyes narrowing as he looked me up and down. I recognized him immediately—Cliff. Some part of me had a sudden urge to punch him, and I had to clench my fists to stop myself. What was wrong with me? Cliff had always been a good friend to Tris. Any friend of Tristan's must be okay.

"Glad to see the pampered princess has finally come to her senses,"

Cliff said, his voice gruff and hostile. "It's a sight to see, isn't it, boys? The Alpha's daughter, here to beg our forgiveness."

I bristled at his tone and glanced at Tristan. "Forgiveness? For what?"

"Are you kidding? For your fucki—"

"Careful, Cliff," Tristan warned, his voice low and dangerous. "Shya is going to be your Alpha. She deserves your respect."

Cliff raised his eyebrows. "A female? As joint Alpha? I thought we were going back to the traditional roles; that's what you promised us."

"And I keep my promises. Shya is vital to our plans. She will bring in the rest of the Bridgetown Pack, those who need an Alpha pair, one from the ruling family, to lead them. But Shya knows her place." Tristan swept my hair from my shoulder. "She'll make an excellent Alpha's mate. She knows who is in charge and will do what I say, won't you?"

I nodded eagerly. "Of course, Tris."

Cliff crossed his arms over his broad chest, and I felt his appraising eyes on me as he looked me fully up and down. It was icky and creepy, and I had that urge again, to go for his throat, but then a petite female with long, dark hair stepped forward, her head bowed slightly. Her hair cascaded down her back in loose waves, the color a rich mahogany that caught the light with hints of auburn. She was slender, almost delicate in build, standing at least a head shorter than most of the others around her. Her features were delicate—high cheekbones, a small, straight nose, and full lips that curved into a tentative smile.

"Welcome, Shya," she said softly, her voice melodious and gentle. There was a hint of an accent I couldn't quite place, adding an intriguing lilt to her words. "It's an honor to have you join us. I'm

121

Lena."

I returned her smile, grateful for the friendly gesture. "Thank you, Lena," I said. "I'm excited to be here, to be a part of this movement."

Lena's smile widened, and she took a step closer to me. "I've heard so much about you," she said, her voice warm with admiration. "Tristan talks about you all the time. You're so lucky to have a mate like him."

Before I could respond, Cliff turned to Lena, his eyes flashing with annoyance. "Did anyone ask for your opinion, Lena?" he snapped.

Lena flinched, her eyes downcast. "I'm sorry," she murmured, shrinking back. "I didn't mean to overstep."

Cliff sneered, his lip curling in disdain. "You never mean to, do you?" he said, his voice laced with sarcasm. "But somehow, you always manage to stick your nose where it doesn't belong."

The urge to tell Cliff to back off was almost overwhelming, but I knew Tristan wouldn't approve. I swallowed it down. "Lena, how long have you been in Tristan's Pack?" I turned to look at Tristan, "You know, I don't know the name of your Pack?"

He smiled at me. "Your Pack, Shya. It's your Pack, too, now. We call it New Bridgetown. We'll keep that name when we take over from your parents and merge the two Packs under my control."

My wolf growled in my head, a sound so sudden after her silence that I almost jumped. Then the chanting rose again, and she slipped away.

I frowned. Why had she growled? Didn't she like the name of our Pack? I loved it. Loved how it acknowledged where we came from but also showed that we were different now, better, with proper ideas, a proper strategy for our people to take back control.

"I joined six months ago. Cliff has been here since the beginning, but you probably already know that." Lena smiled shyly at me.

"Did I ask you to answer for me, Lena? I don't need you sticking that nose in again, do I? Do I, Lena?"

Lena shook her head, her eyes on the ground. "No, of course not. Silly me. I'm so sorry, Cliff. It won't happen again."

"See that it doesn't," Cliff growled, his eyes narrowing.

I watched the exchange with a growing sense of anger and discomfort. The chanting in my head was getting louder; it was almost all I could hear. I reached up and rubbed my fingers on my temples.

"You must be getting tired, Shya," Tristan said, his voice full of concern. "It's a lot to take in. You must go and lie down. I've had Lena make up a tent for you right next to my cabin. After our mating ceremony, you'll move into the cabin, of course, but until then, you'll be right next to me."

I beamed up at him. It was the first time he'd talked about our mating ceremony. I must have pleased him today. I heard the echo of my wolf snarling again, but only for a moment.

"I'll show you the way," Lena said, holding out her hand.

I glanced at Tristan, and when he nodded that it was okay, I took Lena's hand.

Chapter Twenty

SHYA

L ena led me through the camp, weaving between the various tents and structures.

Finally, we arrived at a tent set slightly apart from the others. It was larger than the other tents I had seen, with a thick canvas covering and a wooden frame.

"Here we are," Lena said, pulling back the flap and gesturing for me to enter.

I stepped inside, blinking as my eyes grew accustomed to the dimmer light. This tent was spacious, with a large, comfortable-looking bed, a small table and chairs, and even a washbasin in the corner. It was so different from the cold, damp cage I had spent the last few weeks in.

"This is so lovely," I said, turning to Lena with a grateful smile. "Thank you for preparing it for me."

Lena ducked her head, a pleased flush spreading across her cheeks. "It's my pleasure," she said. "I want you to feel at home here. You're one of us now; it's important you feel like you belong."

I sat down on the edge of the bed, feeling the softness of the furs beneath me. "And you, Lena? Do you feel like you belong here?"

Lena's eyes lit up at my question, and she sat down beside me on the bed, her hands clasped in her lap.

"I do," she said, her voice filled with conviction. "More than I've ever belonged anywhere else."

I knew what that felt like, the utter loneliness of not having a place to belong. I'd felt it the first few weeks in the cage. "Where were you before this?"

She paused for a moment, seeming to gather her thoughts. "I was born a rogue, you know. My parents left their Packs to be together, and they raised me and my brothers and sisters on the fringes of Shifter society. We were always moving, never really fitting in anywhere."

"That must have been hard," I said softly.

Lena shrugged. "It was our life. But then my parents died, and things got even harder. I was the youngest, and my older siblings ... they had their own lives, their own struggles. They didn't have a lot of time for me."

She sighed, as she wrinkled her nose. "After a while, my brother, Matt, he took us to one of the conclave cities, hoping things would be better there. It was supposed to be a new start, and the conclave cities, they're all about equality, right? Humans and Shifters living side-by-side in harmony? But the humans ... it was never overt, but if a Shifter and a human went for the same job, it'd go to the human. Every time. They looked out for their own first. Even if we were better qualified or harder workers. I couldn't get work, no matter how hard I tried."

"I'm so sorry, Lena."

Lena nodded, her eyes clouding with the memory. "In the conclave cities, we were supposed to be equal, but equality meant we had to act like humans. We couldn't Shift whenever we wanted, couldn't live according to our instincts. If we got angry or upset, we had to bottle it up because if we Shifted, if we showed the real us, the humans got upset. They saw it as a threat, and it upset the peace between us."

She shook her head, frustration clear in her voice. "It's not natural for us, you know? Shifting, it's how we express ourselves, how we let off steam. But in the city, we had to keep that part of ourselves locked away. We had to be 'civilized,' had to fit into their mold."

I could see the tension in Lena's shoulders and in the clench of her jaw.

"I felt like I was suffocating," Lena continued. "Like I was wearing a straitjacket every day, pretending to be something I wasn't. And the worst part was, no one seemed to notice. My siblings, they were so busy trying to make a life there, trying to fit in, trying to survive day to day. They didn't see how it was eating away at me."

She paused, taking a deep breath. I could see her struggling to compose herself, to push down the old hurt and anger.

"I tried to talk to them about it, to make them see how wrong it all was. But they just told me to be patient, to give it time. They said we had to adapt, had to make the best of it. But I couldn't. Every day, I felt like I was losing a little more of myself."

Lena looked at me then, her eyes fierce and bright. "That's why, when I heard about a Pack up north, Tristan's Pack, where we could live as Shifters were meant to, without all the stupid human rules and expectations, I knew I had to come. Finding Tristan, finding this Pack ... it changed everything for me." She grew more intense, her voice earnest and impassioned. "Here, I'm not an outsider. I'm not the odd one out, the misfit. I'm part of something bigger, something important. Tristan's vision, his plan for our future ... it gives me hope. Hope that one day, we won't have to hide anymore. We won't have to pretend to be something we're not just to survive in a human world."

I could feel the conviction in Lena's words, the unwavering belief in Tristan's cause. And I could understand the appeal of it, the draw of a place where you could finally, truly be yourself. I could taste that freedom, the ability to finally be myself, no matter what other people thought. No more duty to my family, to others. I could do exactly what I wanted when I wanted.

Just as long as it pleases Tristan.

I frowned as a voice from somewhere far inside of me made me feel uneasy. Was I really free here? Tristan was building a society where he and his friends were on top, where anyone who wasn't like him, who wasn't a werewolf, who wasn't a male werewolf, was lesser. We didn't get our freedom. He wanted us to sacrifice ours to hold up his.

Stay alive, Shya. I'm coming for you.

It was a different voice this time. The one I'd heard before. I clung to it, almost desperate to work out who had said those words.

The chanting in my head spiked, and I clutched at my head as my thoughts scattered like the ripples in a pond after a stone is thrown in.

"Oh, Shya, are you okay? Do you want me to get Tristan for you?" Lena asked, crouching down in front of me.

I pushed a feeling of unease down and forced myself to focus on Lena. "No. No, it's okay. Just a headache, that's all. I'm glad you found your place here," I said. "I hope I can find the same."

Lena reached out, squeezing my hand. "You will, Shya. I know it. You're one of us now, and we take care of our own."

There was a promise in those words, a vow of belonging and acceptance. And as I sat there, listening to the sounds of the Pack going about their evening, I wanted so badly to believe in it, even as some treacherous part of me whispered that just maybe it was a threat, too.

CHAPTER TWENTY-ONE

MASON

The cabin on the hill emerged from the dense foliage like a specter, its weathered wooden facade a natural extension of the surrounding forest. Derek, AJ, and I had been trekking through the wilderness for two days. Whoever lived out here, like AJ, wanted solitude. AJ was stuck in his human form for now; it was too dangerous for him to let his bear out. It meant that Derek and I had been taking turns to Shift and catch food for us all. We didn't want to leave AJ alone just yet. He hadn't earned our complete trust.

We stopped at the bottom of the hill, looking up at the cabin. Derek and I exchanged glances. We knew little about this mysterious contact of AJ's, and the isolation of the cabin only increased my sense of unease. It could all be a trap.

"Milly's a complicated woman," AJ said, interrupting my thoughts. "She's been through a lot, and it's made her tough as nails. She doesn't trust easily, especially not other werewolves."

I nodded, my eyes scanning the treeline for any signs of movement. "What's her story?"

AJ sighed, his face darkening. "Milly had it rough from the start. Her Pack was down south. It wasn't a stable Pack or a big one. It was run by a sole Alpha, a man. When she was a teenager, her Alpha needed cash. Milly drew the short straw. He trafficked her, sold her to the highest bidder."

My stomach churned at the thought of any Pack selling one of their own.

"Her buyers were humans. There's a good market for werewolves, especially young female ones, for rich men. They like the status of owning a pet werewolf. When she wasn't cleaned up and brought out to be on display, Milly lived chained up in the basement. But Milly's a survivor. She bided her time, plotted, waited for her moment, and then she struck. She killed them and escaped. That's when she found Tristan."

Derek glanced up at the cabin. "I can see how someone with that kind of history might be drawn to Tristan's message. A chance to strike back at the humans who wronged her."

AJ nodded. "Milly was part of Tristan's group for a while. She bought into his ideology, thought he had the right idea about taking back power from the humans. But she couldn't stomach the way he treated the females in his Pack."

Derek looked back at AJ. "I've heard his Pack thinks there is a place for females, and it's not by the side of males."

"Indeed. Tristan's views about the supremacy of werewolves don't just extend to humans. It extends to male werewolves being better than females," AJ explained. "He believes women are subservient to the males and shouldn't try to challenge their place in the hierarchy. Milly wasn't having any of that. She quickly realized that she'd swapped one type of monster for another, one who saw women as nothing more than property to be controlled and dominated."

"And she's never joined another Pack?"

"After what her first one did? Milly has a lot of mistrust for Packs. That's why she's up here, all alone. Thinks any Packs will try to force her to join them, and she's done with all that."

This was not going to be easy. "You sure she knows where Tristan is?"

"No, but if anyone does, it's her. Tristan doesn't trust me or my bear. He sends a text to my phone when he wants something done. Uses a different number each time. But Milly, she's been to a few of his camps. If we can get her to help us, she can lead us straight to him."

"Alright then. How do you suggest we approach this?"

"Milly's not one to be underestimated," AJ warned. "She's fiercely independent, and she doesn't take kindly to other werewolves encroaching on her territory."

Derek frowned. "So, what? We sneak round the back and catch her by surprise? Or set a trap out here and wait for her to walk straight into it?"

"No." AJ shook his head. "We knock on the door."

AJ just straight up walked to the cabin door and knocked. Derek and I hung back a few steps, ready in case AJ was betraying us. Nothing happened. AJ knocked again.

A figure darted out from the side of the cabin, knife in hand. It was a woman in her late twenties with short, dark hair that looked like it had never seen the inside of a hair salon. She was dressed in a maroon, threadbare tank top and cargo pants. Her feet were bare, her skin tanned, and her wiry frame was all lean muscle. She moved with the coiled grace of a predator, her body tensed and ready to spring at the slightest provocation.

"What the fuck, AJ?" the woman demanded, her eyes blazing with suspicion and barely contained hostility. "You brought mutts to my door? You know the rules."

"Milly, wait," AJ said, holding up his hands in a placating gesture. "They're not a threat. We just need to talk."

"Talk?" Milly scoffed, her grip tightening on the knife. "Since when do you bring strays to my doorstep for a chat?"

"They're not strays," AJ insisted. "This is Mason and Derek. They're looking for help, same as I was when I came to you."

Milly's icy-blue eyes narrowed, flicking between me and Derek. "I know I owe you a favor, AJ, but Pack wolves? You brought Pack wolves to my door?"

"This isn't about Pack or favors," AJ pressed. "It's about taking down Tristan."

At the mention of Tristan's name, Milly's face hardened. "You think I give a rat's ass about Tristan anymore? I'm done with that psycho and his bullshit. And I'm done with you if you're stupid enough to bring outsiders here."

She took a step forward, the knife glinting menacingly in the sunlight. "Now, I'm only gonna say this once, so listen good. Get the fuck off my land and take your friends with you. I catch you sniffing around here again, I'll gut you like the dogs you are."

AJ opened his mouth to argue, but Milly was done talking. With a snarl, she lunged at him, the knife slashing through the air.

I reacted on instinct, diving forward to intercept her. She was fast, but I was faster. I caught her wrist in an iron grip, twisting hard to force her to drop the knife.

But Milly wasn't going down easy. With her free hand, she clawed at my face, her nails raking across my cheek. I felt the sting of broken skin, the warm trickle of blood, but I didn't let go.

We grappled for a moment, a tangle of limbs and snarls. She was strong for her size, her wiry muscles straining against my hold. I had the advantage of size and leverage, but I didn't want to hurt her.

I tried to grab her other wrist, but she was too quick. She wrenched free and threw a wild punch at my jaw. I dodged, but barely. Her knuckles grazed my chin.

I needed to end this fast. With a growl, I surged forward, using my body weight to drive her back. She stumbled, off balance, and I pressed my advantage. In a heartbeat, I had her pinned against the rough wood of the cabin, my forearm pressed across her throat.

"We're not your enemy, Milly," I gritted out, my face inches from hers. "But we're not leaving until you hear us out. So, you can either cut out the fighting, or I'll truss you up and sit on you until you listen. Your choice."

Milly glared at me, her icy eyes burning with fury. For a moment, I thought she might keep fighting. But then something in her expression shifted.

"Fine," she spat. "Talk. But make it quick. And get your fucking hands off me."

I hesitated for a moment, gauging the sincerity of her surrender. Then, slowly, I eased my grip, stepping back to give her some space.

Milly rubbed at her throat, shooting me a venomous look. But she made no move to attack again, instead crossing her arms and leaning back against the cabin wall.

"Well?" she demanded, her eyes flicking to AJ. "Start talking. And this better be good."

AJ took a deep breath, his eyes locking with Milly's. "We need your help, Milly. This is Mason and Derek Shaw." He indicated us both.

"Mates?" she asked.

"Brothers," I replied.

Derek snorted, a mischievous glint in his eye. "And thank the Goddess for that. Can you imagine being mated to this guy?" He jerked a thumb in my direction. "He snores like a bear and hogs all the blankets. I'd rather cuddle with a porcupine."

I knew Derek was trying to put Milly at ease with us, so I shot him a look, half annoyed, half amused. "Please. You'd be lucky to have a mate as ruggedly handsome and charming as me. I'd have you eating out of the palm of my hand in no time."

Derek laughed, shaking his head. "In your dreams, brother. You'd be bringing me flowers and begging me to move in within a week of dating me."

Milly watched our exchange with a raised eyebrow. "If you two are done with your comedy routine, can we get back to the point? What exactly do you want from me?"

AJ cleared his throat, drawing her attention back to him. "You know Tristan has my mate. Well, he's also taken Mason's mate, Shya. We need to find his camp and get them back."

Milly's eyes narrowed, her lips twisting into a scowl. "And what makes you think I know where that bastard is hiding?"

"You were part of his Pack," AJ pressed, his voice urgent and pleading. "You know how he operates, where he might go. Please, Milly. You're the only one who can help us."

Milly's gaze flicked to me, then to Derek, her expression calculating. "And what do I get out of this little rescue mission? Tristan's not exactly the forgiving type. If he finds out I helped you, I'm as good as dead."

"We'll protect you," I said, stepping forward. "Milly, I know we're asking a lot. But Shya ... you were there. You know what he's like. You must have some idea of what he's doing to her. I can't leave her there."

Milly's eyes bore into mine. I met her look unflinchingly, letting her see the raw desperation and determination in my eyes.

"This isn't just about Shya," Derek added, his voice measured and strategic. "This is about taking a stand against Tristan and everything he represents. You have a chance to strike a blow against him, Milly. To make sure other wolves don't fall into his hands, don't get brainwashed with his twisted ideology."

Milly was silent for a long moment, her brow furrowed in thought. I could see the conflicting emotions warring in her eyes—the distrust, the fear, the hunger for revenge.

"You think you three are just going to waltz in there like some band of avenging superheroes and take Tristan and his Pack out?"

"Yes. I do."

"Then you're as mad as his bear," she scoffed, pointing at AJ.

"Milly—" AJ started.

"Don't Milly me! You brought these two idiots to my land, my home. You're on my shit list, AJ."

"Mill—" Derek tried this time, but Milly held up her hand, cutting him off.

"If I do this, I'm not doing this for you, although someone needs to go with you three dooffusheads to stop you from getting killed," she said at last, her voice fierce. "I'll be doing it for AJ's mate and for Shya. And for every female who's ever had to put up with sick, twisted males like Tristan."

She pushed off from the wall, her posture straightening with newfound resolve. "I'll take you to his camp. I'll help you get your mates back. But after that, we're even, AJ. Understand? I don't owe you any more favors."

I nodded, relief and gratitude surging through me. "Thank you, Milly."

Milly just grunted. "Save the thanks for when we're done. We've got a lot of ground to cover and not a lot of time to do it."

She ducked down, picked up her knife, and sheathed it with a decisive snap. Then she strode past us, heading for the treeline. "Well? You coming or what?"

I glanced at Derek and AJ, then turned to follow her.

CHAPTER TWENTY-TWO

SHYA

M y heart raced as I smoothed down the cream ceremonial robe, a mix of excitement and nerves fluttering in my stomach. The intricate silver embroidery on the cream fabric caught the light, symbolizing the union of moon and night. It was beautiful and fit me as perfectly as I knew it would when Tristan brought it to me yesterday. I wished I could wear the one Mom wore for her ceremony with Dad, but Tristan said it we couldn't wait until we had taken over the Pack. We needed to show ourselves as a united force now so we could present ourselves to Mom and Dad as a fully mated couple, one ready to take over the Pack.

Tristan said that after the ceremony, we'd send a video message to my parents, telling them the good news. They could then abdicate, and Tristan and I would step in and start to make the changes needed to build Bridgetown into a Pack to be reckoned with. I closed my eyes as I remembered I'd pointed out that my parents were unlikely to just abdicate. He'd gotten angry, told me not to concern myself about the details, that he had it all in hand. He'd been right, of course. It was my place to support his decisions, not question them.

"You look beautiful, Shya."

Lena stood behind me, carefully adjusting the folds of the robe. Her fingers were gentle as she arranged the fabric to fall just so, emphasizing the curve of my waist and the slope of my shoulders.

"Tristan won't be able to take his eyes off you when you enter the sacred circle," Asha agreed. They'd been sent to help me get ready, and I was grateful for them being here. My wolf felt distant and muffled, and I missed her. And a discordant chord had started to repeat itself in my mind. One word repeating over and over, slipping into the gaps in the words of the chant. *Mason, Mason, Mason.* It was driving me crazy, especially as I wasn't sure who Mason was.

I smiled nervously, meeting Asha's eyes in the mirror. "I hope so. I just want everything to be perfect. This ceremony ... it's so important."

Lena squeezed my shoulders reassuringly. "It will be perfect. You two are meant for each other. The mating ceremony will bind you together forever, as true fated mates should be. This is it. After tonight, you're going to be so happy."

I took a deep breath, trying to calm my nerves. "I know. It's just ... I thought my family would be here. My parents, my ... I think I have brothers as well. I thought they'd be beside me."

"We're your family now, Shya," said Lena. "And we're going to be right here next to you. You just have to remember this is what you want."

I nodded, the chanting in my head growing louder, drowning out the repeating word. Yes, this was right. This was what I wanted. Even if my wolf felt strangely absent, even if part of me still felt uncertain, this was the path I had to take.

"Man, I can't believe the boss is finally doing it," a gruff voice said from outside the tent.

"Doing what?" another replied, slightly slurred. "Finally getting what he's wanted for years?"

Lena, Asha, and I exchanged glances, stifling giggles. Two of Tristan's men had obviously already started celebrating.

"Yeah, that," the first voice continued. "Never thought I'd see the day Tristan would persuade her that he's her mate."

We moved closer to the left wall of the tent, all of us wanting to hear more.

"Well, he's had help," the second voice agreed. "Besides, it was about time she learned her place. Strutting round Bridgetown, thinking she was going to be in charge of us."

"I just wish I could be there when he tells her about the old man."

The other man laughed. "Fuck yeah! Can you imagine her face when she finds out her new mate killed her dad? I hope Tristan tells her right after he's fucked her."

The words knocked the breath from me. My father ... Michael ... Tristan had killed him? I turned to Asha, hoping to see confusion or disbelief on her face. Instead, I saw horror and guilt. The truth was written plainly in her expression.

"Come on, I want another drink before it starts!" the first man hissed. "And I know Jolie has some stashed in his tent."

As their footsteps faded away, the world around me began to tilt. Nausea rose in my throat, and I barely made it to a corner of the tent before retching violently.

Something snapped inside my mind. The constant chanting suddenly ceased, replaced by an anguished howl.

My wolf was back, and she was furious.

KIRA NIGHTINGALE

"Lena," I turned, reaching out to her. "Asha, please. I can't stay here. You have to help me escape."

For a moment, I thought I saw a flicker of sympathy in Asha's eyes. But then it was gone.

"Shya, honey, you're not thinking clearly," Lena said, her voice unnaturally calm. "You're upset and confused. This isn't the time to make rash decisions."

"Rash decisions?" Goddess, what the hell had I been thinking? I'd been about to mate with Tristan Munroe!

My dad ... could it be true that he was gone? And Mason Shaw! My eyes widened as I suddenly knew exactly who he was and what he meant to me.

What the fucking hell had I been about to do? I felt the bile rising in my throat again and swallowed it down. I didn't have time for that, not now. I had to get away before Tristan's men came to take me to the ceremony. "Lena, they said he killed my father."

She nodded. "I'm sorry. We have to cull the old order so that the new one can bloom, Shya. Some of them are too stuck in their ways. If they can't adapt, if they can't see the opportunities that are open to us, then they need to go. Your family stands in the way. You must see that?"

My jaw dropped. "My family? You mean my brothers, Henry and Tucker? Asha, you know them. You played with them. You ate in our house!"

Asha took a step toward me, her hands outstretched. "It's okay. I know this is a shock, but we just need to talk to Tristan. He'll make everything better."

As she spoke, I saw her eyes dart to the tent entrance. They were

140

stalling, keeping me here until Tristan's men could arrive.

"No," I said, backing away from them. I had to think, had to find a way out. Something deep inside me knew that if I saw Tristan, I would lose myself again. His actions would suddenly make sense, and I'd wake up as his fucking mate tomorrow. I'd do anything to make sure that didn't happen. "I have to get out of here," I whispered.

Lena's expression hardened. "I'm sorry, Shya, but I can't let you do that. Tristan will know what to do. He always does."

Perhaps, but at that moment, I knew what to do, too.

I spun left, my fist connecting with the side of Lena's head. Her eyes widened in shock before she crumpled to the ground, unconscious.

Asha lunged forward, trying to grab me. "Shya, stop!" she yelled, her fingers grazing my arm.

I pivoted, using the momentum to drive my elbow into her solar plexus. The air whooshed out of her lungs, and she doubled over, gasping. I followed it up with a round kick to her head, knocking her out.

"I'm not sorry," I whispered as I backed away from their prone forms. Lena and Asha, they were people I'd thought were my friends, but they'd known about my dad, had been all for killing my brothers. They deserved what they got.

Chapter Twenty-Three

SHYA

I slipped out of the tent. The cool night air caressed my skin, carrying the scents of the forest beyond. My wolf looked out of my eyes, and it felt so right that she was back.

Go west.

I turned and moved silently through the shadows, ducking behind tents and supply crates. Each step was calculated, each breath controlled. We worked together, my senses on full alert, my wolf nudging me in the right direction. The camp, usually alive with activity, seemed eerily quiet, as if holding its breath in anticipation of the ceremony that would never come.

As soon as we cleared the camp's perimeter, I darted into the welcoming embrace of the forest. The trees provided cover, their branches reaching out like protective arms. I ran. Nothing would stop me. I tore off the dress, leaving it in a pool of shimmering fabric on the forest floor as I sprinted deep into the woods.

Now.

I didn't argue, didn't think, just bent over and started the Shift. I felt my bones begin to elongate and reshape. It had been too long, way too long since she'd been out, and I was stiff. My skin prickled as fur sprouted, covering my body in a thick, protective coat. My face elongated into a muzzle, teeth sharpening into fangs. The world around me sharpened into focus, the forest coming alive with new scents and sounds.

And then I stood on four paws, my wolf form powerful and ready. In this body, I felt whole, the lingering effects of the chanting gone.

In the distance, a cry of alarm rose from the camp. They knew I was gone.

I took off, weaving through the trees, paws barely touching the ground as I flew over roots and fallen branches.

Behind us, I could hear the commotion growing. Voices shouted orders, howls filled the air, signaling the start of the hunt.

I pushed harder, needing more speed. The forest floor became a blur beneath my paws as I wove through the trees, their trunks flashing by. My lungs burned with each breath; I was so weak from weeks of being kept captive, but I couldn't slow down. Not now.

The terrain began to slope downward, and I found myself scrambling down a steep bank. Loose rocks and dirt cascaded around me as I half-ran, half-slid down the incline. At the bottom, the fresh scent of water hit my nose.

A river.

There, to the south. I put on a burst of speed and, without hesitation, plunged into the rushing current. The cold water shocked my system, but I pushed through, paddling furiously against the flow. My fur became heavy, dragging at me, but I fought on. Reaching the other side, I hauled myself out, shaking vigorously to shed some of the water weight.

I knew the river would help dilute my scent, buying me precious time. But I couldn't linger. My ears twitched, catching the faint sounds of pursuit still too close for comfort. I set off again, trying not to think about my wet paws leaving damp prints on the forest floor.

The forest on this side of the river was denser, the underbrush thicker. I ducked under low-hanging branches, leaped over fallen logs, my muscles burning with exertion. Brambles caught at my fur, but I pushed through, ignoring the sting of scratches.

But no matter what I did, I couldn't shake them. They were gaining on me. I'd been too long in confinement, too long without exercise and training. I was tiring and they weren't. The yips and howls behind me grew louder, more urgent. They knew where I was.

I dashed over a rocky outcrop and landed on a grassy knoll. A wolf charged in from my left, snapping at my back legs. I swerved sharply, causing him to stumble and fall behind. He wouldn't be alone, though, and I knew it would only be a matter of seconds before others were on me. Panic rose up, but my wolf pushed it back, driving us right with single-minded determination.

I ducked under low-hanging branches, leaped over fallen logs, my muscles burning with exertion.

Ahead, I heard the roar of rushing water. Hope surged within me as I pushed myself harder, faster. The trees began to thin, and I could smell the water mist in the air. Maybe, if it wasn't too tall, I could lose them over the falls.

As I burst through the tree line, I saw the cliff's edge and the waterfall beyond.

Yes!

I skidded to a halt at the edge, my eyes scanning for a safe way down

... and then any way down.

Fuck!

It was at least fifty feet, the water churning violently below. No path down the cliffs. If I Shifted, then maybe my human hands and feet might find a way down, but I had run out of time.

I turned just as they emerged from the trees. Six wolves, stalking forward, heads down, eyes focused only on me. They formed a semicircle around me. Their eyes gleamed in the moonlight, teeth bared in snarls.

I eyed them, calculating my chances. I was my father's daughter. Even in my state, I knew I could take three, maybe four of them, but all six? I backed up to the edge of the cliff. Then, from between them, a figure stepped forward. Tristan, in human form, his eyes locked on mine.

"Shya," he said, his voice calm and commanding. "You're confused, but I can explain everything." He reached out one hand. "Come back with me, and I'll make it all better. You know this is where you belong. With me."

For a moment, I faltered. Chanting seemed to weave through the air, its sounds reaching me from far away. Another figure emerged from the woods. Tall and cloaked, it was the witch from my dreams. He was chanting, his voice low; it mesmerized me. But my wolf snarled, pushing back against the influence. I blinked and realized I had walked three feet closer to Tristan than I had been before.

How the fuck had that happened?

I scrambled back.

Tristan's face hardened. "You don't have a choice, Shya. You're mine. Mine to do with whatever I want. Come to me, Shya. Come to me, now!"

He took a step forward, and I knew I was out of time. I didn't hesitate, just turned and leaped off the cliff.

For a moment, I felt the mist from the falls kissing my fur. I heard Tristan's roar of fury, saw the shocked faces of the werewolves as they rushed to the edge. As I plummeted toward the churning water below, a strange calm settled over me. I didn't know if I would survive the fall, but I knew with absolute certainty that I wouldn't let them catch me. Whatever happened next, I would be truly free.

Chapter Twenty-Four

MASON

We moved through the forest, following Milly's lead. She was in her wolf form, her nose to the ground, tracking something the rest of us in our human forms couldn't smell.

I scanned the trees, my eyes darting from shadow to shadow. The hair on the back of my neck stood up. Every muscle in my body was coiled, ready for action at the first sign of trouble.

The forest here was dense, the trees packed tight together like sardines in a can. The canopy overhead blocked out most of the sunlight, leaving us in a perpetual twilight. The air was thick with the scent of pine and damp earth, and the only sounds were the occasional chirp of a bird or the snap of a twig under our feet.

"You sure she knows where she's going?" Derek muttered, ducking under a low-hanging branch. "Feels like we've been walking in circles for hours."

"She knows what she's doing," AJ said.

Milly let out a low growl, her ears flattening against her head. She clearly didn't appreciate the commentary.

"Maybe we should just let the wolf do her job," I said, keeping my voice low. "Unless you want to be the one to tell her that you think you're a better tracker than she is."

Derek snorted, a grin tugging at the corner of his mouth. "Yeah, I think I'll pass on that. I'd rather not have my ass handed to me by a pissed-off werewolf."

Milly's tail swished in agreement.

Suddenly, a scent hit me like a bolt of lightning. Shya. It was faint but unmistakable. My heart thundered as I inhaled deeply, trying to pinpoint the direction it was coming from.

"This way," I said, my voice urgent. I veered off east, moving swiftly through the trees. The others followed without question.

I pushed through the underbrush, my strides lengthening as the scent grew stronger. Branches snagged at my clothes, leaving small tears in the fabric, but I barely noticed. All I could think about was Shya. I had to find her; had to get to her.

Then I heard something that made my blood run cold. Labored breathing, punctuated by soft whimpers of pain. It was coming from the north, just ahead, beyond a dense thicket of brambles.

I burst through the thicket, branches tearing at my skin. My breath caught in my throat as I took in the sight of Shya, my mate, lying naked and broken on the forest floor.

Her body was a canvas of injuries. Deep gashes marred her skin, and dark bruises bloomed across her ribs and abdomen. Her left arm was twisted at an unnatural angle, the bone likely fractured. Blood matted her hair and trickled from the corner of her mouth, stark against her ashen skin.

But perhaps most alarming was the stillness of her chest, the shallow, labored breaths that barely seemed to move her battered frame. Her eyes were closed, her face slack and unresponsive.

Rage and anguish surged through me, my heart constricting painfully. The smell of river clung to her. We'd crossed one at least a couple of kilometers away. Had she dragged herself all the way from there?

I dropped to my knees beside her, my hands moving gently over her broken body, afraid to cause her more pain. "Princess, baby, I'm here," I whispered, my voice cracking with emotion. "Hold on, please hold on."

Derek and AJ stumbled in behind me, their expressions morphing into shock and horror as they took in the extent of Shya's injuries. Milly went rigid.

I gathered Shya gently in my arms, cradling her against my chest. Her eyes fluttered but didn't open.

"Mase!" Derek hissed.

I looked up as he jerked his chin to the northeast. "Wolves, coming in fast. Probably tracking Shya."

My head snapped up, the sounds of the forest fading away as my focus narrowed to the incoming group.

I gently laid Shya back down, pressing a tender kiss to her forehead. "Don't worry, princess. I'll make them pay," I vowed, my voice a low growl.

I surged to my feet, rage burning in my veins, just as Tristan's wolves burst through the trees, a pack of eight of them, followed by one in human form, probably there to carry Shya back when they found her.

He was a big werewolf with close-cropped hair and a bulky frame that meant he'd fit right in with the army. He took in the scene before him, his eyes lingering on Shya for a moment too long, then he confidently strode forward, palms up, as the wolves spread out around us.

"Easy there. We're not here to hurt anyone. My name is Cliff. That she-wolf belongs to us, so I'm gonna ask that you back up. I'm going to walk over, pick her up, and then we can all be on our own merry ways, alright? There's no need to die over a female."

My wolf growled inside of me, demanding blood. I didn't think, didn't plan, just let the anger take over for the first time in years. I charged forward, a roar ripping from my throat. They were going to regret hunting my mate.

My fist slammed into Cliff's chest, sending him flying back. I was on him before he hit the ground, broke his back over my knee, then snapped his neck. To my left, a wolf came at me fast, but I slammed my knee into the side of its head, then stomped hard on its throat.

Derek and AJ flanked me, their own attacks brutal and efficient. Milly's jaws snapped, her teeth tearing into flesh as she fought a wolf twice her size.

I grabbed a wolf by the scruff of the neck, hurling it into a tree. It yelped as it fell to the ground in front of me, the sound cut short as I kneeled down and crushed its skull with my hands.

Blood splattered my skin, hot and sticky. I reveled in it, in the thrill of the fight.

Two wolves were taking on AJ and Derek. The remaining three circled me warily, fangs bared. I snarled, beckoning them forward. "Come on then, you fuckers! I'll rip you apart."

They lunged as one, a mass of fur and claws. I met them head-on.

I pummeled them with relentless force, my fists and feet finding their marks with lethal precision. Bones shattered, flesh tore, and blood sprayed.

The last wolf fell, and I stood amidst the carnage, chest heaving, knuckles raw.

AJ wiped blood from his brow. "That all of them?"

I nodded curtly. "For now. We need to move."

I strode back to Shya, gathering her limp form into my arms. Her pulse fluttered weakly against my skin.

"Hold on, princess," I gritted out. "I've got you."

I started running, my strides eating up the ground. The others fell into step beside me.

We had to get Shya help, and fast. Nothing else mattered. Our car was at least two hours to the south. I pushed myself harder, faster, my lungs burning with the effort. I ran, my mate cradled against my chest, her blood staining my skin.

I wouldn't let her die. Couldn't. She was everything to me, my whole damn world.

Chapter Twenty-Five

MASON

I sat in the back of the SUV, cradling Shya's broken body in my arms. In the front seat, Derek's knuckles were white on the steering wheel.

Shya's heartbeat was erratic now and getting fainter by the minute.

"Derek, hurry the fuck up," I snarled. "We're losing her."

"I'm pushing as fast as I can," Derek replied calmly. His military training had taken over and when he was like this, he was measured and controlled. Me, my wolf was going berserk. I had to get Shya help, or he was going to lose it and start a rampage.

"The nearest hospital is a human one," said AJ, looking at his phone. "It'll take another forty minutes to get to a Shifter one."

For fuck's sake! We didn't have another forty minutes.

"Head to the human one. She needs help now."

I looked down at Shya, her face pale and still. My heart clenched, panic rising in my throat. I couldn't lose her. Not like this.

Ten minutes later, Derek swung the car into the hospital parking lot, tires squealing. Before he had even stopped, I was kicking open the door, Shya clutched to my chest. AJ scrambled out behind me, leaving the car doors hanging open for Milly to jump out as we raced for the emergency room.

I burst through the doors into the chaos of rushing bodies and barked orders. We must have looked a sight: three huge werewolves striding in, covered in blood and injuries, carrying a woman who was near death, and trailed by a wolf. I was topless, having wrapped Shya's naked body in my shirt. Her blood had seeped through the material and was dripping onto the floor. Conversations cut off as all heads swiveled toward us. I ignored them all; they were insignificant. All that mattered was Shya and anyone here who could help her.

A nurse came out from behind the desk, stepping into my path.

"I need a doctor. Now!"

"Sir, I understand this is an emergency, but we have protocols in place for a reason," the nurse said, her voice clipped and efficient. She was tall, with short blonde hair cut into a severe bob. Her pink scrubs were crisp and unwrinkled, and she had the air of someone used to being obeyed without question. "You need to sit down and wait until the next available nurse is ready to see you. I assure you, it will be as quickly as possible."

My control slipped another notch. "You have one minute to get a doctor here," I declared, each word precise and sharp-edged, "or I'm going to burn this whole fucking place to the ground."

"Sir—"

"He ain't joking, lady." AJ stepped forward. "In case you hadn't realized yet, Mason here is a werewolf, and that's his mate. Now, I'll do what I can to help you nice people out, but if you don't get a doctor here right now, I can't guarantee I can stop him from doing what he's threatening."

The nurse's eyes widened, a flicker of fear crossing her face.

She swung her gaze from AJ to Derek and back to me. I knew my eyes were flaring, that my wolf was peeking out from my eyes. She took a quick step back, then ran to her desk and pressed a button. An alarm sounded throughout the hospital, and through the double doors behind her, a team of nurses arrived at a run with a gurney.

A petite woman in a white coat trailed behind them, her dark hair pulled back into a tight ponytail. Despite her small stature, she radiated authority and competence. "What have we got?" she asked, her voice calm and steady.

Doctor. Will make mate better.

My wolf approved. That was good enough for me.

"We're not sure. We found her like this near a river. She's lost a lot of blood."

The doctor nodded, her eyes sharp as she assessed Shya's injuries. "Let's get her on the gurney."

I hesitated for a moment, then gently laid Shya on the bed, smoothing her hair back from her face. She looked so small, so fragile; it tore at something deep inside me.

The moment she was down, the nurses sprang into action. They rushed her through the double doors into a curtained cubicle. I followed close behind, refusing to let her out of my sight.

Inside, the nurses worked with practiced efficiency. They attached monitors to Shya's body, the machines coming to life with a series of beeps and whirs. IV lines were inserted, bags of clear fluid hanging above the bed.

The doctor moved to Shya's side, her hands gentle as she examined her. The doctor's face tightened, but she kept her focus on Shya. "We'll need to run some tests, get a better idea of the extent of her injuries."

She looked up at me, her eyes compassionate but firm. "I know you want to stay with her, but we need room to work. I'm going to have to ask you to step outside."

Panic surged through me at the thought of leaving Shya. "Fuck no! I'm not going anywhere."

The doctor studied my face; then her eyes flicked to Derek and AJ as they came to stand beside me. She sighed. "Fine. But you need to stay out of my way. Let me do my job."

I nodded jerkily, moving to stand at the head of the bed. I took Shya's hand in mine, careful not to disturb the IV line. Her skin was cold, her fingers limp in my grasp.

The doctor and nurses worked around me, their movements quick and precise. They spoke in low, urgent tones. All I could do was stand there, holding onto Shya like she was my lifeline.

Minutes ticked by, each one an eternity. I watched the monitors, trying to make sense of the numbers and lines. Shya's heartbeat was thready, her blood pressure dangerously low.

Fear clawed at my throat, threatened to choke me. I couldn't lose her. I couldn't.

Chapter Twenty-Six

SHYA

Consciousness returned slowly, my senses awakening one by one. First came the smell, the sharp, sterile scent of disinfectant that could only mean a hospital. Then the sound filtered in, the steady beep and hum of machines. Pain came next, a dull, throbbing ache that seemed to radiate through my entire body.

I struggled to open my eyes, my lids heavy as lead. Fragmented memories flashed through my mind. Tristan's face. The news that my father was dead. Running, desperate to get away. The fall over the waterfall. I tried to piece it together, but my thoughts were hazy, slipping away like wet pebbles.

My Pack bonds were back. I could feel them flowing into me but I couldn't make sense of any of it.

Finally, my eyes fluttered open, the harsh fluorescent light making me squint. There was a face hovering above mine. I blinked and it swam into focus.

"Mason?" My voice came out as a raspy whisper.

"Here." He passed me a glass of water with a straw. I took a small sip, the cool water harsh against my throat.

I tried again. "What are you doing here?" Actually, hold on; that was not the question. "What am I doing here? Where is here exactly?" I asked, looking around the room. It was a standard hospital room with a bed, a cabinet, a tray table on wheels. There were two doors, one I was guessing that led to a bathroom. But this wasn't the medical wing at Bridgetown.

"What do you remember?" Mason asked gently as his thumb stroked my cheek. I closed my eyes at his touch. I was surprised by how safe it made me feel. How comforted I was just by him being here.

Before I could answer, the door to the corridor swung open, and Derek walked in.

"Shya, you're awake," Derek said, relief evident in his voice. He strode over to the bed, his eyes darting between Mason and me. "How're you feeling?"

I shrugged, then winced as the movement sent a jolt of pain through my body. "Like I jumped off a waterfall. Oh wait, I did."

Derek exchanged a look with Mason. "Well, that would explain some of your injuries. What's the last thing you remember?"

I frowned, trying to piece together the fragmented memories. "Jumping. I knew I couldn't let Tristan find me, knew I wouldn't let him take me back there. The water seemed like the best option at the time."

Mason's whole body tensed. He understood what I was saying. "Shya—"

"Don't, Mason. I'd make the same choice again. I won't let Tristan have me. Not again."

Rage filled his face. "You won't ever have to worry about that, princess. He will never get his hands on you again."

157

For a moment, his control, always so tightly leashed, slipped. His presence expanded and filled the entire room. I felt the weight of his power, the barely contained fury that simmered beneath the surface. It should have scared me. But it didn't. All I felt was safe. Protected.

Derek cleared his throat, breaking the tension. "Do you remember anything else? Anything about Tristan, about where he is or his plans?"

"I ... I was held in a camp. Tris ...Tristan, he said I was his fated mate, and I believed him. The things I said ... Oh, Mason, the things I thought! I was going to go through with the mating ceremony, and I was happy!" A wave of disgust and horror swept through me. "I was happy, Mason. He made me think I was happy."

Mason reached out and gently swiped away the tears running down my face. When did I start crying? "There was a witch; I'm sure there was a witch. They came into my dreams, chanting. Every night, they were there. Until all I could hear was the chanting. Over and over." I was rambling now, and I knew it, but I couldn't seem to stop. "I think they did something to my head. My wolf. She shut herself away. I couldn't feel her anymore. But she came back at the end."

I felt inside for her, but she was gone again.

What the fuck was going on?

"She's gone again, Mason," I heard the desperation in my own voice. "Why? What if she's gone? Like, really gone?"

Mason gathered me into his arms. "Hush, princess. It's okay. Your wolf will come back, I promise. There is no witch spell that can separate you permanently from your wolf. Maybe this is just a lingering effect from the spell. If so, she'll come back again."

I pushed against his chest so I could look at his face as another memory crashed into me. "I heard something at the camp. They said ... they said my dad was dead. Please tell me they were wrong, Mason. Please." I curled my fists in his shirt, begging now, but I could see the answer in his eyes, could feel it in my Pack bonds. "No, no, no! You're wrong! It has to be some mistake."

"I'm so sorry, Shya."

I started sobbing and sank into his chest. I cried until I couldn't cry anymore. I don't know how long it took, but after I was done, I fell asleep, my head resting on Mason's shoulder.

When I next woke up, awareness came slowly again, the remnants of sleep still clinging to me. I was warm and comfortable, the pain from earlier now a dull ache. It didn't take long to realize I wasn't alone in the hospital bed. Strong arms were wrapped around me, holding me securely against a solid chest. Mason.

I kept my eyes closed, not wanting to shatter this moment of peace. I knew Mason and Derek would want to talk about what happened with Tristan, would want to tell me about my dad, and I wasn't ready for that. I wanted to forget, to pretend, even if just for a little while, that none of it had happened.

My thoughts drifted, and I found myself thinking of Mason and his wolf. Had my dream about him been real? Or was it just a fantasy made up by my mind to try to get me through the ordeal? I could ask him, but how would I even start? *"So hey, did you come into my dreams, guide me to a river, and give me the most amazing orgasm I'd ever had?"*

Nope. That wasn't a conversation I was ever having with Mason. But not knowing was gnawing at me. I wasn't sure what was real and what wasn't anymore. The doubt scared the shit out of me. If I couldn't trust my own thoughts, what could I trust?

"Princess?" Mason's voice was soft in my ear. "You awake?"

I sighed, realizing I couldn't hide from him forever. I was a Pack princess, and my dad had taught me better. I had to face my problems head-on, no matter how much I wanted to run from them.

I opened my eyes and tried to sit up. Pain lanced through my body, making me gasp. Mason sat up with me, his hands gentle as he helped me into a sitting position. "Careful."

I nodded, gritting my teeth against the pain. "Where are we?"

"It's a human hospital," Mason explained. "Your arm was broken, along with six ribs. You had some internal injuries. You'll feel better after you Shift."

I nodded, trying to ignore the twist of fear in my gut at the mention of my wolf. What if she didn't come back? What if whatever Tristan did to me had driven her away for good?

I pushed the thought away. I couldn't dwell on that now. There were more pressing things to deal with.

I looked at Mason, steeling myself for the conversation I knew was coming. "Okay. Tell me everything."

By the time Mason had finished, I'd cried so much I didn't think there was any water left in my body. Now, I felt completely numb. Part of me thought that maybe that was a good thing.

Mason tucked a stray strand of hair behind my ear. "We'll get revenge for your father."

I nodded.

Mason frowned and then opened his mouth, but before he could say anything, Derek walked in with a tall, bearded man and a petite female werewolf with a scowl on her face. I was guessing Milly. And the other ... My nose wrinkled. Bear Shifter. I narrowed my eyes at him. This must be AJ. A spark of anger rose in my chest before fizzling out.

"You attacked my brother," I said, but there was no heat to my words. Maybe there were no more emotions left in me.

Mason's frown deepened as AJ crossed his arms and nodded once. "I did. And for that, I'm sorry. How is the boy?"

"I don't know. He's just lost his dad, and I've been missing for ..." I glanced up at Mason.

"Five weeks."

Five weeks? Was that all? It felt so much longer.

"Right. So, he's not exactly getting all the breaks right now."

AJ tilted his head and studied me for a moment. "I'm sorry about your father. He was a good man, a good leader."

My breath caught and tears welled up. Okay, so I wasn't totally numb.

Mason slid his hand around my shoulders, and I took a deep breath. I could do this.

"Thank you. And thank you, both of you, for helping Mason and Derek. I understand that they wouldn't have found me if it hadn't been for your help."

AJ nodded. "I know you've been through a lot, but I have to ask, did you see or hear anything about my mate in the camp?"

I wished I had better news for him. "I'm sorry. I was kept away from the main camp and was alone most of the time. I didn't see any other captives when I was there."

AJ's face flashed with disappointment then he lowered his head, looking at the floor while his hand rubbed the back of his neck.

Milly shifted uncomfortably, her eyes darting around the room. Mason had said she wasn't used to being around people, especially other wolves. When her stare landed on me, there was a curious glint in her eye.

"Were they telling the truth?" She jerked her head toward Derek and Mason. "Are you really a Pack princess?" she asked, her voice quiet.

I nodded. "Yes. Or at least, I was. Before ..." I trailed off, not wanting to think about my father.

Milly seemed to study me for a moment. "And you're in line to be Pack Alpha?"

"With my father gone, my mother will be the sole Alpha until she and I decide when it would be best for me to take over. I would have to be mated first, though. It's better for a pair to rule; they work together to balance each other out, to do what's best for the whole Pack."

A strange expression crossed her face, a mix of awe and disbelief. "And you'll get to make decisions for the whole Pack? For real?"

I realized that for her, the idea of a female being in a position of power equal to males was probably a new concept.

I nodded. "Most Packs are run equally by the Alpha pair."

There was something in her eyes, a look; it took me a moment to realize it was hope and desire before she shut it down.

"It's still a Pack, though. I've had enough of those, especially after Tristan."

162

I scoffed. "Yeah, well, Tristan is a fuck—"

Pain lanced through my head at the mention of Tristan, and I winced. Mason's hand was immediately curled around the back of my neck, steadying me.

"What's wrong?" he asked, concern etched in his features.

I gritted my teeth, waiting for the pain to subside. "I don't know. I was just thinking about Tristan, about how much I hate him ..." The pain intensified, stealing my breath.

Milly's face darkened. "It's the witch. It's one of their spells. You won't be able to think bad thoughts about him, not without it hurting."

Bile crept up my throat. Just how much had Tristan and his witch messed with my mind?

"Can it be broken?" Mason asked, his voice tight.

Milly shrugged. "I know nothing about witches. I stay away from them more than I keep clear of wolves."

It was all too much. Tristan, my dad, my mother losing her mate, my brothers their father, and now this. Tristan had had a witch rummaging inside my mind, manipulating my thoughts and feelings. It might not be physical, but it was rape all the same. I curled into a ball.

"Shya?" Mason whispered.

"Take me home, Mason. Please, just take me home."

Chapter Twenty-Seven

SHYA

I'd fallen asleep again right after Mason promised he'd take me home as soon as the doctor cleared me. Goddess, I was just so tired. I could barely stay awake for more than a couple of hours at a time. When I woke up this time, the light was dim, and the only sound was Mason breathing. We were spooning again, and it felt like the safest place in the whole world. With Mason in the bed with me, holding me tight, there was nowhere else I wanted to be.

"How are you feeling, princess?" Mason's voice was quiet, subdued.

"Like a wrecking ball slammed into my chest."

He nuzzled my neck. "If I could take away this pain for you, I would. In a heartbeat."

I felt tears welling up, but I didn't want to cry. I needed a distraction. "Tell me about your tattoos."

"My tats?"

I turned over to face him. He was shirtless, and I cautiously reached out to trace the intricate designs. "When did you get them?"

"When I was a teen," he murmured, watching the touch of my fingers on his skin. Then he took my hand, guiding it to a stylized wolf on his bicep. "This one's for my Pack. My family." He moved my fingers to a small crescent moon near his collarbone. "This is for the people my mom and dad were before it all went to shit."

My fingers slipped down, brushing over a series of intricate lines on his ribs. "And these?"

"Each pattern represents a challenge overcome. This one was the first time I nailed a three-sixty snowboarding. This was when I biked four mountains in twenty-four hours. This one was for Derek and Sam graduating from high school. I thought they were never gonna get there; for sure, they were getting kicked out, but Ryan and I dragged them through their last year, and by some miracle, they passed."

He guided my hand to the intricate tribal design covering his shoulder and part of his chest. "This one's the most meaningful," he said softly. "Got it a few weeks after we met."

"It's beautiful," I whispered. "What does it stand for?"

He pressed my hand flat against his chest, where the tattoo covered his heart. "It's to remind me that no matter how dark it looks, no matter what happened in the past, there is always hope," he said, his voice intense. "You inspired this tattoo, princess. You inspire me to be a better person."

I wasn't ready for this conversation. I needed to change the subject quickly!

"Tell me about your dad. What was he like?"

Mason shifted, wrapping one arm around my waist. "My dad was … complicated."

"How so?"

"He was a good man, once. Before Mom died."

I waited, letting him gather his thoughts.

"After she passed, he just ... gave up. Started drinking. Stopped being a dad."

"That must have been hard."

Mason grunted. "Ryan tried to pick up the slack. Always out hunting, working. Trying to keep food on the table."

"And you?"

"I was at home with the twins and Dad. When he bothered to show up."

I felt Mason's chest rise and fall in a deep sigh.

"He'd get drunk. Call me names. Pass out. Rinse and repeat."

Oh, Mason, "What about Sam and Derek?"

"They saw. Heard. I tried to shield them, but with our hearing ..." Mason's voice trailed off.

I squeezed his hand, encouraging him to continue.

"I begged him to get help, you know. To quit drinking. He'd try for a day or two. Never stuck. The pull of it was too great. He loved the drink more than he loved us."

"Do you really believe that?"

"Yeah, I do. It was an illness, but it was a choice, too. If he wanted to stop, we would have done anything to help him. But in the end, he didn't want it. He liked the oblivion it provided. It meant he could escape everything; he didn't have to feel the pain of losing Mom anymore."

"What happened to him?" In the time I'd known the Shaws, I'd never heard any of them mention their dad.

"He let his anger take over. He lost control. Got violent. Not with Ryan or the boys. Just with me. It started small—I didn't get him a new bottle of beer fast enough, so he'd lash out. Or I gave the twins the last food in the fridge, and it was empty when he got hungry. The drink, it changed him. That wasn't who he really was. He was just so full of anger all the time. It got to the point where he'd hit out if I was in his way or I looked at him funny."

My breath caught. "Did Ryan know?"

"No. He was out all the time, trying to get us money and food to survive on. I didn't want him to know."

"Why?"

Mason's voice was flat. "Didn't want to burden him. He was doing everything he could just to keep us going. He didn't need to know what was going on at home as well. It was my problem. Mine and Dad's. It was up to us to sort it out."

"And? Did you sort it out?"

He fell silent for so long that I thought he wasn't going to answer. Then he said softly, "I'd managed to keep Dad away from the twins as much as I could. Then I got detention at school. It meant I came home later than usual that day. The twins were already there, and I came home to find Dad screaming at Derek. I knew Dad was a hair's breadth away from attacking him."

I looked up at him, wishing I could go back in time and make it better. "What did you do?"

His jaw clenched. "Intervened. Told Derek and Sam to run, and I took the beating."

"Mason, I'm so sorry."

He kissed my forehead, his lips so warm against my skin.

"I knew then I had to do something. It wasn't safe for the twins to be around him, not anymore. I told Dad he had to leave. He was furious, said I was a fucking waste of space, that he was ashamed of me and wished all of us had died instead of Mom."

I stroked his arm. "It was the drink talking, Mason. He didn't mean what he said."

Mason paused. "Maybe. Doesn't change what happened."

"Did he leave?"

"No. He came at me, said he was going to take care of us leeches once and for all. That I was first, and then he'd wait for the others, make sure we all joined Mom."

"Oh, Mason." I cupped his face in my hand, suddenly knowing without a doubt what had happened. It was the only thing that made sense. The Shaw brothers were still here, and it would explain why none of them mentioned their dad.

"You killed him."

He looked into my eyes, and in that moment, he looked so vulnerable. Like he was that kid again, trying to fight off his father. "I screwed up. I became just like him; I lost control. The fight, it wasn't easy, and it wasn't pretty. After ... after I carried the body deep into the woods. I buried him near to the old Dark Goddess temple."

I felt sick imagining it. A boy dealing with something so horrific by himself. And suddenly, the tight rein he always kept on his anger, the balls and fidget toys he used to keep his hands busy all made sense. He was scared of losing control again and killing someone else. "Do your brothers know?"

"Ryan does. He found me a few hours later when he came home. The twins? I think they guessed, but they didn't ask questions when I told them Dad took off and wouldn't be coming back. I think they were all just relieved that he was out of our lives."

It was so different from the happy, loving childhood I'd had.

"Mason, I ... I don't know what to say."

He shrugged, his voice flat. "It was a long time ago."

"You were just a kid. You shouldn't have had to deal with that."

Mason's eyes met mine, filled with a pain that seemed to stretch back years. "Someone had to. Better me than the twins."

I nodded slowly, understanding dawning. "That's why you became a PI, isn't it? To help others who can't help themselves."

Mason's eyes flickered away. "Partly."

"You're trying to save others from what you went through."

He let out a long breath, then pulled me closer. We lay there in silence for a while, just holding each other.

Finally, I spoke. "What do we do now, Mason? About Tristan, about ... everything?"

His voice was hard when he answered. "Tristan is already dead; he just doesn't realize it yet. We'll take down anyone who stands with him."

I nodded, feeling a spark of determination ignite in my chest. "Good. Because I want payback. For what they did to me, to my dad, to everyone."

Mason pulled back slightly, looking into my eyes. "We'll get it, princess. I promise you that."

Chapter Twenty-Eight

MASON

After Shya fell asleep in my arms again, I slipped out to make a phone call. When I was done, I turned to find Derek leaning on the wall outside of Shya's room. I raised an eyebrow in question.

"She's still asleep."

I nodded. "Thanks."

"I heard what you said to her. About Dad."

My face went blank. I hadn't lied to Shya. We'd never talked about Dad after I killed him, and I wasn't sure if Derek and Sam knew what had happened to him.

"You did the right thing, you know. You did what you had to do to protect us."

I studied him, wondering if he really meant it. Derek kept his eyes on mine, and I nodded. His words eased something inside of me that I hadn't realized had been wound tightly all these years.

"Does Sam know?" I asked.

"He suspects. We both did. But he'll feel the same as me. We owe you, Mason. We won't forget that."

I placed a hand on his shoulder. "You're my brother. You don't owe me anything."

Derek nodded. "You sure you want to do this?"

"Do what?"

"Take her back. There's no telling what will happen when she goes back there. Officially, she's still promised to Edmond."

I glanced at the door to her room. She'd looked so small and vulnerable in the hospital bed. "She needs time to heal. After what Tristan's done to her, it has to be her choice, Derek. She has to come to me because she wants to."

He nodded.

"I need to go out for an hour. You'll protect her?"

"You have to ask?"

Three hours later, we were getting ready to leave the hospital. Milly and AJ had gone out and picked up some clothes for Shya. She'd gotten dressed in the bathroom. It had taken her a long time, and she'd refused any help from me or Milly. She wanted to do this on her own, needed to, I was guessing, so we gave her that.

She finally emerged from the bathroom, dressed in blue jeans and a fitted black short-sleeved shirt. Bruises covered her arms and face, but she looked more beautiful than ever.

"Ready to take on the world?" I said, a smile tilting my lips.

Shya raised an eyebrow, a glimmer of her old spark in her eyes. "I don't know about the world. Maybe just a small country to start with."

My smile widened. "I think we can arrange that. Any preference on which country?"

She pretended to think for a moment. "Something warm. With beaches. And those little umbrella drinks."

"Umbrella drinks, huh? I didn't take you for the fruity cocktail type."

"There's a lot you don't know about me, Mason Shaw," she said, a playful smirk on her face.

"Maybe, but I'm looking forward to finding out."

She smiled at me, a glint in her eyes, but it was gone as quickly as it appeared.

I stepped closer, not wanting her to disappear into her head, and gently took her hand. "I have something for you."

I gestured to the pile of boxes stacked in the corner.

"What's this?"

"Well, I know you like shoes, but I wasn't sure what type of shoes you wanted. So I got a selection."

Her eyes widened. "A selection? There are fifteen boxes there, Mason. Fifteen!"

I shrugged. "I don't know much about shoes, so I grabbed a few."

She opened the first box and gasped. "Mason! These are Christian Louboutin 'So Kate' pumps in black patent leather."

She looked at me like this was supposed to mean something.

"So, a good choice?"

"The best, Mason! The best choice. Oh, the Goddess!" She'd opened another box and pulled out the Balenciaga gray running sneakers. "These are supposed to be so comfy you could fall asleep in them."

I smiled, pleased that she liked them. She kept going, pulling out

Jimmy Choo pumps in a soft blue, Dolce & Gabbana slide sandals, and my favorite of the lot, red Valentino Garavani ankle-strap heels.

When she had all the shoes unpacked, she sat down in the middle of a circle surrounded by them all.

She was frowning as she surveyed the choices.

"Did I get the wrong ones?" I asked. "I can buy some more."

"No! No more shoes! These are ... these are beautiful, Mason. But they must have cost a small fortune; you have to take them back!"

Too late; I'd seen her reaction when she'd opened each of the boxes. If I needed to buy her shoes every day for the rest of my life to get her to smile like that, I'd do it.

"I own the most sought-after PI agency in the north, Shya. I can afford a few shoes. "

She looked at the shoes like a child going into a candy shop for the first time and seeing so many sweets that they didn't know where to start.

"No one has ever bought me shoes before. I love them. All of them. But ... how am I supposed to choose?"

"Well." I looked at the shoes around her. "How do you want to feel?"

She glanced at me sharply. "How do I want to feel?"

I kneeled down beside her, careful not to disturb the circle of shoes. "I've watched you, Shya. You love your shoes. It's like, I don't know, like different shoes bring out different parts of your personality. So, how do you want to feel today? We'll find a shoe to match."

She studied my face, then looked down at her lap. "I'm beginning to understand why you are such a good investigator. You're good at noticing things."

"I'm good at noticing things about you."

The most adorable blush crept over her face, and she glanced up at me from under her lashes.

"You really think we're fated mates?" she whispered.

"Yes. I believe it utterly, to the depths of my soul and back again. You are the only one for me, princess. The only question is what you believe."

Her fingers traced the edge of a Louboutin box. "I ... I just don't know, Mason. I honestly don't know what I feel or what I believe. Tristan messed with my mind; he jumbled up all my feelings, so what was up was down, and what was down was up. Until I can work out how I really feel, I can't trust anything. Not even what my heart or my body are telling me."

I arched one eyebrow. "And what are your heart and body telling you right now?" I asked, my voice low.

She smiled cheekily at me. "That I love all these shoes."

I fought the urge to kiss her senseless. I knew, after everything, I was going to have to take things real slow. Instead, I put one hand over my heart and fell back onto the floor as if she'd struck me. Shya giggled. It was a fucking fantastic sound, and I was so relieved that parts of her were coming back.

"And how do you want to feel wearing the shoes you so love?"

"In control. Like I can handle anything."

"And you can," I said firmly. "With or without the shoes. But if they help you feel that way, then that's what matters."

Shya was quiet for a moment; then, she looked up at me with a mix of curiosity and something deeper, more intense. "Why did you really buy all these, Mason?"

I took a deep breath. "Because I wanted to give you choices. Options. I wanted you to know that no matter how you're feeling—strong, vulnerable, playful, serious—you have the power to be who you want to be. You're in control of this, Shya. The shoes highlight part of you, but they don't change who you are. It's all you. With or without the shoes. And I'll be here, supporting you, no matter which pair you put on."

She reached out and placed her hand on my arm. "Thank you. Not just for the shoes. For finding me. For being here with me."

I cupped the back of her head. "I'll always find you, Shya. Always."

Then Shya smiled; a real, genuine smile that lit up her whole face.

"So," she said, a hint of mischief in her voice, "want to help me try these on?"

I grinned back at her. "I thought you'd never ask."

When we made our way outside, the others were waiting for us by the SUV. She'd gone with the Gucci sneakers, saying she wanted to be able to kick the shit out of anyone who was stupid enough to try to attack us on the way.

Derek smiled at Shya as we approached. "Looking good, Shya. You ready to hit the road?"

She offered him a small smile and nodded. I'd seen the spark of who she was back in the hospital room, and I wasn't going to let her disappear into herself again.

"No retreats," I whispered into her ear. "You're a princess, a Little. Never forget that."

Her back straightened, and her chin rose as she looked back at Derek. "I'm ready."

Derek's grin widened. "Damn right, you are."

"Mason," AJ said, stepping forward, "a word?"

I glanced down at Shya. She looked from AJ to me. "Go, I'll do my best not to be kidnapped walking from here to the car."

I watched as Derek opened the door for her, then turned and followed AJ.

"Everything okay?"

"Yes. I just don't think it's a good idea for me to go to Bridgetown."

I frowned. "Why?"

AJ sighed, running a hand over his beard. "My bear attacked Tucker. Brutally. That's not a reminder the Little family needs right now. They've got enough to deal with."

AJ had helped us find Shya, had put himself on the line, but I couldn't deny his point. The Littles were grieving. Having the man who mauled their son and brother showing up wouldn't help matters.

Milly came up behind AJ. "While you boys are nattering about this, I have no intention of going within twenty miles of a Pack. You can drop me off with AJ."

I looked between them, torn. AJ still hadn't found his mate, and I'd promised I'd do all I could to help him. As soon as Shya had been stabilized, both AJ and Milly had headed back to where we'd found Shya. The bodies were gone. They'd followed the scent trails back to the camp and found it deserted. AJ's mate hadn't been there, and Tristan had gone into hiding. Again.

"We'll keep working on finding out where Tristan is." AJ crossed his arms.

I studied them for a moment, then nodded. "Alright. We'll drop you both off at the border."

I kept my word, and when we reached the border of Bridgetown territory, Derek pulled over. Shya was asleep on the back seat. Her wolf still hadn't shown up, and without the ability to Shift right now, she was still healing and fighting off the effects of the witch's spell. AJ, Milly, and I got out and stood facing each other.

"Are you sur—?"

"Abso-fucking-lutely," Milly interrupted.

AJ grinned at me. "You need anything, you call me." His face turned serious. "We find anything, we'll be in touch."

I searched his face, seeing the resolve there. "And I'll be there. Thank you ... for everything."

Milly gave me a curt nod, her way of saying goodbye. Then they were gone, disappearing into the trees.

I turned back to the car, to Shya. One step at a time. Get her home. Keep her safe. Everything else could wait.

We hadn't even come to a stop in front of the Bridgetown Alpha House when the door flew open, and Tucker rushed out.

"Shya!"

Shya jumped out of the car, and he flew into her arms, hugging her fiercely. Camille was next, and in seconds, she had joined them, her arms around them both, tears streaming down her face.

"I'm so sorry, Mom," Shya sobbed. "About Dad, about everything."

"Shush." Camille stroked the hair away from her daughter's face. "Don't you worry about that now. You're home; that's the most important thing. Nothing else matters."

Henry appeared in the driveway, but he didn't join his family. Instead, he stood awkwardly to one side. His eyes met mine, and he nodded once in thanks. It had only been a few weeks since I'd last seen him, but he looked older, grimmer. The teenager I'd known was gone, and a young man stood before me, one touched by death and responsibility.

My princess noticed, too, and wasn't having it. She reached out and grabbed Henry, pulling him into the family hug. Their bodies shook with the force of their shared grief and relief, the reality of Michael's death swirling around them like a tangible presence, a gaping wound in the fabric of their family.

I turned, wanting to give them some privacy, and saw Edmond in the doorway. His eyes were fixed on Shya. He leaned against the doorframe and crossed his arms, his face an unreadable mask. My wolf growled.

Challenger.

Yes, I agreed. We would have to deal with him soon.

CHAPTER TWENTY-NINE

MASON

The leather chairs creaked softly beneath Derek and me as we sat down, the sound mingling with the relentless rhythm of the clock on the mantle.

Across from us in the study, Edmond sat in the chair that once belonged to Michael. He was no Michael, though. His posture was rigid, and his eyes were hard, with a hint of thinly veiled displeasure. Next to him was the man he introduced as his brother, Garrett. Where Edmond was polished, Garrett exuded raw energy. He was slightly taller than Edmond, maybe 6'3", with a muscular build that spoke of hours in the gym rather than boardrooms. Unlike Edmond's formal business attire, Garrett wore trendy, casual clothes that emphasized his physique.

"I suppose I should thank you for finding Shya," Edmond said, his voice aloof and condescending, as if he were thanking workmen for doing a job on his house. "You found and returned her to us, and for that, we are, of course, grateful."

I stayed silent, mainly because I was trying to stop myself from leaping across the desk and punching his lights out.

"I imagine you do this sort of thing a lot in your line of work. Returning lost things to their families."

I leaned back in my chair, wishing I had a ball to squeeze so I could pretend it was his head. "No, this is not the sort of thing I usually do. This was personal. Something of mine was taken. I went out and found it. What about you, Edmond? What have you been up to while we were out there hunting Tristan?"

Edmond crossed one leg over the other and flicked an invisible speck of dust from his knee. "Me? Some of us have to look at the bigger picture, Mason. I was here, holding this Pack together, coordinating the search. We can't all go blundering off in any direction we feel like."

"And yet, blundering off in any direction is exactly what found her."

Garrett opened his arms wide, his movement drawing my attention. A cocky grin spread across his face as he interjected, "Come on, bro. You gotta admit, Mason here's got a point. Sometimes, you need a little less planning and a little more action."

Edmond's jaw tightened at his brother's words.

Was this a coordinated play by them? Garrett insulting his brother to get on side with us? Or was he really just that disloyal? My brothers would never undermine me in front of outsiders.

"But hey," Garrett continued, "I guess that's why you're the brains and Mason here is the brawn, right? Is that what gets Shya all hot and bothered, Mason? Maybe you can give some tips to my brother, seeing as it'll be his job to keep her sweet soon."

I didn't give a fuck if this was a test or not; I had Garrett out of his seat and against the wall before he could blink.

The door swung open, and Camille strode in. Garrett's demeanor changed immediately. He straightened up, and the smirk disappeared. Gone was the frat boy, and instead, there was a respectful member of the Pack.

"Mason, please remove your hands from Garrett."

I stared at Garrett until he lowered his eyes, then released him.

"Cam—" Garrett started, but she held up a hand.

"I don't want to know, Garrett. Please, Mason, take a seat."

I sat back down next to Derek and studied Camille as her eyes lingered on Michael's chair, now occupied by Edmond. Pain flickered across her face, then was gone. She'd lost weight since I'd been here last, and exhaustion lines were etched around her eyes, but there was a spark of hope in them, too.

"I can't thank you enough. You brought my daughter home to me. To us."

"How is she?" I asked. Both my wolf and I were feeling the strain of being apart from her. We wanted her in our sight at all times.

"She's resting. Tucker is refusing to leave her side. They're curled up in bed, and he's reading to her from the latest book he's managed to steal from his brother."

"It sounds like old times," Derek commented.

A shadow passed over Camille's face, and I suspected she was thinking of when Michael was here and reading to his children. She covered it quickly, though, and turned to me. "Tell me everything."

It took over an hour to fill them in on our investigation and answer all of Camille's questions. I'd left AJ and Milly out of it, not wanting to let their involvement be widely known without their permission.

"Now Shya's home, you'll need to look to the future. Tristan is still a threat."

"Yes," Camille agreed, a thoughtful expression on her face. "That's why it is imperative that Shya mates with Edmond as soon as possible."

The words hit me like a throat punch. Mate with Edmond? After everything she'd been through?

"Are you fucking kidding me?"

Edmond's eyes narrowed.

"Our Pack is vulnerable," Camille continued, ignoring my question. "You're right; Tristan is still out there. This isn't over; he will attack again. Michael's death has left a power vacuum. We need to fill it, and fast. A stable Pack that has a clear line of succession is a strong Pack. That's what we need right now."

"Don't you think she's been through enough? Your daughter has been kidnapped and brainwashed. She jumped off a waterfall, for fuck's sake, just to get away from one motherfucker who tried to convince her that he was her mate. She's just learned her dad is dead, and now you want to force her into an arranged mating?"

Camille flinched at my words, but her eyes remained determined. "I know it's not ideal. If there was any other way, I'd take it, Mason. Of course I would. But I have to think of the Pack. Of the future."

I opened my mouth to argue, to tell her exactly where she could shove her plan. But before I could, there was a knock at the door, and Danni walked in.

"Sorry to interrupt, but Jem Parker is here," she said. "And he's brought a girl with him."

Jem strode in, his presence filling the entire room. Though his frame was still thin, and his face bore the marks of his ordeal as Brock's captive, there was an undeniable aura of danger about him. His eyes, once bright with confidence, now held a haunted depth as they swept across us, assessing each one of us with the instincts of a true Alpha.

When he deemed it safe, Jem nodded to someone outside. A slight figure slipped into the room, moving with an odd, graceful hesitancy. Esme, her sandy blonde hair swaying as she walked, looked around with wide, observant eyes that seemed to take in more than just the physical space.

Camille rose to greet Jem, her posture betraying a mix of respect and wariness. "Jem, how nice to see you again."

"Camille," he said, his face grim. "I'm sorry about Michael. Truly."

Camille's composure wavered for a moment. "Thank you," she said softly. Then, almost to herself, she asked, "Does it get easier?"

Jem's eyes darkened. "Not that I've found," he replied simply, his hand unconsciously moving to his chest.

Esme stepped between them, and I wasn't sure if she'd done it on purpose to break Jem's line of thoughts, or to introduce herself.

"I'm Esme Parker. I'll be your witch helper for today." Her gaze swept around the room, lingering on each person before moving on. Garrett tensed when Esme looked at him, and his face went guarded. When her eyes landed on Edmond, a slight frown creased her brow.

"I called Esme from the hospital and asked her to come. She's here to help," I explained. "She's risking a lot to be here. The Wolf Council has made it clear that if Esme performs any magic in the north, she'll be facing a death sentence."

"This is a foolish risk." Edmond scowled. "We shouldn't be involving ourselves with witches, especially not after what they may have already done to Shya. Putting another witch in her head is not the way to protect her."

Esme flinched at his words, her thin frame seeming to shrink even more. Jem's eyes flashed dangerously, a low growl emanating from his chest.

I felt my anger rising again. "Esme can be trusted. This is our best chance to determine if Shya is still under any kind of spell. Esme will be able to see if she is and may even be able to remove it. It might be the only way Shya can be sure that she's free of Tristan's influence."

Esme fidgeted with the hem of her shirt. "Moon star whispers secrets," she murmured. "I can hear the echoes of the spell, even from here. But the shadows ... They're slippery like eels. Hard to catch."

She tilted her head as if listening to something no one else could hear. "This magic has teeth, you know. It bites and gnaws and leaves little crumbs of darkness behind. But I can sweep them away, yes. Sweep, sweep, like fall leaves."

Garrett's eyes glinted with a mixture of amusement and something darker as he spoke. "Let's be real. How do we know this witch isn't just going to make things worse? I mean, come on, she sounds like she's already got a screw loose." He gestured toward Esme with a dismissive wave of a hand. "No offense, sweetheart, but you're not exactly inspiring confidence here."

Edmond turned to Camille. "You can't consider this. It is irresponsible and unwarranted. We're Shya's Pack. We'll help her through this. We don't need to turn to outsiders and witches."

Camille's eyes locked onto mine, studying me intently. After a long moment, she spoke. "This isn't my decision to make. It's Shya's. I'll speak with her and let her choose whether she wants Esme's help."

I nodded.

Esme smiled softly, her eyes unfocused as if seeing something beyond the room. "Sometimes," she mused, her voice dreamy, "the clearest path forward is the one we fear to tread. Like dancing through a moon star garden."

Garrett scoffed and threw up his hands. "Oh, fabulous! The witch is completely kooky, and you want to give Shya to her?"

"Watch your mouth," Jem growled, placing a protective hand on Esme's shoulder.

"Enough, Garrett," I said, stepping between him and Jem. "You've had your say. Shya decides."

Garrett shook his head, but he lowered his eyes and sat his ass back down.

Chapter Thirty

SHYA

I lay in bed, staring at the ceiling. The softness of my childhood mattress felt wrong, like I didn't belong here anymore. My mind raced. Tristan's face kept popping up in my head. I clenched my fists, anger bubbling up. How could he have done this to me? To my family? There was a time, when he was the Beta here, when we were dating, when I honestly thought he cared for us, for me. I saw a future of him and me leading this Pack, of Mom and Dad abdicating and living next door. I'd thought Tristan would be my partner for life, when all he really wanted was the power that came with being my mate. And he was willing to do anything, even killing Dad and getting a witch to mess with my mind and feelings, to get it.

I forced Tristan's face away as Mason's face swam before me. The way he'd looked at me, held me. He was sure, just like Tristan had seemed sure, that we were destined to be together. My parents had believed that Edmond was more suited to me. That as soon as we mated the mating bond would snap into place. It was all so confusing.

The door creaked open, and Mom slipped in, her face drawn and tired. Her chestnut hair was pulled back in its usual neat knot, but stray wisps escaped around her face. She had her usual expertly applied makeup, but it couldn't fully conceal the deep shadows under her eyes. Despite this, her petite frame stood straight, shoulders squared in a deliberate show of strength, but I could see the slight tremor in her hands that she tried to hide by clasping them tightly. It was as if she was held together by sheer willpower, and my heart ached to see her struggling so hard.

"Hey," she said softly. "How are you feeling?"

I shrugged. "I don't know. Confused, overwhelmed, scared. Really, really angry."

Mom nodded, perching on the edge of my bed. "It's okay to feel that way. You've been through a lot."

"Everything is all so mixed up in my head."

She reached out, squeezing my hand. "We're going to figure this out, Shya. I promise."

"How?" I asked, hating how small my voice sounded, scared that my feelings would always be jumbled up this way.

Mom hesitated, then took a deep breath. "Actually, that's why I came up. There's someone here who might be able to help you."

I sat up straighter, suddenly alert. "Who?"

"A witch," Mom said. "It's possible she might be able to break whatever spell Tristan put on you."

My heart raced.

"I don't know, Mom," I said, my voice shaking. "Another witch? After everything ..."

"I know it's scary," she acknowledged. "It is your choice, Shya. You are in control of this. Me, Edmond and Mason will all be there. If she tries anything, the witch will be dead before she can blink. If it works, though, you'll be free of whatever Tristan did to you."

Free. Free from Tristan once and for all. I wanted it so badly. But enough to make myself vulnerable again, to let another witch mess with my mind?

"How do we know we can trust her?"

"We can't trust her; she's a witch. Never forget that, Shya—they cannot be trusted. But Mason called her. The witch has been staying with the Three Rivers Pack. They are vouching for her." She took my hand, her grip warm and reassuring. "I understand your fear, sweetheart. No one's going to force you to do this."

I nodded, swallowing hard. "Okay."

Mom squeezed my hand. "We'll all be there with you, I promise. And I'll be right behind the witch. If she does anything ... "

There was a fierce light in her eyes that I hadn't seen before. Mom had never hated witches before, but now, I felt the ground shift under me. She looked keen for a fight. Like she wanted to kill, to get revenge for what had been done to Dad, to me, to our Pack and family, and it didn't matter who stood in front of her.

"Mom, are you okay?"

She startled at the question before brushing it off. "Of course. It's you I'm worried about. Are you ready for this?"

I took a deep breath and nodded.

The study felt crowded when I walked in, with so many people in it, but also strangely empty without Dad there. Jem Parker stood over to one side, and I didn't need to study him to instinctively know he was a grimmer, more serious, and much more dangerous werewolf than he had been previously. He'd been through so many ordeals and had very little to lose now. Jem Parker had become a wild card, unpredictable and potentially volatile.

Beside Jem, a teenage girl hovered protectively. Her dirty blonde hair was pulled back into a messy ponytail, revealing a gaunt face that seemed too mature for her years. Despite her thin frame, there was a resolute set to her shoulders as she watched me with a mixture of curiosity and caution.

Edmond was there, too, his posture rigid and controlled as always. His blue eyes met mine briefly, a flicker of concern passing over his features before his expression smoothed back into its usual calm mask.

I frowned and turned to Derek, who was leaning against the wall, his muscular arms crossed over his chest. His gray eyes roamed around the room, ever vigilant.

And then there was Mason. I'd felt his eyes on me the moment I'd entered the room, but I only now met his gaze. My heart didn't just skip a beat, it practically somersaulted in my chest just looking at his vision of raw masculinity—tall and powerfully built, his muscular frame straining against his fitted T-shirt in a way that made my mouth go dry.

His close-cropped black hair practically begged for my fingers to run through it, while his sharp blue eyes seemed to undress me where I stood. I felt the heat rise in my cheeks under his intense stare.

I felt rather than saw Edmond scowl at me, and I made myself look away from Mason and step further into the room.

As I did, a sudden movement behind me caught my attention. I turned to see Tucker slipping through the door, his eyes wide with excitement and mischief.

"Tucker!" Mom's voice rang out sharply. "Out, now! This isn't for you."

Tucker's face shifted to an exaggerated look of innocence. "But, Mom," he protested, "I just want to see the magic! Please? I'll be super quiet, I promise! You won't even know I'm here."

Before Mom could respond, Henry opened the door, his eyes landing on Tucker.

"There you are! Come on, Tuck, I have a game all set up for—" He broke off suddenly, his eyes widening as they landed on the teenage girl. "Oh, hello! I don't think we've met before. I'm Henry." Henry strode into the room, his eyes fixed on the girl, his hand outstretched.

The girl looked at his hand and then glanced at Jem. Jem nodded once, and she reached out and shook Henry's hand. "Hello, Henry. I'm Esme Parker."

"Esme? That's a ... er, that's a beautiful name."

A beautiful name? Oh dear, I really had to give Henry some pointers when it came to talking to girls.

"Thank you, Henry," she replied shyly.

Henry didn't say anything, just continued to stare at Esme, his mouth slightly open. I wanted to nudge him, but I was too far away. Jem cleared his throat loudly, stepping between Esme and Henry and glowering darkly at my brother.

I had to save him. "Esme, I'm Shya. I'm the one who needs your help."

"Yes, I know. The shadows in your mind are bright in the daylight. They're poised there, ready to pounce, you know. I can pluck them from you, though."

I felt myself pale.

"The sooner I chase them away," she continued, "the sooner you'll feel better. You want to feel better, don't you?"

Everyone looked at me.

Of course I wanted to feel better, but plucking things from my brain didn't exactly sound fun. I had been raised to be diplomatic, though, especially when all I wanted to do was swear at a teenage girl and run as far away from her as possible.

"Maybe you could explain how this is all going to work first?"

"Oh, I have absolutely no idea!"

I blinked and then turned and looked at Mason. He shrugged one shoulder.

"I know you're scared," Esme continued. "I am, too, moon star true. But I want to help. My magic … it can do good things. Healing things." She looked directly at me, her eyes earnest. "I can't promise it will be easy, but I promise I'll be tippy-toe careful with your mind, Shya."

I paused, considering her words. In the silence, a young voice from the back of the room spoke up. "Try it, Shya! I want to see the magic! Don't be worried; if she does anything you don't like, I'll bite her!"

Chapter Thirty-One

SHYA

"Tucker, I told you to leave." Mom's voice was harsh. "Henry, take your brother out of here. Now!"

I frowned. Mom only talked to Tucker and Henry in that tone if they'd done something really bad.

Henry, who had been staring at Esme, startled at the sound of his name. "Oh, right. Sorry, Mom. Come on, Tuck, let's go."

Tucker frowned. I knew he had picked up on Mom's tone of voice, but he allowed Henry to lead him out, though not before throwing one last curious glance at Esme.

As the door closed behind them, I took a deep breath and turned back to Esme. "Okay," I said, my voice steadier than I felt. "What do I need to do?"

Esme smiled softly. "Just sit down and try to relax."

I nodded, thinking it was easy for her to say to relax. She wasn't the one who was going to have someone digging around in her mind. I settled myself onto the floor and felt everyone's eyes on me.

"I'll be right here," Mason said, his voice soft and reassuring. Our eyes met, and for a moment, the world narrowed to just the two of us.

Then Esme kneeled in front of me, her small hands hovering near my temples. "Close your eyes, Shya. Take deep breaths. Try to empty your mind."

I did as she said, forcing my eyes shut and attempting to calm my racing thoughts. I felt a gentle warmth near my skin. A gasp escaped my lips as I felt something—a presence, a touch—brush against my consciousness. It was foreign, alien, yet somehow not threatening. I could sense Esme's concentration, her careful probing of my mind.

I kept my eyes closed and focused on my breathing. I expected to hear Esme begin chanting, but instead, the quiet stretched.

A strange sensation washed over me, like a cool breeze ghosting across my skin. I fought the urge to open my eyes, to see what Esme was doing. The air around us seemed to thicken, charged with an energy that made the hairs on my arms stand on end.

Suddenly, a voice whispered in my head, making me jump.

Your mind is so sparkly. All these little lights zooming around. It's pretty.

My eyes flew open in shock. Esme sat before me, her own eyes closed, a look of intense concentration on her face. Her lips weren't moving, but I could hear her voice clear as day inside my head.

E-Esme? I thought hesitantly.

Oh! You can hear me! The mental voice giggled. *That's good. Some people can't, you know. Their minds are too noisy.*

I blinked, trying to process what was happening. *How are you doing this?*

It's easy peasy. I just reach out and touch your thoughts with mine.
You can do this with everyone?
Only those I'm physically close to. With practice, I will be able to touch

minds over great distances, but I need to grow more first. Now, try to shush your mind. I need to look for the bad spell. Your sparkly thoughts are hiding it.

I tried to quiet my mind, though it wasn't easy with Esme rummaging around in there. The sensation was strange—not painful, but definitely unsettling.

Shya! There are so many pretty lights dancing around in your mind. Some are bright and zoomy, like shooting stars. Others are soft and floaty, like little fireflies.

I found myself drawn into Esme's vivid descriptions. Suddenly, I could almost see it, too—my thoughts and emotions as tiny, glowing sparks, whizzing and dancing through the landscape of my mind. It was beautiful and surreal.

Oh, no! Oh no, no, no. This is a nasty one. This is really, really nasty. That was a bad witch who did this.

Okay, that did not sound good. *What is it?*

This one here, can you see it? No, of course you can't. Sorry, I always forget you can't see your own brain! But I found the spell. It's all dark and sticky, like a giant octopus. Its yucky tentacles are wrapped around your sparks like a parasite, suffocating them.

I felt my heart rate spike. I wanted it out of me. Now.

Esme's voice in my mind rose in fury. *This is a violation, Shya! A corruption of everything you are. Whoever did this is a very bad person!*

Can you get it out? Please tell me you can get it out!

Of course, I can get it out. I'm a very strong witch, Esme assured me. *I'm going to squish it like the nasty bug it is. Hold on, Shya. This might feel a little weird.*

I braced myself, unsure of what to expect. Suddenly, I felt a swell of warmth spreading through my mind, like sunlight breaking through storm clouds.

There you are! You can't hide from me; no, siree! Out you go!

The sensation that followed was indescribable. It was like a great weight was being lifted, like chains I hadn't even known were there were crumbling away. The sticky, suffocating darkness Esme had described began to dissolve, replaced by a pure, radiant light that seemed to come from deep within me.

Shya! Your sparks are getting brighter! They're dancing faster!

With her words, I felt a final surge of magic and then ... release.

Tristan is a fuckhead shit muffin. I waited for the pain to come, but there was none. The last bits of the spell had fallen. I was free.

I expected to feel relief, to be happy. But as the full extent of what had been done to me came crashing down, rage, pure, unadulterated rage flooded through me. My body began to tremble, my hands clenching into fists. And then, from deep within, I felt another presence stirring—my wolf, now surging to the surface with a vengeance.

No, no, no! Esme's panicked voice echoed in my head. *Shya, you need to calm down!*

But it was too late. With a roar that tore from my throat, I felt my body begin to Shift. My skin rippled and stretched like molten wax, reshaping itself over a rapidly changing frame. Muscles coiled and uncoiled, twisting into new forms as my limbs elongated. A cascade of sensations washed over me—tingling, burning, prickling—as coarse fur erupted from every pore. My face contorted, features fluid as clay, molding into a lupine muzzle. In seconds, my wolf had taken control, blind with fury and the need to lash out at the violation we had endured.

I was dimly aware of shouts as I lunged forward, claws raking across the nearest surface. Something shattered—a vase, perhaps?—and I whirled, snapping at shadows. My wolf didn't care who or what was in our path; she only wanted to let out the pain and betrayal that consumed us.

Through it all, I could hear Esme's voice, high and frightened: "Shya! You're safe now! Please calm down!"

Then Jem grabbed Esme round the waist and yanked her into a corner, out of range. A part of me realized that Jem was protecting Esme. From me. That was wrong. They shouldn't have to fear me.

But my wolf was beyond reason. With another howl of anguish, I threw myself against the walls, desperate to escape, to run, to find the one who had done this to us and make him pay. I knew I was hurting myself, could smell my blood all around me, but I didn't care. I just wanted to hurt something, anything, to make this pain and rage go away.

Amidst the chaos, a single voice cut through the haze of my rage. Mason's voice, strong and steady, touched something deep within me.

"Princess, it's okay. You're safe now. No one here is going to hurt you."

My wolf's ears pricked up, her snarls faltering for a moment.

"That's it, princess. Easy now. I know you're hurting. I know you're angry. I won't let anyone hurt you ever again."

I felt my wolf's hackles begin to lower, her frantic energy slowly dissipating.

A soft whine eased from my throat, the fight draining out of me. Exhaustion washed over me in waves, and I felt my wolf retreating.

The tension slowly seeped out of my muscles.

I collapsed to the floor, human again, my body wracked with uncontrollable sobs. Grief, anger, and a profound sense of violation swirled within me in a chaotic maelstrom.

Oh Goddess, what did Tristan do to me? How could he? He made me trust him. I thought I loved him, and it was all a lie. All of it. I felt hollowed out, as if a fundamental part of me had been scooped away, leaving nothing but raw, aching emptiness.

I became aware of concerned voices around me, hands reaching out to offer comfort. But I flinched away, unable to bear even the gentlest touch.

"Hush, princess. I've got you." I felt Mason's strong arms scoop me up and hold me gently against his chest.

"Does she need the doctor?" Mom asked from behind him.

"No, the cuts aren't deep. She just needs a bath and some sleep."

I felt him moving toward the door.

"You have no right to take her, Mason. As her fiancé, it's my job!"

I heard a thump, then the sound of someone hitting the ground.

"Oh, shit! Sorry, man. I'm so fucking clumsy," Derek said.

"You hit me!" Edmond growled.

"Enough!" Mom used her no-nonsense voice she used with Henry and Tucker. "Mason, get my daughter cleaned up and settled. Edmond, we will deal with this when Shya is asleep."

Then there was the sound of the door opening and then closing behind us.

"Where—?"

"You're safe, Shya. I'm taking you to your bedroom. It's all going to be okay now."

I don't remember getting to my room or Mason lying me on the bed. I think I must have drifted off, but I woke when he came back and picked me up again.

"The bath is ready," he told me, his voice soft.

He carried me to the bathtub and lay me gently in it. The warm water stung my cuts, but the pain was oddly grounding. I hissed softly, blinking away tears as I became more aware of my surroundings. Mason was crouched beside the tub, his eyes filled with concern.

"Easy, princess," he murmured. "Just relax."

I nodded weakly, too exhausted to speak. Mason began to carefully clean my wounds, his touch impossibly gentle. The silence stretched between us, broken only by the soft lapping of water and my occasional whimpers of pain.

As he worked, my mind began to clear. The fog of rage and confusion lifted, leaving behind a dull ache and a growing sense of shame. I remembered my wolf's rampage, the destruction I'd caused.

"I'm sorry," I whispered, my voice hoarse. "I didn't mean to ... to lose control like that."

Mason's hand stilled for a moment. "You have nothing to apologize for, Shya. What happened wasn't your fault."

I felt fresh tears well up in my eyes. "I just feel so angry at myself. I ... I believed him. I let him manipulate me. I thought, after the first time, when he had me convinced, when he was still the Beta here ... after that, there was no way he'd be able to twist my mind against me again. How could I have been so stupid?"

"Hey, look at me," Mason said firmly, cupping my face in his hands. "You are not stupid. They did this. Tristan and the witch. Not you. They're good at manipulation. No one blames you or thinks less of you for what happened. It's the opposite. You are so incredibly brave and strong, Shya. What you went through, what you survived. You broke the spell on your own. You escaped his camp on your own. You did that. Now you have support and love all around you to help you take the next steps. And whatever they are, we'll be here for you."

I met his gaze, seeing nothing but sincerity and warmth in his eyes. Something in my chest loosened, and I felt myself relax further into the water. My eyelids were growing heavy.

"Mason?"

"Mmmm?"

"Thank you for being here."

"Always, princess."

Then I fell asleep, naked, in the bath, with Mason still cleaning my wounds.

CHAPTER THIRTY-TWO

SHYA

The darkness pressed in around me, suffocating and oppressive. I was running, my lungs burning, my heart pounding. Shadows chased me, their clawed hands reaching for me, trying to drag me back into the abyss.

"You can't escape," a voice hissed. "You're mine now!"

I tried to scream, but no sound came out. My legs felt like lead, each step becoming harder than the last. Just as the shadows were about to engulf me, I heard another voice, distant but familiar.

"She doesn't need you in order to deal with this. She has her own Pack, her own family!" It was my mother's voice, angry and insistent.

"I won't leave her," Mason's reply was firm.

"You are not welcome here any longer. You will leave our lands, or there will be war between us," that voice I recognized as Edmond's.

The voices grew louder, more intense, swirling around me like a tempest. I felt myself being pulled in different directions, torn between the nightmare and reality.

"... her choice ..."

"... needs time ...."

"... can't just ..."

"... mine now ..."

"Mason? Mason!" I called out with a gasp as my eyes flew open. For a moment, I lay frozen, my heart racing, my body covered in a cold sweat. The familiar contours of my bedroom slowly came into focus, bathed in the soft, golden light of late afternoon filtering through the curtains. Confusion and fear gripped me as I tried to shake off the lingering tendrils of the nightmare.

What was real and what was not? I just didn't know anymore.

I didn't remember getting into my bed or putting on the soft satin slip that now covered me. Had that all been Mason?

From downstairs, I heard Edmond's voice rise above the others, sharp and commanding. "Mason, stop right there!" he ordered, his tone brooking no argument. "I order you not to go to her. Shya is going to be my mate, and I will be the one to deal with this situation."

I hated that they were fighting. Hated that I was suddenly a "situation." Hated that Dad was dead, and there was nothing I could do to bring him back. Hated that we should be mourning him but instead were bickering with each other. I needed to get up, to stop the arguing, to be the peacekeeper in this, but when I moved, everything hurt. I swung my legs over the side of the bed and then stopped. Everything inside and out was too sore, too raw. I just wanted to crawl back under the covers and pretend none of this had happened.

Fuck! Get up, Shya, you can do this.

A loud, violent thud echoed from downstairs, making me flinch. It was followed immediately by the sound of footsteps pounding up the stairs, growing louder and more urgent with each passing second. The house seemed to tremble with the force of whoever was coming.

My breath caught in my throat as the door to my room burst open, and then Mason was there, his face a mask of fierce protectiveness and barely contained fury. For a moment, he stood there, filling the doorway with his presence, and I forgot how to breathe.

I blinked, and he was by my side, his strong arms wrapping around me. The moment his skin touched mine, it was as if a dam broke within me. I collapsed into his embrace, my body shaking with the force of my suppressed emotions. He was real, he was here. I was so scared that I was going to wake up back in Tristan's cage, or worse, in his bed, and that this was all a dream.

"Princess," Mason murmured, his voice soothing in my ear. "I'm here. I've got you. You're safe now, I promise."

I looked up at him and felt grateful. Grateful he was there, grateful he was taking care of me, grateful that he made everything seem better. And that's when I knew he had to go.

I was next in line to be the Alpha of my Pack. Yes, I'd been kidnapped, had my mind and feelings violated, had been chased through the forest and jumped off a fucking waterfall. But I'd had enough of relying on others to make me feel better. I just wanted to sink into Mason's arms every time I saw him, and when I did, all my worries and fears and hurt went away. I had to find a way to make myself feel better. And I couldn't do that with Mason and his perfect jaw, beautiful abs, and fucking kissable lips, being here.

There was a hesitant knock at the door, then it opened, and Henry stood in the doorway, his expression a mix of concern and something else I couldn't quite place. His eyes darted between Mason and me, his lips pursing into a thin line.

"Henry, is everything okay?"

"Mai Parker and Sam Shaw are here," Henry said, his voice carefully neutral. "They're waiting downstairs."

I felt Mason stiffen beside me.

"We'll be right down," Mason replied, his tone matching Henry's in its neutrality.

Henry glanced at me. When I nodded, he turned and left.

I tightened my grip on Mason, knowing this would be the last time we did this, not wanting to let go.

"Princess?" Mason must have felt a difference in me.

I clung on a second longer, wanting to store his scent and the feel of him deep inside of my brain. I knew I would need it in the coming days.

"I'm okay," I said, finally letting go, not able to meet his eyes. "I need to get dressed. Can you meet me down there?"

Mason studied my face. "Princess, what happened? You can talk to me."

I forced a smile onto my face. "I know. I'm fine, really. I just need to work out what shoes to wear. I'll be down in five."

He looked at me for a moment longer, then sighed and nodded. "Okay, I'll be just downstairs."

Then he turned and left, and I had to sit on my hands and bite my tongue to stop myself from reaching out to him and calling him back.

CHAPTER THIRTY-THREE

SHYA

The warm, pinkish-golden light of dusk spilled across the wooden floorboards of the veranda, creating a deceptively peaceful scene. The air was thick with the fragrant aroma of freshly brewed turmeric and honey tea, my mom's favorite, mingling with the sharp scent of the coming winter on the wind.

I'd chosen my pink Jimmy Choo patent leather "love" pumps; as I stepped onto the veranda, I wanted to feel strong, powerful, in control. My eyes immediately sought out Mason, and when they found his, my lady bits spasmed.

Damn it! I really had to tell him to go.

I forced myself to look away, and my eyes skipped over Derek and fell on Mai. She'd changed since I last saw her. The petite woman before me exuded an air of quiet strength and confidence that hadn't been there before. Her wavy dark hair was pulled back in a practical ponytail, emphasizing her big brown eyes.

Next to her was Sam Shaw, Derek's twin. He had changed, too. He now looked older than his twenty-three years, and there was a new intensity about him, a seriousness that didn't fit with the Shifter with the easy smile and teasing manner that I'd known before.

"Shya!" Mai exclaimed, stepping toward me. "It's so good to see you."

She gave me a hug and whispered in my ear, "I heard about Tristan. I want you to know that you're not alone in this. I'm here for you. Want to go shopping? I'm your girl. Want to eat strawberry Häagen-Dazs in PJs and watch *Firefly*? I'm there. Want to launch a war and torture the shit out of Tristan? I'll be right beside you. Just tell me who to hold down."

And this was why I liked Mai.

"Thank you," I whispered back, hugging her a bit tighter before letting go and turning to Sam. "Hello, Sam."

He jerked his chin in greeting. No smile. No hug.

Hmmm. What had happened to him?

My wolf paced inside of me, unsettled.

Edmond wasn't here, and I wondered if Mom had sent him away to try to keep things peaceful. Jem and Esme had also left, I was guessing back to Three Rivers. I would need to call and thank Esme for what she had done for me.

"Shya," Mom said, gesturing to an empty seat. "Come, sit down. Would anyone like some tea?"

I nodded, grateful for the distraction from my thoughts. I walked over to the table that had a teapot, mugs, glasses, and a pitcher of water on it. I poured myself an Earl Grey. Mason shook his head when I gestured to the drinks, then I settled into the chair, with Mason taking the seat next to me and Henry and Derek leaning against the railing.

"Shya." Sam cleared his throat. "I'm here as the Wolf Council representative. I would like to ask you some questions about the witch you encountered at Tristan's camp, if that's okay?"

I shot a quick glance at Mai, remembering that Three Rivers had nominated Sam for the seat just before I'd been taken. So that was what was going on with him. What the hell happened on the Council that had driven the joy right out of him?

"Sure."

"Can you tell me about your interactions with the witch?" he pressed, his words precise and probing. "Did you ever see him in person?"

I felt my body tense, and my hands began to tremble as the memories I'd been trying to suppress came flooding back. I felt Mason's eyes on my hands and clutched the mug of tea tighter to try to still them. "Only once ... at the end ... at the waterfall. I don't even know if it was a him. It felt like a him." I shook my head. "I know that doesn't make sense."

"Shya, anything you remember is helpful. Even that you sensed the witch was male."

I gave Sam a grateful smile, and he nodded at me to continue.

"I think ... I think I heard him talking to Tristan once. Tristan said something about how if he didn't have me by his side, then phase three would only be possible in three years. The witch was not happy about that; he said three years was too long." I remembered the revulsion and anger I'd felt when I heard that conversation and the frustration I felt when I couldn't wake up and rip Tristan's throat out. "I'm pretty sure they were putting something in my food by then, though. So, I'm not entirely sure about what I heard."

"Phase three? You're sure those were the words?"

"I'm not sure about anything, Sam. But from what I recall, yes,

Tristan said phase three."

"You know what that means?" Mason asked his brother.

Sam rubbed his chin. "I have an idea, and if I'm right, it's a clusterfuck of a problem for us, but I'll need to check some things out. Shya, was there anything else? Anything at all about the witch, what they looked like?"

"Apart from at the waterfall, he always appeared in my dreams. There, he was always covered by his cloak, but ..." I frowned as I tried to picture the witch in my mind. "He did have a scar on his left hand. It ran from his wrist to his thumb and looked old."

"Good. That's good, Shya. Keep going." Sam smiled encouragingly at me.

"At the start, I only heard him chanting while I was asleep. By the end, though, I heard it all the time. A haunting melody that seemed to weave itself into the fabric of my thoughts. It started as a whisper, a faint, ethereal tune that tickled the edges of my consciousness. As time passed, it grew stronger, more insistent, like a symphony of otherworldly instruments playing just for me. It was almost as if I could see the notes dancing and swirling, creating intricate patterns in my mind. Sometimes, it was a gentle lullaby, soothing and comforting, making me feel safe and loved. Other times, it pulsed with passion and intensity, filling me with a sense of purpose and belonging I've never experienced before."

I remembered the feel of those delicate tendrils of sound curled around my memories, my desires, my fears. They caressed my innermost thoughts, slowly but surely entwining themselves with everything that made me who I was.

"The music became a constant companion, a beautiful, seductive presence that I couldn't—and didn't want to—escape. It was ... beautiful," I whispered, and I heard the mix of longing and revulsion in my voice. "Terrifying in its perfection. The way it wrapped around my mind, becoming a part of me ... I didn't even realize I was losing myself."

Mason reached over, entwining his fingers with mine. I clung to his hand. Yes, I was going to ask him to leave; yes, I needed to learn how to deal with this on my own, but right now, I needed this, needed to know he was here, that he was real and not part of a dream.

"You're doing great, princess," Mason said gently.

Mai leaned forward slightly, "Sam, do you think there's a connection between what was done to Shya and the effects of ripple in Shifters?"

Sam tilted his head. "It's a possibility. We know witches are dosing ripple with a powerful spell that not only makes Shifters feel that their Pack bonds are impure and are driving some to break their bonds, but it also prevents them from Shifting into their wolf forms. Mason told me you were unable to Shift, Shya, until recently."

"Yes, it was like my wolf was asleep. She was still there, but I couldn't access her, and she couldn't reach me. Not until I heard that Dad was dead. And then again when Esme—"

Mai descended into a fit of coughs. "Sam ... can you ... water?"

I caught Derek smirking as Sam looked sharply at Mai, then strode over to the table and poured her a glass. While he was distracted, Mason whispered in my ear, "Best not say anything about Esme in front of Sam."

I frowned at him. *What the hell was going on?*

"Yes," Sam said, as he handed the glass to Mai. "Given Esme had

208

been banned by the Council from doing any magic in the north, Shya should definitely not tell me anything about it," he said, his tone light but strained. He flashed me a smile, but it seemed forced, lacking the easy charm I remembered.

Mai sighed. "Esme saved us at the battle with Brock's Pack. The Wolf Council found out about it, though, and wanted to take her. Sam stopped them. They agreed Esme could stay with us but that if she did any more magic here, her life, and the lives of anyone who helped her, would be forfeit."

Oh, well, fuck!

Chapter Thirty-Four

SHYA

I felt a surge of gratitude for the girl who'd risked her life to help me. My parents had trained me too well for any reaction to show on my face, though. "Well, it's a good thing she didn't do any magic. She was here simply to offer her expert opinion on what spell the witch may have used."

Sam flashed me a sardonic smile, "You really are an Alpha-in-waiting. I will need to talk to Esme about her 'expert opinion' on what was used in your case, and if it is similar to the ripple spell."

"And what if it is?" Mom asked. "What are the Council going to do about it? The witches are active in the north again; that much is clear. They are attacking our Pack bonds, our communities, and our way of life with what they are doing with ripple. And now they have involved themselves in this heinous attack on my daughter. It cannot go unanswered."

Sam studied her for a moment before replying. "It won't, you have my word. The Council is fully aware of what is happening in the north, and we're taking steps. But we must ascertain if this is a few rogue witches or a strategic plan from the Inner Coven. The last thing we want is an all-out war with the witches right now."

Mom and Dad had made sure that studying the witches' hierarchy had been part of my training, so I knew the Inner Coven was their equivalent of our Wolf Council.

"After Simon Webster tried to craft a spell to put all werewolves under his control, we should have eliminated them all," Mom replied. "Your Council gave them leniency in simply banning them from practicing magic in the north. It allowed them to regroup, to weave their spells more covertly; it has allowed them to slither their way back into here and plot against us once again. They are already moving against us, even if the Council is too blind to see it. It is already war. You go back and tell your Council that."

My heart froze. *We should have eliminated them all?* I'd never heard Mom say such things before. Genocide on all witches would have been abhorrent to her. My wolf bristled inside of me.

Alpha stinks of grief. Too much grief for one person to hold.

I agreed with her. In our Pack, when your mate died, there was a ritual called the wild wander. Not everyone who lost their mate chose to go on a wild wander, but those who did would Shift to their wolf forms and roam the forest alone for weeks or months on end until they were ready to face the human world again. Some never came back, disappearing forever, but a few returned. With Dad dead and me gone, Mom didn't have the choice to go wandering. She had to stay here and protect the Pack, but she needed that time to grieve. Without it, it could build up inside of her and erupt at any time. Like now.

"I know you want someone to blame, Camille," Sam replied gently. "What has happened here is awful and devastating to you and your

Pack. I understand the urge to find a target for your anger and grief, but killing all witches is not the answer. War with them will kill hundreds, if not thousands, of Shifters. Do you want that for your Pack, for your family? For Shya, Henry, and Tucker?"

"I want my mate back!" Mom snarled. "I want my children to have their father. I want this Pack to be safe and stable and be run by two Alphas, as is our way. But we don't always get what we want, do we?"

I bowed my head as the realization hit that Mom was hanging on by a thread. Living like this, forced to run the Pack by herself, with no outlet for her feelings, was slowly destroying everything she had been. She had been waiting for me to be found so I could come back, be mated to Edmond, and take over. I knew then with a sudden clarity that as soon as I was mated, she would step down.

I glanced at Mason from under my eyelashes, and my heart ached. Any dream I had of Mason and me somehow being together just died. I couldn't leave my Pack now, couldn't leave Henry or Tucker. If I left, either Mom would stay, and I could see the damage this was doing to her, or Henry would have to step up. Henry, kind, gentle Henry. He would be a great Alpha one day with his head for strategy, but right now, he was a seventeen-year-old boy who loved to read and loved his brother more. There would be challenges both inside and outside the Pack from those who saw our weakness and wanted to take Bridgetown for themselves. If I left, my whole family would probably be dead within a year. Would Mason give up everything he had, his Pack, his family, his business, to come and be Alpha with me? Could I ask him to do that, knowing my Pack would hate him from day one?

"Mom!" Henry said, his voice soft but full of reproach. "Esme Parker did us a kindness here. You, of all people, know that you cannot tar a whole species for the actions of a few."

She swung her gaze over to Henry, and he immediately lowered his eyes.

"I know that your father is dead and that your sister was taken and mind-raped by a witch. I know that the witches are involved in ripple, and that drug has been designed specifically to destroy us. We cannot let that lie. We can shut down our borders, throw out the humans here in case the witches try to smuggle some of their own in, only let in Shifters we know and trust, or we take the fight to them. Tell me, what would you decide? How will you live up to your father's memory and protect your Pack?"

And that was enough of that. I straightened my back; I finally knew what I had to do.

"He'll do what's right, Mom. For his family, for his Pack. Just like we all will."

Mom stared at me but for the first time in my life, I didn't lower my eyes. I couldn't read the expression on her face, but for a moment I thought I caught a glimpse of relief flash in her eyes. Then she turned her attention to Mason.

"You found my daughter. Are you going to put your PI skills to good use and find Tristan?"

I almost flinched at the mention of his name, but I stopped myself just in time.

Good. I was getting better. Soon, I'd be able to hear his name without batting an eyelid.

I could feel waves of unhappiness and anger rolling off of Mason. "The camp where he kept Shya is deserted. They obviously left in a hurry, but everyone who was there has disappeared. I have my team on it. He can't hide for long, and when he pops up again, I'll be waiting."

For a moment, my heart beat double time in my chest. The thought of Tristan still out there, still free, made my skin crawl. For a moment, I was back in his cage, helpless, eager for him to visit. Tristan had done that; had made me feel that way. It wasn't me. I breathed in deep through my nose, aware of Mason's eyes on me.

No. I wouldn't let myself go back there, no matter what. I was my father's daughter, and I would get revenge for what Tristan had done. Anger bubbled up inside me, replacing the fear. I would no longer be cowed by a sniveling weasel like Tristan. He had murdered my dad, and I was going to make damn sure he paid for it.

I clung to that anger, letting it fill me up inside. It was so much better than feeling scared. The anger made me feel stronger, safer. I embraced it, welcomed it, using it to steel my resolve.

Sam cleared his throat. "I'll stay and help Mason and his team track Tristan," he said. "Catching him and the witch he's working with is our top priority."

"I want to be kept informed," I said to Mason, my voice steady and hard. "Every step of the way. I want to know everything you find out about Tristan's whereabouts."

Mason's eyes searched my face. I could see the concern there, but I ignored it. I didn't need his worry or his pity right now. I needed his skills.

"After the funeral," Mom interjected. "We need to bury your father first."

Chapter Thirty-Five

Mason

Shya went stiff next to me. "You haven't buried him?" she whispered.

The look on Camille's face softened, thank fuck. I knew she was grieving, but she'd been acting like a complete bitch. At least she still recognized when her children were in pain.

"I wanted to wait for you," Camille said softly. "I knew you'd be found. That you'd come back to us. I wanted you to be here when we said goodbye."

Shya looked stunned. It obviously never occurred to her that they wouldn't have buried Michael.

At that moment, Edmond strode out onto the veranda. His dark eyes swept across the gathered group, lingering on me with thinly veiled contempt. "And when we bury him," Edmond declared, his voice carrying a note of finality, "it will be a Pack affair. No outsiders allowed."

The fucker. If Shya wanted me here, there was no fucking way he could keep me away.

"You must be Edmond, the fiancé," Sam said. "I have to say you live up to everything I was expecting."

A flash of uncertainty crossed Edmond's face; as with most people when they met Sam, he wasn't quite sure how to take him.

"And you are?"

"Sam Shaw. Wolf Council representative."

Edmond's face went guarded. I could almost see the thoughts going through his mind; pissing off someone on the Council could close a lot of doors for him, but Sam was also a Shaw, and right now, Edmond despised all Shaws.

"Is the Council getting involved in this issue?"

"We're hunting Tristan and his witch if that's what you mean. And you, Edmond, are you hunting Tristan?"

Edmond bristled, obviously annoyed at the insinuation that he was sitting on his ass and doing fuck all.

I smiled. My brother always could assess a situation and work out someone's pain points.

"I have our enforcers on it. I have full confidence that they will find Tristan, and we will deal with him. Our focus right now is on seeing Michael laid to rest and making sure Shya is recovering well."

Sam showed Edmond his teeth. Yeah, Sam didn't like Edmond any more than I did.

"That's okay, Edmond. You shouldn't feel bad. Some of us just have better skills in this department. And on that note, I need to go see one of my contacts." Sam's tone was all businesslike.

Mai stood. "As you're my lift back, I'm going to take that as my cue."

"I'll show you out," Henry offered.

Mai hugged Shya one more time, whispering something in her ear

216

that I didn't catch. Then she thanked Camille and nodded to me and Derek.

Sam glanced at Derek and then at me. "I'll be in touch soon."

They disappeared round the side of the house, leaving me, Shya, and Derek with Edmond and Camille.

I turned to face them just as Derek murmured under his breath, low enough that only Shya and I could hear. "Remember, whatever happens, we need to keep the peace."

I nodded, steeling myself.

"It's time we got this sorted," Camille began, her tone brooking no disagreement. "Neither of our Packs can afford conflict between us right now. I appreciate that you have feelings for Shya—"

"It's not just feelings, Camille. She's my mate."

Camille's smile was condescending. "I see. And Shya agrees?"

We all turned to look at Shya. She looked like a rabbit who had just seen me and my brothers in our wolf forms trotting along a trail straight toward her.

She opened her mouth, glancing between me, Edmond, and her mother, and then something in her eyes hardened, and her mouth clicked shut.

Camille sighed. "As you can see, Mason, Shya does not share your confidence in this regard. I think we all appreciate that her emotional state is extremely fragile right now. She needs time and space to heal on her own terms without you clouding the issue."

My heart clenched at her words, but I remained silent, allowing her to continue.

"Our Pack is in a precarious position," she continued. "We must have clear leadership. Shya is supposed to be mated to Edmond.

Having you here ... it sends the wrong signals, dangerous signals, to the rest of the Pack. This arrangement will undermine Shya. Until she makes her choice, she must appear to be neutral. If she eventually chooses Edmond, then you being here now will cause her problems when she tries to exert her authority as the Alpha. There must not be any doubt as to her dedication to this Pack or her mate. Can you understand that, Mason?"

Of course I understood it; I just didn't give a fuck. Shya did, though. Camille was right; I couldn't just think about Shya and me. She was in line to be the next Alpha. I couldn't, I wouldn't do anything to jeopardize that for her.

Camille nodded, her expression softening slightly when I didn't argue with her. "I know you care for her, Mason. But we must do what's best for our Pack now. What's best for Shya and her future."

"You've seen the toll that conflict and bloodshed have taken on our community. Our people are on edge; they are scared. We need to prioritize peace and stability above all else," Edmond said, his tone calm and reasonable. I fought the sudden urge to drive my fist right into his mouth.

"Give us time as a family to heal and move forward. Shya is too confused with you here. Tensions are running too high. You've already pinned one of mine up against the wall." A hard look settled on Camille's face. "If you insist on staying, you're risking a war with the Bridgetown Pack. Is that what you want?"

I stared at Shya, willing her to look at me, to say something, anything. But she kept her eyes fixed on the ground. She looked so vulnerable right then. Had I done that? Was I making things more difficult for her?

"Shya, look at me."

She lifted her chin, her eyes shimmering with unshed tears. "Mason," she said, then took a deep breath. "I think Mom's right. You should go."

The words hit me like a gut punch. I felt my wolf howl in anguish inside me, clawing at my chest.

"Shya," I started, but she shook her head, cutting me off.

"Please," she said softly. "I don't want any more fighting. Not now. Not after everything. We need to say goodbye to Dad. I need time to heal. To find myself again. I can't do that when I'm relying on you all the time."

I clenched my fists, fighting every instinct that screamed at me to stay, to fight for her. But the pain in her eyes ... fuck, I couldn't add to that. This wasn't about me. It was about Shya, about what she needed right now.

"Fine," I growled, not bothering to hide the anger and hurt in my voice. "But this isn't over. I'll go, give you the space you need. But I'm not giving up on us."

Edmond snorted, but I ignored him, keeping my eyes on Shya. She nodded, a small, almost imperceptible movement.

"That's up to you," she whispered.

I turned to leave, Derek following close behind. As we walked away, I heard Camille's voice, soft but clear.

"You did the right thing, Shya. It's for the best."

I clenched my jaw, forcing myself not to turn back. Every step felt like I was leaving a piece of myself behind, but I kept walking. For Shya. Always for Shya.

As we rounded the corner of the house, out of sight from the others, Derek spoke up. "What now?"

"It's time we honor our promise to AJ," I replied. "We need to help him find his mate ... and kill Tristan."

Derek nodded, and I felt his eyes studying me. "You okay, bro?"

I let out a harsh laugh. "What do you think?"

He nodded, understanding in his eyes. "We'll figure this out, Mason. We always do."

I didn't respond. Right now, I couldn't see how. All I could feel was the growing distance between me and my mate and an almost paralyzing fear that I might have just lost her for good.

CHAPTER THIRTY-SIX

SHYA

I stepped out of the Alpha House, breathing in the crisp morning air, wearing my favorite rainbow sneakers. It had been fifty-two hours and thirty-three minutes since Mason left, not that I was counting or anything. It was for the best, but my wolf kept trying to force me to Shift so she could run after him; it felt like my heart and soul physically ached, and I couldn't stop scenting Mason in my bedroom and in the house. It was driving me crazy. I needed to get out of the house, and a walk into town was the perfect excuse.

The familiar sights of my territory greeted me as I made my way down the winding path toward the town center. The sun peeked through the trees, casting dappled shadows on the ground, and a gentle breeze carried the scent of pine and wildflowers to me.

As I walked, I finally felt a sense of calm wash over me for the first time in fifty-two hours and thirty-three minutes (not that I was counting). This was what I needed: some time to clear my head and feel normal again. The shoes helped. I'd been this way hundreds of times in these sneakers.

The town was quiet at this early hour, with only a few early risers going about their business. Everyone nodded at me, though, their eyes downcast.

I passed Mr. Johnson's bakery, the aroma of freshly baked bread wafting through the air. Further down, Mrs. Patterson was sweeping the front steps of her little bookshop. They both waved at me but with wary smiles on their faces. Edmond was right; our people were on edge, nervous, scared about whether another attack might happen.

As I turned onto the high street, a prickle ran down my spine, the hair on the back of my neck stood up, and I felt the unmistakable sensation of being watched.

I smiled as my wolf chuffed.

We knew exactly who was following us.

I continued walking, pretending nothing was wrong. Tucker was getting better. He'd been able to sneak up on all the enforcers, including Danni and Ivan, for the last year. It was only family and, for some reason, Summer, who he couldn't catch unawares. I had no doubt that it wouldn't be long before even that wasn't true.

Not today, though.

I could almost picture him in my mind's eye—his small wolf form, midnight-black fur blending with the shadows, his bright eyes fixed on me as he tried to creep along undetected. My little brother, always up for an adventure, always trying to prove himself.

Deciding I would actually like his company, I slowed. But instead of calling him out, I decided to play along. I made a show of looking around suspiciously, then ducked into an alleyway.

I pressed myself against the wall, trying not to laugh.

I strained, almost not hearing the soft pad of paws on the pavement getting closer. Just as Tucker's nose poked around the corner, I leaped out.

"Gotcha!" I shouted, scooping him up in my arms. Tucker yelped in surprise. When I put him down, his black fur was slightly ruffled, and he wore an expression that could only be described as canine chagrin.

I laughed, crouching down to his level. "Did I spoil your fun? Hey, don't look so disappointed. You're getting much better at this, you know. I almost didn't catch you this time."

Tucker's ears perked up at the praise, and his tail gave a tentative wag.

"Seriously," I continued, reaching out to ruffle the fur on his head. "Give it a few more months, and you might actually surprise me."

At that, Tucker's whole demeanor changed. His tail started wagging furiously, and he pranced in place, clearly pleased with himself.

"Want to come along for my walk?" I asked.

Tucker's response was immediate and enthusiastic. He bounded over to my side, tail wagging so hard his whole body shook with the force of it. I couldn't help but laugh at his excitement.

We set off down the high street together, falling into an easy rhythm. Tucker trotted beside me, occasionally darting ahead to investigate an interesting scent before circling back to my side. It felt good to have him with me, a constant, comforting presence.

As we got further into town, I found myself scanning everywhere, searching for any signs of Tristan's attack. To my surprise and relief, I found none. The shopfronts were intact, the streets clean and well-maintained. If I hadn't known better, I would never have guessed that the attack had taken place here just weeks ago.

"Mom must have worked overtime to get everything fixed up."

At the mention of our mother, Tucker's ears flattened slightly.

I recognized the expression. "I'm guessing she's been extra strict since the attack?"

He let out a small huff. "I know you're worried about her." I thought about him trailing me today. "I know you're worried about me, too," I said, nudging him gently with my knee. "We just need time. We're going to be okay, I promise, Tucker. All of us."

Tucker didn't look entirely convinced, but he bumped his head against my leg just as I spotted two familiar figures walking in our direction. Ethan's hulking form was unmistakable, his closely shaved head gleaming in the morning sun. Beside him, Due-lah's long braid swung with each step, her eager energy obvious even from a distance.

At this time of day, they were probably heading to the Alpha House for their enforcer training. As they drew closer, I saw their eyes widen in recognition.

"Shya!" Due-Lah called out, her face breaking into a wide smile. "It's really you! It's so good to see you out and about!"

Ethan's piercing look softened slightly as he nodded to me. "Welcome back."

Tucker wagged his tail, circling around Ethan's legs. The big man's hand automatically reached down to stroke Tucker's fur, a slight smile twitching his lips.

"Thanks," I replied. "How are things with you both? Are you heading to training?"

Due-lah's eyes lit up. "Yup! It's been so intense since ... well, since, you know. But we're learning so much. Ivan's been showing us some new defensive techniques. Ethan has them nailed down, of course.

Me? Not so much."

Ethan grunted in acknowledgment. "You'll pick it up. Just need to practice, need to be prepared, given how things are these days."

Something in his tone made me pause. "What do you mean, how things are?"

Due-lah and Ethan exchanged a quick look, and I felt a flicker of unease.

"Well," Due-lah said, her voice lowering slightly. "It's just … people are worried, you know? After the attack, and with everything that's been going on …"

Ethan cut in, his voice gruff. "Some folks are wondering if we're as safe as we used to be. There are increased patrols, stricter security measures. It's necessary, but it makes people—Shifters and humans—nervous."

"That's understandable, but Mom's handling it. She's got everything under control."

Another loaded glance passed between them, and my heart sank. I had hoped it had only been me who had noticed how much Mom was struggling. Due-lah shifted her weight, looking uncomfortable. "Of course, your mom is doing her best. No one is denying that, Shya."

Ethan's jaw tightened. "Your mother's a strong leader, Shya. But these are uncertain times. People are scared, and scared people can be unpredictable."

I swallowed hard, trying to keep my expression neutral. "I see. Well, I'm sure once things settle down, everyone will see that we're as strong as ever."

"Of course," Due-lah said quickly, but her smile didn't quite reach her eyes.

Ethan looked down at Tucker, who had been unusually quiet during this exchange. "How about you, kid? You haven't joined us for training in a while. Why don't you come by tomorrow, show those youngsters how a real werewolf works out?"

Tucker's tail wagged furiously at the invitation.

"See you tomorrow, then. Nine sharp, Tucker."

Ethan nodded to me as Due-lah waved goodbye.

"Well, that was weird," I said to Tuck as they walked out of sight.

He bumped his head against my leg, and I laughed. "Alright. I'm going."

I knew where he wanted me to go, I just didn't know why.

Chapter Thirty-Seven

SHYA

As we got nearer to Marnie & Summer's Shoe Emporium, I paused, turning to face Tucker. His tail was wagging with excitement, eyes bright as he looked up at me.

"Alright, little brother," I said, my tone affectionate but firm. "Yes, we're going inside, but there are rules. Remember what happened last time I brought you here?" Tucker's ears flattened slightly. "No chewing on the laces, no knocking over displays, and absolutely no stalking Summer. Got it?"

Tucker gave a small yip that I chose to interpret as agreement. I eyed him warily. "Alright, let's go."

We stepped into the shop and, immediately, something in me eased. I'd spent so much time here, chatting with Marnie, that it felt comforting to be back. This was something normal. Something the old me, before Tristan, would have done.

"Shya!" a voice called out, and before I could even fully turn, I was wrapped in a tight hug, Marnie's familiar scent of lavender and shoe polish surrounding me.

"Marnie," I said, hugging her back just as tightly.

She pulled back, her hands on my shoulders as she looked me over. "Oh, honey, we've been so worried about you. Summer and I tried to visit you at the Alpha House just as soon as we heard you were back, but Edmond said it was Shifter business and that only family could see you. I hope you don't think we abandoned you."

I felt a surge of annoyance, my jaw clenching involuntarily. How dare Edmond turn Marnie and Summer away; they were like family to me. I took a deep breath, trying to calm the frustration bubbling up inside me. Edmond and I were long overdue for a chat.

"How are you?" Marnie continued, "And I mean, how are you, really? No bullshitting here."

She pointed to a sign above the counter that read "Too Busy For Bullshit."

I paused, trying to find the right words. "I'm … managing. It's been tough, but I'm getting there. How about you? The last time I saw you—"

"You saved my life. I can't thank you enough. I've felt so guilty. Maybe if I hadn't run. Maybe if I'd gotten back to the square with help sooner—"

"Marnie," I cut her off. "You can't think like that. You did the right thing. They would have killed you, and then what would have happened to Summer?"

"Shya—"

"No, I won't hear it, Marnes. Tristan is the one to blame for all of this. No one else. Now tell me about you. It must have been scary for you."

Marnie's eyes clouded over, and she let out a heavy sigh. "It's been rough, Shya. The attack … Michael's death, you being kidnapped. It's

228

left its mark on all of us."

She lowered her voice, glancing around as if afraid of being overheard. "Summer's been having nightmares. She tries to act tough during the day, but at night ..." Marnie trailed off, shaking her head. "And she's not the only one. A lot of the humans in town are freaked out. They feel exposed in a way they never have before."

I felt anger bubbling up. I'd been so wrapped up in my own recovery that I hadn't fully considered how the attack had affected the rest of the town. If I didn't already want to rip Tristan's head off, hearing that Summer was having nightmares because of him would have made me determined to tear him apart.

I took a deep breath, trying to calm the rage that threatened to overwhelm me.

"I'm so sorry, Marnie," I said, my voice thick with emotion. "I had no idea it was this bad. You tell Summer there is nothing to worry about. I'm going to find Tristan and make sure he can't hurt anyone ever again. Is there anything I can do to help?"

Marnie gave me a sad smile. "Oh, honey, you've got enough on your plate. Don't worry about us. We'll get through this; we always do."

"Well, I'm back now. If you need anything, you just need to ask, okay?"

Marnie pulled me in for another hug. "Don't be silly. It's you I'm worried about. I was so scared, Shya. Thinking of you out there, with him."

I nodded, not ready to talk about everything that had happened. Not yet.

"What about the rest of the humans here in town? How are they coping?"

"It's been hard. Your mom has closed the town to tourists. She says she can't guarantee their safety. I get why, we all do, but Shya ..." She met my eyes, and I could see the fear there. "Without the tourist money, many businesses are struggling. If this keeps up, some of us might have to shut down for good."

Shit, that was not good. Our whole town was built on Shifters and humans living side by side. If the human shop owners left—along with the humans they employed because there was no work here—then we would have done Tristan's job for him. This wasn't just about money; this was about the very fabric of our community and everything that we stood for being torn apart by fear and uncertainty.

"I'll talk to my mom about reopening the town to tourists. There's got to be a way we can keep people safe without completely killing our economy."

Out of the corner of my eye, I caught a glimpse of movement. Tucker had slunk to the front of the shop, crouching just out of sight of anyone walking in. What was he up to?

Suddenly, the bell above the door jingled, and Summer burst in, carrying a paper bag that smelled delicious.

"Mom, I got the bagels from Mr. Johnson's! He threw in an extra cinnamon one for—" She stopped mid-sentence, her eyes widening as she spotted me. "Shya! You're here!"

Summer rushed forward, nearly dropping the bag in her excitement. She threw her arms around me, hugging me tightly. "I've been so worried about you!"

I hugged her back, feeling a lump form in my throat. "I'm okay, Summer. Really."

She pulled back, her young eyes searching my face. "Please tell me that motherfucker Tristan is dead."

"Summer!" Marnie gasped, her eyes wide with shock. "Language!"

I couldn't help it. The scandalized look on Marnie's face made me burst out laughing.

"Oh Goddess, Summer," I managed between giggles, "where did you learn to talk like that?"

Summer scowled and crossed her arms. "What? He is a motherfucker. After what he did, I think even Mom would agree."

Marnie sighed, shaking her head, but I could see the hint of a smile twitching her lips. "I neither confirm nor deny that assessment," she said primly, but her eyes were twinkling. "Will you stay for bagels, Shya? They smell amazing, and I'm starving. Summer, why don't you put them on the counter and go get some plates?"

"Oh, right!" Summer said, turning toward the counter. As she moved, I noticed Tucker's eyes lock onto her, his body tensing in preparation. He crouched low, his tail swishing in anticipation, and I suddenly knew why he wanted to come here. He was determined to work out why he could never sneak up on Summer, and he thought the only way to do that was to—

"Tuck!"

Tucker sprang forward, but as he did so, Summer casually sidestepped as if she'd known he was there all along. Tucker, unable to change course mid-leap, sailed past her and crashed headlong into a display of running shoes. The stand toppled over with a loud clatter, spilling shoes across the floor. A human shouldn't have been able to sense Tucker like that.

Summer turned around, one eyebrow raised, and looked down at the tangled mess of wolf and sneakers. "Nice try, Tucker," she said, her voice dripping with sarcasm. "Maybe next time."

I felt my cheeks burning with embarrassment. "Tucker! What did I tell you about stalking Summer? Marnie, I'm so sorry," I said, rushing over to help.

But to my surprise, Marnie burst out laughing. "Did you see his face when he missed?" she said between giggles.

I glared at Tucker, who was looking decidedly sheepish. If I knew my little brother, though, he was more annoyed with himself that he'd missed her than being told off. Summer started picking up the scattered shoes. I jerked my chin toward her, and Tucker got to his feet and went to pick up a shoe with his mouth. "Oh no, you don't!" Summer scolded. "We can't have drool marks all over the Nike Air Forces." Tucker blinked, then began nosing shoes toward her.

"You know," Summer said, "one day you'll be a big, scary werewolf, and maybe, just maybe, then you'll be able to catch me out. But that day is not today."

Tucker huffed in a "challenge accepted" sort of way, causing Summer to laugh.

Marnie nudged me with her elbow. "See? No harm done. And tidying up will keep them both busy for a bit, so you can tell me how you're really doing."

I looked down at my rainbow sneakers for a moment. "I ... I don't know, Marnie. Everything's so complicated now. Physically, I'm healing. But emotionally? I feel like I'm all over the place."

Marnie nodded encouragingly. "And Mason Shaw? He's the talk of the town at the moment. We've all heard how he was the one to find you. *And* that he's been staying up at the Alpha House with you." She wiggled her eyebrows suggestively.

At the mention of Mason's name, I felt my heart rate quicken. I ignored it and focused on Marnie's words. If what she said was true, then Mom was right. People had been gossiping about me and Mason, and his being here would only undermine any claim I might make in the future that Edmond was my mate. I had been putting not just Edmond's position at risk, but my own, too. When I took over, there could be no doubt that I was one hundred percent committed to this Pack and to my mate.

"Both Mason and Derek Shaw have been very helpful. We owe them a debt for their help, but they have both gone now."

Marnie stared at me for a beat and then said, "Well done, that was a diplomatic answer worthy of the Pack princess, but I'm asking Shya, not the Alpha-in-waiting."

I bit my lip and sighed. Marnie knew me too well. "I asked him to leave. To give me some space. We need to bury Dad, and I need time to work out who I am again." I paused, my brow furrowing. "Right now, I honestly don't know how I feel about him. Or Edmond. I don't know what's real and what's not. I don't know who to trust. I just know I can't trust myself." I blinked at her. "Everything feels so muddled, but part of me knows that none of that matters. The Pack won't accept Mason. Edmond is what is best for this Pack. What I want doesn't really come into it. Not now."

Marnie's expression softened with sympathy as she put her hand on my arm. "Oh, Shya. I get it, I really do. It's a lot to process. You've been through a lot. But don't give up on Mason. If you think he's the only one who'll make you happy, you have to go for it. You deserve to be happy. But ..." She hesitated, seeming unsure how to continue.

"But what?" I prompted, suddenly wary.

"Look, I don't want to add any pressure, but I don't know how much time you really have to work things out."

"What are you talking about?"

"Edmond was in the shop two days ago. He was asking about you and the types of shoes you like. He ended up ordering a pair for you. Said they'd look perfect for your mating ceremony and that they needed to be here by the middle of this week." Marnie's voice was gentle, but at her words, I felt like the ground had dropped out from beneath my feet.

I leaned against the wall, suddenly feeling dizzy. "He ordered shoes for the mating ceremony? Two days ago?"

We were burying Dad tonight with the moon in its last quarter, a time of release and letting go. The New Moon would rise in five days. It was a phase that symbolized a fresh start and new beginnings. Perfect for a mating ceremony. The fact that he'd ordered the shoes two days ago meant that he had started planning this as soon as he knew I was coming back.

Fuck. Fuck. Fuck!

Marnie nodded, her expression sympathetic. "I'm sorry, Shya. I thought you should know. You might not have much time to figure out how you feel about Mason."

I tried to nod, to say something reassuring, but I couldn't seem to find my voice. I'd wanted time and space, needed it, to come to terms with my decision to mate with Edmond, but I wasn't going to get it.

Chapter Thirty-Eight

SHYA

The pale light of the setting quarter moon cast shadows across the forest clearing as our Pack gathered to say goodbye to my father. Our shared loss hung heavy in the air, thick as the night mist that clung to the ground and swirled around our feet.

I stood at the edge of the clearing, my heart aching as I watched my Pack arrive. They moved silently, with just the occasional muffled sob or quiet sniffle.

"Shya," my mother's voice was soft as she approached, her eyes rimmed with red. "Are you ready?"

I nodded, not trusting my voice. Henry placed a comforting hand on my shoulder, and I felt a small hand slip into mine.

"I miss Dad," Tucker whispered.

I squeezed his hand. "I know, Tuck. I miss him, too."

As one, we stepped forward toward the center of the clearing where, atop a bed of pine boughs, a figure lay wrapped in a pristine red shroud. My eyes were drawn to it, and I couldn't look away. I knew the bundle of red held the body of my father, the strongest and bravest wolf I had ever known. As his immediate family, Mom,

Henry, Tucker, and I were wearing red sashes cut from the same length of material that covered Dad. To the right of my dad's body, a freshly killed deer lay as an offering to the Moon Goddess. Mom had gone hunting this morning. To the left, a small sapling waited to be planted—it was a rare American chestnut, once thought extinct but now making a slow comeback. Like our Pack, I realized, resilient in the face of adversity.

I yanked my eyes away, unable to look at the body any longer, knowing that he would never be coming back. That he wasn't going to sit up and open his arms for a hug. He wouldn't be giving me or my brothers any more lessons in strategy or history. There would be no more secret glances between him and Mom when they thought no one was looking. No more bedtime stories for Tucker or hunting lessons for Henry. He was just gone and had left a hole that the rest of us could never fill.

I glanced around the clearing, taking in the faces of my Pack. Marnie and Summer, and even Ellen, my nemesis on the town council, stood with the other humans, their expressions a mix of sorrow and shock. Danni stood near us, guarding our family as we faced our grief. Ivan, Ethan, Due-lah, and at least ten other enforcers flanked the gathering, their eyes scanning the tree line on the lookout for an attack. It would be just like Tristan to come at us now.

Edmond, who had been standing with his parents and Garrett, nodded once to Mom, and came to stand on the other side of me. His blond hair was neatly combed, and his smart trousers and white shirt projected an air of controlled authority. I felt a twinge of irritation that he was here, with my family, at this moment. We were not mated yet. He was not part of us yet.

As if sensing my gaze, Edmond's eyes met mine. For a moment, I thought I saw a flash of emotion—was it sympathy, or perhaps regret?—but it was gone so quickly I couldn't be sure. He gave me a small, formal nod, his posture stiff and proper, as always.

My attention was drawn back to the center of the clearing as my mother stepped forward, her voice clear and steady, carrying across the clearing. "We have come together as Pack tonight. We set aside our differences, our toils, our kills to honor the life of Michael Blackwood Little, our Alpha, our protector, our friend, and my mate. He was the strength of our Pack, a devoted leader, a loving father, and the perfect partner."

I watched in awe of my mother and her composure. In the face of such profound loss, she somehow found the courage to stand tall, her voice unwavering. The moonlight caught the silver streaks in her dark hair, making them shine like starlight. In that moment, she looked every inch the Alpha she was.

"Michael lived by a code of honor, loyalty, and sacrifice," Mom continued, her eyes sweeping over the gathered Pack. "He believed in the strength of our unity and the power of our bonds. Tonight, we not only mourn his loss, but celebrate the legacy he leaves behind."

Her gaze settled on me, then moved to Henry and Tucker. "He will live on in his children, in the lessons he taught, and in the example he set for all of us."

I felt a lump form in my throat. How was she doing this? How could she be so strong when I felt like I was barely holding myself together?

Mom paused, taking a deep breath. For a moment, I saw a flicker of vulnerability in her eyes, a glimpse of the depth of her pain. But then it was gone, replaced by determination.

"As we say goodbye to our Alpha, let us remember that his strength is our strength. His courage, our courage. We will honor his memory by standing united, by protecting what he loved, and by continuing to build the Pack he envisioned."

She turned to face the shrouded figure, her voice softening. "Goodbye, my love. May you run free under eternal moons. I will run with you soon."

Tucker's small hand tightened in mine.

On a silent cue, the Pack began to move forward to pay their final respects. I felt the tears roll down my face and made no move to brush them away. These tears were for my father; it was my way of honoring him while my mind flooded with memories of him. His kind smile when I'd skinned my knee as a pup. The pride in his eyes when I'd made my first successful hunt. The unwavering strength he'd shown, even in the face of Tristan's first betrayal. Dad always put Pack first. He gave everything for this Pack right up until the end. How could I ever live up to his legacy? I was suddenly keenly aware of the eyes of the Pack upon me. I was next in line to lead, and though the weight of that responsibility threatened to crush me, I knew I had to be strong. For my father. For my Pack.

The moon dipped below the horizon, plunging the clearing into the gray light of dawn.

One by one, people stepped forward to say a few words.

"Michael wasn't just our Alpha." Ethan's voice cracked with emotion. "He was a friend to all of us. When my brother died, Michael sat with me every night for a month. He didn't say much, just ... was there. That's the kind of wolf he was."

Marnie spoke next. "I remember when I first came here and asked to join the Pack, how scared I was. But Michael ... he made me feel at home. He said humans would always be welcome here. That we were part of this Pack. Humans and werewolves in the north? Who would have thought it? But Michael did. He meant what he said, and for that, my daughter and I will forever be grateful."

Marnie's words were soft-spoken and genuine, but I'm sure I wasn't the only one who heard the message in them. My clever friend was reminding everyone that Michael had wanted humans here, in case there were some who were wondering about Tristan and the things he stood for.

Summer's voice trembled as she stepped forward and spoke. "Michael always said that our strength wasn't in our individual powers but in our unity. Looking at us all here today, I know he was right."

I nodded, feeling the truth of those words deep in my bones. We were strong because we were together. We would survive this loss because we had each other. This was Pack. This was what we stood for.

Danni stepped forward, a burning torch in her hand, its flame dancing in the pre-dawn light. She bowed her head and passed it to my mother. Mom's fingers curled around the rough wood, her knuckles white with the strength of her grip. For a moment, she stood motionless, her eyes fixed on the shrouded form of Dad's body. In that pause, I could almost feel her grief as a tangible thing, the enormity of what she was about to do.

With a deep breath, Mom moved forward. The torch did not tremble in her hand as she lowered it to the bed of pine boughs. As the flames licked at the dry needles, smoke began to rise, carrying with it the essence of the forest Dad had loved so much.

We all watched in silence as the fire took hold. The flames grew, reaching upward, embracing the shrouded figure. They danced and swayed, casting flickering shadows across the faces of the Pack. And then dawn broke over the horizon, painting the sky in hues of pink and gold. We stood united in our grief and our remembrance, bearing witness to the passing of our Alpha, my father, and I knew there would be none like him again.

"Your father would be proud of you," Danni murmured as she clasped my hand briefly. Her eyes, usually so sharp, were soft with shared grief. Everyone else had left, all except my family, Danni, and Edmond. We would stay until it was all ash. Tomorrow, we would come back, plant the American chestnut, and scatter the ashes around the base. Dad's remains would nourish the sapling, connecting him to the earth and linking one life to another.

Tucker stood at Henry's side, his small frame rigid, staring into the flames. I longed to comfort him but knew he didn't want that. If I touched him, he would start to cry, and he would want to be the Alpha's son in front of everyone today.

I felt a warm hand on my shoulder. Turning, I found myself face-to-face with Edmond. His expression was a complex mix of emotions—sympathy, yes, but there was something else there, too. A determination that made me uneasy.

"Shya," he said softly, his eyes never leaving mine. "We need to talk. I know this isn't the best time, but we need to talk about the future.

About our future."

I frowned. Was he serious? He wanted to do this now. And here of all places. "This isn't the time, Edmond."

Edmond's eyes darted around before settling back on me. "On the contrary, this is absolutely the appropriate time. Your father is gone. I know it is heartbreaking for you. It is for all of us. It's the end of an era. But we must look to the future. We must make sure the Pack is strong, stable. That it can withstand what is coming. Your father would want that. He would be counting on you to do what is right."

Uh-huh. "And that would be going through with the mating ceremony, would it?"

Edmond sighed, looking disappointed. "I understand you have feelings for Mason. But unless you can tell me otherwise, that is all they are. Feelings. You aren't sure he's your fated mate. If he was, don't you think you would be sure?"

And that was the problem. I'd let Tristan convince me not once, but twice, that he was my fated mate. My heart and body might be telling me that Mason was the one, but how could I possibly trust that?

"I ... I don't know."

"Your parents, your dad, chose me for a reason. Their fated mate bond did not appear until the mating ceremony. Neither did my parents', Shya. It is not unusual. But all of our parents believe we are well suited to each other. That we are the best thing for our Pack. We must be united; we must have strong leadership in these uncertain times."

"I agree, Edmond, but aren't we moving a little fast? I need more time."

Edmond's expression softened, taking on an almost paternal

concern. "I understand, Shya. But Tristan could attack again any day now; there are mutterings in the Pack that, with Michael dead and Camille grieving, maybe it is time for new blood. Perhaps even inviting Tristan back."

All the breath left my body. "That can't be right? Not after everything he's done."

"No? We are Pack creatures, Shya. No matter what else he is, Tristan is a strong leader with a clear vision. Your mother is grieving; her heart isn't here, and everyone can see that, can feel it in the Pack bonds. They want stability. Right now, some are starting to think the best way of getting that is through Tristan."

My hands curled into fists. There was no fucking way we were losing the Pack, especially not to that motherfucker. "We'll show them they're wrong. We'll show them we're still in charge, that we're still able to protect them."

Edmond nodded. "Yes. And the best way to do that ..."

I blinked slowly, knowing he was right, even if my heart was breaking. I thought I would have more time to come to terms with losing Mason, but we needed a strong Alpha pair in place. Now. It was our duty to this Pack, to my dad and his vision for this place, to Henry and Tucker, who would not survive in a Pack ruled by Tristan. He would see them as potential threats that had to be eliminated to protect his rule from future challenges.

"We need to hold the mating ceremony," I said.

Edmond smiled, a soft, condescending smile that irritated the hell out of me. "Well done, Shya. I knew you would do what is right in the end."

CHAPTER THIRTY-NINE

MASON

I stood on Thomas and Wally's porch, my hands fidgeting with the small rubber ball I found in my pocket. Balls and fidget toys helped me think, though it wasn't doing a good job right now. And that was precisely why I was here. Taking a deep breath, I steeled myself and knocked on the door. The sound echoed in the quiet neighborhood, and a moment later, Thomas's tall frame filled the doorway.

"Mason," Thomas greeted me, his warm brown eyes crinkling with a smile. "Come on in."

I stepped inside, instantly enveloped by the warm, inviting atmosphere of Thomas and Wally's home. My eyes swept across the living room, taking in the harmonious clash of styles that somehow worked perfectly together. The walls were a canvas of memories and art, displaying a curated collection that spoke volumes about the couple's shared life.

Framed photographs captured stolen moments of laughter and tenderness between Thomas and Wally, interspersed with abstract paintings that added splashes of color to the space. Each piece seemed to have a story, carefully selected and placed with Wally's unmistakable flair for visual storytelling.

I followed Thomas into the living room, glancing at their grand piano in the corner, its polished surface gleaming under the soft lighting. Nearby, a sturdy, well-cushioned sofa faced a large fireplace, its mantle decorated with various trinkets and mementos. The room was a perfect blend of Wally's flair and Thomas's groundedness.

"Thanks for seeing me, Doc," I said as I continued to take in the surroundings. "I needed to talk to you about something … someone."

Thomas gestured for me to take a seat on the plush couch. I sank into the overstuffed cushions, feeling awkward about asking for help and annoyed with myself for feeling that way. I'd do anything, ask anyone for help if it was for my mate.

"Shya?" Thomas asked, settling into an armchair across from me.

I nodded, my fingers instinctively rolling the small ball in my hands. "She's been through a lot."

"I've heard."

I looked at him sharply.

Thomas spread his hands wide. "You have met Wally, haven't you? He seems to be best friends with Mai and Sofia these days. They talk. Then he comes home, and he talks."

"That sounds about right." I'd been there when those three got together; put them in a room together, and no one else was getting a word in. "I'm worried about Shya. After everything that's happened with Tristan and that witch … I want to help, but I don't know how."

Thomas tilted his head, his salt-and-pepper hair catching the soft light from the table lamp. "Mason, what Shya's been through … it's significant trauma, both mental and emotional. There's no quick fix for that."

"I'm well aware of that, Thomas," I said. "I just ... I need to know if there's anything I can do. Or if there are things I shouldn't do?"

Thomas's expression softened. "The most important thing is patience. Shya needs time and space to grieve, to sort out her own feelings from the ones Tristan and the witch planted in her head. It's a process, and it can't be rushed."

I turned my head as Wally sauntered through the door, his pink shirt and black trousers pressed perfectly. Behind him trailed Amara and Ben, the siblings who had recently moved into Thomas and Wally's home.

"Well, well, well! If it isn't our resident brooding PI!" Wally's eyes sparkled with mischief as he perched on the arm of Thomas's chair.

Amara, all of eighteen and radiating an aura of practiced toughness, leaned against the doorframe with her arms crossed. Her vibrant blue hair framed her face, the bold color accentuating her rich, dark skin and drawing attention to her delicate features—a button nose and full lips set in a guarded expression. Her dark eyes swept over me, assessing.

"Mason." She nodded curtly.

Ben peeked out from behind his sister. His face, a miniature version of Amara's, was framed by a halo of tight, dark curls.

"Hey, guys," I greeted, trying to soften my usual gruff demeanor for Ben's sake. "How's it going?"

"It's going." Amara shrugged, her tone noncommittal.

Ben narrowed his eyes at me, whispering loudly, "Is the dickhead coming?"

Amara's face hardened slightly, her blue hair shifting as she shook her head. "You have to stop calling Jase that."

"Why? He broke your heart. Therefore, he is a dickhead. I'm not going to let him forget that."

I raised my eyebrows at Amara.

"He didn't break my heart, Ben, and I've told you hell will host the women's hockey championship before we start dating again." She switched her glare to me. "And don't you tell him anything about this conversation, Mason."

I grinned at her. "Sure thing. Anyway, to answer your question, Ben, Jase is not coming. I'm here alone, and if I know Jase, he'll be off watching Mai's back."

Ben looked satisfied with that answer. Wally, ever the peacemaker, clapped his hands together. "Alright, you two. Why don't you go wash up and then we can make those cookies you like, Ben?"

Ben's face lit up, his dark eyes sparkling with excitement. He darted toward the kitchen, tugging Amara along by her hand.

Once they were out of earshot, Wally turned back to me, his expression a mix of fondness and exasperation. "Never a dull moment around here, I tell you. Now, where were we? Something about Shya, if my gorgeous ears heard right."

I sighed. I should have known there would be no keeping this conversation from Wally. "I just wanted to know if there was anything I could do to help her."

"Ah, well, I'm sure Thomas has guided you true on that score. But if you need any help, you remember that you're currently looking at a fully-fledged warrior now. I am locked and loaded, as they say, ready for anything you need. Just say the word, and I'll be there, claws out!"

Thomas rolled his eyes affectionately. "Wally, honey, you've been watching too many *Fast and Furious* movies. You're not invincible."

Wally gasped dramatically, placing a hand over his heart. "Thomas!

How dare you try to stifle my inner Vin Diesel? I'll have you know that if you keep this up, I'll be forced to cut off all sexual favors. No more nookie for you, mister!"

And this wasn't awkward at all. Nope. Not at all.

Thomas, however, seemed unfazed. "Wally," Thomas said, his voice soft and full of love, "you're already a bad-assed super-werewolf. And I love you no matter what you do."

Wally's playful demeanor cracked, his eyes welling up with tears. "Oh, Thomas," he whispered, leaning down to place a kiss on his mate's forehead.

I stood quickly, feeling like the third wheel here. "Right, well, I'll leave you to it. Thanks for the advice, Doc."

"Anytime, Mason."

"You sure you don't want to stay for dinner?" Wally asked. He loved cooking for people.

I shook my head. "I need to get tracking Tristan." I held up my hands before Wally could say anything. "I'll let you know if you can help in any way, Wally."

"Good. Don't you forget, Mason, I'm a secret weapon. You just ask Mai. I'm sneaky and stealthy. No one suspects me."

"Apart from me, Wally! I suspect you all the time!" Ben's shout came from the kitchen, making Thomas laugh.

It was nice to see them as a family, but I felt out of place. I missed Shya, my wolf missed Shya, and we needed to start our hunt so she would finally be safe.

CHAPTER FORTY

MASON

I walked into my office at Shaw Investigations, the familiar scent of old paper and coffee hitting me as I crossed the threshold. The room hadn't changed much since I'd last been here, but it felt different.

Derek, AJ, Sam, and Waylen filed in behind me. Milly had refused to come, seeing as my office was in Pack territory. Sam immediately sprawled in one of the chairs facing my desk, his casual posture at odds with the tension in the air. AJ leaned against the wall near the door, arms crossed, while Waylen sat with his laptop on his knees, his fingers already twitching, as if eager to start typing.

Derek moved slowly around the room, his eyes taking in every detail. I glanced at Sam, noting the changes in my brother since he'd left to join the Wolf Council. He seemed older somehow, more serious. The easy grin I was used to seeing was replaced by a thoughtful frown.

"How does it feel, being back?" I asked him.

"Weird," Sam admitted softly, running his hand along the edge of my desk. "Everything seems ... smaller."

I nodded, understanding what he meant. It wasn't just the physical space that had changed—it was us. We'd both grown in different directions since he'd left.

Derek snorted. "That's because you're used to that fancy office of yours at the Wolf Council now, bro. Probably has a view and everything, right? Let me guess, a panoramic vista of perfectly manicured lawns where wolves in suits chase squirrels during their lunch breaks?"

Sam rolled his eyes, but I caught a small smile tugging at his lips. "For your information, it's just a regular office."

"Uh-huh." Derek grinned, clearly not buying it. "No gold-plated door? No mini-fridge stocked with premium raw steaks?"

Before Sam could answer, there was a knock on the door, and Jase bounded in. Behind him strode Carlito Mendez, our second in command at the agency. Carlito had joined us three years ago, bringing with him a wealth of experience and a complex past. Derek had recommended him after hearing about his struggle to find his place after a dishonorable discharge from the Marines. A covert operation that Carlito had been leading went wrong, and the military blamed him. Carlito did, too, but I'd seen the file. He didn't do anything wrong, but the military needed a scapegoat to take the fall. When Derek found him, Carlito had been living as a rogue in one of the conclave cities, drinking to try to forget. Unlike my dad, Carlito was someone we could help. Offered the chance to prove himself, he took it, sobered up, and used his skills to great effect with our agency.

Carlito gave me a sharp nod as he walked in.

Jase's eyes bounced between Sam and me, barely contained energy practically vibrating off him. "Is it true? Is the gang all back together?"

"For now." I turned to the others. "AJ, this is Carlito Mendez."

AJ shook Carlito's hand, his expression neutral, but I knew they were sizing each other up.

"When did Jase join the agency?" Sam asked. "I thought he was working for Mai?"

"He is, but despite his multiple attempts to get them to change their minds, the Alphas are still going by the must-be-twenty-one-to-be-an-enforcer rule. Of course, he's ignoring it and still watches Mai's back, but he's also working here now to get some experience."

"Mainly so that when they do let me join officially, I'll be way ahead of motherfuckers like Cameron Blake."

Sam raised his eyebrows.

"Cameron is twenty-two, already an enforcer, and has asked Amara out three times in the last month," Derek explained.

"This isn't about Amara," Jase said stiffly.

"Kid, I don't even know you," AJ crossed his arms, "but even I know that's bullshit."

Jase's mouth gaped open. He really needed to work on his poker face.

Before Jase could reply, Carlito said, "The boy's got potential. Raw talent, but he's learning."

Jase's mouth clicked close. By now, he knew Carlito almost as well as I did, and that was high praise coming from him.

"Alright, let's get down to business. We need to talk about Tristan." I nodded to Waylen, telling him he had the floor.

Waylen's fingers stopped their constant tapping on his laptop as he looked up, pushing his glasses up the bridge of his nose. His hair was a disheveled mess, as if he'd been running his hands through it in frustration. He let out a dramatic sigh, his lips quirking into a wry smile.

"Ah, the elusive Mr. Munroe," Waylen said, his voice dripping with sarcasm. "Our very own digital Houdini. Let me tell you, folks, this guy's giving me a run for my money."

He stood up, stretching with a series of audible pops from his back. His oversized black hoodie hung loosely on his skinny frame as he started to pace, his movements restless and energetic.

"I've been digging into every nook and cranny of the digital world," Waylen continued, his hands moving animatedly as he spoke. "I've combed through security footage, financial records, known associates—you name it, I've hacked it. But this guy? He's like a phantom in the machine." Waylen's keen eyes darted around the room, taking in everyone's reactions. "Every time I think I'm getting close, poof! He disappears on me. It's like trying to catch smoke with a butterfly net." He paused, a determined glint in his eye. "But don't worry, no one outruns Waylen the Wizard forever. I've got a few tricks up my sleeve yet."

Derek's expression grew more serious. "Any leads at all, Waylen?"

Waylen's lips twisted into a grimace. "Well, that's the rub, isn't it? We've hit a wall harder than a werewolf running full tilt into a silver-plated door." He started tapping his fingers against his leg, a rhythm only he could hear. "We've reached out to our contacts in other Packs, but no one's seen or heard anything. It's like Tristan vanished into thin air, probably cackling like a supervillain as he did it." Waylen's expression shifted, a mix of frustration and determination coloring his features. "But mark my words, I'm going to get him. No one stays hidden from me forever, not in this digital age. It's just a matter of time before he slips up, and when he does ..." He trailed off, his eyes gleaming with the promise of the hunt. "Well, let's just say Waylen the Wizard will be ready and waiting."

I picked up a purple tennis ball from the side of my desk, throwing it against the wall, then catching it. "We need to move faster," I said, my voice low. "Every day Tristan's out there is another day Shya's in danger. We can't afford to wait for him to slip up."

Derek cleared his throat. "There might be someone we haven't approached yet," he said, his eyes flicking between Sam and me. "Someone who might have information."

There was no fucking way. "Absolutely not."

Derek held up his hands. "Whatever you want, bro, but he has contacts we don't."

Fucking hell! The last thing I wanted was to deal with Ronnie fucking Bishop right now.

CHAPTER FORTY-ONE

MASON

I sat in Ronnie's office, my jaw clenched so tight I could feel a headache coming on. I'd always found the contrast between this neat, polished room and the gritty exterior of his biker gang headquarters jarring. It was like he couldn't decide who he really was: the leader of a biker gang or a respectable businessman who took every opportunity to get ahead. In here, it was obviously his personal den away from the chaos outside, with his polished oak desk, pristine countertops, and framed motorcycle photos on the walls. Behind Ronnie's desk, a large window offered a view of the chaotic workshop, bathing the room in light.

Derek, Sam, AJ, and Jase sat beside me. I could sense their unease, mirroring my own mood.

Ronnie rested back in his chair, a smug smile playing on his lips as he studied us. His blue eyes fucking sparkled with amusement, and I knew he was enjoying every second of my discomfort.

"Well, well," Ronnie drawled, his voice smooth and calculated. "To what do I owe the pleasure of this ... unexpected visit?" His gaze swept over our group, lingering on each face before settling back on me.

I clenched my fists at my sides, forcing myself to speak through gritted teeth. "We need information. About Tristan."

Ronnie's smile widened, revealing perfect white teeth. "Ah, yes. I heard about the recent excitement. I would like to thank you, Mason, for returning Shya safe and sound." His tone softened slightly as he added, "I've always been quite fond of her, you know."

I did know. He made it fucking obvious every time he saw her. I bit back a growl, reminding myself that we needed his help, no matter how much it pissed me off.

Ronnie's attention shifted to Sam, his demeanor subtly changing. The smug amusement in his eyes replaced by a calculating look. I tensed, wondering what game he was playing now.

"It's good to see you, Sam," Ronnie said, his tone deceptively casual. "But I have to ask—what hat are you wearing today? You here as a member of the Wolf Council or as a Shaw brother?"

Sam's expression remained neutral, but I caught the slight tightening around his eyes. "Does it make a difference?" he asked, his voice level.

Ronnie's lips curved into a knowing smile. "Oh, it makes all the difference in the world. You see, a Council representative is duty-bound to uphold the laws and maintain peace. They'd have to shut down any ... shall we say, less than legal activities, regardless of the consequences." He leaned forward, resting his elbows on the desk. "But a Shaw brother? Well, he'd be here to back up his sibling who lost, found, and then lost his mate again."

I fought to keep my face impassive. I knew he was baiting me, wanting to see how far he could push me, but inside, my wolf was snarling, and all I wanted was to leap over this desk and strangle the man.

Sam met Ronnie's eyes steadily. "I'm here as a Shaw," he said firmly.

I watched as Ronnie visibly relaxed, a satisfied look in his eyes. He leaned back, spreading his hands wide. "Well then, gentlemen," he said, his voice smooth as silk, "what can I do for you all?"

I clenched my fists once before saying, "We're tracking down Tristan. He's still out there plotting against Shya and her family. He also has AJ's mate, and we want her back. We're looking for any intel you might have on his whereabouts."

Ronnie's expression turned calculating, his eyes never leaving my face. "Interesting," he mused. "As it happens, I've been conducting my own search for Tristan."

My eyes narrowed as suspicion flooded through me. "Oh?" I managed to keep my voice neutral. "And why would you be doing that?"

"Aside from payback for what he did to Shya? Let's just say it's in my best interests to keep tabs on someone with Tristan's ... particular views on humans. What is it you're offering here?" He glanced at each of us in turn. "A temporary alliance?"

Derek looked at him intently, his eyes sharp. "If we pool our resources, we both stand a better chance of hunting Tristan down."

Ronnie's grin widened, his eyes sliding back to me. "Now, now, Derek. I appreciate your enthusiasm, but I want to hear it from the man himself." He settled back in his chair, folding his hands on the desk. "Is this really what you want, Mason?"

I wasn't going to strangle him; that would be too easy. No, I was going to slam his head against his pristine desk until I cracked it open like a boiled egg.

I took a deep breath, forcing myself to relax my fists.

"Yes," I growled, the word coming out more like a challenge than an agreement. "We're proposing a temporary alliance, Ronnie. Your information, our resources. We work together to find Tristan and AJ's mate."

Ronnie's smile was all teeth as he nodded. "There, was that so hard? Now, let's talk about what I know and how we can help each other, shall we?" Ronnie's tone shifted to something more businesslike. "I'll be honest, I haven't had much luck so far. But I do have a lead that might pan out. There's a contact of mine who I believe has been supplying Tristan's men with goods."

No one moved, but the atmosphere in the room changed subtly; all of our attention sharpened.

"I've sent some of my men down there to track Tristan's people back to any possible camps," Ronnie continued. "With any luck, we'll have a location soon."

My mind raced with the possibilities. "Waylen's been following supply lines, tracking movements."

A grin spread across Ronnie's face, his eyes glinting with amusement. "Well then, it seems we have ourselves a race, don't we? Whose contacts will come up with results first?"

I narrowed my eyes at him, fully aware of how much he was enjoying this situation. Part of me wanted to tell him to shove his race up his ass, but I knew this was our best shot at finding Tristan quickly.

"Agreed," I said, giving a reluctant nod. "We'll share whatever we find."

I stood up to leave, eager to be out of there and back hunting Tristan.

"By the way, Mason," Ronnie said, his tone dripping with false casualness. "I've got a little bonus information for you. Free of charge—not something I usually do, mind you, but I find I can't pass up this opportunity."

I turned back, my guard instantly up.

"My sources tell me Shya has set a date for her mating ceremony with Edmond. It's due to take place in three days."

The words hit me like a physical blow. For a moment, I forgot how to breathe. Three days? Shya was going to mate with Edmond in three fucking days. My mind reeled, struggling to process this information.

I kept my face blank, even as I felt my heart hammering against my ribcage. Thank fuck Ronnie was human and couldn't hear the telltale racing of my pulse.

"Is that so?" I managed to say, my voice steady despite the turmoil inside me. "Well, I appreciate the information, Ronnie."

As we filed out of the office, my mind was in turmoil. Three days. I had three days to somehow stop this mating ceremony and get my mate back.

CHAPTER FORTY-TWO

MASON

I slipped through the shadows of Bridgetown Pack territory, every sense on high alert. This place had never been home, but now it felt downright hostile.

My feet glided silently over the damp earth, leaving no trace of my passage. The scents of pine and jasmine hung heavy in the air, but beneath them, I caught the faint musk of wolf—patrols, but not close enough to be a concern. A twig snapped nearby, and without breaking stride, I cataloged its source: a rabbit about twenty feet to my left. Irrelevant.

Memories of holding Shya in the hospital flashed through my mind, of me admitting I'd killed Dad. What the fuck was I doing? She was a Pack princess, for fuck's sake. I was a killer who ran a PI agency. She deserved better than this. My wolf growled at me, and I shoved those thoughts aside. No time for that self-pitying crap. I had to concentrate. I had a job to do. Get to Shya. Stop this mating ceremony. Nothing else mattered.

The Alpha house loomed ahead, dark and imposing. I pressed on, keeping to the shadows of the trees. A patrol passed north of me, two wolves padding silently through the undergrowth. I tensed. The wolves paused, sniffing the air. For a heart-stopping moment, I thought they'd caught my scent. But then they moved on, disappearing into the night.

I waited another minute before setting off again. I was almost there. I could see Shya's window now, a faint light glowing inside.

I ran, reached the base of the Alpha House, and leaped. My hands found holds in the rough stone. My muscles strained as I pulled myself up, each movement precise and controlled.

Shya's window was just above me. I slid the window open and slipped inside.

My eyes immediately found Shya, sleeping in just her panties and a pale pink vest. She looked so fucking beautiful. Delicate, vulnerable, soft. For a moment, I just stood there, drinking in the sight of her.

Then reality crashed back in. We didn't have much time.

"Shya," I whispered, moving closer. "Princess, wake up."

Her eyes snapped open instantly, alert and focused. In one fluid motion, she was out of bed, a knife seemingly materializing in her hand. The blade pressed against my throat before I could blink.

Delicate, vulnerable, soft? Yeah, not my princess.

I was oddly proud of her, even as the blade broke my skin.

"Mason," she hissed, her voice low and dangerous as the knife disappeared as swiftly as it had appeared. "How did you get in? We've tripled our patrols, and you sauntered past them! What the hell are you even doing here?"

"What the fuck do you think I'm doing here? I heard about the mating ceremony," I growled. "You can't go through with it."

Shya's eyes widened, a flicker of pain crossing her face. She took a step back.

"Mason, I—"

"No. Don't give me the bullshit excuses your mom has put in your head. Tell me why the fuck you would agree to this?"

She took another step away from me. "Mason, try to understand. I have a duty to my Pack, to my father. We're facing threats all around us. I have to ensure we're safe, that we're protected."

"And you think mating with Edmond will do that?"

"Yes." She said it so matter-of-factly.

I held her gaze. "What about you?"

Shya frowned. "What about me?"

"Is this what you want? Not for your father, or your mother, or your Pack. Is Edmond who you want?"

She shook her head. "It doesn't matter what I want."

"You're wrong. What you want is everything."

"Really?" She threw her hands up. "You make it sound so easy. 'Hey, Shya,'" she said, trying to imitate my voice, "'even though you don't trust your own feelings, why don't you give up everything you've been brought up to believe, abandon your family and friends, go off and have hot, sultry sex with me for the next year.'"

"The hot, sultry sex sounds fucking awesome."

She ignored my quip and started pacing. "You're asking me to give up all my responsibilities, to forget my duty, to leave everything I've ever known, all for something I'm not sure about. I hardly even know you! If you think what you want is everything, what is it you want, Mason?"

I didn't have to think about that for even a second. "You."

Shya blinked. "What?"

"You, Shya," I said, my voice dropping to a husky whisper. "I want you. Every fierce, stubborn, beautiful inch of you. I want your fire, your passion, your strength. I want your laughter in the morning and your sighs at night. I want to stand beside you, whether it's here in the heart of your Pack lands, beneath the pines of Three Rivers, or in some distant corner of the world we haven't even dreamed of yet. I don't care about the where, Shya. I just want you. Your hopes, your fears, your dreams. All of it. All of you." I raised one eyebrow. "And especially the hot and sultry sex."

I took a step closer, close enough to see the flecks of gold in her eyes, to feel the heat radiating from her skin. "I want a future where we face every challenge together, where we make something that's ours. Not your Pack's, not your parents', not anyone else's. Ours." I could hear her heart thumping quickly in her chest. "I want the chance to show you that what we have isn't just a passing attraction. It's real, princess. It's powerful. And it's worth fighting for."

She seemed frozen on the spot. Petrified.

"Princess, look at me," I said softly. When she locked eyes with me, I slowly reached out, giving her time to pull away if she wanted. She didn't. My hands cradled her face, my thumbs brushing her cheeks.

"You have to start trusting yourself again," I murmured, looking deep into her eyes. "Right here, right now, what is your heart telling you? What is your body telling you?"

Her breath caught, a shiver running through her at my touch. I could feel her pulse quickening under my fingers, see the flush spreading across her cheeks. My own body responded, a rush of heat and need coursing through me.

"Mason," she whispered, her lips parting slightly. The hunger in her eyes matched my own.

"Tell me to stop, princess. Tell me, and I will."

But she didn't. Instead, she closed her eyes. Slowly, ever so slowly, I lowered my mouth to hers. My lips hovered there for an eternity of seconds, a breath away from contact. Waiting for her signal to stop. When none came, I closed the distance and captured her mouth in mine. She melted against me instantly, just like I knew she would. Her arms wound around my neck, pulling me closer as her body sank into mine. The taste of her lips was fucking intoxicating. This was what I wanted. Every day for the rest of my life.

I lifted her up, her legs wrapped around my waist, kissing her so completely. Her hands buried themselves in my hair, tugging slightly. A low growl rumbled from the back of my throat. She liked that. She kissed me harder, as if she was pouring all our pent-up frustration and longing into it.

Holy hell, she was fucking amazing.

Something bright flickered in her eyes, a spark of something wild and untamed. She reached up and slipped off my shirt, revealing the expanse of skin beneath. Her eyes widened as she took in the sight of me, a soft gasp escaping her lips.

"Like what you see, princess?"

Her cheeks flushed crimson as she looked at me sharply. "You said that before. In my dreams."

I arched an eyebrow. "Really? And what did you say?"

"I said ... I said, 'Oh, yes.'"

I surged forward and kissed her.

"Mason," she whimpered as my fingers trailed downwards, skimming the delicate curves of her body, and I reveled in the sound.

We crashed into the wall, and my hand skimmed lower until I met the waistband of her panties. I couldn't take my eyes off her, and her chest heaved as she sucked in a sharp breath, anticipation making her pupils dilate. I wasn't wasting time putting her down; I ripped off her panties, then whipped her vest off. She was finally naked, thank fuck, and I took a moment to drink her in.

"Goddess, princess, you're so fucking beautiful."

Her cheeks flushed a deeper shade of crimson at my words.

"And fucking adorable."

"Mason—"

"I'm going to suck your clit until you come all over my face, princess."

Her eyes widened as she squirmed, a fucking delightful combination of shock and anticipation painted across her face.

Her back arched as I brushed my fingers lightly over her nipples, a soft whimper escaping from between her parted lips. I watched as they tightened under my touch, the sight of it driving me wild with lust. Unable to resist any longer, I dipped my head down and captured one in my mouth, teasing it gently with my tongue. She gasped, her hand fisted in my hair.

"Mason," she moaned out my name like a prayer, her voice shaky with need. The sound sent a jolt of heat straight down my spine, making me so fucking hard. I switched to her other nipple, giving it the same attention, eliciting another ragged moan from her. Her hand slipped down my back, fingers tracing the designs inked into my skin.

I moved lower still until I was kneeling between her thighs, my breath fanning her heated core. Her breath caught in anticipation as I hitched one of her legs over my shoulder, then parted her with my fingers, gazing in deep admiration at the sight before me.

"Your pussy is a sight to behold," I whispered. Her scent filled my senses, and I leaned in, flicking my tongue against her folds. The taste of her on my tongue was intoxicating, and I groaned, unable to resist delving deeper.

"Holy hell, you taste amazing, princess."

She writhed as I continued to explore her with my mouth. It was pure bliss watching her lose herself like this, feeling the way she responded to every lick of my tongue. Her thighs tightened around me as she whimpered again, louder now, the sound swallowed by the room. She moaned as I found her clit with my tongue. My hands rested against her hips, holding her steady while I began to devour her with an intensity that had her bucking her hips.

She was so sweet, so fucking divine. The taste of Shya was something I knew I would never grow tired of. I swirled my tongue around again and again. I was relentless, picking up the pace as I found just the right rhythm to have her shaking with pleasure. Her gasps grew louder with each pass of my lips.

"Mason!" she cried out as she hit her peak. Her entire body shook with the force of her orgasm. She clung to me tightly as she rode it out, her nails digging into my shoulders, and I fucking loved it. Loved that I could do this to her.

"Mason," she moaned, and her eyes were hooded with desire again as they met mine; a light sheen of sweat coated her body, making her skin glisten in the dim light.

I chuckled. "My greedy princess. So eager for more."

I stood up and kissed her, filling her mouth and mine with the taste of her.

My hand drifted up her torso, caressing the soft skin there before resting over her heart, where I could feel its rapid rhythm beneath my palm. Her whimpered response vibrated against my lips, and she shifted uneasily against me, her body still throbbing from the intensity of her climax.

I picked her up and placed her on the bed. My fingers trailed down the valley between her breasts before cupping them gently. I marveled at their fullness, the weight of them in my hands as they spilled over my fingers. I caught one hard nipple between my thumb and forefinger, rubbing it lightly to tease a soft cry from her lips. She pressed her chest harder against my hand.

"Mason," she pleaded, the sound dragging out of her throat in a low moan.

I fucking loved the sounds she made. My free hand trailed lower until my fingers found her opening. She was warm and wet and ready. Her hips bucked against my hand as I slipped a finger inside. She gasped, and I added another finger. Her legs spread wider for me without any prompting, inviting me to delve deeper.

"Such a greedy girl."

I finger-fucked her with a rhythm that had her writhing underneath me. I watched her beautiful face, captivated by the way she looked so relaxed, so blissed out. Her eyes locked on mine, and I saw the moment she realized I was watching her. Her breath hitched, and her pulse sped up. Without breaking eye contact, she reached out, her delicate hand tracing down my torso and under my waistband. Then my sweet little princess wrapped her hand around my cock. She started slowly, mirroring the pace I was setting inside of her.

Her touch was hesitant at first, fingers lightly stroking me as she watched my face closely for any reaction. Then, her hand moved more confidently, exploring every inch of me with a curious touch that had me fighting back a groan. She twisted her wrist slightly, her fingertips tracing light circles over my sensitive head before taking a firmer hold. She pumped her hand faster, and I increased the pace of my thrusting fingers. My thumb swirled around her clit. She gasped, and her grip tightened on me in response. Her eyes went wide and unblinking, her gaze never leaving mine as she watched my face.

"Fuck," I hissed through gritted teeth, struggling to keep control of my body.

She grinned wickedly up at me, and I almost came right then.

I added another finger, and leaned down and kissed her. Our bodies rocked in perfect harmony to our shared rhythm. It was intoxicating. I could feel the tremor growing within me, a tight coil ready to explode. The sensation was electrifying, coursing through my veins like wildfire. Her inner walls clenched tightly around me as her body arched into me.

"Mason," she all but screamed, her voice high and desperate.

I felt her tighten around me once more, and with a shudder that rocked her whole body, she came apart beneath me. The sight of her, the sound of my name on her lips in that moment of absolute bliss, was enough to push me over the edge. I groaned low and deep as my own release exploded. My vision blurred, and my muscles tightened. Every nerve ending in my body lit up like a fucking Christmas tree; the pleasure was so intense it was almost painful. Her eyes were still locked onto mine, wide and full of unadulterated pleasure as we rode our joint orgasms out together. And I watched every flicker of emotion cross her face, knowing I was the fucking one who put it there.

CHAPTER FORTY-THREE

SHYA

I felt so relaxed; my muscles were like liquid beneath Mason. My fingers relaxed their grip on him, and I traced lazy circles over his beautiful abs as he brushed back my hair from my face and kissed my forehead lightly.

"Princess?"

"Mmmmm?" I could definitely get used to feeling this way.

"Don't go through with the mating ceremony," Mason said softly. And my whole body went stiff.

He had to go and ruin it, didn't he?

"Mason—"

"Don't. Don't fucking talk to me about responsibility and duty when my fingers are still wet from you coming all over them."

Did he really just say that to me? How the hell did he get away with talking like that all the time?

I pushed him off of me and jumped to my feet. "What do you want me to say, Mason? That I'll give up everything, leave my family, and Pack when they need me the most ... and what? Come live with you in Three Rivers? I've trained to be an Alpha my entire life. What do you expect me to do there?"

"I don't fucking know!" he admitted as he buttoned up his pants. "You can do whatever you want; we can work that out together. But that's the key, we do it to-fucking-gether."

"What if what I want is to be the Alpha?"

"Do you?"

I blinked, not expecting him to ask me that. No one had ever asked me that. I had never asked myself that; had always just assumed that it was what I would do.

I sank down onto the bed. "I don't know, Mason," I said, my voice husky. The weight of expectation, of duty, seemed to press down on me, making it hard to breathe. I closed my eyes, remembering the countless hours of training, the lessons in Pack politics, my father's hand on my shoulder as he told me how proud he was of me. "It's all I've ever known. It's what I've trained for."

I could see the faces of my Pack members in my mind. This wasn't just about Henry and Tucker. It was about Marnie and Summer, Danni and Ivan, Ethan and Due-lah. How could I turn my back on them now, when threats lurked at our borders, and uncertainty plagued our future?

I opened my eyes to find Mason staring intently at me.

"I never thought I had any choice, but right now, my family needs me. I can't abandon them. It's not in me, Mason. It's just not."

He studied me for a beat, and I couldn't tell what he was thinking. Then he sat down next to me, our knees brushing against each other. I leaned into him, my head resting on his shoulder. For a moment, we just sat there in silence.

Finally, he spoke. "Then I'll leave the Three Rivers Pack. I'll come here."

I stared at Mason, my heart pounding so hard I was sure he could hear it. His words echoed in my mind, a siren song of possibility and passion. For a moment, I allowed myself to imagine it—a life with Mason here, doing what I was born to do.

"Do you even want to be an Alpha of a Pack? Do you realize what's involved? How this would completely change your life?"

"I'm a quick learner, princess."

I looked into Mason's eyes and felt a yearning so deep it frightened me. This connection between us, this pull—it was unlike anything I'd ever experienced. But was it real? What if I made him leave everything for me, and this thing between us was just a temporary attraction to the hot bad boy from the next town? Could I do that to him? He would hate me forever. I would hate myself forever.

What if I chose duty over desire? The thought of mating with Edmond, of living a life dictated by obligation rather than love, made my stomach churn. But could I live with myself if I chose my own happiness over the safety and well-being of my Pack, over the safety and well-being of Mason?

"Being here means giving up everything you've ever known to be the Alpha of the Bridgetown Pack with me. It will be dangerous, Mason. Edmond is already accepted. You? They won't accept you. Not easily. We'll be challenged for at least the first six months, and they'll all be challenges to the death."

"I'll handle the challenges, princess."

I shook my head, frustration building. "You don't understand. This isn't just about physical challenges. It's about politics, traditions. We do this, and we're changing how we've done things for hundreds of years. They'll fight us every step of the way."

"Then help me understand, Shya. What exactly are we up against?"

I took a deep breath. "First, there's the issue of legitimacy. You're not from our Pack. Many will see you as an outsider trying to usurp power."

Mason's brow furrowed. "Okay, so we'd need to prove my loyalty. What else?"

"The internal politics. Every decision you make would be scrutinized. Many will resist any changes we try to make simply because the order came from you, and one wrong move could turn the entire Pack against you."

Mason was quiet for a moment, absorbing all this. "It sounds like a political minefield. And if I get it wrong, they'll turn against you for choosing me."

I nodded. "Yes. By choosing you, I'd be risking everything—my position, my family's legacy, the Pack's stability. I'm opening the whole Pack up to even more infighting, which outsiders would try to take advantage of. Just when this Pack needs stability the most, we'd be throwing the doors open to chaos. It's not just about us, Mason. It's about the lives of everyone here, and your life, as you know it, would be over. If you take the place Edmond is supposed to have, you'd be coming into a Pack that hates you, doesn't trust you, and wants you dead." I couldn't do that to him. "Mating with Edmond is for the best, Mason. Can't you see that?"

He stared at the wall, his face lost in thought. "I'll have to win them over, then. Do something for this Pack that is irrefutable."

He turned to me, cupped my head roughly, and kissed the living daylights out of me, his lips determined and delicious against mine.

Okay, wow!

"I promise you, I'll prove myself worthy to be your mate, to be the Alpha here."

"Mason," I whispered. "I don't want you to put yourself in danger for me. I can't lose you, too."

He stared deep into my eyes. "Don't worry about me, princess. You're my mate. My reason for breathing. My heart, my soul, my everything. I'd tear down mountains, challenge the Goddesses themselves, and walk through the fires of hell to keep you safe and by my side. There's no force in this world or any other that could keep me from you. I'm yours, completely and utterly, until my last breath and beyond."

I steeled my heart, knowing that was the most romantic thing I would ever hear. There would be no sweet words or passionate declarations from Edmond.

"I'm still going through with the ceremony."

He grinned again. "No, you're not. But it's cute that you think you are."

The cocky bastard kissed me one more time, then he ran, leaped, and slid feet-first out of the window. At the last second, his hand reached out and grabbed the sill, holding himself in place. "I like that you can use your knife but tell Edmond he needs to increase the patrols again. It's way too easy to break in."

Then he dropped out of sight.

CHAPTER FORTY-FOUR

MASON

I dropped silently to the ground as the cool night air rushed against my skin, carrying with it a complex tapestry of scents. The manicured lawn of the Alpha House's garden offered a subtle green fragrance, mingling with the sweeter notes of night-blooming flowers. But beyond that, the unmistakable smell of town life permeated the air.

A figure emerged from the shadows, and my muscles tensed instinctively. Camille. The moonlight filtering through the canopy cast harsh shadows across her face, accentuating the lines of grief and anger etched deep into her features. She walked rigidly, her shoulders tense and squared, as if bracing for a fight. Her hands were clenched at her sides, knuckles white with strain, and there was a fierce, almost feral energy about her. Her lips were pressed into a thin, unforgiving line as she fixed me with a look that could have frozen fire. In that moment, I realized just how formidable an opponent she could be. My wolf stirred, recognizing a potential threat, but I pushed him down. This wasn't about dominance or territory. This was about Shya, about love, about doing what was right. And this was a woman pushed to her limits, teetering on the edge of desperation. The Camille I knew—the strong, intelligent Alpha, the proud mother—was barely recognizable beneath this hard, unyielding exterior.

"Mason." Camille's voice was cold. She took a step forward, her eyes never leaving mine. "I thought I made it clear you weren't welcome here anymore."

I shrugged, meeting her gaze with my own. "I needed to see Shya."

Her lips thinned even more, disapproval radiating from every pore, though whether it was from me refusing to lower my eyes or the fact that I had seen Shya, I didn't know and didn't give a holy fuck.

"My daughter is no longer your concern. You need to leave, Mason. Shya has responsibilities to this Pack. A duty to fulfill."

The word "duty" ignited a spark of anger in my chest. How many times had I heard that word used to justify what they were doing to Shya?

I took a step toward Camille. "That's some fucked up bullshit, and you know it. Her duty? Forcing her into a false mating for the sake of Pack politics?"

Camille's eyes flashed dangerously, a low growl rumbling in her chest. "Watch your tone, Mason," she warned. "You don't understand—"

"No," I cut her off, taking a step closer. The anger within me surged, but I kept a tight rein on my control. "I understand perfectly. You're locking her in a relationship that will slowly eat away at her."

The thought of her stuck in a relationship with someone who didn't see the real her, the wild and free and strong and confident her, made my chest ache.

"Tying her to Edmond, to anyone who isn't her true fated mate, will kill her day by day. You're sacrificing your daughter's happiness for your own agenda."

Camille's face contorted with a mix of anger and pain. Her eyes, so like Shya's, flashed with a dangerous light. "How dare you! How dare you presume to know our family? Shya's bloodline has ruled here for the last two hundred years. This is what she has been molded for since she was born." Her voice dropped, taking on a tone of reverence and determination. "She knows she must do whatever is needed to secure this Pack against all threats. Her happiness is secondary."

I shook my head, rage bubbling up at how cruel parents could be. "If I had a child, their happiness would be my only concern." The wolf within me was snarling, demanding action, but I knew that violence wouldn't solve this.

When I spoke again, my voice was low and intense, each word deliberate. "What you're doing to Shya is no different from what Tristan did. You're just perpetuating the same cycle of abuse and control." I watched as Camille's eyes widened, shock replacing anger for a moment. But I pressed on, knowing I had to make her understand. "You claim to love her, but you're stripping away her choices, her freedom. Just like Tristan did. You're using your authority to force her into a situation she doesn't want while ignoring her feelings and desires. That's not love, Camille. That's control."

I took another step closer, my voice dropping to a near-whisper. "You saw what Tristan's manipulation did to her. He and his pet witch took her mind apart piece by piece. And now you're doing the same thing, all in the name of duty and tradition. You're teaching her that her own happiness doesn't matter, that she exists only to serve others' needs."

She took a step back as if I'd physically struck her.

"You're wrong—" she started, but I wasn't finished.

"Am I?" I challenged, my voice softening slightly. "Camille, I know you're hurting. I know you've lost so much. But ask yourself, truly ask yourself: if you love Shya, how can you do this to her?"

Camille's face crumpled, the mask of anger giving way to raw pain. For a moment, I saw the grieving mother beneath the Alpha face.

"She's our future," she whispered, her voice breaking. "With Tristan out there, she will always be vulnerable. Always be at risk. Mating with Edmond will secure her place. I'm trying to protect all my children. I'm trying to protect her."

I shook my head. "By crushing her spirit? By denying her the chance at true happiness?" I took a deep breath. "If you really love her, you'll let her make her own choices. Even if that means going against Pack traditions. Even if it means letting her be with me. Letting us rule together."

Camille's eyes flashed with a mix of emotions—anger, fear. "You honestly think you can replace Michael? That you, above all of our own people, can rule here?"

"Yes," I said simply. Of that, I had no doubt. I held her shocked gaze for a moment, then turned and walked away.

She was right about one thing. Shya would never be safe while Tristan was still out there. And I knew just what to do about that.

CHAPTER FORTY-FIVE

MASON

My eyes scanned the forest terrain constantly, searching for any sign of Tristan or his Pack. I could sense Derek and Sam flanking me, their movements as familiar to me as my own after years of working together. The sound of AJ's footsteps brought up the rear, while Milly's almost silent tread put her just ahead of him.

Ronnie's call from that morning replayed in my mind. His tip about a possible campsite in this area had been our first solid lead, even though he had given it to the Bridgetown Pack as well. I had finished the call to find Waylen in front of me, holding a piece of paper, the triumphant look on his face falling. The language he used about Ronnie beating him to the location by two minutes was enough to make even Derek blush.

"Anything?" Derek's low voice broke into my thoughts.

I shook my head. "Not yet, but we're close."

It was another half hour before we reached the clearing. It was roughly circular, about thirty feet in diameter, surrounded by towering pines and thick underbrush. In the center, a makeshift fire pit had been made using a ring of stones, probably gathered from the nearby creek, which I could hear gurgling softly in the distance.

Around the fire pit, the ground was bare and compacted, evidence of recent activity. Distinct areas were flattened where tents had stood, the grass still bent and struggling to right itself. Scattered around these areas were small personal items left behind—a dirty sock, a broken comb, an empty water bottle.

To one side of the clearing, a crude lean-to had been constructed using fallen branches and what looked like a tarp.

I breathed in deeply, logging the lingering scents of unwashed bodies, fresh animal kills, cooked food, and the acrid smell of cigarette smoke. Overlaying it all was the unmistakable musk of werewolf—a Pack had definitely been here.

Sam crouched down near the fire pit, holding his hand above it. "The embers are still warm."

We were on the right track, thanks to Ronnie, but we had just missed them.

I nodded, my eyes still scanning the area. Near the edge of the clearing, I spotted several sets of footprints leading off into the forest. They were fresh, the edges still sharp in the soft earth.

"They left in a hurry," Milly observed. "You think they got a tip-off we were coming?"

Before I could answer, AJ called from inside the forest. "Over here. I've got tracks leading north."

I headed toward him as my phone vibrated in my pocket. I pulled it out to see the screen lit up with Waylen's name.

"Mason," Waylen's voice crackled through the speaker, urgency clear in his tone. "We've got movement at the camp where they were holding Shya."

I put the call on speaker so the others could hear. "What kind of movement?"

"As ordered, we've been keeping tabs on that campsite ever since you found Shya. I set up some motion sensor cameras, real discreet-like, and I send a high-level drone over it every day. I got pings on all my cameras about twenty minutes ago. We can't get a visual of who's inside yet, but there's definite activity. Carlito is on his way to see if he can verify who's there."

"It could be Tristan," Milly said.

"Or it could be a trap," Sam countered, his tone grim.

I rolled a squash ball between my fingers, weighing our options. The fresh trail from this campsite beckoned, luring me with the possibility that it would lead us to Tristan. But the activity at the other camp couldn't be ignored. If Waylen was right, they were probably there to pick up anything they left behind or scout if it was being watched. They wouldn't stay long, especially if they found any of Waylen's cameras.

"What's our move, Mason?" Derek asked.

I took a deep breath, knowing that whatever decision I made could change everything.

"We head to the other camp. We might get lucky, and Tristan will be with them. If not, we might be able to capture one of them, see what they have to say."

I took one last lingering look north at the trail left by the people who had been here, then turned south. As I did, though, a scent caught my attention. I held up a hand, halting the group, and tilted my head slightly, focusing my senses.

"We're not alone," I whispered, my eyes scanning the treeline.

Derek and Sam immediately tensed, ready for action. AJ's massive frame shifted slightly, positioning himself to protect the others. Milly's eyes narrowed as she scanned our surroundings.

I twirled my forefinger in a circle, indicating we should spread out and encircle the area. We moved with practiced stealth, each of us taking a different approach. Derek and Sam flanked left and right while AJ and Milly covered the rear. I took point, then caught a fleeting glimpse of movement behind a large oak tree. I signaled the others, then crept forward slowly. The scent grew stronger—definitely a werewolf and female.

Suddenly, a twig snapped under AJ's foot. He froze. Fucking bear Shifters, they could never get the hang of being stealthy. Almost immediately, a blur of motion erupted from behind the tree as our target made a run for it.

"There!" I shouted, abandoning stealth for speed.

The chase was on. The werewolf, in human form, was fast, weaving between trees and leaping over fallen logs with grace. But I was faster. I could hear the others spreading out, trying to cut off her escape routes.

I was closing the gap when she suddenly pivoted, using a tree trunk as leverage to change direction.

"Milly! Left!" I yelled.

Milly appeared from between the trees, forcing our prey to veer right—straight into Derek's path. The female werewolf skidded to a halt, realizing she was surrounded.

Her eyes darted around, searching for an escape. Then, with a snarl, she lunged at Milly, clearly seeing her as the weakest link. It was a mistake.

Milly side-stepped her attack and drove her elbow into the back of our target, using her momentum to throw her off balance. I seized the opportunity, tackling her mid-stumble. We hit the ground hard, rolling through the underbrush.

She fought like a wildcat, clawing and biting. Her elbow caught me in the ribs, forcing out a grunt of pain. I managed to keep my grip, using my greater strength to pin her arms. Then AJ's massive hands appeared, helping to secure her flailing legs. Even then, she continued to struggle, her eyes blazing with defiance.

As we pulled her to her feet, I got my first good look at our captive. She was petite, with long, dark hair, now disheveled from the struggle, cascading down her back in loose waves.

Her delicate features were contorted in anger.

"Let me the fuck go!"

"What's your name?" I replied calmly.

She lifted her chin, a sneer curling those full lips. "Lena. And you're making a big mistake."

"Really? I think you'll find the mistake is yours, Lena," Milly retorted, stepping forward. "You allowed yourself to get caught."

Lena's eyes flickered to Milly and widened. "You! You're a fucking traitor, Milly! I should kill you where you stand."

"Do try to be a bit original, Lena. I heard that from the whole Pack. You still running with Tristan?"

Lena glared at Milly, and her lip curled in disgust. "Of course I am! I'm not scum like you. I don't abandon my Pack."

Milly took a step forward, her face a mix of disbelief and frustration.

"Abandoned? I escaped, Lena. I thought you, of all people, would have seen through Tristan's lies by now."

"The only liar here is you," Lena snarled. "You turned your back on everything we stand for. Everything Tristan taught us."

"Fuck Tristan! Fuck him and his lies!" Milly countered, her voice rising. "Can't you see through the bullshit he spouts? The way he treats women, the things he makes us do—"

Lena's eyes blazed. "I do what he wants, what he needs, willingly, Milly! I'm finally part of something bigger than myself. We're going to change the future for all Shifters, so what does it matter who does what? We all have our roles to play. None of you fuckers will ever understand that. You can't stop Tristan or his movement. There's a change coming, and I'm going to be at the forefront of it."

"A change?" I interjected, trying to keep her talking.

"A revolution," Lena declared. "We're going to take back control, and afterward, the world will be better; werewolves will finally be where we belong."

Milly scoffed, her voice dripping with disdain. "You mean with male werewolves on top? That's part of Tristan's vision, too, isn't it? The males don't want to share that top spot with females."

"Maybe that's for the best. You ever think of that? I feel sorry for you, Milly. Always trying to be something you're not instead of embracing the good you can do if you just accept your place. Females weren't built for the same things as the males. We should be proud of that fact. Our job is to support our males, do whatever it takes to make sure they come out on top."

"Listen to yourself," Milly pleaded, her voice softer now. "This isn't you, Lena. This can't be what you dreamed of when you were younger."

Lena's face hardened. "You know fuck all about my life. You're the scum that left, remember? I don't see anyone else lining up to take care of me. Tristan and his Pack do. They're my family, and we're going to achieve something amazing."

"Yeah? And where are they now?" I asked. "It looks to me like they abandoned you here."

Her eyes swung to mine, and she raised her chin. "I was sent to watch. To make sure the last of us to leave weren't going to be followed."

"Followed?" Sam asked, his brow furrowed. He was probably wondering the same thing Milly had earlier: had they received a tip-off we were coming, or were these just their usual precautions?

"You think we're not one step ahead of you at all times? We know what you're going to do before you even do it! Tristan will reward me. I did my job; I distracted you. Hell, I still am distracting you." Lena laughed, her joy in doing good for Tristan all over her face. "They'll be long gone by now."

I eyed AJ and Milly. Ronnie had tipped both us and the Bridgetown Pack off about this site. If Lena was telling the truth, one of us had a mole.

"What were you all doing here, Lena?" I pressed, hoping she might reveal more. "What's Tristan's endgame?"

Lena's eyes glittered with pride and defiance. "You think I'd tell you anything that could harm our cause?"

"Your cause?" Derek scoffed. "You mean Tristan's cause? He must be laughing his ass off; you know that, right? He's got you so brainwashed, he's got you believing that you're not worth the ground he walks on. That all females are worthless. He's using you; can't you see that?"

"No," Lena snarled. "You're the ones who can't see. Tristan has

282

a vision for our future. Just because my part is different, doesn't make it any less important. We're all working toward a future where werewolves no longer hide in the shadows."

I could feel we were getting close to something important. "And how does he plan to achieve this vision?"

Lena's face twisted into a cruel smile. "By any means necessary. The humans will fall, and the strong will rise. That's the natural order of things."

"Natural order?" Sam interjected, disgust evident in his voice. "There's nothing natural about what Tristan's planning."

"You're all so blind. Reality has a way of punching you in the face, doesn't it? And I can't wait for when it hits you. The reality is that Tristan's vision is the only way forward for our kind."

"Forward to what?" I demanded. "What exactly is Tristan planning?"

A smug smile played across Lena's lips. "You'll see soon enough. You'll be too late to stop it, as usual. When everyone is distracted, Tristan will strike. He'll take the mate the Goddess saved for him and kill them all, every last one. And from the ashes of the old order, we'll build a new world."

When everyone was distracted.

The mating ceremony.

Fuck!

And Tristan wasn't just planning to disrupt the ceremony—he was planning a massacre.

Chapter Forty-Six

SHYA

I sat on my bed and stared at the shoes Edmond had bought me for the mating ceremony. Pale pink Dolce & Gabbana Bellucci pumps with a lace-covered mesh and crystal brooch. They were gorgeous, even in their box. So far, I had refused to take them out. I felt like as soon as I did, it would make it all real. It would be me admitting that there was no going back. When I picked them up, I would be mating with Edmond.

A soft knock at the door interrupted my thoughts. Before I could answer, the door creaked open, and two familiar heads poked in.

"Shya?" Henry's voice was quiet and hesitant. "Can we come in?"

Without waiting for my answer, Tucker ducked under Henry's arm, his eyes wide with excitement. "Of course we can come in!" he declared, grinning. "Shya would never keep us out, not even on her mating day!"

"Oh, really?" I put on my most stern face and arched an eyebrow at him. He hesitated, one foot raised, until I winked at him. "Get in here, both of you, before someone sees you."

Tucker bounded into the room while Henry followed more

sedately, closing the door quietly behind them.

"Wow, Shya! In this dress, you'll look like a proper queen!" Tucker exclaimed, his eyes fixed on my ceremonial dress hanging on the wardrobe. It was the one Mom had used for her mating ceremony with Dad.

Henry's eyes, however, were on me. "Are you okay? Shouldn't you be dressed by now?"

I forced a smile. "I'm fine. Just running a little late."

"That's okay," Tucker climbed onto the bed beside me, his small frame vibrating with barely contained energy. "I watch movies. The female is supposed to be late. It's expected."

I smiled at him. "Well, that's good for me, I guess. What are you even doing here, anyway? I would have thought Mom had you busy with the preparations."

"We came to talk to you about something," Henry said softly.

"No, we came to tell you important things," Tucker said, his voice dropping to what he probably thought was a conspiratorial whisper.

I looked between my brothers, curiosity piqued. "Alright, what do you need to tell me?"

Tucker's face grew serious, all trace of childish excitement gone. "It's about Mason and Edmond."

Uh-oh. I did not like where this was going. "What about them?"

Henry sat down on my other side, his movements careful and composed. "We've been watching, Shya. Watching them. Watching you."

Tucker nodded, his small face set in a frown. "Edmond isn't right for you. He won't make you happy. He doesn't act like a true mate should."

I felt a lump forming in my throat. "It's not that simple, guys. The Pack—"

"It is that simple," Tucker interrupted. "A real mate should do anything for you. Edmond didn't do that."

Henry placed a hand on my arm. "When you were taken, Mason was desperate to find you. He came here and nearly started a war between our Packs when Mom tried to kick him out. When he realized he wasn't going to get any coordinated help from here, he looked for you on his own. He didn't stop."

I swallowed hard.

Henry's eyes darkened slightly. "Edmond ... we know he has other skills. He organized things from here. He sent others out looking, but he didn't go himself. He said it was more efficient that way."

It didn't surprise me. That was exactly how I would have expected Edmond to react.

Tucker scoffed. "That's not what you need in a mate. He's like a cyborg—Edborg, with no feelings. You need someone who will fight for you, no matter what."

I looked down at the shoebox in my lap. "It doesn't change anything. It's too late."

"It's never too late to do the right thing," Henry said, his voice soft but firm. "Dad always said that, remember?"

"Dad wanted me to mate with Edmond."

"Dad didn't see Mason when you were taken. He would have changed his mind. I know he would have."

Tucker stood up. "Mason swore he'd find you or die trying. You deserve that."

I looked at my brothers, feeling a surge of love for them both. They were trying to protect me in their own ways. "The ceremony is still happening."

Tucker's young face scrunched in confusion. "But you love Mason."

I felt a pang in my chest at his words. "It's not that simple, Tucker. Love isn't always enough."

Henry's hand tightened on my arm. "This is about the Pack, isn't it? About trying to stabilize it after ...?" He trailed off, his eyes reflecting a wisdom beyond his years.

I nodded, always amazed by Henry's perceptiveness. "Edmond is the safe choice. The one the Pack will accept without question. With Mason ... we would be opening ourselves up to challenges, both from inside the Pack and out."

Tucker's voice dropped to a whisper. "Is this about the people talking about inviting Tristan back?"

I felt my blood run cold. "How do you know about that?"

Tucker shrugged. "People don't see me. Ninja Tucker, remember? And when they do, all they see is a kid, not someone who might understand what they're saying, even if they do try and say it in code."

I smiled sadly at him, feeling my heart ache for the little boy who'd had to hear his own Pack talk about welcoming back the one who killed his father. "Yes, Tucker. That's part of it. The Pack longs for a strong leader. Leaders protect us and guide us. Under a strong leader, we are all safe, and life is stable; there is food, there are jobs, there is medicine and education for all—all of us thrive. I need to mate with Edmond to show we still have strong leaders here."

"I don't get it. They're saying it because they see Mom as weak, right? They want you to take over, and they want Tristan as your mate not the Edborg, because the Pack thinks Tristan used to be one of us, that he has proved himself to be a strong leader, and that's what we need?"

I nodded. "He is a strong leader, and we are at war with him. If we invited Tristan back to be Alpha with me, the war would end. We would have one less enemy to worry about. But everyone has a choice, Tucker. You have to ask yourself if he is someone worth giving your allegiance to. He is strong, yes, but what does he stand for? Is he going to make life better for everyone or only for those he thinks are worthy? Will he bring a Pack together or splinter it, pitting those he says deserve to be rewarded against those he says don't? I'm sure it will be great if he decides you are worthy. But will you stand by and watch as he treats those more vulnerable than you like they are worse than rats? And if you did, what sort of person does that make you? We all crave strong leadership, Tucker, that's who we are, but I would choose chaos and war every time over bowing down to a person like Tristan, and I would die before I let my family be ruled by him."

"You could run?" Henry suggested. "Go with Mason; start a new life somewhere else."

I looked at him. As our eyes met, I saw the exact moment Henry understood.

"You're doing this for us!" He looked horrified. "If you ran, I'd be next in line. You think I'm not a match for Tristan. You think he'll kill me and then Tuck. You're staying for us. You're mating with Edmond to protect us!"

Tucker blinked up at me, his young face colored by shock and dawning comprehension.

"I'm doing it to protect all of us, Henry," I said softly.

"But, Shya," Tucker's voice was small, "what about your happiness?"

"Being a strong leader isn't about brute strength. It's about understanding the needs of everyone and working to make life better for all; it means putting others before yourself. And right now, keeping you both safe ... that's what matters most."

Henry's eyes glistened with unshed tears. "We never asked for this sacrifice."

"It's not a sacrifice," I lied.

"I won't allow it!" Tucker jumped back on the bed with one finger pointed at me. I almost laughed at the stern expression on his face. "You mate with any one you want. You want Mason, you take Mason. You want to be single, I'll make them all disappear! Me and Henry will kick their butts. You just wait and see!"

Goddess, I loved my brothers so much. I'd do anything for them. "I want to mate with Edmond, Tuck. It's the best thing for everyone."

Tucker deflated before my eyes, his shoulders slumping as he stepped off the bed.

"Well, that sucks. I guess I have to put on the horrid jacket Mom got me, then."

I smiled softly at him. "I guess so. Don't worry about me. I'll make sure I'm happy, I promise. I'll see you both there, okay?"

They left the room together, Henry glancing sadly back at me as he said, "You know, Dad also said one more thing. He said a great leader always carves her own path." Then he closed the door.

I took a deep breath, picked up the shoes, and slipped them on.

CHAPTER FORTY-SEVEN

SHYA

The ceremony began as twilight descended, the new moon rising in the sky like a silver sickle. Its ethereal light bathed the grove, casting long shadows that danced among the ancient trees. The air thrummed with anticipation as I stood at the edge of the grove, my heart pounding. The sky-blue ceremonial dress felt too tight, too restrictive. I took a deep breath, trying to steel myself for what was to come. This was it. If Mom was right, the fated mate bond with Edmond would snap into place soon.

I reached inside me for my wolf, but she just stretched and went back to sleep.

Okay. Not exactly the reaction I was hoping for.

Bridgetown—humans and Shifters—had arranged themselves in six concentric circles, each leaving a small gap for me to pass through. The chanting that had begun half an hour ago swelled around me, a living, breathing thing.

I stepped through the gap in the outermost circle, the voices of those furthest from the center a low, steady hum. As I walked along the perimeter of the fifth circle, searching for the next gap, the chanting

290

grew slightly louder. Eyes followed my every move.

With each circle I entered, the voices grew stronger, the melody more intricate. By the time I reached the third circle, the sound vibrated through my bones, seeming to pulse with my very heartbeat. I caught glimpses of familiar faces as I walked. There was Marnie, her eyes shining with unshed tears. Summer, beaming with what looked like pride. Danni watched me with a solemn expression. As I reached the final circle, my eyes found Henry. His face was a mask of concern, his eyes far too knowing. He was turning into a man, no longer the sheltered, sweet teenager I'd known.

The chanting reached a fever pitch, a crescendo of sound that filled the grove and seemed to touch the very stars above. As I stepped into the center where Edmond waited, the harmony peaked in a note so pure it brought tears to my eyes, and then everyone fell silent. The sudden quiet was deafening after the overwhelming sound, and in it, I could hear my own heartbeat, loud in my ears, as I turned to face my future. Edmond's face set in a neutral expression, and he turned to me. Garrett, standing behind Edmond, winked.

Brilliant. As if I didn't need the reminder that I was tying myself not just to Edmond but to his brother.

I walked forward, coming to a stop next to Edmond.

"We now call upon the representatives of each family to present their ancestral totems," Mom's voice rang out.

Garrett stepped forward, holding a beautifully carved wooden wolf. Its eyes seemed to gleam in the moonlight as he placed it on the altar before us. "I present the totem of the D'estry," he said, his voice ringing out clear and strong. "May it symbolize the strength and unity we bring to this union."

Henry approached next, his young face solemn as he carried our family's totem. It was an intricate carving of an oak tree, its branches spreading wide. "I present the totem of the Little family," he said, his voice only wavering slightly. "May it represent the deep roots and enduring legacy we offer."

As the two totems sat side by side on the altar, I felt a pang in my chest. This was really happening. Two Packs, two families, joining together through Edmond and me.

I tried to focus on the ceremony, on Edmond standing beside me, but Mason's face kept popping in my head. His intense blue eyes that seemed to see right through me, the way his hair felt when I ran my fingers through it, the intricate tattoos that snaked up his right arm. I could almost feel the warmth of his muscular body, the strength as his arms pulled me close. And the way he talked to me. I was a Pack princess, but he didn't give a shit about that. No, he was crass and explicit and honest, and it drew me in like a magnet.

I shook my head, trying to clear it. I couldn't think about him now. I had made my choice.

Inside, my wolf sat up, her ears pricked.

Mom's voice took on a rhythmic cadence. "We call upon the four elements to bless this union," she intoned. "Earth, to ground them in stability and abundance."

She sprinkled soil around our feet, and I felt a tremor run through me. But it wasn't the comforting connection to my Pack bonds I usually felt—it was something else, something unsettling.

"Air, to bring them clarity of thought and freedom of spirit."

As she waved incense around us, the scent making me dizzy, I found my gaze drifting to the edge of the circle. For a moment, I thought I saw Mason standing there, his eyes locked on mine. I blinked, and he was gone.

"Fire, to ignite their passion and light their way."

The flames of the ceremonial candles flickered, casting dancing shadows across Edmond's face. But instead of warmth, I felt a chill run through me.

"Water, to flow through their lives with adaptability and emotion."

As Mom sprinkled blessed water over our joined hands, I felt a rush of emotion—but not the one I was expecting to feel. Instead of a bond with Edmond, all I could feel was an overwhelming sense of wrongness. My wolf chuffed at me.

Silly pup, not listening to heart.

I thought you were asleep?

Want to be awake for what is coming.

I could feel her smugness, as if she knew something I didn't. And suddenly, with crystal clarity, I knew the connection I felt with Mason wasn't just love or a passing attraction. It was deeper, primal. He really was my fated mate. The realization hit me like a physical blow, leaving me breathless as my wolf howled with joy.

I stared at Edmond, panic rising in my chest. How could I have been so blind? How could I go through with this when my very soul was calling out for someone else?

I had spent my whole life trying to be the perfect daughter, the ideal future leader, always doing what my parents and the Pack expected of me. But in this moment, I understood that true leadership wasn't about following a predetermined path. It was about having the courage to forge your own way.

My wolf's words echoed in my mind: *Silly pup, not listening to heart.*

She was right. I had been foolish, ignoring what my heart—and my very soul—had been trying to tell me all along. A leader doesn't just do what others want; they do what's right, even when it's hard. They trust themselves, and they're strong enough to know that sometimes they need to lean on others. I'd let Tristan take that from me. He'd managed to tie me in so many knots that I didn't trust myself or my feelings. I had relied on others to guide me, even when I knew their path was wrong. I had pushed Mason away in the mistaken belief that isolating myself from the people who supported me when I needed it was the strong thing to do.

No more. It was time for me to take back control of my life. To take back control of me.

With that thought, a sense of calm settled over me. I knew what I had to do.

"Stop," I said, my voice ringing out clear and strong, cutting through the ceremonial chants. "I can't do this."

A collective gasp went through the assembled Pack members. My mother froze, the blessed water dripping from her fingertips. Edmond stared at me, his eyes wide with shock.

"I'm sorry," I continued, my voice growing stronger with each word. "But I can't go through with this mating."

"Shya!" Mom's voice was sharp, but I ignored her. I kicked off the delicate ceremonial shoes. They clattered on the stone altar, knocking over a candle. Then I turned and ran.

I sprinted through the gaps in the circles, Pack members too stunned to try to stop me. The forest welcomed me, branches seeming to part as I raced through them. Behind me, I could hear shouts of confusion and alarm, but I didn't look back.

I burst through the treeline onto the lawn in front of the Alpha House and skidded to a halt. There, idling on the road, was a red Aston Martin Vantage. And leaning against it, a grin on his face, was Tucker.

"Took you long enough," he said, throwing a set of keys up then catching them. "I knew you wouldn't wanna go through with it, so I got you a car. I stole it from Garrett." He gave me a wolfish grin. "Do you think he'll mind?"

He threw the keys up again and I caught them. "Tucker, you're my little ninja! How did you know?"

He shrugged, his eyes sparkling with barely contained excitement. "You're my big sister. No way were you gonna mate with that butthead. Now go before they catch up!"

I didn't need to be told twice. I jumped into the driver's seat, the ceremonial dress billowing around me as I slammed the door shut. The engine roared, and I spun the wheel, kicking up a cloud of dust as I accelerated down the road.

As the lights of the Alpha House faded in my rear-view mirror, I felt a blend of exhilaration and fear. I had no idea what would happen next, but I knew one thing for certain: for the first time in a long time, I felt truly alive.

Chapter Forty-Eight

SHYA

The Vantage roared beneath me, matching the thundering of my heart. The wind whipped through my hair, carrying away the last remnants of that damned ceremonial incense. I was finally completely in control.

I hadn't made it far when a figure appeared in my headlights, standing dead center in the road. My breath caught as I recognized the broad shoulders and dark hair.

Mason.

I slammed on the brakes, tires screaming in protest as the car skidded to a halt a foot from where he stood. Our eyes met through the windshield, and holy hell, it was like touching a live wire. My wolf howled inside me, urging me forward.

Time seemed to slow as I drank in the sight of him. I couldn't think straight, couldn't draw breath. All I could focus on was the way his lips parted slightly as if he was about to speak. Those lips that had haunted my dreams for so long, now so tantalizingly close.

Without thinking, I flung open the car door and sprinted toward him. We collided in a tangle of limbs and need, our lips crashing together in a kiss that set my world on fire. His arms wrapped around me, and his mouth claimed mine with a ferocity that stole my breath away, and I matched his intensity, pouring all my denied feelings into the kiss. Every nerve ending in my body seemed electrified by his touch. A growl rumbled deep in Mason's chest, the vibration sending shivers cascading through my flesh. It was a primal sound, one that spoke to the wolf within me, igniting an answering howl in my soul.

This. This was right. This was where I belonged. In Mason's arms, with his scent enveloping me, his taste on my lips. The rest of the world fell away, and all that existed was us, this moment, this connection that defied all reason and logic.

When we finally broke apart, gasping for air, I looked up into those pale blue eyes that seemed to see right through to my soul. In them, I saw a reflection of my own desire, my own need, my own love.

"Mason," I breathed, the words tumbling out. "It's you!"

Why? Why did I always have to state the obvious?

He smirked at me. "I would hope so, given your tongue has just been in my mouth."

"I mean, you're here."

"I told you I couldn't let you mate with anyone else."

"I didn't. I didn't go through with it."

His expression was so fucking knowing and smug. "I figured, what with the aforementioned tongue in my mouth."

"I don't know how we're going—"

"I'm giving up my Pack, princess. We'll stay here, protect your family, protect your—our—Pack, and I'll make them accept me even if I have to fight every single fucking one of them."

His words hit me like a tidal wave, washing away every doubt, every fear that had been clawing at my insides. Mason was willing to give up everything—his Pack, his position, his home—all for me. For us. In that moment, I saw our future unfold before my eyes. The challenges we'd face, the battles we'd fight—together. I saw lazy Sunday mornings and fierce Pack meetings, stolen kisses, and shoulder-to-shoulder stands against our enemies. I saw a life filled with love, adventure, and partnership.

My heart swelled, threatening to burst from my chest. The words I'd been holding back, the feelings I'd been too scared to fully embrace, suddenly seemed so simple, so right. Looking into his eyes, I knew there was only one thing left to say.

"I love you, Mason Shaw."

He grinned at me. "I know. I'm just glad you finally figured it out."

I drew back from him. "You're supposed to say you love me back!"

Mason's eyes sparkled with mischief. "Oh, am I? I must have missed that part in the 'How to Respond When Your Mate Finally Comes to Her Senses' handbook."

"I can't believe I love you! You're impossible!"

"Impossibly charming, you mean," he said, pulling me closer.

"Impossibly arrogant is more like it,"

"You know," Mason said, his voice dropping to a husky whisper, "for someone who just declared her love for me, you're being awfully sassy."

I leaned in, my lips brushing against his ear. "Get used to it, wolf boy. You're in for a lifetime of sass."

He shivered slightly at my touch, then pulled back to look me in the eye. His expression softened, all traces of teasing gone. "A lifetime, huh? I like the sound of that."

My heart skipped a beat. "Yeah?"

"Yeah," he said softly. Then, with a dramatic sigh, he added, "I suppose if I have to put up with your sass for the rest of my life, it's only fair you know I'm not giving you up, princess, not for anything or anyone. You're stuck with me from now on. I love you, too, even if you are an infuriating, beautiful, stubborn wolf."

I couldn't help the grin that spread across my face. "Was that so hard?"

"Excruciating," he deadpanned. "I may need mouth-to-mouth resuscitation to recover."

I laughed, feeling lighter than I had in weeks. "I don't care what we do, as long as we do it together."

"It's a good thing you feel that way, princess because we're about to be attacked by Tristan."

My heart, which had been soaring just moments ago, now plummeted to my stomach. "Tristan? How do you know?"

Mason's eyes hardened, his jaw clenching. "We met one of his Pack. They let it slip."

Fear gripped me, icy tendrils wrapping around my heart. "My family, the Pack, I have to warn them."

Mason shook his head. "There's a mole. Someone has been feeding Tristan information. You warn them, and Tristan will be in the wind."

As I stared into his eyes, something shifted inside me. The fear didn't disappear, but it transformed, igniting into a blazing anger. I would not allow Tristan to threaten my happiness, my Pack, my future.

"This is our chance to get him," I growled, my wolf rising to the surface. "We're going to end this. Tonight."

A predatory grin spread across Mason's face. "There's my princess."

Without hesitation, I tore the fastenings of my mating ceremony dress. The silk whispered against my skin as it fell away, pooling at my feet in a sea of blue. I stood before Mason, naked and unashamed, my skin prickling in the cool night air.

Mason's eyes roved over my body. "Shya?"

I met his gaze, feeling the power of my wolf surging through my veins. "I'm going hunting." I tilted my head to one side. "Think you can keep up?"

Then I closed my eyes, surrendering to the change. My bones shifted, realigning themselves, muscles rippled, and fur spread across my body. It was fast, fueled by my rage and the need to protect our Pack. When it was done, my wolf howled in anticipation.

Mason kneeled before me, running his hand through the thick fur at my neck. "You're breathtaking," he murmured.

I nuzzled his hand, then turned toward the forest. We had prey to find.

CHAPTER FORTY-NINE

MASON

T he streets of the town quickly gave way as we raced toward the forest's edge. Streetlights faded behind us, replaced by the soft glow of the moon overhead. As we hit the tree line, the world transformed. The forest was alive with whispers of the night. Moonlight filtered through the canopy of towering maples and oaks, their leaves rustling softly in the cool breeze. Stands of white pine and eastern hemlock added to the mix, their evergreen scent sharp and invigorating in the crisp air.

I ran silently, and beside me, Shya's wolf form moved with deadly grace. Her fur gleamed in the dim light, muscles rippling beneath her coat with each powerful stride.

I leaned in close to Shya. "Tristan will have been planning to hit after the ceremony when the Pack is most distracted with the celebrations. If his mole is still in contact, he'll know you left. He'll be reassessing right now."

Shya's ear twitched in acknowledgment, and she pressed further into the forest, her nose following a scent.

I tilted my head back and inhaled deeply.

Ah. She wanted to see who I'd brought with me.

As we went over a small rise, a cluster of familiar figures came into view.

Derek stood at the center of the group, his arms crossed over his broad chest. His eyes were alert and calculating, on a constant scan of the surroundings.

Flanking Derek were Sam and AJ, their faces wearing matching expressions of grim determination. Milly's petite frame was barely visible behind Derek, but her presence was undeniable. Her lean, muscular body was tense, ready to attack.

Jem and Esme stood slightly apart from the others, Jem standing protectively in front.

I felt Shya tense beside me.

"I brought help. Ryan and Mai wanted to come, but there's a situation in Three Rivers that they need to deal with."

Shya relaxed slightly as she moved toward them. Esme's face lit up as Shya got nearer. "Shya! Lookee at you. I saw your wolf once before, but I didn't realize just how pretty you are! I will be a beautiful wolf, too, one day. Mine will soar on the winds and—"

Jem coughed loudly, drowning out what Esme was saying, though I thought I heard something about tiny flailing pieces of ash, screaming in pain, but that couldn't be right.

"It is good to see you again, Shya," Jem said after he had finished coughing. "Esme and I are here to help in any way we can. Hopefully, we will end this today."

Esme bounced up and down on her heels, radiating excitement. "Oh, yes! You'll have our top level of help today. Not the tippy-toe careful help. No, not that. Today is for bold action. Jem told me. He's my brother, you know. And I've been practicing my magic. Though that's supposed to be hush-hushy. But I trust you all. Even Sam. He's the Wolf Council now, but his heart tells me things. He won't betray me to a horrid death."

Sam frowned, his eyes darting from Esme to Jem and back again.

"And I can do all sorts of magic—"

"Esme," Jem said gently. "Remember what we talked about? Careful with the details."

Esme's face fell slightly, but she nodded. "Yes, yes. I remember. Tippy-toe careful with details. But I was only telling what I can do, not that I do it." She placed a finger over her mouth, holding her lips shut. Then tried to speak around her finger. "See, I can do tippy-toe careful!"

Derek nodded to me. "We spotted Tristan's forces. They're positioning themselves upwind of the ceremony clearing."

Milly moved to stand beside Derek. "From what we could see, he's brought a small army with him."

"He must have brought most of his Pack. I counted at least two hundred."

"Two hundred and seventeen, to be exact," Milly replied. "I did a thorough count while we were scouting. And they're well-armed. I spotted quite a few with silver weapons. They came prepared for battle."

"Are they moving to attack?" I asked, feeling the tension ratchet up a notch.

AJ shook his head, his eyes never leaving the treeline. "Not yet. If we're quick, we might be able to get the drop on them before they can make their move on the Bridgetown Pack."

"We stick to the plan, then. Everyone know their roles?"

The others nodded.

I sensed Shya's doubt radiating off her in waves. Her green eyes darted between our small group and the direction of Tristan's forces. I knew what she was thinking—we were vastly outnumbered.

I smiled, a touch of mischief in my eyes. "We have a secret weapon they won't be expecting. Something that'll even the odds."

Shya tilted her head, then with a sharp huff, she turned and began trotting toward where Tristan's forces waited.

I pivoted to the others. "You heard the princess. Let's move out."

Chapter Fifty

SHYA

There were too many unfamiliar beings in the woods today—the forest had fallen silent; all the small creatures were in hiding. As I crept forward, my nose twitched, catching a whiff of something out of place. I slowed my pace, every muscle in my body tense as I followed the scent. It grew stronger with each step, a cocktail of aggression and anticipation that made my lips curl back from my teeth. Then, as I neared the crest of a small rise, I caught sight of movement through the trees.

At first, it was just a flicker—a shadow downwind passing between trunks, barely distinguishable from the swaying branches, but then I saw more. Bodies, low to the ground, slinking through the underbrush. Their movements were coordinated, purposeful. I could make out the sleek forms of wolves interspersed with the upright figures of those still in human form.

They moved like a dark tide through the forest, weaving between the trees with practiced stealth. Every now and then, moonlight would catch a glint of metal. I saw ears twitch, noses lift to scent the air, and eyes gleam with anticipation.

At the front of the group was Tristan. I shuddered, a mixture of fear and revulsion coursing through me. My heart rate spiked as dread, disgust, rage, all tangled up inside of me, each fighting for supremacy. My wolf snarled, thirsting for revenge, for justice. I could almost taste Tristan's blood on my tongue, could almost feel the satisfaction of ripping into the flesh of the man who had caused so much pain and destruction.

Then Mason was there, putting a warm hand on my back. My heart rate calmed slightly as I forced the rage back down. I couldn't attack now. I knew without a doubt if I did, Mason and the others would follow me, and I would be signing all our death warrants. No, I had to wait for Mason's secret weapon.

Ahead of me, Tristan raised a hand. As one, his Pack froze, becoming as still as the trees around them.

Tristan pointed one finger left, then right, signaling to his followers. They began to spread out, forming a wide arc that I knew would soon circle my Pack.

"It's time," Mason whispered as he turned to face the others behind us.

AJ's eyes darted between Mason and me, a question on his face. I could smell his uncertainty, his fear.

"I give you my word, AJ, we'll protect the Bridgetown Pack. We won't let you hurt them."

I whipped my head around. Had Mason lost his mind? Was he seriously about to unleash a crazed bear Shifter into these woods? There was no rational thought, no controlling AJ when he was in his bear form.

"Derek and Sam are going to flank AJ the whole time. They'll herd him. They'll make sure he only attacks Tristan's Pack."

I flicked my gaze to the twins and took in the look of resolve on both their faces.

We were vastly outnumbered. Mason was right. AJ would be able to go through Tristan's ranks and leave carnage in his wake. It was incredibly risky but right now it was our only chance.

I nodded. Immediately, Sam and Derek stripped off and started their Shifts.

AJ muttered something I couldn't catch, then closed his eyes. The air around him seemed to shimmer, and then his form began to change. It started slowly, almost imperceptibly. His skin rippled like water and then began to thicken, taking on a leathery texture. Suddenly, a low, rumbling growl emanated from deep within his chest, growing in volume as his body expanded.

The change accelerated. AJ's frame swelled, his muscles bulging and reshaping. Bones cracked and popped, elongating and thickening to support his massive new form. His fingers shortened, nails extending into wicked, curved claws.

Coarse, dark fur erupted from his skin in waves, starting from his spine and cascading down his body. His face contorted, his jaw jutting forward, teeth growing into fearsome fangs. His ears rounded and shifted position, and his nose flattened and widened into a broad muzzle.

Where AJ had stood moments before, now loomed a massive grizzly bear, easily twice the size of our largest wolves. His small, dark eyes glittered with a primal rage, and his nostrils flared as he scented the air. The sheer power radiating from him was incredible, wild and uncontained.

He swung his head around and glared at me. Mason moved, stepping in front of me as Derek darted in behind AJ, nipped at his back leg, then took off toward Tristan's forces. AJ twisted his body about and charged after Derek, Sam keeping pace with him on his left.

There was a solitary warning yell, then chaos erupted. Screams and howls filled the air, mingling with the sound of snapping branches and bodies hitting the forest floor.

Alright, then. My turn.

CHAPTER FIFTY-ONE

SHYA

I raced forward, teeth bared, claws digging into the soft earth. The scent of fear and blood filled the air as wolves were flung aside by AJ's enraged form. Bodies collided, snarls and yelps echoing through the trees. Then all thoughts disappeared as I slammed into a fleeing wolf. I ducked under a swinging claw, then countered with a bite to my attacker's flank. Blood filled my mouth as my teeth sank deep into their flesh. They yelped and twisted, trying to break free, but I held on, trying to drag him down. As we hit the ground, I released my grip and immediately lunged for his throat. He barely managed to roll away, scrambling to his feet with a snarl.

We circled each other, hackles raised, teeth bared. From the corner of my eye, I caught a flash of movement. Another wolf was charging at me from the side. Then Mason barreled into them, sending them flying in the opposite direction. I didn't hesitate; I pounced on my wolf attacker, my claws raking across his throat. He whimpered, dashed out of range, and then collapsed in a pool of blood.

A few yards away, I glimpsed Mason locked in his own fierce battle. He was poetry in motion as he faced off against three wolves. He ducked and weaved, his movements fluid and precise. One attacker lunged at him, but Mason side-stepped and whipped his hand out, grabbed the wolf's hind leg, and used the momentum to slam him into a nearby tree.

I didn't have time to get distracted. I spun around, narrowly avoiding a set of snapping jaws. I darted in, my teeth finding his soft underbelly. He howled in pain and ran for the trees.

Coward.

There was no time to catch my breath. Two werewolves in human form were sprinting toward me, trying to get away from AJ, both holding silver knives. I growled low in my throat, my muscles coiling, as the first one lunged, knife slashing through the air where my throat had been a moment before. I feinted left, then abruptly changed direction, throwing myself to the right. The silver blade whistled past my ear as I pivoted and launched myself at the attacker, my jaws aiming for his knife arm.

He jerked back, but not fast enough. My teeth grazed his forearm, drawing blood. He hissed in pain, his grip on the knife loosening. Seizing the opportunity, I clamped down harder and wrenched my head to the side, feeling tendons and muscle tear beneath my fangs.

The knife clattered to the ground, and I released his arm, ready to finish him off. But his partner had circled behind me, and I felt the sting of silver as his blade nicked my flank. I yelped, more in surprise than pain, and whirled to face him as I felt the knife slice across my hide. Then a weight slammed into my side. The first man had recovered, picked up the knife with his uninjured hand, and thrown himself at me. We rolled, a tangle of fur, limbs, and flashing silver. As we came to a stop, I found myself on top, pinning him down with my weight. His eyes widened in fear as I loomed over him. I didn't hesitate but ripped this throat out with one bite.

Before his partner could come at me, I charged forward. As he crouched to block me, I leaped high, sailing over his head. I twisted in mid-air, landing behind him. He half-turned and slashed with his knife, but my teeth found their mark on the back of his neck. He collapsed beneath me, screaming, more in terror than pain, as I drove him face-first into the ground. He went still under me, and I was up and off to face the next attacker.

Through the mayhem, I caught glimpses of AJ. He was a force of nature, his massive form leaving a wake of broken bodies wherever he went. Derek and Sam darted in and out, herding him toward the thickest clusters of enemies.

I had just killed another wolf when a chill shuddered through me, and I heard it. The chanting, soft and insidious, trying to weave its way inside my head. I turned my head and spotted a figure on the edge of the clearing—Tristan's witch.

He was shrouded in a black cloak that seemed to absorb the moonlight. His face was hidden in the depths of his hood, but I could feel his eyes on me.

The chanting in my head grew louder, a deep, resonant hum that seemed to vibrate through my very bones.

I shook my head, trying to clear it, but the chanting just got louder. Out of the corner of my eye, I saw Mason stumble, his movements becoming erratic. I looked left and saw Derek, Sam, Milly, and Jem all on their knees, clutching their heads.

Panic rose in my chest. I knew this feeling, this invasion of my mind. My wolf growled, pushing back against it. I couldn't go back under

Tristan's control, not now. I had no doubt that if the witch won this, I would end up mated to Tristan by dawn, Mason and his brothers dead. And without Derek and Sam to marshal AJ, the bear would tear into my Pack and family. I could feel the tendrils slipping through my defenses and wrapping around my mind, squeezing tight.

What was I doing? Why was I fighting Tristan? He was my true mate. He was a visionary. I should be protecting him, not attacking him. I felt a rush of guilt and shame. What had I done? I lay down on the ground and whimpered.

Stay alive. I will come for you.

My eyes fell on Mason. He was on his knees, one hand braced against the forest floor, the other holding his head. His face was screwed up in concentration and pain, and my heart jolted as I saw a wolf heading straight for him, teeth bared.

Stay alive. I will come for you.

Mason had said that in my dreams. He had kept his promise; he had come for me. I would not let him down. The chanting faltered for a second, then came back, stronger this time.

No! I would not be a puppet again.

I stood up, one limb at a time. It was so fucking hard. Like I was encased in compacted mud and was trying to break free.

Stay alive. I will come for you.

I'm coming for you, baby.

I had broken free before; I could do it again. My wolf slammed into the front of my mind, howling with rage, and I pulled free. A loud snap echoed in my head, but I didn't have time to think. I took a running jump and leaped over Mason. I sailed through the air, my body a taut line of fur and muscle. Time seemed to slow as I arced over

Mason, my eyes locked on the charging wolf, and I used every ounce of my strength and momentum to slam into the attacker.

We collided with a bone-jarring impact, sending us both skittering away from my mate. This wolf was larger, but I had the advantage of training and desperation. I fought with a ferocity born of love and fear, my teeth clamping onto the wolf's throat. The wolf thrashed and bucked, trying to dislodge me, but nothing was going to make me loosen my grip. His struggles weakened, then stopped as he went limp beneath me.

I spun around, my eyes searching for Mason. He was still on his knees, still in pain, still fighting it. That's when I saw Esme. She was a hundred yards from the other witch, her small frame radiating power. Her face, usually warm and kind, now blazed with an inner fire. She raised her hands, palms out toward the witch, and I felt a shift in the air around us.

The witch's hooded head jerked toward Esme.

"Naughty, naughty!" Esme scolded.

The witch whirled his hands around as if throwing a baseball toward Esme. She smiled, flicked one finger in an upward motion, then made a scooping gesture with her other hand. The witch stumbled back, and Mason surged to his feet, shaking his head. Around the clearing, others were rising, too—Derek, Sam, Milly, Jem. The witch's hold on them had broken.

The witch took a step back. His cloak billowed around him, and in a blink, he vanished into the shadows of the forest.

Sam darted after him. AJ roared ferociously to the right, and Sam immediately changed course. The others wasted no time and followed Sam back into the fray.

Chapter Fifty-Two

SHYA

The battle raged on, intensity undiminished. Tristan's Pack, though battered, was far from defeated. I caught glimpses of Tristan barking orders, rallying his forces. His eyes blazed as he directed them, trying to regain control of the fight.

Mason and I locked eyes, a silent understanding passing between us. We needed to keep Tristan's Pack off-balance, prevent them from mounting an organized counterattack.

"To me!" Mason yelled as he and I moved as one, diving into the thickest cluster of enemies. We fought back-to-back, a whirlwind of claws, teeth, fists, and feet. Derek flanked us on the left, his powerful form bowling over two wolves at once. Sam darted in from the right, quick and agile, nipping at heels and keeping our opponents off-balance. Milly circled the perimeter, her eyes sharp, picking off any stragglers who tried to escape or regroup.

We were relentless. We pushed and pulled, scattering Tristan's wolves away from each other. Each time they tried to come together, we were there, breaking their formations, sowing chaos in their ranks.

Through the melee, AJ was still on his rampage, his roars shaking the very ground beneath our feet.

Good. He was keeping Tristan's forces busy so they couldn't attack us with more men.

Suddenly, a chorus of howls pierced the air. It was a sound I recognized, would recognize anywhere. One by one, the Bridgetown Pack arrived. Mom, in her massive wolf form, led the charge. Behind her, I saw Danni, Ivan, Ethan and Due-lah. Henry came next, and my heart skipped a beat. I couldn't lose him, but he was seventeen now, and this was his fight, too. Our enforcers came next, thundering through the trees in a wave of moving bodies intent on killing any who stood against them. After them ran a contingent of humans. Marnie was there, next Mrs. Patterson, and Mr. Johnson, and Ellen, of all people. They were fighting for our Pack, for our way of life, and I couldn't be prouder.

They hit the lines of Tristan's Pack, and the forest descended into a cacophony of snarls and screams. I yipped to get Mason's attention. With my Pack here, AJ needed to be gone. He would not differentiate between Tristan's Pack and ours.

He was already ahead of me, though.

"LULLABY!" Mason shouted, and immediately Derek, Milly, Jem, and Sam veered toward AJ. They began to circle him, taking turns to dart in to nip at his legs, attempting to herd him away from the main fight. It was a dangerous dance—one swipe from those massive paws could be fatal.

"Jem!" I heard Esme call out. "Now!"

I saw Jem dash to Esme's side, positioning himself protectively in front of her. Esme's face was a mask of concentration as her hands wove intricate patterns in the air.

AJ's movements became slower, more lethargic. His roars turned to confused grunts as he swayed on his feet.

I ran and joined Jem, Mason on my heels. We formed a protective triangle around Esme. Her spell was working, but it left her vulnerable. We couldn't let Tristan's wolves interrupt her. The thought of AJ going after my family made a surge of adrenaline spike inside of me.

A snarling wolf lunged at Mason, but he was ready. He ducked under the attack, then drove his fist up into the wolf's jaw with a sickening crack. The attacker crumpled to the ground, unconscious, as Mason swung round to block a silver knife slashing at him from the left.

I spun, keeping myself between the wolves and Esme. A low, threatening growl rumbled from my chest, a clear warning: They would not get past me.

Jem was a blur of motion, his speed making him hard to pin down. He zipped around the legs of a wolf, then darted in to sink his teeth into its haunches. The wolf howled in pain and tried to shake him off, but Jem held on.

Behind us, I could hear AJ's grunts becoming less frequent. I risked a glance over my shoulder and saw AJ swaying on his feet. His eyes were heavy-lidded, his massive head drooping. With a final, confused grunt, the bear slowly toppled over. The ground shook as he hit the forest floor, sending leaves and debris flying.

For a moment, everything seemed to pause. Then Esme's voice rang out, clear and triumphant: "Lullaby complete!"

Tristan's head swung about at the sound of Esme's voice. His eyes locked onto mine.

Yeah, that's right. You're beaten.

I snarled.

I'm coming for you.

Tristan's eyes widened as he read the intent in my eyes. Then he spun on his heel and bolted. He slipped between the trees with the fluid grace of a predator, his form blending into the shadows of the forest. The rest of his Pack had seen his retreat, and they scattered.

Without a second thought, I took off after him. My paws pounded against the forest floor as I gave chase.

This ended now. One way or another, Tristan would never threaten me or my loved ones again.

CHAPTER FIFTY-THREE

SHYA

The forest blurred around me as I ran after Tristan, my paws flying over the ground. His scent hung thick in the air, and I followed it with a single-minded determination. He tried to throw me off, doubling back and veering sharply, but nothing could stop me from finding him. My world had narrowed to a single point: Tristan.

I could hear his ragged breathing, see flashes of his form as he darted between trees. He was fast, but in wolf form, I was faster. This was my Pack, my land, and the forest itself seemed to bend to my will, branches swaying out of the way, clearing my path, roots and stones rising in just the right points to offer me sure footing on the uneven terrain. The very earth beneath my paws seemed to propel me forward, lending me strength and speed.

My muscles burned, but I pushed harder. This wasn't just about me anymore. It was about my family, my Pack, everyone Tristan had threatened. With each stride, I felt them all driving me on.

I hurtled forward, closing the distance between us.

He ducked left under a pine tree, breaking into a small clearing, and I knew I had him. I knew this place. Had come here as a child hunting with my dad. I slowed as he raced to the far side and skidded to a halt. A sheer rock face loomed before him, too steep to climb. He spun around, his hazel eyes wide as they met mine.

My lips pulled back in a snarl as I circled him.

He turned as he followed my movements, watching me carefully. "Shya," he smiled. "My mate. I knew if anyone could catch me, it would be you. Look at you—so powerful, so magnificent. This is exactly why we belong together."

Tristan's voice dropped to a seductive purr. "This is why we're destined for greatness, you and I. Together, we could lead our kind to reach their true potential. We'd be unstoppable, and you know it."

He extended one hand toward me as if offering me the world. "Embrace your destiny. With your support and my vision, we could reshape the very fabric of our society. Isn't that what you truly want? To be strong? To be feared? To be worshipped? I can give that to you." Tristan's eyes blazed with fervor. "Join me. Let's show everyone—wolves and humans alike—what real strength looks like."

His words hung in the air, charged with promise and temptation. Tristan stood there, hand outstretched, utterly convinced of his own irresistibility and the inevitability of my submission.

I growled low in my throat, the sound rumbling through the clearing. My eyes never left Tristan's as I stalked toward him, each step deliberate and menacing.

For a moment, confusion flickered across Tristan's face. His outstretched hand wavered, then slowly lowered. The confident smile began to fade as understanding dawned in his eyes.

"Shya," he said, his voice losing its seductive edge. "Think about what you're doing. We're meant to be together."

I didn't stop. My lips drew back to show him my teeth.

"No," he ordered. "Shya, you will obey me!"

Tristan's eyes widened, the last vestiges of his certainty crumbling away. He took a step back, then with a sudden burst of movement, he lunged to the side, attempting to dart past me.

But I was ready. I sprang forward, my powerful legs propelling me through the air. My jaws snapped shut on his leg. I sank my teeth into his calf, and I heard him cry out in pain and terror.

"You stupid fucking bitch! I'll kill you for this!"

A deep, familiar chuckle resonated through the clearing. I released Tristan's leg as he twisted around to see Mason emerging from the treeline.

"Well, fuck me over with a feather," Mason drawled, sauntering toward us. "What do we have here? The great Tristan Munroe, brought low by a female? This is fucking priceless, you know. I can't wait to see the Pack's faces when they hear about this. They'll be laughing their asses off for weeks."

Tristan's face contorted with rage and humiliation. He struggled to his feet but fell when he tried to put weight on his injured leg. Blood dripped from the wound and ran onto the ground in a steady stream.

"Face it, Tristan, it's over. Shya beat you. She showed you who's stronger, who's smarter."

Tristan swung his head from side to side, looking for a way out as I stalked closer. His arrogance melted away, replaced by naked desperation. I could see the calculation in his eyes, he wanted to Shift but he knew he'd be leaving himself vulnerable; we'd kill him before he'd transformed a paw.

"Please," he begged, holding up his hands. "I'll do anything you want. I'll leave the north, never come back. I'll give you whatever you want. Just let me live."

"There is nothing you have that we would ever want," Mason growled.

"Shya, you made me do those things. If you had just accepted me, none of this would have had to happen! If you're looking for someone to blame, then blame yourself. Not me!"

I snarled, and Tristan's eyes darted between us, realizing his words were having no effect. In a flash, his hand went to his boot, pulling out a silver knife. With a roar of desperation, he threw himself at me.

As one, Mason and I moved. I ducked under Tristan's swing and sank my teeth into his abdomen, ripping and tearing. At the same time, Mason's powerful hands gripped Tristan's head.

There was a sickening crack, followed by a wet, tearing sound. I danced back as Tristan's body went limp, blood pouring from his eviscerated midsection, and watched it topple over. Mason stood, Tristan's head dangling from his hand, a look of grim satisfaction on his face.

It was done. Tristan was dead.

Mason and I made our way back through the forest, leaving Tristan's mutilated body behind. The sounds of life were muted as we reached the edge of the clearing, and I paused to take in the scene.

The remains of Tristan's Pack, those who weren't still and bloody from AJ's rampage, were surrounded by our Bridgetown enforcers. Some looked lost, defeated; others were snarling defiantly.

Mom was supervising the enforcers and directing the clean-up. Derek and Sam were with Milly, Jem, and Esme, all guarding AJ while he slept. Henry sat beside Marnie by the treeline, tears falling silently down her face as she took in the devastation in front of her. There was no Edmond or Garrett here, nor their parents. I wondered if they had left already or if they had never come.

My fur brushed against Mason's leg. He glanced down at me, a small smile playing on his lips.

"You ready for this? I meant what I said. I'm not giving you up. Not for anything or anyone. We do this, and you're stuck with me, princess."

I just looked at him. There was nothing he could say to change my mind.

"So be it," he said and strode into the clearing, his presence commanding immediate attention.

Mason hurled Tristan's severed head into the center of the clearing. It landed with a sickening thud, rolling to a stop in front of the Bridgetown Pack. Gasps and murmurs rippled through the crowd.

"Listen up!" Mason's voice boomed across the battlefield. All eyes turned to him. "We killed Tristan," Mason announced, his voice hard and unyielding.

I stepped forward to stand by him, still in my wolf form, my head held high. Mason's hand came to rest on my back.

"I am Shya's mate," he declared, his eyes sweeping over the assembled wolves. "We're together. We will always be together. We're your future Alphas. You have a problem with that, now's the time to challenge us."

I watched as all eyes swiveled to Tristan's head, then back to me and

Mason.

Silence radiated out, and not one person said a fucking word.

Chapter Fifty-Four

SHYA

1 *day later*

The night air was cool against my skin as I stood at the edge of the sacred grove, my bare feet relishing the feel of the soft earth. It had been only a day since Mason and I had defeated Tristan, but it felt like a lifetime ago. Tonight, under the light of the full moon, Mason and I would be bound together as mates.

The grove was alive with energy, filled with members from both the Three Rivers Pack and the Bridgetown Pack. I could see Mai, with Ryan's arm around her waist, staring up at him with such a look of love on her face. I wondered if that was what I looked like when I looked at Mason. Derek stood nearby, his eyes doing their perpetual scan of the area, only resting when they hit Sofia, who was chatting with Marnie and Summer. Wally and Thomas were there, too, holding hands and looking dashing in matching black suits. Sam wasn't here, and I knew Mason was missing him. The witch had disappeared after the battle; there was no trace of him, not even a scent to follow. Sam had set off as soon as Mason and I had returned, hoping to track him down, and hadn't returned yet.

AJ and Milly had left, too, as soon as he woke up in human form. They were going to search more of Tristan's camp for signs of AJ's mate.

A bell chimed, and everyone moved to their places. Earlier today, Ryan had severed Mason's bond with the Three Rivers. It had been painful to watch him lose his Pack, his family. I had thought he was going to collapse with sudden loss, but then his eyes had sought out mine. I did the only thing I could: I held his gaze and willed my love and admiration for him to shine through. Then, Mom had sealed his new Bridgetown Pack bond. It would take him time to get used to it, for the bond to settle into place, but he was one of us now. I could feel him through the Pack bonds, and he could feel me.

For my second mating ceremony, I'd asked Henry and Tucker to walk the circles with me, to show unity in our Pack and support for Mason.

I smiled as my brothers walked toward me, both looking handsome in their formal attire. Henry looked so grown up in his suit, his lanky frame somehow more dignified. His watchful brown eyes, so like our mother's, scanned the area before settling on me with a warm smile. Tucker, in contrast, was practically bouncing with excitement, his whole being vibrating with energy.

"Ready, Shya?" Henry asked softly, offering me his arm.

I nodded, taking his arm and reaching for Tucker's hand. "Thanks for doing this, both of you."

Tucker beamed up at me, his ever-present smile even wider than usual. "Are you kidding? This is so cool! I get to be part of the ceremony!"

Henry shushed him gently. "Remember, Tuck, we need to be respectful."

"I know, I know," Tucker said.

I glanced down at my little brother and grinned. "So you don't have a car on standby this time?"

Tucker looked thoughtfully toward the circle where I knew Mason was waiting for me.

"Nah. He'll do. Though if he hurts you ..." His voice turned serious, and for a moment, I could feel the power coming off my brother. I almost took a step back; the threat was so real. "He'll have to answer to me."

He might only be seven, but Tuck was going to be one hell of a powerful Alpha one day.

"Sounds like a good deal, Tuck."

As we began our walk to the outer circle, I felt everyone's eyes turn to me. The simple white dress I wore fluttered gently in the breeze, and I held my head high. This time, there was no pretense, no forced smiles. I was barefoot and unadorned. This was me. For better or worse, I had no armor anymore. Mason was mating the real me.

The chanting began, a low hum that grew in intensity with each step I took. This time, the sound seemed to buoy me forward, propelling me to my future. I searched the faces in the crowd, no longer seeing expectation or judgment but hope and acceptance.

We walked the circles in no time at all, and as I reached the innermost circle, I saw Mason waiting for me next to Mom. She was smiling at me. After seeing Mason throw Tristan's head into the ranks of the Bridgetown Pack, Mom had relented. She would bless our union and step down from the Alphahood in the next few weeks. I didn't think she would stay for long after that. I could see in her eyes that she yearned to mourn Dad properly.

My gaze swept over Mom and came to my mate. The rest of the world dropped away as our eyes met. Mason's eyes were locked onto mine, igniting a fire that coursed through my entire body. In that moment, I felt as if I could see into his very soul and he into mine. It was as if every step I had taken in my life had been leading me to this exact moment, to him.

Mason's lips curved into a smile that was meant only for me. I felt my own lips respond in kind, unable to contain the joy and love that threatened to overwhelm me. The air between us seemed to crackle with electricity, charged with the promise of our future together, and in that moment, I knew with absolute certainty that this was right. This was where I belonged. With Mason. I was home.

Edmond and Garrett waited for most of the ceremony to be completed before they put in an appearance. As they stepped into the sacred grove, a hush fell over the gathered werewolves, and I knew something was wrong. The circles parted as Edmond and his brother strode forward. Edmond's face was a mask of calm composure. Beside him, Garrett's eyes darted around, a mix of defiance and contempt in them.

"Edmond," Mason growled in warning.

"Enough, Mason. This is wrong," Edmond called out, coming to a stop in front of us. "Shya's mate should come from our Pack, not an outsider. This is what we agreed, Camille."

"It was." Mom inclined her head. "Of course, that was before

327

Mason and Shya put their lives on the line to stop an attack on our Pack and killed the one who murdered my mate while the insider, the one from our very own Pack, ran and hid."

Edmond's mask cracked a little as he drew himself up and hissed, "I did not hide. Someone had to oversee the defenses. If Tristan had broken through, the whole Pack would have fallen."

Mason stepped forward. "You keep telling yourself that."

Edmond glared at Mason, and his fists clenched.

Yeah, Edmond's cool, calm exterior was definitely under some strain.

"Whatever your opinion of my actions, it is immaterial. The next Alpha must come from our Pack."

"I come from our Pack, Edmond." I took a small step toward him. "And Mason has joined us. He is one of us now." I lowered my voice. "Please don't do this," I pleaded, searching his face for any sign of the man I'd known and respected.

Edmond's mask slipped even more. His blue eyes flashed with fury, his frame trembling with barely contained rage. "It's not right," he snarled, all pretense of calm evaporating. "You're the link to the Alphahood, Shya, but it's not your choice. The fate of a whole Pack and its future should not rely on the fickle reasoning and passing fancies of a woman."

Garrett moved closer to his brother, his voice low but carrying. "That's right, Ed. Show them what real leadership looks like."

"Of course," Mason murmured behind me, as if he had just worked something out. His hand found mine, squeezing gently before he addressed Edmond. "You're the mole. You tipped off Tristan about what we were doing. Did you tell him where to find Shya the day she was taken, too? Did you tell him where to find Michael?"

I heard the collective intake of breaths from the Pack around us.

"Don't be ridiculous!" he scoffed. "I was supposed to mate with Shya. I'd be Alpha. Why would I hand the Pack to Tristan?"

And there it was. I wasn't a person, just a thing to pass around. The key to the kingdom for anyone who mated with me.

Mason's gaze swung to Edmond's brother. "Why indeed, Garrett?"

Edmond's face paled, his composure cracking further as he looked between Mason and Garrett. "What is he talking about, Garrett?"

When Garrett didn't answer, Edmond stared at him, horror etched across his features. "Did you tip off Tristan?"

For a moment, silence reigned in the grove. Then Garrett laughed, a harsh, bitter sound.

"You're damn right I did," he declared, squaring his shoulders and lifting his chin defiantly. His eyes, so similar to Edmond's, now blazed with anger and twisted pride. "I saw the way Shya treated you, brother. The way she treated our family. As if we were beneath her."

Garrett's eyes swept over the crowd, his voice rising with each word. "We're better than the Littles. We always have been. Our bloodline is pure, our heritage unmatched. Why should we bow to them?" He spat the last word, his face contorted with disgust as he turned to me. "To her? She's a prissy little bitch. And she made you plead to mate with her, all while she was fucking an outsider behind your back!"

Edmond looked aghast, but Garrett paid him no mind. He was on a roll now, years of pent-up resentment and twisted ideology pouring out of him. "Tristan understood the truth of the world. Werewolves should have their pick of females. We should have our pick of the humans. Tristan was going to make sure we all got what we deserved. A return to the old ways, where real wolves ruled by strength and right."

"How could you?" Edmond was horrified. "You betrayed this Pack; you betrayed our family. And for what? So you could fuck whatever little tart took your fancy?"

Garrett's lips curled into a sneer. "I was proud to help him."

Edmond snapped. I saw it a moment before he lunged at his brother, hands reaching for his throat.

Mason saw it, too, and slammed into Edmond, pushing him back before he could attack Garrett.

The crowd murmured in shock and anger. I could feel the tension building, the air thick with the promise of violence

Danni and Ivan were there immediately, glancing between me and Mason.

"There will be no bloodshed on my mating day," I said firmly, my voice carrying the weight of my newfound authority. I nodded to Danni and Ivan. "Take them away. We'll deal with them later."

Neither of them went quietly. In the end, Garrett was unconscious as Ivan and Ethan carried him away. Edmond hadn't put up much of a fight. After all, he wasn't a fighter, more a strategist.

I waited until they had left, then turned back to Mason. "Now, where were we?"

Chapter Fifty-Five

SHYA

All during the celebrations, I felt Mason's eyes on me. The heat from them followed me around, making me squirm with anticipation. I put up with it for precisely one hour (and I only managed this through my many years of hard-core Alpha training), and then something within me snapped. I had to have Mason. Now.

He was standing with Ryan, Derek, Mai, and Due-lah. I wasn't sure how much attention he was paying to the others, as his eyes tracked me as I walked toward them.

"So, there I was, covered in motor oil and holding a rubber chicken—" Due-lah was saying, gesticulating wildly.

Mai's face was one of careful blankness. "I'm not sure I even want to know how this story ends."

"Earth to Mason," Derek said, waving a hand in front of Mason's face. "You still with us, bro?"

Mason blinked. "Sorry, what were you saying?"

Mai followed Mason's line of sight, a knowing smirk on her lips as she caught sight of me. "I think someone's a bit distracted," she teased.

"Sorry to interrupt," I said, my voice steady despite the adrenaline rushing through me. "Mason, can I borrow you?"

"Of course, princess."

"Have fun!" Mai winked at me, and I grinned back at her. I fully intended to.

I reached out, taking Mason's hand. "Come with me," I whispered, tugging him away from the crowd. "I want to show you something."

We walked hand in hand through the forest, the sounds of the celebration fading behind us. The earth was cool beneath my bare feet, and I reveled in the feeling of freedom. No more pretenses, no more masks. Just me and Mason, exactly as we were meant to be.

"You know," Mason said as we ducked under a low-hanging branch, "when I imagined our mating day, I didn't picture a nature hike. Though I'm not complaining about the view." His eyes trailed over my white dress.

I felt a blush creep up my cheeks. "Eyes front, wolf boy. We're almost there."

We ducked around a tall oak, and there it was. The small wooden hut stood nestled among a sea of wildflowers. The flowers, usually a riot of colors during the day, swayed gently in the night breeze, their petals shimmering like pale ghosts in the moonlight.

Behind the hut was a small lake, its surface a mirror, perfectly still and reflective, and capturing the full moon's image, creating a second celestial orb that seemed to float just beneath the water's surface. Fireflies darted here and there, their bioluminescent flashes creating a living constellation that mirrored the stars above.

"What is this place?"

I smiled. "This was my hideout when I was a kid. Whenever the pressure of Alpha training got too much, I'd come here to escape."

Mason turned to me, his expression softening. "And now you're sharing it with me?"

I nodded, suddenly feeling a bit shy. "It seemed fitting. This place has always been my sanctuary, and now ... well, you're my sanctuary, too. With you, I don't need my armor; I can just be me."

Mason's expression turned wolfish. "Really? Shall we put it to the test, princess? Tell me, Shya, in explicit detail, exactly why you brought me here. What is it you want me to do?"

Oh, fuck.

My eyes widened as I felt heat spreading over my entire body. I couldn't. I just couldn't say out loud all the things I wanted him to do to me.

Mason must have seen my face because his grin turned predatory. "If you say it, princess, I'll do it."

I took a deep breath, keeping my gaze steady on him. My heart thumped in my chest, anxiety and excitement scrambling for dominance in my mind. This was it, that moment of complete vulnerability. The idea of speaking my thoughts, my desires, felt like diving off a cliff into the unknown, as thrilling as it was terrifying.

"I want ..."

"Yes, princess?"

I was a future Alpha, for fuck's sake. I could do this. I stood up straight, took a breath, and started counting off the things I wanted on my fingers. "I want you to undress me. I want to feel your hands on my breasts, tweaking my nipples until I beg for more. I want you to put your ..." I could do this. "Your fingers inside of me while you lick and suck my clit until I come. Then ..."

"There's more?" Mason said, pretending to be shocked.

"A lot more, yes. Then I want to feel your ... um ... your cock inside of me."

Oh, the Goddess, I was going to die of embarrassment.

"Uh-huh." Mason started to stalk toward me. "And what will my cock be doing inside of you?"

"Oh. Um. Moving?"

"Moving?"

"Yes, moving. In and ... and out?"

Mason laughed. "Well done, princess. I'll let you off the rest. For now."

Well, thank the Goddess for that.

Mason's grin lingered as he strode to me, his dark eyes filled with a wicked promise. "Step one, princess," he said, his voice a sultry promise in the nighttime air. He reached for me, his hands finding the hem of my dress. I gasped as his fingers brushed against my skin, a flurry of goosebumps erupting in their wake.

Slowly, he began to lift the fabric. His eyes never left mine, that wicked grin still playing on his lips. He pulled it higher, revealing my thighs first and then my hips. Then he pulled it up and over my head.

My panties were next, sliding down with a silky whisper until I was standing there, almost fully revealed under the star-streaked sky. Mason's eyes went to my breasts, which were pressing against the material of my bra. I felt a flush creep up from my chest to my face.

"Now," he said, his voice husky with desire. "Step two. Let's see about these nipples you want me to play with."

I watched as Mason reached out and traced his thumb over the peak of my breast through the fabric. With his other hand, he unclasped my bra, and it fell away from my body. I was utterly laid bare now in front of him under the moonlight.

My nipples hardened instantly under the sensation, and a wave of heat flooded through me. His thumbs brushed back and forth over my bare nipples, the slight pressure sending sparks of pleasure through my body. Then he rolled my nipples between his fingers, tweaking them slightly.

Oh, wow!

"More," I breathed. He bent down slightly, his breath fanning against my skin just seconds before his lips closed around my nipple. A jolt of intense pleasure shot through me, causing my knees to buckle slightly. His arms moved around me instantly, holding me steady while his teeth gently grazed one nipple, then the other. The sensation was electric, and I found myself pressing closer to him, craving more.

His hands moved lower now, skimming over my flat belly to pause at the juncture between my thighs. His wicked grin told me that he was about to take it up a notch, and I braced myself for it.

"Step three," he whispered as he picked me up and lay me down on the ground. His hot breath ghosting over my sensitive flesh, he settled between my thighs, sending waves of pleasure washing over my skin.

"You are fucking drenched, princess," he murmured. "And I get to lick this all up."

I gasped as his tongue traced the line of my folds, exploring the damp heat of me in broad strokes at first.

"You taste divine," he said before his attention became more focused. His tongue began to circle my clit, applying just enough pressure to make my hips jerk upward. An involuntary moan escaped from my lips as Mason's tongue flicked against my most sensitive spot. Then my legs trembled as he slowly sucked my clit into his mouth. I could feel his firm hold on my hips, his other hand splayed wide against my abdomen to ground me, to keep me from completely losing myself. His tongue swirled around the small bud before he gently nipped at it with his teeth. The sensation was so intense that a shocked cry tore from my lips.

Mason chuckled low against me, sending warm vibrations through me that made me squirm and moan louder. Just when I thought I couldn't take anymore, he slipped a finger inside of me.

"Oh Goddess, Mason ..." I groaned out, feeling my climax beginning to build within me. "Don't stop."

The intensity of it all was overwhelming, far beyond anything I'd ever experienced before. Each flick of his tongue was like a strike of lightning, illuminating every nerve in my body.

His tongue circled my clit faster now, his lips sucking and nipping until I was crying out, bucking against him in a desperate search for release. Every touch felt amplified tenfold as I neared climax; each stroke of his tongue was a whiplash of pleasure through my veins.

His tongue danced as each stroke of his fingers sent shockwaves through me, and then his fingers inside me curled upwards slightly, hitting a spot that had my back arching and my mouth opening in a silent scream of pleasure. I couldn't think, couldn't breathe; there was just Mason and the things he was making me feel. I cried out, my hips bucking in time with his thrusts as the orgasm crashed over me.

I collapsed against the ground. The scent of Mason and me, of our desire, mingled with the wildflowers, and it was intoxicating.

"Step four," Mason's voice was deep and full of desire.

I squinted my eyes at him. "I don't remember a step four."

He grinned. "It's cute that you think that."

Oh. Right.

"Mason, I've never ... I mean, yes, in dreams, and I have a very effective vibrator, but with another person ... That is, I—"

"It's also cute when you get so nervous you ramble."

"I am not rambling!"

"You're rambling."

"I'm trying to explain, I'm—"

"You're a virgin, princess. I know."

"Oh."

"Oh? That's it? Just 'oh'? No more rambling?"

I crossed my arms over my chest, feeling strangely vulnerable.

"No," I said simply, a slight blush creeping up my face.

"Princess, look at me. If you don't think that this is a fucking wonderful gift you are giving me, you are out of your mind. I'm going to be the first to sink my cock into you. To watch you come while I move—yes, in *and* out—inside of you is a fucking honor, one I will cherish and treasure for eternity."

"But what if ... what if it's bad? What if I'm bad?"

Mason laughed. "Where have you been on this journey of ours? Our chemistry is insane, princess. How can anything physical between us be bad?"

"I don't know how—"

"I do. I'll show you. You don't need to worry about a thing, princess. You're going to lie back and let me do all the work this time."

"This time?"

He grinned wickedly at me. "This time," he repeated.

My heart pounded heavily in my chest as his eyes bore into mine, the look in them making me shiver with anticipation. He gently brushed a stray lock of hair away from my face, his touch soft and tender. "Ready?"

I swallowed hard, the word "yes" barely a whisper on my lips. A slow grin spread across his face as he leaned down to capture my lips with his own. The passion in his kiss left me breathless, all thoughts of doubt fleeing from my mind. I stopped thinking and let my body take over.

His fingers traced the curve of my hip before sliding down to my inner thigh. He spread my legs wider, granting him more access. His eyes never left mine as he positioned himself at my entrance.

He paused, looking deep into my eyes.

"Say it," he ordered. "Say what you want."

I swallowed. "I want ... I want your cock inside—Oh!"

My eyes widened as he pushed himself inside of me, not fast, but not slow, either. Just a steady pace of him filling me up, stretching me until he was fully inside. Then he paused, allowing me to adjust.

It felt fucking amazing. My vibrator had never felt like this. The heat coming off him, the silky-smooth feel of his cock pressing against my walls. No one had ever told me about this.

"Princess, you okay?"

I could barely form a coherent thought, but managed to nod faintly.

"You want me to move? In and out?"

He was teasing me, but I didn't care. I didn't want him to move; I needed him to.

"Mason, please," I gasped, urging him on.

His smile was wolfish. "That's my princess," he murmured before beginning to move. The motion was slow and steady at first, a rhythm that had me gripping on to him, my breath hitching at each stroke.

It was overwhelming and intoxicating all at once, an exquisite fullness that had nothing to do with just how much of him there was inside me. It was more. It was this connection, tangible and electrifying, that we were creating; it was raw, beautiful, and I needed more.

I rolled my hips, bucking, meeting him thrust for thrust.

"Yes!"

He drove himself deeper within me, his pace quickening, his thrusts becoming harder, deeper. I could feel him hitting places inside me that I didn't even know existed.

Then he hooked one of my legs around his waist, allowing him to go deeper inside me. He delved into me again, each powerful thrust echoing through the night air. I was reduced to a writhing mess beneath him, the pleasure intense and all-encompassing.

"Fuck," he growled, his voice strained. "You, this, everything, it's so amazing, princess."

His words sent a violent shiver through me, igniting something primitive within me, and I felt his control slipping, the pace increasing as he lost himself in the moment. I wanted him to lose control, wanted to show him it was nothing to be scared of. He wouldn't hurt me. I wrapped my legs around his waist, pulling him in, urging him on. His control vanished. He went wild with desire, thrust into me again and again and again. He was everywhere all at once. His scent filled my nostrils while his muscular arms held me against him, his strong body moving above mine in a rhythm that promised to break us both. The pure pleasure that spread through me was intoxicating; each thrust pushing me closer and closer to the edge.

All rational thought left me as pleasure started to coil tighter and tighter within me. "Mason," I gasped again, pushing up to meet him with each thrust. "I'm... Oh Goddess ... I'm ..."

His movements grew erratic as he neared his own peak. His breath hitched when he pushed himself even deeper into me one last time before I shattered underneath him, screaming out his name as he emptied himself inside of me. It was mind-blowingly incredible.

Why the fuck had I waited so long to feel this with Mason?

Then all thoughts fled as my entire body seized. My back arched as my Pack bonds erupted; one flaming red thread, my bond with Mason, set fire to the whole lot. In that moment, I could feel everything, see everything that Mason could. His love for me, his fierce need for me. I was drowning in him, in his thoughts and emotions. I felt like a ship caught in the maelstrom, tossed around in an ocean of love and desire so profound that it made my heart ache. The shockwave hit me so fiercely it was as if I had been thrown against a wall—Mason's emotions bled into mine until I didn't know what was mine and what was his.

Then the world spun, the fire banked, and I was back in Mason's arms, panting heavily and wishing I could feel that again.

"The fated ... the bond ..."

Mason grinned. "I know. It sealed. I felt it, too."

"I saw ... The things I saw ... felt ..."

He reached down, still panting, and placed a hand over my stomach. "I particularly liked the one with our pups in it."

I frowned. "Pups?"

"You didn't get that one?"

I shook my head, not sure what he was saying.

"I saw the pups that we just made. They're very cute, just like their mother."

"Pups? As in plural?"

He didn't answer, just grinned, then leaned down and kissed me.

EPILOGUE

M^{ason}

The sun hung low in the sky as I led my team through another of Tristan's camps. Usually, on a mission like this, I'd have a ball in my pocket to help me think. Not today. Ever since my bond with Shya sealed, I'd found I didn't need the balls and fidget tools so much. Behind me, Derek, AJ, Milly, Ivan, and Ethan fanned out, searching for any sign of life.

"Another dead end," Milly muttered, kicking at an empty can. The clatter echoed through the silent camp, emphasizing its emptiness.

I saw AJ's face fall, hope dimming in his eyes. "No sign of her here either," he said, his voice subdued.

I placed a hand on AJ's shoulder. "We'll find her, AJ. We won't stop looking."

This was the fifth of Tristan's camps that we'd searched. After Shya and I had killed Tristan, his Pack had fallen into chaos. His Pack had been built on the charisma and vision of one person. With their leader dead, it didn't take long before they turned on each other, desperate to shift blame for their actions under Tristan's rule. In their scramble to save their own skins, they'd given up the locations of all Tristan's camps. We'd been methodically working our way through them, hoping to find AJ's mate and any other captives Tristan might have taken.

As we turned to leave, a rustle from one of the cabins caught my attention. Ivan and Ethan immediately flanked me, ready for any threat.

"Come out," I called, keeping my voice firm but not threatening. "We're not here to harm anyone."

A moment passed, then another. Finally, the cabin door creaked open, and a young woman cautiously stepped out into the fading light.

She couldn't have been more than twenty years old, but her eyes were wary as she looked at us. Her frame was slight, almost lost in an oversized black T-shirt that hung loosely over a pair of worn and dirty jeans. Despite her disheveled appearance, there was a scrappy, determined set to her jaw that suggested she wouldn't go down without a fight.

"Who the hell are you people?" she demanded, her voice carrying a hint of a warning.

"We're not here to cause trouble," I replied. "My name is Mason Shaw, Alpha of the Bridgetown Pack. We're searching Tristan's camps. Can you tell us your name?"

The young woman's eyes narrowed at my words, her stance shifting slightly. I could see her weighing her options, deciding whether to trust us or not.

"Ruby," she finally said, her voice guarded. "My name's Ruby. What do you want with Tristan's camps? I mean, you're welcome to take what you want. There ain't much here, is there? I'm guessing he's dead, seeing as he ain't been back here in weeks?"

I nodded, taking a careful step forward. "He is. We're here looking for people he might have taken captive. How long have you been here, Ruby?"

Ruby's shoulders sagged slightly, some of the fight going out of her. "A few months," she muttered. "They left me to watch the camp and … and no one came back."

I exchanged a glance with Derek. "How did you end up here?"

Ruby hesitated, then seemed to make a decision. Her words came out in a rush, as if she'd been holding them back for too long. "I came looking for my sister. Tristan found me. He told me he knew my sister but that she was dead, and I didn't know what to do after that. So when Tristan offered me a place here with food, shelter, a Pack, well, I didn't have anywhere else to go, so I thought, why not?"

I felt a pang of sympathy for the girl. "What do you want to do now? We can take you back to Bridgetown. The rest of your Pack are being held there for the moment."

She hesitated. "Do I … do I have to?"

"No," Milly replied. "You don't have to if you don't want to."

Ruby stared out at the camp and then back at us. "Okay, then. I think I'm going to stay here for a bit."

"Alright. Would you mind answering some of our questions before we go?"

Ruby nodded eagerly, relief evident in her posture now that we weren't a threat. "Yeah, yeah, I can do that."

AJ took a step toward her. "My name's AJ. My mate … she was being kept hostage. Have you seen her?"

Ruby's expression turned thoughtful. "I've heard of you. Tristan's pet bear Shifter who has been twice cursed—once by a witch, and once by the Goddess, giving him a human mate."

Derek's eyebrows shot up.

I turned to AJ. "Your mate is human?" I asked, unable to keep the surprise from my voice.

"Yes," he murmured. "She's human."

Milly narrowed her eyes at AJ. "Does she know you're a bear Shifter?"

AJ shook his head, unable to meet our eyes. "She doesn't know what I am. She doesn't even know she's my fated mate."

Fuck!

I clenched my jaw, processing the new information. AJ's situation was fucked up; no two ways about it. A human mate? That was almost unheard of. And this one didn't even know her mate was a bear Shifter, a cursed one, at that.

We had to find her.

I turned back to Ruby. "Do you know anything about his mate?"

"I know of your mate," she said quietly. "She was here for a time."

AJ's head shot up. "What happened to her?"

Ruby bit her lip, clearly uncomfortable. "Because she's human, they ... they sold her."

Rage twisted AJ's whole body, and Ruby stumbled back. I put a hand on AJ's shoulder.

"We can't have your bear putting in an appearance, AJ. Not here."

He took a deep breath, then another. Then nodded to me.

"Who is 'they'?" Derek asked Ruby.

Ruby pointed to a cabin at the far end of the camp. "The

werewolves who stayed there. They were from the army. They're the ones who sold the humans."

Without a word, we moved toward the cabin. The structure loomed before us, weathered wood darkened by age and neglect. Its windows were grimy, offering little view of the interior.

I pushed the door open, wincing at the loud creak that echoed through the camp. The smell hit us first—musty and stale, with an underlying tang of something metallic. Blood, maybe.

Derek stiffened beside me.

"You recognize a scent?"

Derek's face paled, but he shook his head. "No, it can't be him. He's dead."

I frowned as I moved inside; it wasn't like Derek to get a scent wrong. The inside was dim, light filtering weakly through the dirty windows. Dust motes danced in the air, disturbed by our entrance. The cabin was sparse; the main room had a few rickety chairs scattered around, and a worn table stood in one corner, its surface covered in scratches and stains.

The place felt ... off. Like it was holding its breath, waiting for something.

"In here," AJ called. I strode to the back room. It was just as sparse as the other one, with a bed frame and a dirty mattress in one corner.

Derek had followed me in but stopped dead, staring at the wall AJ had uncovered. It was covered with photos—all of the same woman. Curly red hair, button nose, a determined set to her jaw.

What the fuck?

"What?" Milly asked, seeing our reactions. "Who is the woman?"

Derek's eyes hardened, his fists clenching at his sides. "Sofia. My mate."

Milly frowned, looking at all the photos; there had to be at least sixty of them. All of Sofia going about her daily life.

"But why? Why would they be targeting her?"

"Because of me," Derek growled. "Because of what I did in the army. And if it is who I think it is, Sofia's in a fuckload of danger."

The Reluctant Mate, Book 5 in the Shifters of the Three Rivers series.

How far would you go for a second chance?

A Derek and Sofia story, coming 2025! Preorder now!

Want to know what happened on Derek and Sofia's hot and dangerous first date? Sign up to my newsletter at www.kiranightingale.com for a *free* prequel novella!

COME JOIN US IN THE SHIFTER REALM!

Kira Nightingale
Mystically Dark, Wildly Romantic...

Sign up to my newsletter and get Fairground Fling, a free prequel short story about Derek and Sofia's first date!

As an author, I write paranormal romance books that are mystically dark and wildly romantic. I send out my newsletter every two weeks, and in it you can get exclusive content and snippets from my current work-in-progress, news about what I'm up to, and sometimes even photos of my clumsy cat, Scout. You can sign up to my newsletter at www.kiranightingale.com

THE RESCUED MATE

Fairground Fling, Shifters of the Three Rivers 0.5

No way will I let fate decide my destiny, but Derek Shaw is back and proving impossible to resist...

Sofia

All I wanted was to run my coffee shop in peace, avoid my fated mate, and forget about our Shifter bond. Is that too much to ask for?

Apparently it is, because Derek Shaw just walked back into my life, all rippling muscles and piercing eyes. The man sets my blood on fire, but there's no way I'm giving in. I've seen what happens when "fated mates" are torn apart, and I won't let that happen to me.

Derek left to join the military, turning his back on our bond. Now he's back in the Three Rivers Pack, determined to win me over. But I've built walls around my heart that even an Alpha wolf can't break through. At least, that's what I keep telling myself...

Derek

I left Three Rivers to serve my country, but I never forgot Sofia. Every day, her fiery hair and captivating scent haunted my thoughts.

Now I'm back, and the pull towards Sofia is stronger than ever. My wolf won't rest until I claim what's mine. But Sofia's determined to keep her distance. That's okay, though. I'm a Shaw, and we never back down from a challenge.

ALSO BY KIRA NIGHTINGALE

Shifters of the Three Rivers series

The Runaway Mate

The Renegade Mate

The Resolute Mate

The Rescued Mate

The Reluctant Mate(coming 2025)

The Relentless Mate (coming 2025)

A Three Rivers Holiday Tale: A Shifters of the Three Rivers Novella

Boxsets

Shifters of the Three Rivers, Omnibus of Books 1-3 (ebook only)

Mai and Ryan's story with ***an exclusive epilogue!***

Audiobooks

The Runaway Mate (available on Audible and Amazon)

Coming Soon

The Renegade Mate
The Resolute Mate

About Kira Nightingale

Kira Nightingale is a Scot living in Canada. She has always wanted to be a writer, and can't believe how lucky she is to finally be able to write romance stories all day long. She lives with her husband, her two children and a massive cat called Scout. Kira loves to drink tea (her favorite is Long Island Iced Tea, but unfortunately she only gets to drink this occasionally) and likes to dunk cookies in it (yes, even the Long Island kind.)

ACKNOWLEDGEMENTS

P utting together a book for publication is no small project and involves many steps after the author has written 'The End.' Once again I'd like to thank my wonderful editor, Brigitte Billings, and my amazing PA Team, The Nerdy Girls Collective for all their support. Any mistakes are mine. The awesome cover was created by 100 Covers – thank you, Jamie Ty!

Printed in Great Britain
by Amazon